HANNAH CURIOUS

AND THE

DARKHIVE OF LOST WORDS

Neil Scott

ISBN: 9798475589274

For all the curious ones...

CHAPTER ONE

Hannah Darnell reluctantly lifted her eyes from her bowl of porridge and saw the gathering storm in her grandmother's sagging face.

'Who the devil's that knocking this early on a Saturday?'

Her grandmother chewed on her false teeth accusingly, her chins wobbling as she folded her morning newspaper and slapped it on the tablecloth. With a heavy sigh, she pulled her faded dressing gown tighter around her plump frame and acted out the extended charade of imminent movement.

'I'll go.' Hannah took her cue and slid back her chair, silence her only gratitude.

Unlike most girls of fifteen, weekends weren't a beautiful sunrise at the end of a dreary, rain-lashed week of school. Saturdays for Hannah meant lists of chores and odd jobs around the fading Bluebell House. Sunday mornings brought an eternity in a draughty church and supervised homework in the afternoon. After that, school on Monday morning wasn't dreaded it was an escape.

Hannah passed her grandmother as she renewed her interest in her newspaper, her scowl recharging. Sweeping from the kitchen, Hannah's socked feet softly swished across the cool black and white chequer board tiles of the long hallway, the grey morning light grudgingly seeping in through the fanned windows over the door. Previous occupants of the Victorian mansion peered judgementally down from the walls, the grandfather clock filling the space with its sedate rhythm. She tapped her hand on the curled banister at the foot of the sweeping staircase just as there was a further knock at the door. Skipping forward the last few strides, she secured her dressing gown over her pyjamas and after turning the large key in the lock, heaved open the heavy door.

A restless postman asked her name and took her wobbly, scribbled signature on his handheld gadget. Thrusting a damp brown-paper package into her hands, he forced a weak smile and bounded back down the damp steps. She locked out the tepid May drizzle and eyed the splattered parcel suspiciously as his idling van crunched its way back up the gravel driveway.

Secured haphazardly with reams of brown tape, it was the size of a football, yet soft and oddly shaped. Stuck across the top of the packet, the dozen misaligned stamps varied in price from five pounds to two and a half pence. The address beneath simply read:

Hannah Curious

Bluebell House

Bramley-upon-Thames

Hannah Curious? Why she'd not been called that since she was…

'Who is it girl?' Her grandmother bellowed distantly, her voice sharp enough to cut glass.

Hannah flinched and stared at the parcel, knowing instinctively she had to keep it a secret or risk never seeing it ever again.

'Erm…' She paused, not able to deny the knock at the door but unable to think of a more plausible reason instead.

6

'Postman!' She yelled back, wincing.

She thought about rushing the parcel up to her room, but if she did, her grandma would be more suspicious than ever. She crept up a few steps, threw it gently onto the first landing and darted back down the hallway on tiptoes.

She paused by the kitchen doorway, curling her long black hair behind her ears before strolling indifferently in to retake her seat. She felt the heat of her grandma's eyes lift from her paper and follow her across the room. As Hannah silently drew her chair in to the table, she forced herself to look up from her lukewarm bowl and feign surprise.

'Oh, it was just some books for me. I'll take them up after breakfast.' Hannah spooned some gloopy oats into her mouth.

Her grandmother narrowed her eyes, making no comment but for a sucking noise as she rearranged her dentures. Hannah had had a few deliveries of books before, ordering them online at school with the help of a kindly teacher who turned a blind eye in exchange for what was left of her dinner money. She always told her grandma the packages contained schoolbooks, but over time, she'd allowed a sliver of her rebellious streak to resurface and become a little more adventurous. Feeling the laser-like heat of her grandma's judgemental glower return to the scandals in her paper, Hannah released her breath and tried to remember how to sit naturally. Scraping the last of the porridge from her bowl, she stretched with her best impression of contentment.

'More tea Grandma?' Hannah's hand rested on the teapot's handle.

Grandmother Johnson's eyes twitched before she gave an almost imperceptible nod and turned the page to sneer at the obituaries. Hannah poured the steaming amber liquid into her china cup, a finger securing the teapot lid. A splash of milk, a cube of sugar and a gentle winding were all coyly scrutinised from under half-closed eyelids. As Hannah replaced the spoon neatly beneath the handle on the saucer, a growling snuffle and a flick of the corner of her paper acknowledged her efforts.

'I'll get dressed and start on the lawn grandma.' She stood up.

Her grandmother's face snapped up from her paper and Hannah's chest tightened, thinking she'd overdone it. She kept her expression blank until a sharp sniff and a dismissive mumble signalled the all clear and Hannah ambled stiffly from the room.

'Yes and afterwards you can come back and do the dusting properly, that girl has never understood English standards.' She shouted after her.

That girl was hardly a girl. Magda was the woman who looked after the house and her grandmother throughout the week. She practiced her English with Hannah, told terrible jokes and was good for a clandestine hug when her grandmother was safely away for her afternoon nap.

Bounding up the stairs two steps at a time, Hannah scooped up the parcel and darted across the landing on tiptoes. Rushing past her grandmother's bedroom and the unused guest rooms, she headed down the dim corridor to the smallest, coldest bedroom at the back of the house; her sanctuary from the world.

She leapt onto the thick itchy blanket on her bed, the dark wooden wardrobe rocking gently by the door. The old furniture and pale wallpaper made it look like an old person's bedroom, but when Hannah had put up posters or brought home keepsakes over the last three years, they'd routinely disappeared whilst she'd been at school.

'Frivolity is the devil's doings, girl!' Her grandma always cried, nostrils flaring.

Hannah learnt the lesson slowly, glancing impishly at the groaning bookshelves beside her window. Sitting cross-legged, she peered at the unfamiliar spidery handwriting on the brown-paper parcel, checking the rear for a return address but finding it blank. She was breaking her grandma's rules just holding it in her trembling hands. She licked her dry lips as they twitched into a grin as mischievous as it was nervous.

'I really shouldn't.' She mumbled as her thumb poked through the brown paper.

With a gasp, she dropped it on the bed and flinched back against the wall.

An unblinking black and white eye peered out through the torn strip of brown paper, confusion battling with her curiosity. She swallowed and tore into the parcel with her fingers. A brown threadbare nose with frayed black stitching abruptly poked out, a head flopping to one side to stare at her.

Lifting him from the packaging, she looked into the unseeing face of a teddy bear, *her* teddy bear. A puzzled smile curled her lips upwards and she shook her head. How long had it been since they'd looked at each other nose to button; ten,

9

eleven, twelve years? She ran a finger along her mother's stitching holding on his damaged ear, feeling the rough singed fur on his back from when he'd sat too close to the fire. There was no doubt it was the one she'd had as a young child; the randomly named Mr Bloggs.

Although a little self–conscious, she couldn't resist giving Mr Bloggs another tight squeeze. He smelt musty but closing her pale blue eyes, she tumbled back through the years in an instant to the carpet of the sunny living room in Manchester. Her mother bent down to her, smiling, caressing her cheek and tapping a finger playfully on Mr Bloggs' nose. She revelled in the soft touch of her hands and the scent of apple blossom from her hair.

Tentatively she opened her eyes to the dim walls and held him out once more, his head nodding gently with a glazed smile. She glowed with warm memories as she sat him down on her crossed legs and together they examined the torn brown paper. In the bottom, she found a folded white note.

Now do you believe me?

Now will you trust me?

Your loyal friend.

Alex.

16711677. 202. 311. Friday 11am.

Hannah read it three times before putting Mr Bloggs aside, leaping from the bed and pulling a well-thumbed copy of To Kill a Mockingbird from her bookshelf. Jumping back on the lumpy mattress, she repositioned Mr Bloggs and opened the book. Pulling out a note secreted in its middle pages, she matched it to the newer notes' handwriting.

Hannah

You maybe think you don't remember me, but you do.

You maybe believe it was all in your imagination, but it wasn't.

You maybe won't believe me, but you're in great danger.

You may be blind, but they are not.

Your loyal friend.

Alex.

16711677. 202. 311.   *Friday 11am.*

The trouble was, Hannah did remember. Alex was her best friend from her first memory to her seventh birthday. He'd always been there when she'd wanted to play, talk, or have a tea party with Mr Bloggs. Her memories of Alex were full of smiles and of a time when she trusted no one more, not even her mum and dad.

Only Alex was never real, he'd been her imaginary friend.

She hugged Mr Bloggs and placed him and the two notes in front of her on the bed as if arranging evidence. She pulled her legs up under her chin and hugged them.

Was she going crazy? She'd dismissed the first note as an odd hoax, as she'd never told anyone in Bramley about Alex. She'd almost forgotten about him herself. The arrival of Mr Bloggs though, was beyond a joke, it was impossible.

She'd lost him during an Easter holiday to Scotland, on a fateful day-trip to Edinburgh. Whereabouts she couldn't be sure, all she remembered was the nauseating panic when she didn't know where he was and the utter world-ending despair when her parents couldn't put him back in her empty hands. She'd bawled her eyes out, sniffling on and on even as they retraced their steps, her mum asking in all the shops and museums, her dad pacing up and down all the streets. Yet Mr Bloggs was gone. As her dad carried her back to the car on his shoulders, a bag of sweets clutched tightly in one hand and a too-new teddy bear in the other, she'd got her first taste of sorrow and loss.

It wouldn't be her last.

'What are you doing up there!' Her Grandma's piercing voice jolted Hannah back into a world of lawnmowers and furniture polish.

'Coming!' She yelled back.

She scooped up the notes and returned them to Scout's custody between the pages of Harper Lee's book. After a moment's hesitation, she flipped over the square beanbag in the corner of the room and carefully unzipped the bottom. Apologetically stowing Mr Bloggs in a plastic bag containing some other contraband, she carefully buried it in the white polystyrene beans and zipped it back up.

Flattening the envelope, she managed to roll it up and slide it down the hollow tube of her metal bed-frame until she could think of somewhere better. She screwed the brass knob tight on top and looked around her. Almost as an afterthought, she pulled out two new-looking books on Art History and cast them casually on the bed. Hurriedly changing into jeans and an old fleece, she rushed downstairs, tying her hair back as she went.

The rest of the weekend dawdled past. Yet Hannah no longer willed the hands around her watch, her curiosity refusing to let go of the numbers on the notes.

16711677. 202. 311. Friday 11am.

She guessed Alex wanted to meet her on Friday, the first part a code for where. Cursing Alex – or whoever it was - for being so cryptic but secretly enjoying the challenge, she set about her chores without complaint. Whilst mowing the lawn she'd tried to form the code into a phone number, but couldn't make the idea work. Cleaning the windows of the conservatory, she'd wondered about map co-ordinates, but again failed to make any sense of it. Changing the beds, she'd pondered on bus routes, train times and road numbers before conceding she could probably make them into anything if she concentrated hard enough.

School lessons resumed on the Monday and her attention returned to a blur of graphs, diagrams and scribbled notes. As Tuesday, Wednesday and Thursday passed, mathematical equations, chemical symbols and historical dates buried Alex's cryptic code deeper and deeper in the recesses of her mind. He surfaced occasionally, but she didn't focus on him properly until late on Friday morning. Her anxiety grew as the deadline neared, but wherever Alex was at eleven o'clock, it wasn't in, around or anywhere near Mrs Perkin's Science Class. The bewildering sense of disappointment didn't replace her triumphant cynicism until she lay staring at the dark ceiling above her bed with Mr Bloggs in her arms.

13

Alex would be mad she hadn't solved the riddle and met up with him today.

'But he's imaginary!' She murmured without conviction. 'Isn't he? Wasn't he?'

She pulled the covers higher under her chin and gave Mr Bloggs a tighter squeeze, getting a slight sinking feeling.

She couldn't really be in great danger, could she?

She wrinkled her nose, but snuggled herself deeper under her covers, eyes darting beyond the dark wardrobe to the back of her bedroom door.

Only Alex knew about Mr Bloggs or called her Hannah Curious.

Hannah opened her mouth but closed it again. She'd not been called Hannah Curious in years and if it wasn't Alex or her father, it could only be one other person. She shut her eyes and drew in a long pained breath, her brain's reason and logic silenced.

Bluebell House had become her prison.

She chewed on her lip, not wanting to play this game any more. The thought of the world turning with its infinite wonders while she shuffled endlessly from Bluebell House to the Wesleyan church and Bramley High School was overwhelmingly depressing.

'What do you think Mr Bloggs? Should I just forget about it all?' She listened to his silence. 'I guess you'd tell me if I shouldn't?'

She clung to Mr Bloggs until sleep came, his existence the one impossible doorway she couldn't keep closed.

Despite a growing scepticism about the whole charade, she still felt somewhat disappointed when Saturday passed without a further knock on the door. In fact, but for Magda hiding a chocolate bar under her pillow, a class field trip organised at short notice for the end of the week and her grandmother saying she liked someone in the paper, her life had resumed to one entirely devoid of surprises. The week idled past, routine re-established and Alex returning to her distant, distorted memories. As the weekend approached - almost a fortnight after Mr Blogg's return - Hannah Curious was in hibernation again, if not forgotten. She would have remained hidden too, had something odd not happened on their school trip to London.

'...Yes Emily, I know you're missing double Science, but this is important too. Now listen up class!'

Hannah lifted her eyes from the blur of shops and offices to Mrs Perkins swaying awkwardly at the front of the coach.

'I know we sprung this trip to the Science Museum on you suddenly and you'd all rather be learning about Amino Acids back in class, but it's not just an excuse to escape school for the day. The truth is our Education Authority - in its infinite wisdom - has entered the school in a drawing competition to commemorate the anniversary of the Great Fire of London.'

There was a collective groan around the coach.

'Settle down!'

'Waste of time!' 'Stupid.' 'Drawing Miss? What's drawing got to do with Science?'

'I...It's.' She faltered, cheeks colouring. 'Look, no arguing! Just sketch the monument and meet back here in one hour. And need I remind you; you're representing the school; so straighten your ties and tuck in your shirts!'

Armed with paper and pencils they slunk off the coach into a cacophony of traffic and road works. The reverberating thunder of a pneumatic drill bounced back off the tinted windows of the towering office buildings, drowning out the traffic, conversation and any further directions from their teachers. Splitting naturally into cliques and groups, they shuffled away through the flows of uncompromising city-dwellers with their briefcases and umbrellas. Hannah tagged onto the back of a group, but stopped as they rounded the corner onto the pedestrianised Monument Street. A tall fluted pillar of Portland stone with a crown of gold leaf flames stood improbably amidst the eight and nine storey office blocks like a lit candlestick left in a model village.

Her wide eyes sensed movement and she realised the tiny figures at the top were tourists on a narrow viewing platform, the grey clouds behind them dizzily racing across the hazy sun. A gust of wind ruffled her hair and she pulled her black blazer tighter around her slender frame, glad she'd worn trousers and remembered her favourite pink and lemon gypsy scarf.

She wandered nearer, ignoring her classmates as the idle majority headed for a coffee shop and the studious minority claimed the benches opposite. Stood in its shadow she marvelled at the carved dragons and ornate frieze on the Monument's

16

base, itself the size of a modest house. Beneath the frieze was a large white information board.

THE MONUMENT

This Monument designed by Sir Christopher Wren was built to commemorate the Great Fire of London 1666. Which burned for three days consuming more than 13000 houses and devastating 436 acres of the city. The Monument is 202ft in height. Being equal to the distance westward from the bakehouse in Pudding Lane where the fire broke out. It took six years to construct 1671-1677...

Her day lurched sideways.

16711677. 202. 311. Friday 11am.

'They were years!' She muttered, only vaguely aware of the sideways glances she garnered from the foreigners alongside her.

...The Monument is 202ft in height...

Her eyes jarred on the number and she dizzily scanned the rest of the plaque.

...The balcony is reached by a spiral staircase of 311 steps...

She gasped, the tourists at her elbow quietly drifting away.

'Get a grip Hannah, get a grip.' She murmured before her eyes widened, pulse racing as noisily as the road-workers around the corner.

She cautiously turned her trembling wrist over and lifted her black sleeve.

It was quarter to eleven.

It was Friday.

Mr Bloggs, the notes and Alex forced their way back into her mind as if they'd drilled through her skull. Her breath trapped high in her chest. Any sense of elation though was fleeting, as they brought with them the nerve-ruffling weight of Alex's warning. She peered back up to the coffee shop, feeling isolated amongst the camera-wielding tourists. Without knowing why, she glanced further over her right shoulder and found a man in a brown fedora hat hastily looking away.

You may be blind, but they are not.

Unease tightened its chilling grip on her. She swallowed hard and self-consciously moved in the opposite direction around the base of the Monument, her ankles tight, toes clenched. She pulled up on the other side as she spotted two men in black fedoras talking further down the street. One whispered in the other's ear before looking at his watch. Not knowing exactly why, the panic within her rocketed skyward.

Without hesitation, she turned towards the Monument and rushed out of sight through the open doorway.

Noticeably cooler inside, she peered nervously back outside, sure the men would burst inside any second.

'One is it?'

Hannah stared at the cashier in his ticket kiosk and nodded numbly. Stuffing the paper and pencil in her bag, she handed the money over and stiffly took her ticket. Glimpsing a dark hat move past the doorway, she turned to the spiral staircase and bolted upwards. Hand skimming the wooden banister on her right, she counted the black limestone steps as she climbed around the inside of the column.

Nine, ten, eleven.

Over her shoulder, the entrance hall disappeared from view, her legs flooded with adrenaline.

Forty-one, forty-two.

She thought she heard someone below her but her pounding footsteps drowned them out.

Ninety-six, ninety-seven.

She heard voices and looked up just as a couple of gleeful kids bounded downwards followed by a chastising mother.

'Jonathon, be careful! Sophie come back here now and hold onto my hand!'

Hannah slowed, embarrassed to be rushing as she hugged the steep inside. Looking over the banister, she saw nobody was following her and tried to relax a little.

One-hundred-and-forty-two, one-hundred-and-forty-three.

The monotonous curved view of identical black limestone steps became almost mesmerising as she counted from the rhythmical thud of her feet.

One-hundred-and-eighty-two, one-hundred-and-eighty-three.

Her calves tightened and complained, reminding her of frenetic games of hockey at school. A train of a dozen people came down full of the joy of gravity. The noise of their footsteps deafening after she'd seemingly had the stairs to herself for so long.

'Not much further love. Views are worth it.' A jovial Yorkshire voice soothed.

With panted breaths, she half leaned on the rendered white wall and sped onwards.

Two-hundred-and-fifteen, two-hundred-and-sixteen.

'Here's an eager one!'

'Yes dear.'

She passed an older couple who stood silently as she darted up their inside.

'Gawd knows where they get the energy from Frank!'

'No Dear.'

Two-hundred-and-forty-seven, two-hundred-and-forty eight.

Hannah's chest burned, her throat hurting with every breath. She slowed, her gaze raised desperately upwards in search of anything but steps. The walls were lightening above her, but so was her head. Swaying slightly, she walked the last few steps, her hands clamped on her thighs. Above her, the stairs abruptly stopped at a white door, daylight streaming through a doorway in the wall on her left.

Three-hundred-and-nine, three-hundred-and-ten, three-hundred-and-eleven!

She'd made it! Hannah leaned heavily on the flat banister, her sides heaving like a cat readying to be sick, her back clammy beneath her school-bag. She stared down the centre of the staircase at the dizzying anti-clockwise spiral, willing her pounding heart to slow.

Hannah sucked in a couple of deep breaths and wiped her temples with a tissue. Her watch read five minutes to eleven.

'I'll just have a look. Still plenty of time to do the sketch.' She reasoned, still gasping.

Look for what exactly?

Scepticism bullied her fragile optimism. The sound of people stomping, huffing, puffing and encouraging one another drifted up the spiral steps. She waited until they arrived, kidding herself she was simply curious to see if they wore hats rather than delaying stepping outside. She smiled as two couples reached her, playfully rolling their eyes and blowing out their cheeks.

Following them outside, the cool breeze pleased her as much as the amazing panorama over the rooftops of London. She'd spooked herself with the riddle and bolted upwards like a startled squirrel up a great oak. Now her fright fell away as the vastness of the skies beyond the protective wire mesh belittled her paranoia.

Beyond a pair of fluttering Union flags, the River Thames carved a wide brown path through the clutter of stone and glass buildings. Far off to the right across the rooftops the London Eye turned and the Houses of Parliament shimmered through the haze. Opposite her, the imposing glass Shard skyscraper glinted and scratched at the clouds. On her left, Tower Bridge stood like a miniature gateway, the imposing grey warship HMS Belfast behind it like a guard dog waiting for the postman.

Hannah shuffled around the cramped square platform, her left hand skimming the stonework, right on the stainless steel balcony. Passing a man feeding coins into the telescope in the corner, Hannah gripped the cage and looked to the east. Decorated church spires reached skyward amidst a sea of concrete and glass, the ornate imprisoned by whirring air conditioning units and the stark lines of modernity. Further round to the left, she recognised the inside-out Lloyds building

21

and the wonderful curves of the Gherkin amidst the sparkling towers of the financial district.

She'd seen so much of London on the television and in her books, yet now the views fell onto her own blue eyes. A cool breath of wind touched her round face and raked its fingers through her dark hair. She smiled, despite the cages all around her, up here she was free.

'Regardless of what happens,' she thought, 'regardless of what punishment she'd face if spotted up here instead of drawing, this made it worthwhile.'

She moved past a Chinese couple, the man taking in the view whilst his wife snapped pictures of St Paul's Cathedral across the rooftops. The views to the north were much like the east, rooftops to the horizon interspersed by the occasional tall building and splash of greenery. Back facing west once more, the return of unease replaced the novelty of new vistas.

A tap on her shoulder made her stiffen, her heart instantly beating at a million beats a minute. She swallowed, brought her head around and there he was. Full of smiles and utterly gracious, the Chinese man held out his digital camera and pointed at himself and his wife. With a barely masked sigh of disappointment, Hannah's shoulders sagged and she took his camera. As they posed with broad grins, Hannah clicked the button and took their photograph. As they thanked her with a display of synchronised bowing, Hannah reciprocated and turned around.

Stood before her with the same soppy grin from her childhood, was Alex.

CHAPTER TWO

Her chest tightened so sharply, she thought her heart had stopped.

She stared numbly, her brain overloaded; thinking difficult, words impossible. Lips tight and head shaking, she leaned on the balcony behind her and sucked in a few shallow breaths.

Alex stood between her and the doorway in a simple baby blue shirt, black trousers and shoes, a leather belt snug around his waist. It was a vast change from the cloaks and colourful tunics she recalled in her memories, looking more like a relaxed office worker than an extra from Camelot. Yet the thick glossy brown hair sweeping across his forehead, the high cheekbones and square chin were just as she remembered. The light glinting in his bright, cobalt blue eyes unlocked a hundred forgotten memories, her mind overflowing with shared laughter, mocking stares and fevered colouring-in competitions. He timidly came forward as if approaching a wild horse, stopping as she backed further away.

'Alright, I'll stay here.' He managed a lopsided smile, eyes creasing with an odd mix of amusement and awkwardness. 'Hello Hannah Curious.'

Behind him, a string of breathless middle-aged Germans filed out of the doorway murmuring appreciative noises of the view and cool air. He glanced back at them before leaning on the flat rail and looking out to the river.

He stood in silence, a hint of a wry grin lingering on his lips. She stared wide-eyed at him. Despite thinking of little else since the return of Mr Bloggs, she realised now she was far from ready to meet a figment of her imagination.

After the first note had arrived, she'd clung to her belief he'd been a fantasy, as real as the tooth fairy or the man in the moon. She'd dredged her memories for a time when Alex had lifted a teacup or pushed open a door or when her mum and dad had interacted with him instead of humouring her, but she'd always come up blank.

As a young child, she'd been convinced he was real.

Ever since he'd become an embarrassing memory.

'And now?' She asked herself.

She swallowed hard and reached her hand out, letting it fall back to her side as he turned her way.

'I'm sorry. This must have all come as a great shock to you.'

Hannah stared, shoulders trembling.

'What do you want?' Her voice sounded strangely distant.

Alex stared out at the horizon before refocusing on her face.

'There's someone who wants to meet you.'

She met his eyes and swallowed subconsciously. 'Who?'

'The Guardian. You may be in great danger.'

'Who?' Hannah exclaimed again numbly.

'The Guardian.' Alex said patiently. 'The secrecy around you might be compromised and as such I don't know all the details. I was simply instructed to arrange for you to be here.'

'Arrange...?' She exasperated. 'What...with...silly riddles and...and...'

He waited for her frustration to blow itself out.

'It saddens me we've had to take such precautions.'

Hannah waited for him to continue, but he returned his eyes to the jumbled rooftops.

'But I've got school...How could...?' She stumbled, glancing down at her class scattered about the street below. 'I...I wouldn't be here at all if my class hadn't had a school trip!'

'Ah, glad it worked,' he grinned, 'not entirely my idea, but-'

'What?' Hannah murmured, eyes narrowing.

He nodded, smirking at her reaction. 'Took a bit of lateral thinking after two no-shows, but it was thought a funding prize from the local education authority might tempt your school to inadvertently help us out.'

Hannah looked away, eyes unable to focus.

How could he arrange to get her class out of school for the day?

How could anyone?

She turned back, irritation fuelling her bravery. 'You can't just cancel lessons for the day!'

He grinned and looked her up and down.

She gritted her teeth and changed tact. 'Well, who is this...this...*Guardian*?!'

25

'Just...wait until they get here.' He said neutrally.

Hannah sighed.

'Why me?'

'I told you, it's believed you're in great danger. Just don't ask me why.'

Her intrigue lost its battle with frightened anger.

'Why?'

Alex laughed before noting Hannah's straight face.

'I don't know.'

'You must know.'

'I don't.'

'You must!'

'How long do you want to do this for?'

'How long you got?' She snapped.

He sighed. 'Look Hannah, I don't know what the Guardian wants, I'd tell you if I did. All I know is, we're all to meet here, well away from your home.'

'But why am *I* in danger?' She said incredulously. 'I'm of no interest to anyone.'

Alex shrugged awkwardly. 'I'm sure that's not true.'

Hannah examined her shoes, as if they could somehow help her.

Why was this...this...Guardian stranger warning her? What interest was it to them?

Hannah's shoulders tensed, her lips tight as Alex looked calmly away to a boat surging upriver.

'And I'm not Hannah Curious any more; no-one's called me that since I was seven years old! In fact, this has been a complete waste of time.' She folded her arms and stared at Alex who showed no alarm she was going anywhere.

'I should never have come up here, I must be mad. Have you any idea how much trouble...?' Hannah's cheeks burned at his lack of reaction and with a disgusted sigh headed for the doorway.

'Have you seen them?' He said without turning.

Hannah paused, tried to resist before rounding on him with annoyance.

'What?'

'Have you seen them?'

You may be blind, but they are not.

The line from the letter resurfaced in her mind, her stomach tightening.

'Who?' She muttered, the fire gone from her anger.

He turned towards her. 'The watchers, those growing number of unnoticeable types who you only see when you know they're there. In particular,' he held her gaze, 'those wearing fedora hats?'

Hannah started and Alex's eyes narrowed.

'Where?'

She dropped her gaze to the ground below and Alex pushed himself back from the edge.

'Here! Are you sure? How many?'

'Erm…' Hannah swallowed hard. 'Two, no three. Two of them were talking but the other looked right at me.'

Alex rubbed his cheek and gingerly peeked over the edge.

'Did you ever notice them back in Bramley-upon-Thames?' He whispered in close but she no longer pulled away. 'Think Hannah. It's important.'

Hannah frowned and thought back to her sheltered existence in and around Bluebell House. It seemed impossibly distant, a dreary montage from another world.

'I don't think so, the only time I'm outside at all is in the garden and walking to school or church.'

'Are you sure?'

'I think so.'

'You *think* so?'

'Yes.'

'They mustn't find out where you live.'

He sighed and glanced back down towards the ground.

'How many have you seen today?'

'I said, one watching and two talking.' She squinted and pointed to a figure in the shadows reading a paper. 'Is that another one down there?'

'Don't point!' He snapped, forcing her hand down. 'Never point!'

'Sorry.' She said jumpily.

He pressed himself back into the stonework again and rubbed a hand over his mouth.

She eyed his panic and wrinkled her nose. 'Look what is this? You can't jump at your shadow every time you see someone in a hat! Whatever next, avoiding people in sandals or running from anyone with a beard?' Hannah thought for a second, 'Actually, that last one-'

'Don't mock what you don't understand!' Alex fizzed. 'The fedora-wearers keep to the background, always watching but never noticed. People up here aren't supposed to see them.'

'And what if I do see them!' Hannah challenged, almost derisorily.

Alex looked to be biting back his anger.

'Hannah,' He shook his head, 'if you see them, and they see you've seen them, and you've seen they've seen you've seen them, well...you'd wish you hadn't seen them.'

Hannah blinked and allowed an untethered eyebrow to soar.

Alex sighed. 'But that's beside the point. The fact you saw them probably means they're not after you. They're more than likely just monitoring the location or tourist movements. Hopefully it's nothing more, hopefully they're not onto us.'

'Us!? What do you mean us?'

'I didn't mean it like that, I meant my...organisation.'

'But why should they be monitoring me, I'm just a girl from Manchester.'

'Hannah, I don't know your full story, such is the level of secrecy around your protection, but I do know you're not *just* anything. Even in your early years, when I was assigned to watch over you up in Manchester, I never knew why. That's for the Guardian and Elders to know, not the likes of me.'

Hannah's eyes widened, the drama of the last couple of weeks morphing into part of an operation going back fifteen years.

29

'Ridiculous!' She murmured but with less conviction.

Besides, Protection? Protection from what, a few strangers in peculiar hats?

She tried to voice the absurdity of it all but movement made her self-conscious and she leaned back on the railing beside Alex, surreptitiously watching the Chinese couple as they drifted away towards the stairs.

As they disappeared inside, raised voices echoed out from the doorway.

'Yes it is your fault Edward, you blithering buffoon!' A clipped voice berated. 'If you hadn't lost track of time, we wouldn't be late in the first place.'

'Sorry George.' A despondent public-school boy accent replied, the name drawn out.

'*Sorry George* simply won't cut it this time Edward. If we've missed them again because of your forgetfulness, well-'

The voices increased in volume as they moved out into the open air.

'-let's just say I'm not taking the blame for you this time. Just you wait until the Guardian and the Elders hear we were late three weeks running, well I'll tell you for certain, they'll not be best pleased.'

Hannah's eyes flared.

The pair stood taking in the view but the similarity with all the other tourists ended there. The taller of the two wore black pinstripe trousers and a shiny gold waistcoat beneath a burgundy coloured frock coat. His gentile face was long but distinguished, his eyes keen and thin handlebar moustache finely groomed. He clutched a large copper coloured top hat with a chocolate coloured band at its base. In his other hand, he dabbed a gold silk handkerchief to his brow before returning it

30

to his chest pocket. Drawing in a great breath, he leaned confidently on his black cane, examining the clouds as if he was expecting rain.

The smaller of the two stood nearer to her and looked much more uncomfortable, staring downwards like a claustrophobe having his first formal introduction to a fear of heights. The black three-piece suit hung awkwardly from his rounded shoulders, his arms dangling limply by his sides, sleeves retreating from his hands. His face was round with dark bushy mutton-chop sideburns, a black bowler hat sat low on his head, seemingly balanced on his ears and eyebrows. At least until the taller one tapped the hat with his cane and he hurriedly took it off.

Without thinking, Hannah gave Alex a nudge with her elbow and flinched at having struck solid flesh. Not noticing or too polite to draw attention to her shock, he followed her gaze to the pair still staring out over the city.

'Oh…here we go.' He mumbled under his breath.

'Sorry?'

'Nothing.' He said, returning his gaze to the horizon.

He might not be interested, but Hannah couldn't keep her eyes off them.

'I'll never get to be a professor at this rate.' The taller one said shaking his head resignedly.

'Why'd you want to do that George?' The smaller one asked, the pronunciation of his friend's name almost as long as the rest of the question.

'Do what?'

'Turn into a Prof-verb.'

31

'For the umpteenth time Edward, I want to become a professor because my untapped philosophical depths are completely wasted having to babysit you.' As he spoke, he bent down and picked up a silver coin by his foot, placing it in his pocket as he straightened up. 'Besides, I think Professor Found has a rather meaningful ring to it.'

'But, but what…would happen to me?'

'Never mind, just keep hold of your train of thought and try not to lose your footing on the way down like last time.'

'Have we missed them George?'

George brushed his coat aside and reached into his waistcoat pocket, producing a gold hunter-case pocket watch on a chain. With a flick of the thumb, the cover opened and he pulled a face, the annoyance still in his voice.

'Twenty past eleven. What do *you* think Edward?' He said sarcastically. 'The Guardian's message said to be here at eleven with humble apologies, now we're the ones who are going to have to apologise!'

Hannah's gaze slid across to Alex, who had his eyes shut. She looked back as the pair turned to the doorway, George indicating with an open palm for Edward to go first.

'Erm...' Hannah took a step forward, unsure what she was going to say. 'Excuse me?'

The pair looked back at her, behind them, at each other and back at her with puzzled faces.

'You can see us?' George said with an inquisitive frown.

She'd never been asked that before, let alone by two men dressed as if they'd stepped straight out of a Dickensian street scene. Were they questioning her eyesight or her sanity?

'Well…yes!'

Another exchange of Victorian glances, whispers and shakes of the head.

'By Jove! So you're from Lexica?'

Hannah's eyes narrowed briefly. 'Where? No, I'm from Manchester!'

The back of the burgundy coat turned her way as the pair partook in another hushed conference. The smaller of the two gormlessly peered around his friend's arm to look her up and down.

'Most irregular George. Most irregular.' The shorter man muttered.

'Yes I know Edward, now let me handle this.' The man called George stood up straight and almost looked embarrassed. 'I'm sorry Miss, there seems to have been a misunderstanding. We were informed to meet the expected arrival of A-' He checked himself as if he'd nearly said too much. 'A gentleman and his friend.'

The truth dawned on Hannah and she pointed over her shoulder. Alex reluctantly stepped forward, hands in his pockets.

'No you see…' The man began. 'Good heavens! Aldwyn Claviger? Is that you?'

'George Found lives up to his name once more.' Alex said carefully.

George bowed politely and swapped his hat to his other hand. Alex half-heartedly lifted his own imaginary hat and ignored George's outstretched hand. George let his arm fall away and gawped at Alex's clothes.

33

'I'm sorry old chap, I didn't recognise you. What are you doing here?'

'I'm here on private business. What are you doing here?' Alex's voice had changed to the restrained manners of a frigid Victorian gent.

George's lips twitched, his eyes narrowing as he peered at Alex. Hannah stood awkwardly, sensing an unresolved argument bubbling just beneath the strained pleasantries.

'Private business…?' George queried.

Alex nodded and remained quiet.

'I see.'

'I doubt it.' Alex mumbled.

'Hmmm?'

'Nothing.' Alex shook his head.

George's mouth twisted, moustache twitching. 'Well, this *is* a turn up. And here was me thinking you were far too busy with your caretaking work…'

'Key-keeping work! I'm a Grade four Nouner Claviger, as you well know.'

'Sorry old chap, slip of the tongue.'

'That's alright old man; I know I was never quite as busy as you. Tell me, how's the black market these days?'

Muted anger flashed across George's eyes, much to Alex's amusement.

George chewed his tongue but Alex's wry grin melted his guard. Another unspoken conversation passed between them and Hannah sensed they'd agreed a temporary truce.

'Of course you have met Edward Lost before, haven't you?'

The man with the bowler hat shook hands with Alex or Aldwyn - or whoever he was. They were all still nodding to one another when the group of Germans shuffled past Hannah and walked right through George and his friend Edward as if they weren't there.

The set walls of her reality swayed as her brain distrusted her eyes and she staggered backwards. She blinked hard, but the Victorian pair didn't so much as flinch, still chatting to Alex as the tourists moved away around the platform.

She bumped into the rail behind her, still gawping as ghostly thoughts bubbled and fizzed through her brain. Real and fantasy blurred into one muddied mess, a thousand paranoid questions raising their hands in her head and shouting, 'Me, me, pick me!'

Her overworked logic waved a white flag, confusedly willing her to be asleep, so she could press the reset button and wake up back at Bluebell House.

'George, I'd like you to meet an old friend of mine.'

Hannah centred her swirling attention on Alex's smiling face. George beamed too, tucking his hat under his elbow and smoothing his dark hair with his other hand.

Once more, his outstretched hand remained empty.

Hannah' s heart pounded, trapped within her chest like an irate prisoner in a cell. She empathised, pressing herself further into the bars behind her. She belatedly forced the weakest of smiles and managed a stiff nod of her quivering head. George mirrored her greeting and gave a solemn bow from his shoulders.

35

'George Found, Grade four Verbman; adventurer, merchant, impresario, diplomat and entrepreneur at your service madam.'

'And purveyor of quality, stolen items.' Alex whispered just loud enough for all to hear.

'Sssssssssshhhhh-ut up…caretaker.' George murmured indignantly from the corner of his mouth. 'All items found are legitimately lost items!'

Alex's eyes slid across to Edward Lost - who stood frowning at a woman's compact polka-dot umbrella in his hands – raising an eyebrow as he returned his gaze to George.

George stared at it uncomfortably as if thinking of an obvious explanation. A few painful seconds passed before he snatched it and secreted it deep in one of his coat pockets.

'Yes, well...this is my erm...this is Edward Lost, Grade two Verbman.'

'Pleased to meet you.' Edward grinned as he leaned forward and bowed awkwardly.

'Right, well…shall we get down to business?' George said to Alex.

Distracted by loud, olive-skinned tourists appearing through them from the doorway, Hannah stepped into the corner, their chattering voices blanking out much of the conversation. She heard fragments from George and Alex's lips, but understood even less. It sounded like English, but she'd never come across such terminology: Heartisans, Lexica, Feds, Pandemonia.

After five minutes, Alex turned to Hannah as if he'd only just remembered she was there.   'Ah, if you'll afford me a couple of minutes George. I believe I've some explaining to do.'

'Absolutely old bean, we'll wait just inside the door. Come along Edward.'

Alex stepped towards her, his normal accent and mannerisms returning. He unsuccessfully tried a smile.

'It seems dangerous developments elsewhere have meant your meeting with the Guardian is cancelled until further notice. I'm sorry for wasting your time Hannah. I'll be in touch if it's rearranged. Remember to avoid the figures in fedoras. Here…'

He reached in his pocket and produced a key on a long silver chain. He held it open and she cautiously put her head through the loop.

'This is my key, use it if you're ever in trouble.'

'Why? Hey, where do you think you're going?'

He stepped towards the doorway.

'It's not wise for us to linger up here in the open. So I'm going to return to Lexica with George and Edward.'

'But, you can't go now….' She pulled up, hearing the desperation in her voice. Despite the craziness threatening to overwhelm her mind, the thought of not seeing him again troubled her more than she'd like to admit. Besides, he was….a growing buzzing noise interrupted her thoughts.

'Noooo! They heard us!' Alex's eyes widened.

Before Hannah could follow his gaze, he'd pulled her roughly down onto the hard floor, her left shoulder banging into the stone wall. She twisted round to shout at him but the words evaporated from her lips. Clinging to the outside of the cage was the largest wasp she'd ever seen. Easily as tall as her, it buzzed furiously like a power drill, wings rattling against the wire mesh as its knife-like stinger stabbed violently through a gap where she'd just been stood.

She frantically pushed herself back into the wall with her feet, scrambling desperately to put some space between her and this monstrous insect. Her pulse pounded deafeningly in her ears as a large shadow crossed her body. Looking up, a second crawled down the outside of the sloping cage above her head, its glassy wings still.

She was hallucinating; had to be, absolutely had to be! Alex plucked her up in one fluid movement and bundled her inside the doorway.

'You alright old chap?' George understated, leaning on his cane by the handrail.

'Buzzwords! We need to leave now before they attract other Fiends!'

'Cripes! What about your friend?'

They all turned to Hannah.

'It's alright Hannah,' Alex said breathily, 'they're after George and me, not you. Keep quiet and they'll not even notice you leave. Take care, Hannah Curious.'

He turned to George. 'We should go. Now!'

George nodded to a bewildered Hannah and pulled open the white door, which she'd assumed only headed up to the golden flames at the top of the Monument.

38

Following George and Edward through, Alex gave her a final nod of the head and slammed the door shut behind him.

Hannah trembled against the banister at the top of the stairs, afraid to take her eyes off the open doorway lest the horrible creatures somehow got in through the cage. Every time the silence grew and she thought they'd flown away, frantic buzzing returned and they drifted past the entrance. She saw a woman lean on the railing right next to one of them without flinching or even seeming to notice it was there.

This is it Hannah, you've gone mad. First, you hallucinate, next you believe your visions and finally you act on them. Welcome to Insanityville Miss Fruitcake, enjoy your stay.

She frowned, wondering if hearing such a mocking voice in her head helped or rather proved the point.

A family with excited children appeared through the doorway and she turned away lest they see the terrified look she must have on her face. She listened to their rhythmical footsteps and gleeful shouts, allowing a few moments of reality to soothe her jagged nerves.

She'd just met Alex.

Her imaginary friend from her childhood wasn't imaginary, she'd just met him so she hadn't lost her mind. She tried to block out the buzzing from outside and uttered the latter part repeatedly.

She hadn't.

As her heart rate returned from three figures to two, her thoughts moved to the steps. If she hurried she could rejoin her class, make a hasty sketch of the monument, call it impressionism and nobody would be any the wiser. As she lifted her foot over the threshold of the top step, she couldn't resist looking over the banister at the dizzying spiral one last time.

A gasp filled her lungs, freezing her in place. She was already too late.

CHAPTER THREE

A dozen right hands moved up the handrail like the legs of a caterpillar. Hannah stared, transfixed by the jerky rhythmical movement as they spiralled up towards her.

About a third of the way up, they abruptly stopped. Twelve faces slowly leaned out, left hands lifting their fedora hats from their heads as they peered upwards straight at her.

Hannah jumped and snapped her head back out of sight, belatedly realising her mistake.

'I just know I had it when we left the Hotel!' A strong Lancashire accent protested. 'Are you listening Frank?'

Hannah turned numbly to a grey-haired woman coming in from outside, her hands searching in her cavernous shoulder bag.

'Yes dear, but it's not going to rain, forecast said so.' A tall, balding husband lumbered along in her wake.

'That's not the point Frank…oh sorry love, are you going down?'

Hannah numbly shook her head and stepped aside, watching them gingerly feel their way down the first few steps. It all felt surreal, chaos swirling with reality, danger hidden in plain sight. The couple slid out of view, but she knew she couldn't follow, knew they couldn't help her. She glanced dizzily outside at the

Monument's caged gallery and whilst she no longer glimpsed any gargantuan wasps, she recognised the folly of trying to hide out there from the men in hats.

They couldn't actually be after her, could they? They surely couldn't.

She tried to force herself to believe that, but it was like trying to put a reluctant cat in a box. As the sound of heavy footsteps rose up the centre of the stairwell, panic gripped Hannah with paws and claws and refused to let go.

'This can't be happening.' She muttered, head throbbing with disjointed thoughts.

Nausea washed over her, her hand numbly reaching up to calm her pounding chest. Cold metal pressed against her skin. With a yelp and fumbling fingers, she pulled out the long silver key.

She hadn't lost her mind.

A shadow crossed the doorway and she glimpsed yellow and black stripes outside.

She hadn't.

Gripped between numb fingers and thumb, she brought the dulled key up to the shiny gold lock in the white door. She saw instantly it was about two centuries out of date. Yet as she pushed the key nearer to the Yale lock, a prickle of electricity crossed her hand, like an army of ants marching towards her wrist. The puffing and panting of the Feds on the stairs grew louder but she daren't turn around. The key touched the metal facing, glowing and sparking as it morphed itself into a slender gold key that slid effortlessly into the lock.

Wide-eyed, she turned it and the door popped open an inch. In one fluid movement, she flicked the door from her left hand to her right, the key coming free and bouncing back onto her chest. She slid through the gap without looking back, almost trapping her fingers in the doorjamb as it closed with a satisfying click.

She stepped back in the dim light, waiting anxiously for it to burst open or at least judder in its frame. Neither came and gently she dared to release her breath. Footsteps behind her relinquished the door's grip on her attention. She turned to another stone staircase, a figure bounding up the spiralling steps towards her.

'Alex!'

'What's happened?! More Buzzwords?'

She rushed down a couple of steps, but as he slowed, she stopped short, her raised hands hovering before curling her hair behind her ears. George and Edward loomed into view behind him, out of breath, the latter without his hat.

'Men in hats, fedoras, they're coming, about a dozen, more, coming up the stairs, running...' The jumble of words tumbled from her lips.

Alex and George exchanged worried looks.

'Most irregular George. Most irregular.' Edward piped up before frowning as he patted the crown of his bare head.

'Don't worry, they can't get in here.' George soothed.

'They said that about the other side of the Monument!' Alex exclaimed.

'True enough, but there's a difference between out of bounds and out of reach.'

Hannah reached for a banister on her right, thoughts alternating between the grotesque yellow and black insects and the men chasing up to get her. Her head swam slightly, the walls pulsating and swaying. She sucked in a deep breath and let it out gradually.

'Troubled times Aldwyn. Deeply troubled...Oh I say, are you alright?' George enquired.

'No...I'm just...' Hannah uttered as Alex grabbed her arm and forced her to sit down.

'Damn Feds!' George exclaimed.

'Ladies present!' Edward chirped from behind.

'Quite, I do apologise.'

'It's alright. I'm alright.' Hannah managed, not wanting their attention or a fuss.

She gripped the wooden banister and hauled herself back up onto her feet. A flickering flame drew her gaze on to a gaslight on the wall, her eyes staring sceptically at the clockwise curve of the handrail. Leaning tentatively over the banister, she looked down a mirror image of the spiral she'd seen on the other side of the white door.

'But that's impossible!'

She looked at Alex who seemed amused at her curiosity.

'Nothing is impossible.'

His words fizzed in her mind for a moment as if she'd rushed a glass of pop. Here she was standing with the impossible, in the impossible, having just been attacked by the impossible. She took a step back up towards the door, distrusting of the black steps underfoot.

'Don't worry Miss Lady Hannah, it's natural to feel a certain amount of disorientation at first.'

'Remember that lad!' Edward chuckled.

George's gaze slid cautiously to his companion.

'Remember? He was so scared he clambered over and jump…'

'Yes, well I am sure we don't need to hear about that right now Edward.' George chastised, his forced grin all teeth and no humour.

'What am I going to do now?' Alex looked from Hannah to George.

'Well she can't stay down here.'

'She can't go back out there to the Feds!'

'Goodness, what a quandary,' George sighed, 'trapped between worlds and no safety in either.'

'Most irregular!' Edward added.

The three of them stood deep in contemplation like a strange image from a fashion catalogue.

'Who are the Feds exactly?' Hannah said despondently.

They stirred from their daydreaming, Edward and Alex turning to George who seemed more than happy to speak.

'Well, Miss Lady Hannah, I suppose you would describe them as our secret police, they watch Heartisans-'

Alex read her frown, 'Heartisans are our term for people, humans like you. Sorry George, do carry on.'

George let his eyes linger on Alex before returning them to Hannah. 'They watch Heartisans up in Pandemonia-'

'Pandemonia is our word for your world up on the surface.' Alex cut in and held his hand up to George in apology again.

George glared at Alex before unclenching his teeth. 'Up on the surface, they look for suspicious characters and Words who shouldn't be up there.'

'Words like you and Edward?'

'I guess you could say that.' George said indignantly.

'She just did.' Alex grinned.

'Oh I'm sorry, I didn't mean-'

George waved away her apologies. 'No offence taken.'

Alex wiped his hand across his chin and licked his lips. 'You know in a way this could be a blessing in disguise.'

George looked up at the door and down the steps, blowing out his cheeks, Edward mimicking his every move. 'Some disguise.'

'-disguise.' Edward mumbled shaking his head.

Alex pulled a face sardonically. 'If Hannah can't leave right away, maybe I should take her to see the Guardian instead?'

George's eyes widened, telling Hannah everything she needed to know about such an idea.

'Steady on old chap, I don't mean to be harsh but those days are behind you.'

'-hind you.' Edward muttered, innocently.

Alex looked sternly at George as if he'd just blown his nose on their temporary peace treaty.

'For the last time, I was innocent!'

The atmosphere became frostier.

'Sorry Aldwyn, I wasn't…' He glimpsed Hannah's upturned face and drew himself back to his full height. 'I just think we should leave all that in the past and deal with the present. You've moved on, we've all moved on. Being a Claviger is a dignified position. Obviously, the Guardian holds no grudges or you wouldn't have been entrusted with this minor task.'

Alex scowled.

Edward lost interest.

'Yet,' George continued, 'recklessly risking the safety of yourself or Miss Lady Hannah here will almost certainly make it your last.'

'Maybe.' Alex managed.

'Besides Aldwyn,' George lowered his voice, 'things have changed. The Guardian and the Shrouded Guild don't operate from the secret offices in the Bibliography any more, they move from place to place to evade detection.'

George fiddled with his moustache and gave a stiff shake of his head. 'No, I think it better if you take her straight to another entrance and spirit her back home to afternoon tea and her needlework before she's missed.'

Hannah raised an eyebrow, guessing it'd been some time since George had been around teenagers.

47

'Moreover Aldwyn, do it quickly lest the Feds contact the authorities and set the Author-tarian Guard down here on full alert.'

'We don't know they'll do that.' Alex said unconvincingly. 'They could just be heading up to investigate the Buzzwords.'

'Yes and when they get up there and find no cause?' George looked at him almost with pity. 'Oh dear, what a mess. Ironically, I think the Guardian was meeting the two of you, precisely to warn you both of the growing threat from the Feds. '

Hannah shook her head at the ridiculousness of arranging a meeting to warn her about Feds, in a place teeming with Feds.

'What a stupid...' She began.

The three of them looked up at her and she saw the snapshot of a dozen Fed faces looking up at her again.

She swallowed hard. 'They saw me.'

George's eyes narrowed.

'The...Feds.' She said timidly. 'They saw me inside the staircase.'

'You looked at them? Without their hats?' He asked.

Alex closed his eyes resignedly even before Hannah nodded.

George looked back at Alex smugly. 'So, she's probably in the Fed's incident report now, good work Aldwyn.'

'It wasn't Alex's fault!' Hannah blurted, her cheeks reddening as George eyed her cautiously. 'The meeting shouldn't have been arranged-'

'It's alright Hannah,' Alex cut in, 'George knows he spoke as much jargon in the open as I did.'

George's moustache twitched as he ground his teeth.

'But,' Alex added before George could come back at him, 'George is right about the Feds reporting it to their superiors. They'll forward your description to the Author-tarian Guards who patrol the borders on the upper floors. Of course they won't know you're a Heartisan, they'll assume you're a Word like us.'

Hannah didn't know whether that was good news or not.

'And with only one way in and out of the Monument, they know there's a secret entrance up there too.' George added gloomily.

'They can't get in here can they?'

George half-smiled to alleviate her fears. 'No, we should be safe here, but it will mean Alex will have to get you out of Lexica another way. Preferably another entrance away from here and away from patrolling Feds.'

'Perhaps you're right. The Guardian will just have to wait.' Alex conceded through tight lips.

She caught up with George's words. 'Sorry, wait, what?!'

George innocently turned her way. 'Hmmm?'

'Another entrance away from here? What about the rest of my class?'

'Oh I don't think they'll be able to come, will they George?'

George looked sardonically at Edward fidgeting with his coat, fingering a thread where a button should have been. 'No Edward.' He forced a smile for

Hannah. 'You're worried you'll get in trouble with your schoolmistress, aren't you? Well, I think we're a little past that now, aren't we Aldwyn?'

He tried a mocking smile with Alex, but it wasn't shared and he tapped the step twice with his cane. 'Now, may I suggest we head down?'

Hannah roused herself and tugged sharply on Alex's arm.

Alex paused for a second, noting her stern expression. 'We'll be along in a second, George.'

George glanced at Hannah and concurred with an elegant tilt of his head. 'Don't linger too long up here.'

George set off sedately with a swish and regular dull tap of his cane on the black limestone steps, Edward following with a melodic plod.

Hannah searched Alex's face for explanations.

'What? Where are…How…?' She took a breath and kept her voice low. 'What on earth's going on? I can't stay down here!'

'We'll work something out, try not to worry.'

'Try not to *worry*?!' She hissed, half turning to an imaginary audience. 'My teachers are going to go mental if I don't get back to the coach on time! Not to mention I got attacked by two five-feet-high Buzzwasps and you just walked off and left me!'

'Buzzwords, they're called Buzzwords…and yes, but you see they weren't after you, so…'

'And the Feds?'

'Oh!' Alex's mouth formed a perfect circle. 'Oh, I-I think I see now, you're angry with me because I left you. So, you are probably wanting some kind of,' he gestured with revolving fingers, 'explanation?'

Hannah bit her tongue, the mouthful of unladylike words valiantly restrained.

'Right well, they were Buzzwords. They're parasites who feed off terminology and jargon people don't understand.'

'What would've happened if it'd stung me?'

'Don't worry yourself about that right now.' He moved down a step but she held onto his arm.

'What would've happened?'

He looked at her gravely and her eyes opened wide.

'Don't worry about it.' He pulled out of her grip and stepped down. She stubbornly watched him descend. 'Unless you'd like to head upwards and get yourself arrested by the Feds?'

She glanced back up to the door, checked her watch and resignedly plodded down the steps after him.

George eyed their whispering from below as they came into view and misinterpreted her expression. 'I suppose you're wondering how it's possible to be descending clockwise when you climbed up clockwise?' He smirked.

'I know!'

'Yes Edward, I know you know but Miss Lady Hannah doesn't. By the way Edward, will you do the count?'

'Right you are George. One, two, three…' Edward continued to mutter numbers as he plodded down the steps.

George looked up at them arrogantly. 'It's very difficult to explain the intricacies of inter-world travel to those more interested in science than religion. In many ways, a believer is much more open to the concepts and details than a logical mind. One merely has to mention passing to the other side and…'

'Where are we exactly?' Hannah cut in abruptly, her mind numbed by her sudden descent into deep trouble.

George glared, briefly startled.

'Sorry,' she placated. 'I mean...'

'She means tell her where we are, please?' Alex placated.

George looked sternly at Alex as if it was somehow his fault, gaining a bemused shrug in return.

'Very well, I can see you aren't one for anecdotes. We're descending the staircase hidden from view in your world. Technically speaking it's a Number Well, a kind of numerical airlock between our world and yours.'

Hannah tried to focus, the greater calamity too large to face. 'So are we in the Monument or not?'

'Well, I suppose technically we *are* still within the walls of the Monument, but the staircase and all you see around you doesn't actually exist. It relies on our collective belief to keep it beneath our feet.'

Hannah wrinkled her nose.

'Just because you don't understand it doesn't make it untrue. Think of matter in your world; solids, liquids and gases, they're formed by invisible atoms, yes?'

Hannah nodded, unsure if she could ever fully focus on a Science teacher in a copper-coloured top hat.

'Yet, those atoms are empty space but for a few miniscule electrons whizzing around a tiny nucleus. Everything you take for granted as solid in Pandemonia is actually 99.99% emptiness between Protons, Neutrons and Electrons. If you eliminated all that space, you would fit all the Heartisans in Pandemonia into a space about the size of a sugar cube!'

'I know a horse who likes sugar cubes.'

George ignored Edward's contribution. 'Likewise in Lexica this staircase is 99.99% empty space collectively held together by our imaginations.'

Hannah curled her lip, wishing she could hear her shrill alarm clock more than ever before in her life.

'Maybe a demonstration will help?' Alex piped up.

Hannah stopped and glared at him.

'Splendid idea young Aldwyn, showing is always better than telling, although we must be quick.' George continued down a few steps and pressed himself and Edward against the wall. 'Now Miss Lady Hannah, I want you to stand like this and stare at the banister.'

Alex grinned at her and nodded encouragingly until she reluctantly obliged.

'Now picture the wall and stairs without a handrail, just a curve of black stone steps and a bare stone wall. Concentrate and imagine it isn't there.'

Hannah silently glared through the handrail at George.

Nothing happened.

'This is stupid.' She thought. 'I'm in so much trouble and-'

'Forget your worries and concentrate. Let your disbelief go.'

She focused back on the curved wooden rail. Still nothing happened.

'Clear your mind.'

She sighed and with reluctance buried her fear and scepticism, the silence growing longer and oddly somehow thicker. Hannah imagined the press of cold metal on her lips, her tongue numbed.

The banister flickered in front of her. She blinked, thinking she'd imagined it but it did seem to be lightening in colour, fading away until she could make out the opposite wall through the wood.

'Keep concentrating, nearly there.' George rasped as if out of breath.

Hannah shook her head, denying the message provided by her eyes.

'That's impossible.' She murmured.

The handrail gained more colour until she smothered logic and concentrated hard.

'It doesn't exist. It doesn't!'

It dimmed until with a pop like burst bubble gum, it disappeared completely. Beyond it, Hannah made out an indistinct curve of steps mirroring their own, two ghost-like figures trudging upwards, one with an expensive camera round his neck.

Alex gave her an exhilarated grin. 'Bloomin' mental, isn't it?'

'Ladies Present!'

54

Alex held up his hand by way of apology to Edward's disapproving scowl. Hannah meanwhile had tentatively shuffled nearer, the unhindered curve of stone steps intersecting with the ghostly one repeatedly up and down the tower. The lack of handrail made the drop quite terrifying.

'Don't get too close to the edge!' George ordered, his voice full of strain. 'It's gone, look?'

He waved his cane up and down, unheeded through the air where the handrail should have been.

'Now if you'll all think of something else, a fruit bowl perhaps, it'll be updated.'

Hannah pictured a bunch of bananas curled around some apples and oranges, blinked and the ghostly steps opposite disappeared, the banister returning as if it'd never been away. Her fingertips caressed the warm, polished wood.

'How did you do that?' She exasperated.

George dabbed at his brow once more with his handkerchief.

'You did as much as me. Collectively disbelieving erased it, collective distraction brought it back from our memories.'

'What about those people? The other steps?'

'Merely a glimpse of the Heartisan side of the Monument, normally as hidden from our view, as our side is from theirs.'

'This is crazy, I must be dreaming. You're all utterly insane!' Hannah muttered, her eyes alive.

'Numbers Mr Lost!' George demanded, stooping to pick up and return Edward's hat to his head.

'Ninety-two, ninety-three…' Edward muttered as they continued downwards.

'What's with the numbers?' Hannah asked.

'Ah,' George looked uncomfortable but got a nod from Alex. 'Well, Miss Hannah, there are many types of Fiends out there - like the Buzzwords you just met - who aren't best friends of the English Language or its Words; Slangsters, Whyjackers, Grammarauders, Spellbinders, Text-Pirates, Interjectors, Digiter8s, Thought-Bandits, Punc-Robbers, to name but a few.'

'Were the Punc-Robbers on the Illustrations level rounded up in the end George?' Alex queried.

'Oh, I keep forgetting you haven't been home for years, yes I think we rounded them up before they could do too much damage to the Collective Noun Gallery and the Hall of Synonyms.'

'Punc-Robbers?' Hannah wore the irritated frown of the new girl at school.

'Sorry Han, I forget this is all new to you. Punc-Robbers steal punctuation. Last time I reported in, over three years ago, there was a frenzy of looting on a couple of the upper floors in our sector.'

George waited for him to finish. 'As for the number counting Miss Lady Hannah you'll be wise to remember this fact, down here numbers act as a way of scrambling conversations from those who may want to overhear us. In Lexica, Text and Numbers mix about as well as oil and water.'

Beyond George the staircase ended at another chequered tile floor. Hannah recalled her own counting from the entrance on the way up. 'Is that why you have your Number Well thingy based in the Monument?'

George tilted his head, obviously impressed. 'Yes, so many people have counted the steps on the way up over the centuries the walls have become deeply impregnated with numbers. It's one of the reasons the government of our Language commissioned Sir Christopher Wren to build it in the first place back in 1671.'

Hannah missed a step and stumbled down onto the black and white tiles of the lobby.

CHAPTER FOUR

The Number Well lobby looked much grubbier than the Monument entrance, the white floor tiles yellowed and the black greyed. Dust lay in heaps along the skirting boards and in the corners as if drifted like grey snow. There were no pictures on the walls, a small typewriter on a table in the stairwell the only furniture. Two gaslights threw quivering shadows across the dreary mustard walls and filled the air with a sulphurous burning smell. At the far end, a slither of fluorescent light seeped under an ill-fitting door.

'Right, time we weren't here.' George said, glancing at his pocket watch.

'Good luck down there Aldwyn.' Edward piped up.

George swept around, knocked Edward's hat to the floor with a flick of his hand before tapping the head of his cane rhythmically on his bald head. 'I told you in con-fi-dence. You stu-pid little man.'

Eyes nearly shut; Edward shrank with every tap until the collar of his shirt had devoured much of his neck. With a heavy sigh and a gentle dab at his brow, George turned sharply and smiled guiltily at Alex.

'Sorry, I don't know what came over me. Must've been something I ate.'

'Good luck down there?' Alex frowned. 'What does he mean *down there*?'

'Hmmm.' George said, his face full of restrained distraction.

'Edward said, "Good luck down there"'

'Did he?' George shared his surprise with a bewildered Edward. 'Did you Edward? Did you?'

Looking from behind, Hannah could see George's head shaking beneath his top hat and his cheeks twitching as if mouthing the word 'no' to his friend. A deeply puzzled Edward looked from George to Alex and up to his brow.

'Erm…' Mirroring George, he tentatively shook his head from side to side. 'Yes I did! Down there in the Glossary Atrium, that's where the Guardian is, you told me, remember.'

George slapped himself on his forehead and dragged his hand down over his face.

'…and others have witlessness thrust upon them.' George muttered with a resigned huff. His shoulders heaved before he turned around wearing a wide-eyed smile.

'Very well, I heard a whisper about something happening near to the entrance of the Glossary. They didn't actually say that's where the Shrouded Guild had relocated, but-' His smug, self-importance evaporated into concern. 'But, that's not the point. Stay well clear Aldwyn, no good can come of you going down there unannounced.'

'What's the Glossary?' Hannah interrupted.

George's eyes flared 'And that sort of stupid question is precisely why you need to stay away Alex!'

'Manners George!'

George sighed and held up his hand. 'Quite right Edward, my humble apologies Miss Lady Hannah.'

Hannah shrugged as he bowed.

'Still Aldwyn, questions like that within earshot of the wrong sorts could get you both into the gravest of trouble. I cannot stress to you enough how much has changed since you were down here last.'

George gritted his teeth, his eyes flickering to Hannah and back.

'Anything you say to me you can say in front of Hannah.' Alex said.

George looked to his left and right before lowering his voice.

'We live in troubled times Aldwyn my friend. The growing number of Feds patrolling in Pandemonia is a concern, but not half as worrying as developments down here.'

'There's always been problems George. The Guild wouldn't exist without enemies of the Language, dissenters and-'

George vehemently shook his head, sighing as he leaned in closer. 'It's...It's all changed. We're not in the shadows any more Aldwyn.'

Alex's frown hung heavily over the silence.

George chewed on his thoughts before continuing. 'Words whisper about marching boots, futile scuffles and muffled cries of distress in the middle of the night. Some of the tales of monsters are fanciful, some of the rumours of government hit squads frightening, but when day breaks there are always fresh traces of spilt ink in the corridors and more dissenting Nouners, Verbmen and

Adjectivores have disappeared. It appears as if someone is systematically rounding up key Words from every floor.'

Alex sucked in a breath as if he'd just sat in bathwater much cooler than he'd expected. George empathised with some more concerned working of his eyebrows.

'Indeed. Except nothing is reported, nor protest made. Everyone pretends life is normal, despite all knowing someone who's lost a friend or is missing an acquaintance.'

He shook his head grimly. 'All we hear from the WPs in the House of Commas and the House of Words are bland statements about the ongoing fight to make our corridors safe from terrorists and rebels. Even the normally impartial BBC Word Service on the wireless seems disinterested in the disappearances.'

'What about the Daily Narrative or The Yarn on Sunday?' Alex frowned.

'There's nothing in any of the newspapers, not even in the gossip columns of the News of the Word!' George smoothed his moustache. 'Now you know me Aldwyn, I don't take any notice of tittle-tattle, but I can't help thinking they're hiding more than they're telling.'

'Hiding what?'

George took off his hat and gripped it with both hands in front of his chest, the concern on his face speaking a thousand words. He repeated his sideways glances, drew in closer and lowered his voice further.

'I don't know Alex, there's something in the atmosphere down here, you see it in every face. Every Word is nervous. Cautious. Careful. Everyone moves like a ghost, frightened of their own shadow. Wordminster peddles fears of insurgents

61

from other Languages, but all anyone sees are more Author-tarian Guards and fewer freedoms. Suspicion of one another is growing, fear abundant.'

'Fear?' Alex frowned.

George nodded eagerly. 'Yes Aldwyn, I think the English Language is at its most perilous since the French invasion of 1066 and is seeing the most seismic of changes since the tumultuous Great Vowel Shift of the late Middle Ages!'

He looked haunted, as if he'd already said far too much. Carefully returning his hat to his head, George smoothed his ruffled collar and his composure.

'Look old bean, all I'm saying, is don't waste any time down here, just get yourself and Miss Lady Hannah out of Lexica as quick as possible, you hear.'

'But how?' Alex shrugged. 'I suppose the Number Wells in the Contents Atrium would be nearest-'

George shook his head vigorously. 'Awash with Author-tarian Guards and Spellcheckers; totally out of the question.'

Alex tapped his chin. 'The exit by the Abbreviations and Acronyms Academy on the fortieth floor?'

'The A.A.A.A.?' George pondered. 'Author-tarian Guard patrols. I wouldn't risk it.'

'Well, what about the Number Well opposite the Proverbial Idiomography?'

'More Guards than you can shake a stick at!'

Alex's eyes flickered without seeing until he blew out his cheeks. 'What about the Science Terminology lab?! Any chance Kelvin's experimental Number Well will be unguarded?'

George stared at him. 'Absolute zero.'

'Shame.'

Hannah opened her mouth but she didn't like to interrupt.

'I can't think of any more. Are all the Inter-world Number Wells guarded by Author-tarian Guards and Feds?'

'All except this abandoned one, and I think we've just blown that too.' George moved shiftily from one foot to the other. 'There is one place where you might still find an unguarded Number Well.'

Alex narrowed his eyes.

George leaned in slightly. 'It is rather a long shot.'

'It would be.' Alex mumbled.

'Hmmm?'

'Too good to me.'

George narrowed his eyes. 'There's an old Number Well in the disused west wing of Bookingham Palace.'

'Buckingham Palace!' Hannah exclaimed.

Alex glanced at her and back at George.

'With the Royal family supposedly on an extended tour of the American English sector-'

'Supposedly?' Alex frowned.

George's tongue poked out between his lips and he lowered his voice further. 'There's a strong rumour they've been forced to flee, exiled to Pandemonia.'

Alex gawped.

'Quite.' George's moustache drooped. 'But, it does mean the mothballed building won't be so heavily guarded, so you'll be free to find the secret Number Well and get Hannah home before anyone notices.'

'I like it in there.' Edward grinned.

George looked alarmingly at Edward before forcing a hearty laugh and elbowing him. 'Ha ha ha! Good one Edward!'

Edward grinned confusedly as he rubbed the top of his arm.

George ignored their bemused faces. 'It's in the Mirrored Words room in the west wing, I believe. I'm sure it will be all locked up, but no problem for a key-keeper like you, right?'

Alex paused and nodded. 'Thanks George.'

'You take care Aldwyn, both of you take care.'

'We will.'

George winced unconvincingly and offered Alex his hand.

'I'm sorry we can't come with you, but we're already running late for a hush-hush meeting in the Welsh sector.'

'We're shifting some surplus L's we shouldn't have.' Edward whispered loudly.

George closed his eyes and pinched the top of his nose.

Alex suppressed a grin. 'Bye George. See you Edward.'

'Farewell my friend.'

'Goodbye.' Hannah and Edward chirped amid the false bonhomie of the briefly acquainted.

The pair rounded the wrong side of the banister, squeezed past the small table and stooped to open a small door concealed under the stairs. Bundling his crouching friend through first, George followed with all the elegance of a Giraffe folding itself through a cat-flap. As a flailing hand reached back and closed the door behind them, Alex blew out his cheeks.

'Don't get on you two, do you?'

'George and me? We used to.'

'Really? Did he steal your teddy-bear too?'

'No it's more complicated…' He frowned, 'how could you possibly know…?'

She shrugged.

'Ah, he told you, didn't he?'

Her pride took a blow and she came back punching.

'Is it so surprising I worked it out by myself?'

He paused too long.

'Newsflash for you Alex, my world no longer revolves around dollies, tea parties and lurid pink sweeties. I'm *not* five years old any more! While you've been off doing whatever it is you do, I've grown up and can – believe it or not - actually have independent thoughts of my own, thank you very much!'

Alex stared, backing away to the door in the far wall, as if she were an unexploded bomb. Hannah fumed as he drew a loop of keys from his pocket, sighing as he picked a key and turned it in the lock. As he tentatively twisted the door handle and poked his head through the gap, she shrank from her outburst. All she had to do was find this Palace exit and get back to the coach before anyone noticed she was missing, getting angry wouldn't make it happen any quicker.

She sucked in a deep breath, flicked her bag further up onto her shoulder and crossed to place a hand on Alex's shoulder as a gesture of apology. He jumped at her touch, banged his head on the door and shuffled back inside like a startled mouse. Scrunching up his face, he vigorously rubbed his ear, much to Hannah's amusement.

'I'm sorry. About before, and,' she gestured awkwardly, 'about your head.'

Lowering his hand, he almost allowed himself to smile. 'Come on trouble.'

The straight corridor appeared to stretch into infinity in both directions. Uniform white doors ran along both of the cream walls, two lines of stark strip lights above, white and black polished marble floor below. Identical plastic plants and red fire extinguishers were the only objects regularly breaking up the monotony.

Hannah trudged along behind Alex, pulling at her scarf in the warm stuffy air, her nose twitching at a faint aroma she couldn't quite place. She kept looking over her shoulder, twitching at every door clicking open and every soft thud as they closed. She saw fleeting glimpses of figures scurrying from one door to another but nobody seemed to linger in the corridor long. They shuffled on, Hannah's eyes drawn to the words printed at the top left-hand corner on some of the doors.

Ambivalence it said on one. *Amble* on the next.

Alex cautiously peered left and right around the corner of every interconnecting corridor, oblivious to Hannah's growing curiosity.

66

Ambrosia, Ambulance.

She frowned, realising they were in alphabetical order.

Ambulatory, Ambush.

The latter wasn't a word she particularly wanted to read especially as she became increasingly nervous of the subtle movement far ahead of them. The end of the corridor darkened, a look over her shoulder showed the same thing in the distance, blackness with a hint of scarlet.

'Alex?'

'I see them.' He said firmly. 'Author-tarian Guards. We need…there!'

He didn't point but instead quickened his pace and pushed on a door, which - to Hannah at least - looked identical to all the others. She followed him through into a naked concrete stairwell, a number fifty-nine painted in black at the top right of the wall ahead of her.

Alex scampered down the steps, swinging round to the next flight with a hand curled around the leather handrail. Hannah followed, two steps at a time, pushing herself off the walls in an effort to keep up. Only as he drifted out of sight did she call out his name. He waited for her beneath the number sixty-six on the wall. She eyed it curiously but he spoke before she could ask the question.

'Alright, this should be far enough.'

He held a finger to his lips and peeped out of the door, whispering. 'No Guards on this floor yet. Whatever happens, not a word and do keep up.'

He didn't even give her chance to nod before rushing along the corridor, Hannah scurrying to keep up. Almost identical to the floor above, the same distinct smell filled her nostrils. She spied *Aromatic*, *Arose* and several doors for *Around* before her subconscious delivered, the corridor had the heady aroma of old books; the warm, reassuring smell of knowledge starched into wood fibres. Despite the fearful whirlwind life had sent her way, she drew in a deep breath and let the aroma soothe her anxiety.

Alex sharply changed direction and she stumbled into him. Apologising, she concentrated on staying close as he stomped off to the left, right at the first junction and left at the next. On he went, darting down side corridors and across junctions until Hannah was completely disorientated, the stairs all but a memory. This time around, she heard no doors opening nor saw any movement.

As Alex stopped ahead of her, she rested on his shoulder, hand clutching the ache in her side. Half of the strip lights overhead abruptly dimmed, the other half flashing an unsettling red. Yet no alarm sounded, no wailing siren or ear-piercing bell filled the air, leaving Hannah and Alex in an eerie silence.

'It's a lockdown.' Alex muttered coldly.

In the distance a black and red mass appeared, blinking on and off beneath the lights. She swallowed drily, eyes wide.

Alex counted the doors they passed with an outstretched finger. The keys reappeared and almost without breaking stride, they were inside a tiny bare room beneath a single bare light bulb. In one corner a floor-polishing machine stood amidst some bottles of chemicals, in another a mop and bucket. Large grey cabinets surrounded them on the walls, two of which Alex threw open revealing several columns of switches. Hannah's shoulders trembled, her nerves stretched by

68

warning lights and patrolling guards. She pulled her bottle of water from her bag and took a sip, wiping a dribble from her chin with a shaky hand.

'Alex?'

Ignoring her, he opened a third cabinet door, flicked some switches, closed it and opened a fourth.

'Alex, I can see you're busy but I was thinking, maybe it'd be best if I just went back up to the top of the Monument. The Feds have probably given up by now anyway.'

'Can't.' He said moving to the next cabinet without a backwards glance.

'No, Alex I don't think you understand. I can't stay down here. I'll be late for the coach, they're probably already looking for me. I'll get detention, or worse.'

'Out of the question.'

'Alex!'

He pulled open the cabinet behind him and tapped a finger on his lips.

'Alex! Please?' Hannah's voice cracked slightly.

He stopped, turned and narrowed his eyes.

'Are you alright?'

Hannah nodded, shook her head and with a sigh simply shrugged. 'Just tell me what's happening?

'Ah right, well we're in what I like to call, a *bad* situation. The Author-tarian Guard are scouring all the upper floors looking for you, I'd guess the Feds are doing much the same on the streets of central London. They may even have linked you to the coach from your school in Bramley-upon-Thames, fingers crossed they haven't.'

Hannah kept quiet.

'What I'm trying to say is if I were you, I'd just forget all about what your Teacher or Grandmother will do to you if you're late home. If those Author-tarian Guards catch up with us first, you can forget about ever seeing Pandemonia again.'

He returned to tracing his finger down the rows of fuses and left Hannah staring wide-eyed at the back of his head.

'Better?' He asked obliviously.

She stared numbly as he flicked one last fuse, closed the cupboard and squeezed past her to peek out the door into the darkened corridor.

'Alex, you don't understand, I have to get home...Alex?'

He slid out of the door and dragged Hannah after him by her wrist. She plodded along in the dark behind him, trying to reject his words, trying to laugh them off and not believe they could possibly be true.

How could they be? They couldn't keep her down here against her will, could they?

Stumbling along, she stared at his hand on her wrist and questioned everything, even down to whether Alex was truly on her side. Was he actually trying to save her or was he actually kidnapping her?

She had no answers only suspicions, anxiety and a dull thumping rhythm growing behind her right eye. She eased herself from his grip, but kept with Alex, for she had nothing else. In a world of strangers, his familiar face was the nearest she had to a friend.

Arriving at a junction, Alex pulled up sharply.

'Damm! Missed one.' He cursed.

The corridor ahead of them opened out into a dark lobby area, before continuing under flashing red lights on the far side. Unfortunately, a brightly lit corridor intersected their path. They hovered in the semi-shadows, skulking from doorway to doorway. Hannah tried an office door, but the handle wouldn't budge.

Alex shook his head. 'Even my keys won't open the Office doors during a Lockdown.'

They crouched behind a tall plastic plant close to the junction. Twenty guards noisily jogged past in one direction, followed by another four walking the other way.

'They don't trust the dark.' Alex whispered pensively. 'We'll have to run through it to get to the lifts beyond.'

Hannah's stomach scurried away to hide behind her liver.

'On three.' Alex murmured.

'Just go!' Hannah ordered, nudging him up with her elbow.

Teeth gritted, she sped towards the light, jacket flapping and bag bouncing around on her back. Alex surged ahead as the lights got nearer, both of them moving stealthily but for the sound of their footsteps and the swish of their clothes.

She kept expecting to see someone step out in front of them but the light came and went in a split second, distant yells and the sound of movement chasing them into the darkness. Alex's shadow made for the middle set of lift doors in a row of five, leaving Hannah squinting in the gloom. In the corridor beyond the lobby, overhead strip lights were coming back on one at a time, an ugly crowd with riot shields shuffling forward in the light.

'Whatever you're doing, do it quicker!' Hannah hissed, groping her way towards Alex.

He didn't reply but she heard his keys jangling and some murmured curses.

Guards arrived at the intersection of the fully lit corridor behind them, trapping them by the lifts but advancing no nearer. In the other direction, the Guards waited by the edge of the lobby, riot shields glinting in the light.

'That's odd...' Alex muttered, jabbing a button behind her, two red arrows lighting up on the wall.

She backed against the lift doors, head darting from one wall of glimmering helmets to another, waiting for them to charge with their batons and shields. She thought of Magda, Mr Bloggs and Bluebell House, wishing for normality. She cursed herself for trying to escape her world, for daring to believe she could go back to being that happy, carefree girl again.

Hannah Curious was gone, just like her childhood.

To think otherwise had just been childish naivety.

Abruptly, the lift doors opened and Alex bundled her inside, the stark fluorescent strip lights almost blinding her. She staggered slightly, hands over her squinting sensitive eyes. The doors snapped shut behind them and the lift lurched into movement. Alex guided her forwards and turned her round to sit down. She

72

held her head in her hands restlessly, sucking in long breaths until her shoulders stopped shaking and her head stopped buzzing.

'We're safe now Hannah.' Alex sat next to her, still staring at his keys.

She couldn't bring herself to answer, feeling as if she was treading water in the middle of an ocean, her fear conjuring up sharks and jellyfish beneath the imaginary waves. Numbed with dread she tried simply to exist as the seconds and minutes passed, to survive for survivals sake.

Trying not to think, she blinked her stinging eyes against the light. The lift bumped and shuddered occasionally as it whirred onwards but it looked pretty much like every other lift. Except - and even she had to admit they were big exceptions - they sat on a white leather sofa, a drinks machine sat on the left of the doors and on the right, a curtained alcove hid what she guessed was a toilet. Guessed being the word, as she had no desire to investigate further, if she could cross her legs on a train, she reasoned she could cross her legs anywhere.

'That was close.' He sighed.

She didn't reply, didn't want to look at him. What she feared she'd see she didn't know, but for several minutes she kept her eyes on the metal floor. Forcing herself to look, she turned and only saw Alex; someone who'd once been her best friend.

'Got something to show you.' Alex said cryptically as he got up off the sofa and pressed a button behind him.

Hannah turned at a whirring noise as the back wall of the lift split, each side sliding back revealing a glass window and a vision that tested her sanity one stage

73

further. Hannah shielded her eyes with her hand, but while she dealt with the dazzling sunshine, she wasn't ready for the view.

Kneeling on the white leather, she peered through the glass with a mixture of awe and a fear of heights, the former only just outweighing the latter.

They were incredibly high up, looking out over a city bearing more than a striking resemblance to Manhattan in New York. Buildings of varying heights, shapes and styles covered the island, all vying for the most sunshine like trees in a forest. Only to Hannah's eyes, it looked out of perspective, the buildings too big and land too small. The doors rolled back around the corners revealing a dizzying one hundred and eighty degree view along the sides of a gothic skyscraper.

Built with honey-coloured limestone, leaded glass windows, gold leaf and ornate carved gargoyles, the building stretched far away on either side of them, resembling an unlikely offspring of the Empire State building and the Houses of Parliament. Surging downwards past mullioned windows and carved stonework pillars, they soared outwards down the spine of a colossal flying buttress, one of a line of giant arches supporting the stepped walls.

Directly opposite their skyscraper, stonemasons had somehow created a soaring chateau as staggering in its intricacy as its size. Hewn from ghostly-pale khaki stone in a French renaissance style, it looked impossible the ground could ever bear such an enormous weight. Her gaze drifted over the stout round towers at each corner to its sleek façade filled with tall narrow windows. Near the top, the round towers stepped inwards to a taller four-towered keep, her view finally

74

settling on the steeply pitched dark slate roofs cluttered with an eclectic mix of bell-towers, steeples and smoking chimneys.

She leaned forward until her forehead touched the glass, mistakenly allowing her gaze to plummet past wispy clouds to the distant ground. Her stomach instantly lurched upwards and fumbled for the handle to its ejector seat. If it hadn't been so empty, it may well have been after such a mistake. Head throbbing, she pushed herself back upright and away from the glass, until she recovered her breath, if not her nerves.

To the right, construction cranes perched precariously on the open concrete and steel floors of a tapered tower. Curved red eaves, terracotta tiles and ornate jade dragons festooned the completed lower floors. Looking out to the edge of the island, she glimpsed much smaller buildings in various states of ambition and disrepair.

'The United Repositories of Lexica.' Alex said with arms wide.

'Repositories?' She frowned.

'Yes, not a captivating title for our realm is it? We lobbied at the Lexican Council for the World of the Written Word, but were outvoted.' He shrugged. 'Rumour had it the French Language found out we'd been stockpiling W's from two bumper harvests and decided to teach us a lesson. Luckily with the internet being so prolific we found a way to use up the surplus.'

'What is this place? Is it a model?'

He laughed warmly. 'No, this is Lexica, our world of Languages. Each of these buildings represents one of the eight thousand or so Languages used in Pandemonia.'

Hannah looked out at the buildings anew. 'Eight thousand!'

'Yes according to the last census at least. I suppose it seems a lot to the uninitiated but the number changes all the time as dialects drift in and out of use or new fictional languages like Vulcan and Klingon are invented.'

Her eyes drifted over all the small and large buildings, imagining what was going on behind every window, wondering if there could be someone somewhere looking back at her.

Alex broke into her daydreaming, pointing like a tour guide.

'Here in the centre we've all the main languages. Opposite us with all the towers is the Académie Française. On your right, the one with all the cranes is the ever-changing Mandarin Pagoda. Behind us on the right is the Real Academia Española and at our rear but no less impressive are the Russian and Arabic buildings. Collectively we make up the L6 and regularly hold summits as well as attending the much larger URL council meetings, where representatives of all Languages can attend.'

Hannah stared agog. 'The L6?'

'Yes, it's similar to the G8 up in Pandemonia, where the leaders of your richest industrialised countries get together for meetings and policy-making.'

Hannah nodded numbly.

'Of course, Lexican representatives of the L6 also attend the G8 conferences up in Pandemonia, but in total secrecy obviously.'

Hannah stopped nodding.

'If you look to the west,' Alex pointed to the right away from the sun, 'across the Amper Sands and Lake Tilde you may just be able to make out the edge of the vast Latin fields swaying in the breeze.'

She followed his pointed finger to her right and strained to see the vast fields through the haze. Sloping gently down to the water's edge, there appeared to be a hedgerow-bordered patchwork of pastures. The fields looked like they were full of wheat only much darker.

'What? The dark grey areas over there?'

'Yes, that's the edge of the land used by Alphabet farmers to cultivate all the letters you use and recognize across Europe, the Americas and much of Africa. The Cyrillic letters prefer a cooler climate so are grown much further to the north whilst Arabic, Hebrew and the Indic alphabets thrive in the warmer south.'

Hannah frowned. 'You grow letters?'

'Well not me personally, but yes the Alphabet Farmers do and the Languages buy the letters from them wholesale. Only the likes of Mandarin and Japanese still paint their own words from scratch.'

Hannah shook her head.

'Most of the Font Merchants deal out of Lower Glyph.' He waved a hand toward a distant town nestled by the coast, the smudge of red roofs shimmering through the haze.

77

She knew she wasn't dreaming, deep down she'd known for some time but only in the light of the mind-blowing view from the lift could she openly accept it. Even her imagination was incapable of imagining such detail and ordered beauty amidst the madness. The Buzzwords and the eerie Guards could've been a bad dream but here she knew the truth.

This world was no fantasy, Lexica was real.

CHAPTER FIVE

'209 Incorruptible – Indignity.'

'How much further?' Hannah pushed her sleeve back over her watch.

Alex pretended not to hear, flicking the curling corner of his well-thumbed copy of Up & Down magazine - Summer edition. After closing the view of Lexica again in the interests of security, they'd argued about why the floor numbers rose even though the lift was descending. Alex had fobbed her off with a strange explanation comparing floor numbers with the pages of a dictionary, but when she asked him if he was doing precisely what George had warned him not to do, he'd become evasive.

'I just thought it'd be easier and safer to get to the Palace from a lower floor.'

'How is deeper into this nightmare better than-'

'Who's in charge?' He bristled.

'Well there's no need to be like-'

'Why don't-' He shook his magazine and lowered his voice. 'Why don't you rest your voice for a bit.'

Hannah fumed but bit her tongue, the pair of them falling into an uneasy silence.

'210 Indigo – Inexpensive.'

The numbers on the L.E.D screen above the doors moved like a milometer on a tortoise.

'211 Inexperienced - Information.' Chimed a seductive female voice, who appeared to be having way too much fun simply reading out floor numbers.

Fascinatingly it only became audible if Hannah looked at it, something she did on and off for nearly eighty floors before Alex snapped and told her to stop playing Peek-a-boo with a machine!

'Buy us a drink Alex?'

Alex sniffed stuffily. 'Can't.'

'Why?' Hannah said, crossing to look absent-mindedly at the nine pictures on the front of the machine. While she recognised the top three as Lemon, Lime and Orange, the others looked like Steak, Brick, Pen, Ball, Autumn and bizarrely two men shaking hands.

'I just can't, why don't you sit down.'

She glanced at him, his focus back behind the pages of the In-lift magazine. Bored, she blew out her cheeks and pressed the buttons randomly. Nothing happened, so she prodded them again. The machine emitted a low whine, a faint glow coming from a hole at eye-level. As she curiously leaned closer, a red laser shot out and danced over her eyes.

'Arrgh!' Hannah shrieked unable to move.

'Hannah!' Alex leapt forward and tugged her aside. 'What did you do?'

'Nothing.' She said automatically.

'Definition not recognised. Please reposition for re-scanning.' A stern male voice demanded from the machine.

Hannah blinked at the drinks machine, her eyes instinctively flicking upwards.

80

'231 Leghorn - Level.' The sultry voice purred.

'Stop looking at the stupid display!'

'Definition not recognised. Please reposition for re-scanning.'

'It scanned your eyes! Tell me you didn't let it scan your eyes?'

Hannah winced but Alex didn't look annoyed, more pensive.

'Ignore it. It'll probably turn itself off in a minute or two, especially if you stop looking at it.' He read the question on her lips and sighed impatiently. 'All Lexicans have a barcode across their retina detailing their identity and definition. It's used as Identification at the borders and for charging expenses to your department...'

'Such as drinks in lifts.' Hannah whispered.

'Definition not recognised. Please reposition for re-scanning.'

'Such as drinks in lifts. I'm guessing it didn't recognise you as an imposter or the alarms would have gone off.' He shook his head. 'Now please just sit down and behave yourself, if you know how.'

'Sorry granddad.' Hannah mumbled to herself and curled up on the sofa, shutting her eyes for a sulk.

With a twitch, she stirred. Squirming against the bright light, she pulled the duvet over her head. She didn't want to get up and do her chores, she just wanted to lie there and snooze through the morning. Yawning, she wondered what nonsense Grandma Johnson would come up with over breakfast; polish the gravel on the drive perhaps or trim the lawn edges with scissors, again.

'Definition not recognised. Please reposition for re-scanning.'

Hannah stiffened and drew the duvet down over one eye.

'Hey sleepy head, back with us? Good, we're almost there.'

She groaned as Alex came into focus.

'Nice to see you too.'

She flung off her jacket, sat up on the white sofa and rubbed her squinting eyes. Lexica mocked her with the hum of the moving lift.

'451 Appendix A'

'I thought we should walk the last couple of floors.'

Hannah sat up, wishing she'd brought her hairbrush.

'452 Appendix B'

'This will do us.' Alex stretched his spine as he got up and prodded the button by the doors.

Hannah hauled herself to her feet and yawned again, glad to be getting out of such a small space. Her knees bent slightly as the lift decelerated and eased to a stop. With a satisfying ping, the doors slid open and a cool draft of air caressed her skin as they stepped outside onto a mildly damp flagged floor.

'Definition not recog-'

The lift doors slid shut, Hannah's mouth dropped open. Dusty old red brick walls surrounded a large courtyard on three sides of them. Two dark green warehouse doors on cast iron rollers hung on the wall opposite. Her eyes settled on some faded whitewashed lettering off to one side:

Appendix B – English Language Graphemes

82

Craning her neck back, she followed the four walls high up into a murky darkness, wooden walkways and cranes criss-crossing the space.

'Been raining.' Alex sniffed.

Hannah let her gaze float down like a raindrop from the sky. She'd not thought about where they were, yet now she found herself increasingly confused.

'Wait, I thought we were on the inside of the building?'

Alex looked bemused. 'You have to forget all those Pandemonia rules. This is Lexica, every floor is its own world, some bigger than others.'

Hannah's mind boggled, coughing up another complaint.

'Wait, wait, wait, wait, the view from the lift, all those buildings and fields beneath a hot sun, how can that be when we're hundreds of floors underground?!'

Alex looked at her with weary bemusement.

She frowned. 'Aren't we?'

Alex sighed. 'It'd be easiest all round if you left your physics and fancy logic at Lexica's door. Languages, whilst governed by their own rules and laws, aren't restricted by such ridiculous notions as reality.'

Hannah's eyes fell onto him, her own grip on 'ridiculous reality' being gently prised free one fingertip at a time.

'We'd best keep moving.' Alex said, heading for a door beside the lift.

Hannah took one last long look around and followed him into another concrete stairwell. Plodding down six flights of stairs, Alex waited for her beside a door bearing the sign for *Floor 455 - The Glossary.*

Hannah ground her teeth. 'You lied!'

'Come on.'

'You lied to me and you lied to George.'

'George Found isn't the boss of me!' He snapped, yanking the door open.

'Alex!'

'Sssssssshhh!' Alex closed the door and brought a finger to his lips. 'It's none of your business, now come on!'

He disappeared through the doorway but Hannah didn't follow. She sat on the cold concrete steps in a fug of utter misery. She'd hoped Alex would help her, she'd wanted to believe in him. Only now, that just seemed stupid and childish. He only cared about himself.

She drank the last of her water and sat fighting the tears before the door creaked open.

His irritation faded away when he saw her face.

'I'm sorry. Look Hannah, as soon as we find the Guardian, we'll get you out of here and back home, I promise. But you saw all those Guards on the upper floors, they weren't on patrol, they were after us.'

She sniffed. 'Alex, I just want to go home.'

'I know, but if we can find the Guardian and the Elders, they'll help us. They'll know a safe, quick route out of here, not some hare-brained royal trespass. We might even get an armed escort too. Alright?'

She sighed and wearily nodded as he helped her back to her feet.

Through the door, they entered a great open square that mirrored her mood. Yellow paint peeled from faded wooden benches, raised flowerbeds lay overgrown and the scant water in the ornate fountains sat green and stagnant. A dank, swampy smell hung in the air making Hannah wrinkle her nose and breathe through her mouth. On three sides of them, rows of lift doors were set into the stonework, too many for her to count.

At the far end, a grand entrance stood at the top of some wide stone steps. A row of imposing Ionic columns held a triangular pediment aloft, its front carved with an intricate relief of figures and machines. With an *A* missing and an *R* hanging upside-down from one nail, several large golden letters hung across the columns declaring it as the entrance to *THE GLOSS__Y*. If the entrance square was anything to go by, she imagined it'd been a long time since the interior could've lived up to its new title.

Following Alex as he cautiously crept across the square, she crossed several huge mosaics of figures and inventions welcoming visiting Words to the *Home of Explanation*. In the shadows behind the columns, she glimpsed wooden boards nailed haphazardly across a line of doors.

Again, the feeling of unease she'd repressed bubbled back to the surface. Before her adrenaline had ebbed away and she'd dozed in the lift, she'd wondered how exactly they'd evaded the Author-tarian Guards back up in the darkness of floor sixty-five. The truncheon-wielding, heavily armoured Author-tarian Guards had surrounded two unarmed strangers, yet they'd somehow let the pair of them escape their grasp. The guards could've seized them but they didn't, they could've

85

charged at them with their batons and riot shields, but they didn't. They simply stood and watched them escape. The more she thought about it, the more she worried and the more she found to worry about. Why had the Guards not simply switched off the power to their lift? Or recalled it back to the sixty-fifth floor? The Guards had plenty of time to trap them, yet they'd allowed the lift to run for...

She lifted her sleeve and realised with some alarm it was already half past three. Her teachers must be frantic! Despite what Alex had said, she'd still somehow hoped to find her way out, if not back to the Monument, at least to a phone by now. The two threads of worry interwove with one another into a cord of angst. She instinctively knew they needed to get away from there.

'Alex, why didn't the Guards stop the lift?'

He squirmed, confirming he'd had similar doubts. 'I don't know. I also don't know why the lift was waiting for us on floor sixty-five or why – during a Lockdown - the lift doors were left unlocked.'

Her stomach cramped.

He twitched at her widening eyes.

'This isn't right Alex, I think we should-'

She didn't get any further.

All the lift doors opened simultaneously. Four huge yellow-helmeted Author-tarian Guards emerged from each and lumbered forward into an unbroken line around the edge of the square. More Guards stepped out from behind the columns at the top of the steps, completing their encirclement.

'It's going to be fine. You'll see, just fine.' Alex whispered without conviction.

86

It was a prognosis Hannah failed to see any grounds for, concluding they were about as far from fine as she could imagine. In fact, on a vertical scale from fine down to unpleasant, they weren't just at the lower end, but in a deep hole and still digging.

The Guards were near-identical to the red ones on the upper floors, looking like tall, bionic riot police with body armour, jack-boots covered in chrome and intimidating faceless helmets with tinted visors.

'The door!' He whispered in Hannah's ear.

'There's no way out.' She exclaimed.

'Run for a lift?'

'Through them? After you.'

Hannah eyed the guards nervously, but they didn't move or say a word.

'What are they waiting for?' She whispered in Alex's ear.

'I don't know. Look, if they ask any questions, just plead innocence and stupidity. We'll have to pretend to be Words from one of the floors upstairs!'

The long shrill ring of a phone echoed across the square, but no one moved or even registered the noise. It rang twice more before an ominous, clipped voice answered and projected out across the yard as if in a conference call.

'Yes, Ambush team?'

'Boss, we 'ave got two more!' The guttural reply came from a man with a mouth bigger than his vocabulary.

'Is that so?' The voice sounded surprised. 'There should be no more; are you sure they're not just rebel sympathisers, cause you can throw them straight in with the Fiends.'

'I dunno boss, one of 'em has strange clothes.'

Hannah glanced at Alex who was staring at her jacket, tie and dark trousers.

'Right,' the voice said wearily, 'I suppose I'd best have a look at them.'

The other voice gave an affirming grunt.

'Reset the trap and bring them down to me.'

The phone slammed back into its cradle, silence settling over the stand-off once more. Alex twitched as the majority of the Guards retreated into their lifts, four on each side remaining as still as Granite gateposts.

'There's only four now.' Alex muttered, nodding back to the stairs.

'Right!' Hannah snapped sarcastically. 'You take the two huge massive ones on the left and I'll take the two even larger ones on the right.'

A single set of lift doors remained open opposite the steps and the remaining sixteen guards lumbered towards them, one of them jabbing awkwardly at the lift. They shepherded Hannah and Alex towards the open doors like rhinos herding chickens. Hannah sensed her imaginary friend was still searching for a gap and grabbed his arm.

'Don't do anything silly Alex, I need you.' It sounded more desperate than she'd planned but she knew she wouldn't get far down here without him.

He glanced at her before glaring at the advancing guards. Guiding her behind him, they backed away into the lift.

'Don't forget, you're a Word from a higher floor.' He said anxiously.

'I won't.'

'And try to act terrified and way out of your depth.' Alex added.

'Who's acting?' Hannah mumbled.

The journey down the last fifty floors of the English Language was even more unpleasant than the first four hundred and fifty, the intimidating sight of four unflinching guards replacing the boredom from before.

As the doors closed and they hurtled downwards, Hannah expected the helmets to shout at them or taunt them, but they remained rigidly still. She noticed the black names etched on the sides of their yellow helmets for the first time. Only there were no O'Connors, Smiths or Davies here, instead their names read: Ensnare, Corner, Seize and Detain.

Despite the tension of their unswerving gaze making every one of her muscles stiff, Hannah soon realised whatever unpleasantness was to come, it wasn't going to happen in the lift. Her eyes strayed upwards once more.

'479 Index – X, Y & Z'

'How much further?' Hannah murmured almost inaudibly out the corner of her mouth.

Alex leaned on his elbow, his hand covering his lips as he spoke in a low voice. 'This can't be happening. We can't be...Oh no! Floor Four-Eighty! The Checkpoint!'

'The what?'

89

'Checkpoint, listen, have you got any objects from Pandemonia in your pockets?'

'No, it's all in my bag.'

'Anything else? It's important.'

She pulled an anxious face and patted her jeans pockets, finding a bulge. She arched her back to dig the object out when Alex grabbed her wrist. He shook his head and seeing the fear in his eyes, she mouthed 'Phone' in return. He spat out a silent curse, eyed the blank helmets sideways and rubbed a hand across his chin.

'When I stand up, stuff it down the back of the sofa and drop the bag over the rear. Best lose your watch too.'

The lift slowed and Alex pushed himself up to his feet, grinning awkwardly at the nearest guard.

'I...erm...wish to make a complaint about our treatment. There's been a terrible mistake. Can I make a complaint? Hello?'

He moved to the second and knocked on his armoured chest plate.

'Hello, is anyone available to deal with my complaint? We're not meant to be down here. Hello?'

He moved across to the third, shaking his head. 'Have you all taken a vow of dumbness? Hello?'

He stood on the steel-toecaps of the fourth, hands on hips, glaring cockily up at the visor. 'You sir have very hairy nostrils. Hellarrrgghh-ugh!'

Alex hit the wall with an almighty crash, his feet slapping high above his head before he cascaded on top of the sofa in a tangle of curses and flailing limbs. As he

90

grimaced and squirmed into a position where he could see Hannah's face, the lift doors opened.

'Are you alright?' She said. 'That was…amazingly…'

Alex looked at her expectantly, rubbing his neck.

'…stupid.'

Alex's eyes narrowed disappointedly, Hannah grinning wryly at his expense. He managed a frustrated sigh before his eyes flared more intently. She understood and gave him an almost imperceptible nod.

'Good girl.' He managed before the guards roughly hauled him to his feet and propelled him out the lift doors. They turned back to Hannah but she was already scampering along in his wake.

CHAPTER SIX

The Guards shoved them out of the lift towards an unassuming cream hut and a red and white striped barrier, both protected by sandbags and coils of barbed wire. Her feet barely touched the cracked tarmac floor before an electrical whine fixed her to the spot. Two dark green tanks emblazoned with large white letter E's flanked the checkpoint, their massive guns swinging around to point menacingly at her and Alex's head. With encouragement, they shuffled forwards, trying to ignore the threatening glare of the rifled barrels as they tracked them across the floor. Hannah breathed deep and focused on the sign atop the hut's felt roof:

CHECKPOINT CHARLES

You're Leaving The Modern English Sector.

Carrying Weapons Beyond This Point Forbidden.

Obey Grammar Rules.

Alex caught her eye and not for the first time that morning, attempted a reassuring look that missed by several metres. Inside the hut, a slight figure in a smart black suit and homburg hat sat hunched on a high stool. As the yellow-helmeted Guards approached, his hand strayed tenderly to his face where the beginnings of a violet bruise blossomed on his cheek. He lifted a clipboard from the desk and clutched it tightly in his thin bony fingers like a meagre shield. Swallowing hard, he slid awkwardly off his stool and stepped outside.

'Names?' He mumbled.

92

'Eh?' The leading Guard grunted.

'…' The man in the suit opened his mouth.

'You again! Talk up Prep-o-sish-oner!' The Guard spat, much to the amusement of the others.

'I'm-' The Prepositioner squeaked. 'I'm supposed to write down all your names.'

Without warning, the Guard flung the back of his gloved hand across the man's face with a sickening whack, sending him crashing into the door-frame and down onto his knees.

'Put dat in yor reck-ords!' He chuckled and waved all of them forward, squashing the Prepositioner's hat underfoot.

Hannah took a crash course in having a panic attack, her heart leaping around inside her chest like an over-caffeinated monkey learning to breakdance.

The guard pushed down on the concrete block, lifting the red and white barrier. Hannah glanced towards the checkpoint hut as they passed underneath, glimpsing more clipboards, neatly arranged stationery and a terrified pair of eyes peering over an Imperial typewriter. Stepping over a thick white line on the road, a stereo whine of electrical engines came from behind them. She defied her curiosity, the menacing feel of the guns pointing at her back as strong as if she'd stared deep down down their dark barrels.

Without thinking, she lengthened her stride and rushed onto the black leather sofa in the open lift in the far wall. She kept her head down as the Guards shoved Alex in after her, the grisly sound of the fist hitting that poor Word's cheek playing repeatedly in her tormented mind. Alex wore a blank far-away look as the doors

closed and the lift plunged downwards, her expectations followed.

She stared at her pale wrist and wondered what was happening where time still

existed. She guessed it must be some time after four, the atmosphere at her school

and at Bluebell House no doubt getting stormy, her Grandma's scowl thunderous.

She cringed as she wondered whether anyone had called the police yet. The

thought darkened her mood, the faceless guards pushing her further into misery.

Just where were they taking them?

Had Alex been afraid they'd scan her eyes at the checkpoint?

What would have happened to her if they had?

Hannah discovered no comfort in the hard questions or the stark answers she

found in reply. It conjured up a spy-hole to her worst fears, through which she was

compelled to peer: questioning, interrogation, punishment, imprisonment...

Torture?

She pulled up before it could go any further, telling herself they wouldn't do

that, they couldn't. She looked back at Alex, his foot tapping relentlessly on the

floor and her confidence ebbed away. If Alex was scared, she'd every right to be

terrified.

Hope deserted her.

This wasn't Wonderland and she wasn't Alice. Nor were a click of her silver

shoes or a talking lion coming to her rescue. There was no shape-changing dæmon

or a wise white wizard going to save her from this misadventure.

94

'This can't be happening. This is nothing to do with me.' She muttered under her breath. 'I don't belong here.'

The delicious thought of explaining the mistake to the first authority figure she saw glowed in her mind and she savoured the sweetness of an express lift rushing her back up to Pandemonia, to London, to fresh air and her own bright skies. She'd take weeks of detention and Grandma's punishment in an instance if she could just feel the wind in her hair again. Far from home, hungry and hollow, she didn't think she could feel much worse.

The lift slowed and the doors opened on Floor 500, instantly proving otherwise. The tight, dark stone tunnel with its dripping vaulted roof looked about as inviting as the entrance to a disused railway tunnel, at midnight, on Halloween.

The same heavy-handed shoves encouraged them out of the lift into the damp passage. The moss-covered walls glistened with trickling water, while underfoot their shoes slipped and splashed over slimy cobblestones. The first of two rusty portcullises loomed out of the gloom. A blue helmet covered in water droplets peered at them from the other side, a flaming torch on the wall reflecting menacingly in his dark visor. He coughed gruffly and tapped the portcullis three times with a black metal baton.

The portcullis clanked ominously upwards until they were able to duck underneath and step into the small space beyond. The guard waited for the first portcullis to crash to the floor with a jarring clang before grunting, and turning to tap the second. It threw Hannah off-balance, the noise ringing in her ears as she ducked under the second portcullis and squelched forward into the darkness. She heard three metallic taps behind her, just getting her hands over her ears before the second portcullis crashed to the ground.

'Yurg awlgight?' Alex seemed to say beside her through the whistling noise.

She nodded anyway, blinking and swallowing hard to try to pop her ears.

The tunnel ended in a flight of worn stone steps heading down into an eerie dark void. Looking about as inviting as an abandoned castle dungeon, even the weak light from the torches only dared venture down to the fourth step. Hannah dug in her heels; only Alex's hand on the inside of her elbow, half a dozen guards, two portcullises, two tanks and five hundred floors preventing her from hot-tailing it out of Lexica.

Alex guided her tentatively down the first three steps, the sound of dripping water the only noise. 'It's alright.' He whispered in her ear. 'We'll be alright.'

One by one, the torches went out, the darkness rushing in to suffocate them, smothering them with fear.

'We, we best keep moving.' Alex said meekly, coughing to cover his wavering voice.

Helped by Alex, she took a tentative step downwards and gratefully found stone beneath her foot. Alex moved down again and she followed, a hand on his shoulder. Her thoughts drifted to the Monument and counting steps, her shoulders sagging at the thought of doing this for hundreds of steps. A low rasping noise unbalanced her further, but Alex kept her upright.

She gasped as a match sparked and flared brightly in the darkness, the orange streak settling into a small flame maybe twenty metres in front of them.

96

'Hello?' Alex cried out cautiously, his voice echoing.

Hannah felt the vibrations of his voice through her fingers but her eyes were wide, fascinated by the only point of reference in an empty universe. The flame floated unhurriedly upwards to light the tip of a fat cigar clenched between pouting lips.

'Who's there?' Alex cried louder.

The cigar repeatedly flickered with flames, puffs of white smoke emanating from its burning end until with a wave of the match, it left only a glowing ember and the suggestion of a face.

'Show yourself stranger!' Alex shouted, a hint of terror seeping into his voice. Hannah stared at the red dot, mesmerised by the sound of the stranger's slow breathing. After an eternity of seconds, the loud click of someone's fingers broke the peace.

Murmured movements of careful action came at them from all angles. A match flared on their right, another on their left until with an orchestral rasp the darkness filled up with a line of struck matches. Only the matches didn't move to cigars this time but to fuel-soaked torches. One by one, they whooshed into tall yellow flames, the glow reflecting across dozens of shiny helmets, the radiated heat warming Hannah's face. The smoke and haze shimmered over the Guards' heads, the glow hinting at a soot-covered vaulted ceiling. A straw-strewn floor stretched out between them and the semi-circular wall of Author-tarian Guards, a glance down revealing they stood on the bottom step.

The Guards blocking their path wore identical black riot gear as those by the Glossary, only with blue helmets that flickered orange and yellow in the flames. They pulled crude homemade weapons from their belts and beat their body armour. The clamour of glistening meat cleavers, lengths of heavy chain and iron bars thudding into their chests cramped Hannah's stomach and tightened her stiff legs.

'Order!' A loud screech from the man with the cigar cut through the noise like a Sergeant Major on a parade ground.

All the uniformed yobs stopped their unintelligible grunting.

'And what have we got here? Two more rats from the trap?' His lip curled. 'Two more deluded heroes answering the call to save their beloved Language?'

The Word at the centre of the line was unmistakably the voice from the Glossary phone, but in person, he sounded even more eroded and raw. He stood shorter than the muscled heavies around him, but otherwise differed from them predominantly in the colour of his copper helmet and his appetite for Cuban tobacco.

He pushed his visor up onto the top of his helmet revealing a pasty, angular face. His cheekbones were sharp, his lips thin and moustache wiry, but the intense shine in his eyes gripped Hannah most, making her feel they reached for her soul. He smirked at her discomfort and took another long pull on his cigar. He blew the smoke from the corner of his mouth before clamping it back between his teeth.

'Saw the notice did we?' He looked Hannah up and down. 'Thought you'd put on some ridiculous disguise and come join the resistance?'

Without haste, he pulled at the fingers of his black leather gloves, individually inching out each finger and thumb, pouting as he pulled the glove off his hand. Nobody made a sound as he repeated the process on his other hand, pulling it off and moving both to a trouser pocket. He took another long draw on the cigar and let his eyes settle on Hannah and Alex. They narrowed inquisitively.

'No? Well, why don't you tell me why you *were* outside the Glossary Main Entrance?' He questioned, his words heavy with quiet accusation.

Alex visibly gulped and lost any colour he had left. 'Well, erm…'

'Step forward when you're talking to me!'

Alex flinched before tentatively crossing the dusty floor. Hannah paused before joining him.

'Halt!' He screeched. 'Now if you weren't there to make contact with the Resistance, why were you outside the Glossary Main Entrance?'

'Right, well…' Alex began, Hannah straining to leave her face expressionless even as her head quivered uncontrollably.

The man shrieked over Alex. 'Were you both not aware of the recent Decree of Prohibited Movement? The Ministry of Internal Security contacted all offices through the Imperial network. Or do you habitually give scant notice to Orders of the Ministry?'

Both Alex and Hannah looked blank.

Hannah suspected it didn't matter what they said, speaking to him akin to throwing words in front of a gale-force wind.

'I'm Cyril Law, Chief Constable of the Author-tarian Guard.' He fiddled with some dirt under his nail and pulled a face. 'Well, joint Chief Constable, but nonetheless, all you need to know is I'm in charge and your presence has caused disorder to break out amongst my men.'

Hannah heard a muffled earthy guffaw behind her and turned to see four huge guards had crept around to their rear as Law spoke. She turned back to him, wanting to point out they'd hardly strayed down here on their own, but her tongue was much happier hiding in the dark.

'Even Scuffle there,' He gestured over Hannah's shoulder, 'He knows how much I dislike disorder.'

He smirked and a few brown-nosing laughs came from behind him. He let them continue before raising his hand and silence instantly returned. He dropped his half-smoked cigar to the floor and meticulously screwed it out beneath the toe of his heavy-duty boot.

'Enough! May I remind you of the Government Decree of Prohibited Movement, subparagraph seven clearly states: *All free movement between eight pm and seven am is subject to a curfew and access below Floor 450 is forbidden at all times*.'

He looked at them with an expression of both tedium and disgust.

'With this in mind I'm arresting you both for Wilful Trespass, Breach of Curfew and Treason. You do not have to say anything, but it may harm your defence, blah, blah, blah, etc, etc, guilty as charged. Now come with me.'

Law turned to walk away but neither of them moved, Hannah feeling as if the flagstones had encased her feet.

Wilful Trespass? Treason?!

The searing anger of injustice burned through her frozen veins and arteries. After giant insect attack, secret Word police and threatening ambushes, their unlawful arrest melted through the last of her restraint.

'What the heck do you…you can't do that! You can't just do that and walk away!'

'Hannah…no!' Alex managed to croak, his hand reaching for her shoulder.

She shrugged his hand off and took a pace forward. 'Oi! I'm talking to you!'

The Chief Constable stopped moving without turning round. Hannah looked at the intimidating row of blue helmets beyond him, more than a dozen jaws dropping open.

'We have rights; you Police can't just arrest us without reason. We've done nothing wrong!' Hannah blurted, her hands gripped tightly into fists. This nonsense had to stop and if Alex was happy to stand by, she certainly wasn't.

A guard grunted behind her, another growled and within seconds, all the rest were shouting and whooping like a frightened band of gorillas. CC Law turned round with his hand raised, a look of murderous hatred on his face.

'Order! Order! I won't have disorder down here!' He visibly simmered as the Guards took much longer to settle than before.

Hannah tried to stare back but had to lower her gaze, as his eyes seemingly bored into her brain, searching for her brittle confidence so he could snap it over his knee.

He tilted his head, his nostrils flaring. 'Police is a Pandemonia term. What are you doing using a Pandemonia term?'

She stood open-mouthed as the ground fell away beneath her.

They weren't the Police, they were the Author-tarian Guard and her slip of the tongue had heightened his interest. She turned to look at Alex who stared back aghast.

Law's eyes narrowed, unsure what he'd caught in his net but realising they'd just let some precious detail slip. She stood exposed like a mouse before a lion.

'Name, Floor and Grade?' He spat out angrily.

Alarm rang loud in her brain. Whatever Name she gave, how would she know what Floor and Grade they were? Chances were someone as stern as C.C Law would know every Word and Location in the whole of this demented world. Her eyes widened to the size of moons as she scoured the ground for answers. She slid her hands into her pockets, certain they were shaking.

'I'm, I'm just a girl from upstairs, who shouldn't be down here.'

Alex blurted out from behind her. 'Hannah Curious! Grade one Adjectivore-'

As soon as he spoke, Law waved his hand and the guard behind Alex picked him up by his belt and collar and discarded him aside like a bag of rubbish. CC Law watched with cruel glee as he hit the flagged floor with a sickening thud and tumbled towards the vault wall.

'Another word and I'll shoot you myself.' Law glanced back at Hannah and examined his nails nonchalantly. 'Do go on.'

Hannah quivered as a winded Alex gingerly pushed himself up onto his hands and knees, wheezing for breath.

Hannah Curious, why had he picked her old nickname again?

What was Alex trying to tell her?

A memory jarred in her head; she'd heard someone say it already today. If possible, her eyes grew wider, her mind whirring despite Law's intensive gaze.

'I'm just a girl…' She muttered, stalling, thinking, glancing at Alex who was now touching his lip and checking his fingers for blood.

'Name, Floor and Grade? Answer now or I'll have them beat it out of you.'

Hannah met his gaze, his head tilting as a cruel sneer formed on his lips.

'It's Hannah,' She heard her voice go higher and swallowed hard. 'It's Hannah Curious, a Grade one-' she glanced at Alex 'Adjectivore.'

She stopped and thought, dredging her memory for where she'd heard her name. She blinked, instinctively looked upwards and the female voice in her memory fell into place. She looked back at Law and fumbled the words out breathlessly.

'Floor 121 - Crystalline to Curious.'

Law looked down his nose at her and sniffed. Eyes narrowing, he flicked his gaze onto Alex almost as an afterthought.

'And you?'

Alex gingerly got to his feet, his hands resting on his knees.

'Alex Guide, Grade two Nouner, Floor 190.' He muttered between coughs.

Law stared at the pair of them with inquisitive distrust.

'Search them.' He clicked his fingers and waggled a hand in their general direction.

Hannah folded her arms tightly across her chest and squirmed as rough gloved-hands frisked her and patted her empty pockets. The disappointment on CC Law's face grew into a suspicious growl.

'Come!'

With his boot leather creaking, he turned on his heel and strode through the lines of guards, the ranks parting before him. Hannah waited for Alex to hobble over to join her and followed. He caught her eye as he limped forward clutching his ribs but didn't speak, her guilt eating at her selfishness as he winced with every other pace.

'Sorry.' She muttered awkwardly but if he heard her, he didn't acknowledge it.

As they walked, Hannah glared up at the immovable hulks clutching their weapons. Again, there were names etched on the sides of their helmets, only this time in white on blue rather than black on yellow. The nearest two on her right were Yob and Bruiser, on her left was Thug, beyond him Brute, Hoodlum and Bully. She passed the fourth, fifth and sixth rows of Guards, the lines blurring into an army.

Ahead of them, a set of large wooden gates opened, the bright light dazzling Hannah's eyes. C.C Law eyed them with a sick leer.

'Welcome, my prisoner friends, to the last journey you'll ever make.'

CHAPTER SEVEN

Hannah hugged her thin jacket tighter to her body as a frigid breeze whipped in off a green sea and clawed at her hair. A causeway - little more than a thin ribbon of cobblestones – meandered out over the menacing water, like the spines of several open books face down on a ruffled green tablecloth.

The path headed across the waves to the dirty red walls of a most foreboding place under the heaviest of skies. Sat on a rugged outcrop of jagged rocks, the impenetrable curtain wall of bloodied stone rose up to sinister towers and intimidating turrets. The twinkling flames of countless braziers sat along the parapet, making the sharp crenulated battlements look like a row of shark's teeth.

'The Emergen Sea.' CC Law said bringing Hannah's shuddering focus back to the water. 'The last line of defence against escape from the Darkhive, its waters are said to contain many secrets best left unfound.'

He caught Hannah's alarm and smiled cruelly.

'Let's just say, you wouldn't want to get your feet wet.'

He calmly turned to Alex. 'Been here before with the Guild?'

Hannah nearly swallowed her tongue.

'Guild?' Alex responded coolly to Law's fishing. 'I'm Alex Guide, not Guild. I was showing Hannah Curious here the old Appendix warehouses and the Glossary, didn't know it was out of bounds, did I?'

'You know Don Curiosity?' His lip curled in disgust at Hannah.

'The infamous cat-killer? I doubt it; he's still locked up in there isn't he?' Alex nodded to the fortress over the water.

A cruel sneer slithered across Law's lips as he looked back at Alex. 'I didn't ask you, I asked the girl. You appear to have learnt nothing from your dance across the floor just now.'

He lost interest, screwing up his face as he checked his watch. 'The tide's turned, no chance of getting across today. We'll have to wait for low tide tomorrow afternoon.'

'Law.' A grizzled voice uttered.

All three of them turned to see a colossal Guard stood awkwardly in front of them.

'That's Chief Constable Law to you, Tough!'

Tough blinked indifferently.

'Well?'

'Messenger.' Tough grunted.

Hannah peered around Tough's bulky frame to see a Guard hovering apprehensively just inside the doorway, a note crumpled in his hand. Several of Law's guards eyed his red helmet with unease.

'A message from the Response team?' Law frowned. 'Right, Tough watch these two.'

Hannah stared at Law as he strode up the path back to the entrance.

'Do you think it's about us, Alex?'

He didn't reply.

'Alex...?'

She turned left and right, finding him scurrying down the dusty path, his arm cradling his bruised side. Tough watched Hannah as she cautiously backed away, spun on her heels and bolted after him. Bounding over tufts of grass and loose stones, she caught up with him as the path levelled out and changed to cobblestones.

'Alex! What are you doing? Alex?'

'Move!'

They'd just tiptoed their way onto the slippery stones of the causeway when Law's voice echoed from above.

'Hey! Get back here! Stop them!'

Several guards lumbered into an unsteady pursuit whilst Law screamed in the face of an apathetic Tough.

'Alex!' She panted as they sped away from the shore, but he wasn't for talking.

After a painful minute, she looked over her shoulder again. Law now stood alone, pulling a cigar from his top pocket and tapping it on the back of his other hand, the familiar sneer just about visible on his cruel face.

Hannah did her best to keep up with Alex, who despite his discomfort still pounded over the cobbles. She urgently pumped her arms but the hard, uneven ground deadened her legs. A noise and a yell turned her head back to the Guards behind, three of them staring down the slope into the turbulent waves. She slowed to a backwards walk but couldn't see anything amidst the pounding surf. They glared at Hannah before turning away and jogging back towards their master,

107

leaving her with a nagging doubt as to whether there'd been three or four Guards chasing them.

After she caught up with Alex, they settled into a hasty walk, neither ready to speak. Hannah sensed Alex's anger at her for ruining their chance of bluffing Law. Although, as she crossed the windswept causeway, voluntarily heading for what appeared to be a high security Word-prison, she failed to see how she could've made matters worse. Besides, he could hardly be expecting an apology when he'd just run off without her, leaving her stood with a burly Author-tarian Guard.

'Tough.' She muttered.

As they got further away from Law and his Guards, the wind felt stronger on her cheeks, seemingly blowing from all directions at the same time. The sea either side of them grew choppy, waves whipped up into crested peaks by the incessant wind. Overhead, the dulled metal sky grew darker, the clouds trapped in a tumultuous swirl directly over the causeway. They plodded on, their destination becoming larger but no clearer in the flat, overcast light.

Nearing halfway, Hannah chanced a look behind her at the tiny blue-helmeted Author-tarian Guards. Ahead, the slits in the towers and Darkhive gatehouse remained impenetrably dark, the battlements deserted.

'Why did you run Alex?'

He glanced back at her. 'The messenger.'

'The Guard in the red helmet?'

'Yes.'

She waited for more but Alex just trudged on.

108

Her fear morphed into resentment and she cursed him for returning into her life. People always said never to meet your heroes, they never mentioned your imaginary friends.

She eyed the skies wishing she knew what was happening five hundred floors above them, what the Feds were doing or those in charge of the Author-tarian Guards. She knew she should have been fretting over anxious teachers and police searches but right then those problems felt a world away.

Alex plodded on ahead of her.

Maybe all this wasn't about her at all. Maybe they were after Alex and he'd simply dragged her along for the ride?

She gritted her teeth and shook such destructive thoughts from her mind.

The waves still washed menacingly up the slopes on either side of them. Although the waves ebbed and flowed erratically, she sensed them gradually creeping higher. Movement out the corner of her eye turned her head, but she only saw the frothy surf breaking on the smooth slopes.

Alex's paces noticeably shortened until he stopped.

'What? What now?' She sagged.

'You shouldn't be here.' He looked at the floor. 'I've let you down, I've let the Guardian down! I should have let the Feds take me away back at the Monument.'

She stared at him, but he didn't raise his gaze.

'I've never been further down than the Appendices, let alone this deep. I...' His voice cracked. 'I don't know anyone who's been through Checkpoint Charles and returned as the same person.'

She realised for the first time, he wasn't much less out of his depth than she was and felt sympathy nudge her anger aside.

'Look, we are where we are, finger pointing or feeling sorry for ourselves isn't going to do us any good right now, is it?'

'You're right.' He looked over her shoulder at the Darkhive looming large.

'So, what is it?'

'It's nothing. It's just...' He licked his dry lips. 'It's just this place.'

Hannah looked at him awkwardly.

'We've all heard stories...' He trailed off. 'It's just...most Words pass through these gates kicking and screaming as they know they're not coming back.' He faltered on the last couple of words but tried to cover it with a cough. 'No Word has ever escaped from the Darkhive.'

Hannah looked at Alex anew, his genuine fear contagious. She'd already nearly cracked and now the rock who'd got her into this mess, the rock she was relying on getting her back out again was crumbling before her eyes.

'Don't be telling me that! Alex don't!'

He looked into her eyes.

'I'm sorry. I didn't mean it to sound so bleak. We'll come back, I'll sort this mess out somehow and get you home, I promise.'

Hannah didn't hear him. She felt sick, her body whirling as if all her emotions were on the Waltzers and screaming to go faster. She'd craved an answer to her curiosity and been rewarded with a one way trip to oblivion, in a world built on foundations of mistrust and hate.

110

She crammed her despair back into its box, swallowed hard and reached out to straighten his shirt collar.

'Listen. I'm clinging on here Alex,' she said, lips trembling 'clinging on to my mind with the varnish on the end of my nails. If you give up, if...'

She couldn't bring herself to finish the sentence. She looked past Alex, beyond the green waves lapping frothily over the road, to a millimetre high blur of black and blue dots at the other end of the Causeway. She fought off a shudder and jerked her eyes back to the disappearing cobblestones. She stared for several seconds before the message got through.

The waves reached across the road in several places like white hands clawing for purchase on the smooth stone. She whipped around wide-eyed at the rising water. The waves broke below them with a thunderous clap, the surf surging up the slopes, reaching for them with a bubbling hiss.

Reaching for them?

The loose thought found purchase in her mind like a windborne seed landing on barren soil. She stared at the waves and the hands in the surf formed from froth and foam, groping blindly for victims to pull down into the depths. She shook her head, as if disbelief could somehow bring back her scepticism.

'Alex! The tide! We've got to beat the tide!' She blurted, tugging on his sleeve to get him moving towards the Darkhive walls.

She surged forward, moving with utter abandon, sprinting as if a ravenous dog snapped at her ankles. She bounded forth over the uneven ground, feet barely kissing the cobbles. Chancing a glimpse over her shoulder to ensure Alex was still at her heels, her luck ran out.

Her toe stubbed into a raised stone, time slowing as her foot stopped.

She tripped.

Micro-seconds passed as her body came alive with tensed panic, her chest surging ahead of her feet as she went from running to flying. Her jarred foot instinctively whipped through beneath her, trying to catch up in a race to keep her upright. Her shoes hit the ground in short steps as gravity pulled at her leaning body. She flailed her arms, her torso straightening as she regained her balance with every step. Alas, she wasn't on a flat floor but damp, greasy cobbles and as she tried to correct herself, she inadvertently veered to her left.

Her recovery ran out of room.

Her left foot slapped onto the wet stone at the top of the slope and she skidded forward, hands flapping frantically as she swivelled and overbalanced backwards.

'Hannah!' Alex cried, her name seeming to fill the air around her forever.

She twisted sideways and slid downwards, coming to a stop on all fours, her shoes lower down the wet slope, her eyes just below the level of Alex's tiptoeing feet. It took all of three seconds but to Hannah the world whirled for minutes. The three or four metres back to Alex and the top of the causeway looked like a cliff face.

She peered down at her feet and dug in her toes, the Sea below sucking in the last of its previous wave as if drawing in a deep breath. The water level dropped and dropped until the great wall of green water collapsed in to fill the gap. The

112

Emergen Sea seized its opportunity and sent a freak wave after her. Her feet scrabbled at the wet surface searching for an elusive grip as she clawed at the smooth rock with her nails. Her soles kept slipping on the slimy rocks, but inch by inch, she edged up the slope. The deafening rumble and wet slap of the wave crashing below her shook the causeway beneath her, the vibrations spurring her on ever more frantically.

Her right leg slipped.

Her toes lost grip and her foot slid down from under her, her knee dropping to the wet slope and soaking her trousers. She panicked and stared down between her legs, the white frothy hands within the water surging up towards her ankle.

'Hannah!' Alex leaned downwards, his arm outstretched, his white fleshy hand reaching for hers.

She drew in a deep breath and pushed upwards with all her strength as the wave hit the sole of her shoe. Alex's hand slapped hard onto her left arm and clamped tightly round her wrist. At the same time, the water surged over her foot, instantly soaking it to the skin. Her screeches at the coldness changed to screams as icy fingertips scraped down her calf and grasped at her ankle, seeking purchase through her soggy socks. More pulled on her toes, her arm taking the strain as they tried to pull her from Alex's grip. She shivered and instinctively kicked out. Alex tottered forward a foot before straining backwards, moaning through a tight grimace.

They stretched Hannah out like a medieval prisoner on the rack. Alex's hands slipped down her wrist to her hand as he screamed through gritted teeth. She looked at his contorted face, her eyes begging him to hold on, willing him to tighten his grip.

Abruptly the pain in her stretched arm went away.

The wet numbing cold around her clutched foot also disappeared.

She could see Alex screaming but couldn't hear a sound. Lifted completely off the ground, she was stretched and strained, but the panic and stress fell away, as if she was an observer watching the struggle from afar.

This was it, she thought, the coin toss moment.

Heads you win, Tails you lose.

Each outcome greeted with a shrug and confused indifference. She looked around this new state of mind and knew she should be feeling fear and dread but all she had was an infinite emptiness.

The wave crested and fell back.

The pain returned with a flash of white light.

A finger and thumb pinched the skin of her ankle but the water sliding back down the slope dragged them away with a disappointed hiss. Alex tumbled over backwards and Hannah slammed back onto the wet slope with a soggy thud, wincing as she scrambled back up on to the top of the ridge.

They stared at each other wide-eyed, a long terrified conversation transmitted between them in a single look. Hannah paused before shaking her head.

'Go!' He yelled.

Hannah turned and with adrenaline still overloading her veins, ran so fast she was like a passenger in her own body. All her senses were on overload, her head

114

swimming, the sound of her breathing flooding her ears. Despite blocking out the noises and sense of panic, the thunderous crash and sizzle of the angry waves continued pounding the ground underfoot.

The end of the causeway grew nearer, her vision blurred by the uneven cobbles jarring her legs. In places, the waves already climbed the slopes on either side to within inches of each other.

'Close enough to shake hands.' A part of her thought perversely.

She squinted at the point where the causeway rose up to the Darkhive's imposing gates, something not right about the junction of cobblestones and the threadbare island.

Panic pushed her onwards, her throat grating and legs burning. They splashed through the topmost foam of the crowning waves, fingers in the surf crushed and kicked aside before they could hook onto her laces or grip onto her sodden trousers.

'Faster Hannah, Faster!' Alex urged with a scream and a hand in the centre of her back.

As they neared safety, Hannah's hopes sank. Where the path had once gently sloped upwards to the island, she now saw a huge gap in the causeway. Splashing on through the surf, they slowed on the dry, loose cobbles before inching their way towards the crumbling edge.

The gaping hole in the eroded causeway writhed with frenzied waves, the white water scything through the remains of the road and its foundations. She sighed wearily across at the cliff of dirt at head-height opposite her, only fifteen metres from her, but as good as in another country. The sea surged through gaps from both sides and crashed over exposed rocks as if knowing they were there.

It looked impossible.

'I can't...' She shook her head, but more through fear than decision.

Peering down into the craggy abyss, Hannah guessed Law knew they wouldn't survive and had allowed them to run to their deaths. Yet thinking of Alex stopping midway and her stumble, she realised painfully they only had themselves to blame.

'Hannah? When you're ready.' Alex said calmly at her shoulder.

She looked down at the ever-decreasing patch of dry ground around their feet, the causeway behind them all but covered by green waves.

'May as well die trying.' She thought, trying to overwhelm reality with faux courage.

She clenched her fists and waited for a ferocious wave to surge up the broken remnants of the slope. As it subsided, she leapt for a broken concrete block and bounced straight onto another. A wave rocked a huge jagged boulder on her left as she skipped over three smaller ones in its lea, the spray falling icily over her back. With a hand on a loose rock, she scrambled up onto a large crumbling spine of cobblestones. Steadying herself and sucking in a misty breath, she waited for Alex as he followed her path up onto the jagged, unstable remains of the causeway. He clutched at her as a large wave crashed behind them making the ground tremble.

Hannah set off across a thin ridge, the line of cobbles atop a crumbling earth tightrope. Arms outstretched for balance, the vibrations shook her legs as one after

116

another the waves pounded either side of them, clawing at the foundations. She kept moving even as the cobbles shifted beneath her feet and rocks tumbled into the white and green water below, each wave snapping at her ankles like a yapping terrier. Raising her eyes, she saw the island almost within reach and broke into a run, bounding from stone to awkward stone with abandon. With a final large leap over a surging wave, she hit the gentle slope and ran a few steps to safety.

Alex followed, skipping and jumping across a disintegrating ridge of jagged stones. He leapt high, his knees tucked into his chest as the largest wave yet threw itself at his departing feet. For the briefest of seconds, it looked like Alex surfed down the wave on the soles of his shoes. He landed on the edge, threw his weight forward into a roll and raced past a frozen Hannah.

Leaning on her legs, her chest heaved and sides ached, the fizz of elation eroding her dread. She clenched her fists and sucked in some deep breaths. The water had soaked her and grabbed at her ankles but she'd got away. It was such a tiny victory but after so much misfortune, it was one worth celebrating. Strolling up the thin, grassy slope, she couldn't hide the broad smile on her face.

'We did it Alex! We did it!'

Laid breathlessly on his back, Alex didn't reply. Her eyes fell onto several parallel lines etched down the soles of his shoes, as if scratched by long sharp fingernails.

She looked back out over the angry green water, shuddering as the remnants of the causeway disappeared beneath the waves.

117

CHAPTER EIGHT

Hannah dropped down next to Alex on the thin grass; chest aching and throat dry.

'What the...heck?' She murmured, eyeing the green water.

Alex said nothing, her exasperation withering into self-doubt, as if she'd imagined the level of danger they'd just survived.

She eased her shoe from her right foot and pulled down her sock, wincing as her fingers explored the angry red marks on her ankle and several scratches on her calf.

'You alright?' Alex said over the thunder of frustrated waves pounding the juddering island.

'I'm fine.' She muttered, pulling up her socks and rolling down her trouser leg before he could make a fuss.

She tied her shoe and eyed him cautiously, the question reaching her lips twice before she let it escape.

'Who *are* you exactly?'

'Hmmm?' He murmured, looking back from the angry sea.

'You, Alex...Aldwyn Claviger, who are you?'

'What do you mean?'

'Well, yesterday I was a nobody, today everybody thinks I'm...somebody.'

He frowned. 'I still don't-'

She rolled her eyes. 'Alex, I'm...this morning I was on a school trip! Now I'm stranded on some god-forsaken underground island, sat at the gates of some kind of weird...Alcatraz!'

He stared.

'It's that tiny gap between normal life and...'she waved a finger about her, 'whatever this is?'

His eyes narrowed slightly.

'I mean, if it's not too much trouble?' She added. 'You know, it might pass a few minutes before we're inevitably tortured to death!'

'Sarcasm?' He sighed wistfully.' I'd almost forgotten about sarcasm...' He caught her patient glare. 'Well, there's not much to tell. As George said, I'm a Grade four Nouner, a Key-keeper. I joined the Shrouded Guild as an apprentice of course, but...it didn't work out.'

'And *who* are they exactly?'

'The Shrouded Guild?' He asked softly.

She nodded.

'It's a secret group set up centuries ago to protect English Words in times of trouble.'

'And this demanding Guardian figure?'

'The Guardian runs the Guild, with wise counsel from the Elders.' His eyebrows flicked upwards. 'It all seems such a long time ago since I was properly involved now though. I've been up in Pandemonia for the last fifteen years; with you...and then, travelling and learning Heartisan ways. I used to get my coded

119

instructions through the Times Cryptic Crossword, came as a bit of a shock to see my call-sign in there again after all these years. Truth be told, I was just as eager to meet this Guardian as you to meet me.'

Hannah blushed slightly, her eyes narrowing. '*This* Guardian?'

'Yes, they change from time to time. Some retire, some are...less fortunate.'

Hannah resisted and changed the subject.

'What did you do before living with my family?'

Alex smiled at the memory and opened up.

'I spent ten years running messages and distributing leaflets for them before earning the right to be trained as one of the Guilds' elite agents; a Knight Watchman. I proved my knowledge and skills in the entrance exams and was all set to commence my training, but...'

He froze, staring at the sea. 'But there was...They discovered evidence I'd cheated. They said whilst unsubstantiated, it still "cast doubt on the integrity of my character." I was surreptitiously dropped and another apprentice selected instead.'

Hannah thought for a moment. 'George Found.'

His eyes flared and answered her question.

'Yes, although a week later he got kicked out too on some other misdemeanour. He never talks about it, but it was rumoured his references didn't check out.'

'And you naturally think he *found* the evidence for your downfall. No wonder you're still mad at him.'

120

Alex sighed. 'I don't know what to think any more. I've tried to put it all behind me.'

'Right, but you still kept checking the crossword each day for your call-sign, didn't you?'

His eyes narrowed at her.

'Just in case they ever needed you again?'

He sighed inwardly. 'Pretty stupid eh?'

'No, not at all.' She murmured, looking out at the choppy green waters, the causeway but a memory. 'Sometimes, you'll do anything to get back what you've lost.'

He stirred. 'You mean...?'

Hannah didn't look at him.

Alex stared at her but didn't pursue it.

She coughed into her fist.

'So!' She said a little too eagerly. 'Come on, who are you? Not Alex the imaginary friend but this Nouner called Aldwyn, I don't even know where you were born? How old you are? Where you live? Do you have family? A home?' She raised an eyebrow. 'A wife?'

He looked at her sympathetically. 'Those are Pandemonia questions.'

'And?' Hannah frowned.

He shook his head. 'They've no relevance here in Lexica, our World's populated by Words, Letters and Punctuation, not humans, flora and fauna. We've no concept of birth and death in your sense of the word.'

121

'But...' Hannah struggled.

'Words aren't born Hannah, we're created. I came into existence through popular demand at some time in the Middle Ages; *Claviger* coming from *Clavis* - the Medieval Latin word for key and *Gerere* - the Latin word meaning "to carry".

'In the Middle Ages? But...But that makes you at least 500 years old!'

'Oh yes and the rest. Could be up to 1500 I guess.'

'You guess? You mean you don't know!'

He shrugged. 'What does it matter, Words don't age, they just become redundant or if they're lucky gain new meanings.'

'Is that what happened to you?'

Alex shook his head. 'I drifted out of fashion, replaced largely by Servant, Caretaker, Custodian and Warden. Fortunately, I'm not totally unused or they'd send me the same way as Words like Quotha, Sweven and Gardyloo.'

'Why what happened to them?'

Alex pointlessly checked they were alone before leaning towards her and whispering. 'They were erased. No-one talks about it.'

'What do you mean erased?'

'No-one talks about it.'

'But why?'

'Hannah, I said *No-one* talks about it.'

Hannah bit her tongue and waited, hoping he hadn't totally clammed up.

'As for family, I've got the Claviger office, but they're more like colleagues than relatives. Margaret and Toby Claviger work on my side of the office, Gregory

122

and Walter work on the other. They focus more on the other definition of Claviger – a club-bearer. To be honest, I don't get back much.'

'You don't like them?'

'They're just slightly...' He paused and looked diplomatically for the right words before his shoulders sagged. '...dull! Conversations about hitting objects with clubs can get a tad repetitive. Chatter about key-carrying isn't exactly a hotbed of sparkling conversation either. They're keen though, I'll give them that. They're all ambitious to work up from understudies to head the office or become a suffix or plural. It's nice knowing I don't have to worry about all the mundane allocation, replication and stocktaking nonsense.'

'I'm not sure I can get my head around all this.'

'The Four Words on floor four would be able to explain more; they're the grammatical gurus of the English Language. They help with the introduction and context of new ideas.'

'Forewords?'

Alex nodded. 'Yes, four of them.'

Hannah thought better of asking again. 'Are they your leaders?'

He shook his head. 'No, the leaders of the English Language are Mr Prim and Mr Proper, a coalition brought together to bring down our full-stop deficit. Although listening to George, they're doing almost nothing to stop the terrible changes, they're either power-mad or...someone else is manipulating them.'

Hannah never much liked politics and found her interest weakening. 'So where do the Shrouded Guild-'

'So many questions!'

'I'm just curious.' She said without thinking.

He smiled wryly. 'Some things never change.'

Hannah saw herself distantly through Alex's memories, that Hannah; the girl full of questions, with her nose in her books and summer in her eyes.

She leaned back on her elbows and basked briefly in joyful memories full of dollhouses, colouring-in and storytelling in a den under the kitchen table. Lifting her head, she glanced out contentedly over the water. All the ferocity had subsided, the tranquil green water now more like a rippling lake than a raging sea. The winds had calmed, the clouds parting, a lemon-coloured sun warming Hannah's skin and drying her clothes.

A dull resonating thud broke the tranquillity.

Rolling onto her side, Hannah eyed the Darkhive entrance as the slow meticulous clanking of heavy chains announced the opening of its colossal doors. Alex pulled her to her feet, and they stood stretching limbs and brushing dust from their clothes.

The noise ceased, the wooden doors parting just enough to reveal a tall, thin strip of inky blackness between them. A yellow light flickered on, throwing a huge approaching shadow onto the edge of the left-hand door. They heard footsteps and a small shuffling figure appeared, peering at them over the rims of his half-moon glasses.

'Oh no.' The dark haired man said disapprovingly as he looked Alex and Hannah up and down before disappearing back the way he'd come.

124

Hannah raised an eyebrow enquiringly.

Alex tilted his head unenthusiastically. 'Another Prepositioner.'

'Like at the Checkpoint?'

He nodded, lip curled.

The Prepositioner returned with a bulging clipboard and a worn black Homburg placed haphazardly on his head. His wrinkled black suit hung limply from his bony frame as he approached with the air of a worried butler.

'No, no, no, this will never do.' He flicked between the top sheet and the one below. 'Names? Give me your names?'

'We're meant to be inside Prepositioner.'

Hannah frowned at Alex, he noticed and briefly shook his head.

'I'll be the one who decides where you're meant to be Nouner! Names?'

Alex sighed. 'Alex Guide.'

'I've no records of any more Nouners being Darkhived today. You can't be here, the tide has turned. No, no this'll never do!'

He tapped his clipboard with his pen. 'I've no paperwork! Rule 4.3c of the Prepositioner handbook states: It's forbidden for Nouners to move around at liberty in the lower floors without a green slip sub-stamped by the three relevant Prepositioners, furthermore-'

Alex cut in. 'I care not for your rules Prepositioner.'

The Prepositioner looked at him sternly. 'You mustn't obstruct me in my work. I must know both your names! Rule 26.7d clearly-'

'I care not for *any* of your rules Prepositioner.'

125

Hannah stood awkwardly.

The Prepositioner looked lost.

'But what will I record? This is most irregular without any paperwork. I must have the details to be able to do my work.'

Alex had no sympathy. 'Put what you want old man! It's of no concern to us.'

'But without the details, I'm without purpose. My reason for being is to record where Nouners are in relation to those around them. Without that, I'm...I'm...' He trailed off.

Hannah was sure he was going to cry.

'Hannah Curious, my name is Hannah Curious.'

Alex glared at her.

'An Adjectivore.' The Prepositioner said, lip curling with disdain.

Alex cut in as he saw Hannah bristle.

'Alright Prepositoner, just put,' He waited impatiently as the Prepositioner scrambled for a pink sheet on his clipboard, his pencil hovering expectantly, 'Alex Guide and Hannah Curious are *within* the Darkhive.'

He scribbled, let a sneer smear his lips and ordered them inside at once.

'Alex?' She said with a sense of foreboding.

'Trust me.'

At another time Hannah would have laughed.

'Inside, now. In, go on in, you can't be out here! Get inside now, in. That's it, in you go!'

126

He hustled and harried them between the doors into the yellowy gloom, the doors creaking closed with an ominous thud. The Prepositioner's shuffled away to his open door and kicked it shut without a backwards glance.

Hannah gasped as the darkness smothered them, the noise of the slammed door reverberating around them like an explosion in a Cathedral. As it subsided, she heard a bell tinkle faintly somewhere away in the darkness.

'Alex?' Hannah reached for him, the panic barely disguised in her voice.

'Right here.' Alex guided her hand to his arm and disguised the disgruntlement in his own voice. 'Don't worry, we were always going to end up in here whatever we did, if not from the sentries, from Law and his Guards when the causeway cleared at low tide.'

'What about the Prepositioner?' Hannah asked, still full of questions.

'He's not going to help us.'

'But maybe he's just…'

'Hannah he won't. Don't you get it? Alex and Hannah are *within* the Darkhive.' He sensed her frown even in the darkness. 'A Prepositoner doesn't care about anyone or anything but his work. As long as his paperwork is up to date, he's as content as a Buzzword at a business conference.'

Hannah bit her tongue, fast concluding Lexica was no place for anyone with even a trace of goodness in their body. It was a cold, heartless place where the worst of human nature seemed not just tolerated but positively encouraged.

'What do we do now?' She whispered.

'Ssssh.' Alex hissed.

127

Hannah tilted her head, picking out faint noises in the darkness; quiet footfalls, the squeak of boot leather and the swish of careful movement.

'You said we'd finished?' A voice moaned.

'Quiet back there. To your positions!' A hushed voice barked.

Hannah took a breath, her head jerking to the left and the right with each new noise, her stomach tightening. She flinched at a low rasping noise as a match flared into a small orange flame.

'Oh no, not again!'

CHAPTER NINE

The flame floated upwards, illuminating the bulbous bowl of a smoking pipe.

'Law?' Alex cried.

'It can't be.' Hannah murmured.

The pipe flared, leaping flames briefly revealing a mouth and some stubby fingers. The match waved and went out, only a faint glow remaining.

'Show yourself!' Alex shouted.

Someone's fingers clicked and a single cone of light illuminated a rectangular black dais.

'Step up please.' A dry voice commanded.

'Who's there?' Alex yelled defiantly.

The pipe glowed.

'Step up please.' The same unruffled voice spoke with a calm malice.

'Maybe we should do as he says.' Hannah murmured as Alex continued to stare up at the pipe smoker.

Feeling numb from the neck down, Hannah stepped up onto the dais, Alex reluctantly following.

'Good.'

A further snap of the fingers and another cone of light revealed a second raised platform opposite them. A black helmet and black sleeves sat behind a polished walnut pipe. He lifted a creased pink sheet from a high desk.

'Alex Guide and Hannah Curious, you're to be tried by twelve Words good and true.'

Another click illuminated two long benches on their left with six Author-tarian Guards in each row, black names written on the sides of their matt silver helmets. Hannah groaned, knowing whatever was about to happen was already inevitable.

Further finger-clicks from who she now saw as the judge revealed a helmeted stenographer bashing away at a miniature typewriter, a helmeted public gallery opposite the jury, a silver-helmeted prosecutor – a black gown over his body armour - and much to everyone's amusement, an empty seat where the public defender should have been. The judge banged his pipe like a gavel on his desk until the laughter subsided.

'You're brought before the court today charged with...' The judge flicked through his notes, his confusion growing, 'with...I'm sorry I don't appear to have you on my Court List.'

'We're just visiting.' Alex proffered nervously.

'Hmmph!' The judge snorted, dropping his notes. 'Oh I doubt that. We've not had a visitor since, well...ever. No, no we'll have to think of some other charge, public gallery, do you have any ideas?'

Hannah frowned incredulously across at the public gallery, squinting at the names on their helmets.

'Making us work late!' Injustice said bitterly.

'He never listens to me anyway, so...' Discrimination muttered from the jury opposite.

'Ssssh. Anyone else?'

Several of the Guards scratched their helmets.

'Breaking and entering?' Prejudice leered over at them.

The judge snorted with amusement, heartily banging his pipe before peering down his nose at Hannah and Alex, 'You are hereby accused of breaking and entering into the Darkhive judicial courts, how do you plead?'

'Not…Guilty?' Alex said without conviction.

The judge drew the pipe from his mouth and guffawed. Everyone in the jury and gallery joined in as his laughter grew, rocking back and forth in their seats with the hilarity of the answer. All, except the stenographer who furiously hammered the shorthand for *Ha*.

The pipe banged again and gradually the riotous roars descended through hearty chortles and weary chuckles to complete silence.

'Good now, Prosecutor? Without going into too much detail, please present the case against the guilty.'

The Prosecutor pointed at Alex and Hannah. 'The guilty were found here just now acting guiltily, right here, over there, just now.'

He sat down.

The Judge banged his pipe again, seemingly for no other reason than he enjoyed doing it. He ignored the empty chair and turned directly to the jury.

'It's usual for the jury to retire before deciding on a verdict but as this is overtime, I suggest we move straight to a decision. Foreman of the jury, have you reached a guilty verdict?'

131

Inequality leapt to his feet in the jury. 'You always ask the foreman!'

'He never listens to me anyway, so...' Discrimination muttered again.

With a heavy sigh, the judge's hand disappeared behind the pipe and pinched at his nose.

'Sit down Colin, for the last time, it's not personal, just procedure.'

Inequality crossed his arms as if refusing to sit down, before immediately sitting down.

'Foreman - *and only the foreman* - have you reached a verdict? '

A guard with Bias on his helmet stood up, leaning a little as if one leg was longer than the other one.

'Yes boss. Guilty boss!'

'Good!' Order blew out his cheeks and tidied his papers. 'A little chaotic, somewhat unprofessional, but we get there in the end. I hereby sentence you both to indefinite imprisonment in the Darkhive. Courtroom dismissed.'

Hannah barely had time to take in his words before the pipe slammed into the desk and eight Guards stepped out of the darkness, surrounding the raised dais. Beyond their huge frames, the Author-tarian Guards filed from their positions in the odd courtroom, muttering to one another as they drifted away into the darkness.

Two Guards stepped aside on the left of the dais revealing the judge in his black helmet, the pipe still clenched between his teeth. He was a wiry figure, his face gaunt but grizzled, the first shadow of silvery stubble appearing on his chin, matching the colour of the lettering on his helmet. His hooked nose had been broken at some point, giving him the overall air of a retired boxer who knew when to quit. His dark, empty eyes glinted in the strong spotlight, dominating his face and holding Hannah's gaze like a hawk eyeing a mouse.

'I'm Chief Constable Reginald Order. You have been sentenced by the Darkhive High Court, please come with us.'

Neither Alex nor Hannah moved.

'Bravo, bravo!' Order mocked with deliberate clapping. 'Your continued resistance is courageous and I admire that, but let's get the facts straight shall we? You're within the Darkhive, escape quite impossible. You are now officially my property, mine until I find you a purpose within the prison or see fit to discard of you.'

He enjoyed their discomfort.

'I can offer you two paths from here to your eternal incarceration. One is direct and largely painless, the other…less so.'

He sucked on his pipe and blew out the smoke, smiling to the guard beside him. 'I do enjoy it when they resist Nigel. It's always so…*inspiring* watching hopes being crushed.'

Hannah swallowed hard and stepped down from the dais, Alex reluctantly followed.

'Now, walk in silence or I'll have Garrotte and Strangle here use a little subtle persuasion.' He gestured to a couple of urban gorillas behind them.

Hannah glanced over her shoulder at their square chins and wished she hadn't.

133

'Oh yes, don't be fooled by the Grade one buffoons in my courtroom, these Guards are my most vicious and dangerous.' He leaned forward conspiratorially. 'To be honest, I do well to control them at all.'

A tremor shook her shoulders, shivers zigzagging down her spine.

Order took a last draw on his pipe, bent a leg up behind his other and whacked it against his boot. After the smouldering tobacco spilled to the floor, he handed the pipe to a Guard with a line of them clipped onto his belt.

Smirking at the look on Hannah's face, he turned and walked away, Killer and Slayer at his shoulders, Slaughter, Assassin, Murder and Vengeance forming a muscle-bound cage around them. As rough hands shoved them around the back of the jury box, Hannah instinctively knew these Guards were more ruthless than any they'd encountered so far. Whilst they took Order's orders, they obviously weren't answerable to Law's laws.

As the Chief Constable approached a long horizontal crack of light, two huge doors opened in time with his strutting stride, bathing them all in subdued light. He nodded to someone on the right and with fury, Hannah saw the Prepositioner grinning from a doorway, yellow light flooding out around his ankles.

Marching outside onto a dusty road between thin, windowless buildings, the earthy smell of dust replaced the stuffiness of unwashed clothes and stale smoke. High above them the detached buildings almost seemed to touch; the narrow, grubby ribbon of sky running above them like a continuous strip light. Glimpsing through the gaps between the clanking musclemen, Hannah realised the buildings

134

weren't buildings at all, they were the ends of rows of shelving running gloomily into the distance, each filled with small metal boxes.

It resembled a huge storage warehouse, only one without a roof and with weeds growing underfoot.

'Where are they taking us Alex?' She whispered.

He looked paler than ever, his eyes glazed. Her words seeped through his thoughts and he helplessly shrugged his shoulders.

She blinked hard and tried to think of somewhere else, anyone else. Her grandma seized the opportunity and elbowed her way into Hannah's thoughts. She paced around Bluebell House, not in concern but fury at Hannah bringing shame on her name. She scowled furiously, raging at Magda, the irresponsible school and the incompetent Police.

'I'm in serious trouble when I get out.' Hannah twitched. 'If I get out.'

A short sharp gasp came from her lips, her Grandma disappearing like a popped balloon.

If she got out.

She'd dreaded getting home, but what if she didn't return?

What if there wasn't a mistake?

What if the great danger Alex warned her about, had been the danger of capture by the Feds and Author-tarian Guards?

They'd tried to imprison her and she'd obliged by rushing across the causeway to get into their prison a day early. She wanted to blame someone; Alex, George, Law, Order, her Grandmother, but deep down she knew the truth.

135

Sadness shivered gently behind her softening eyes, but she fought it with all she had left, determined not to let them bring her to tears. Teeth clenched, she blinked away the fuzziness and focused on Order's heels ahead of her, counting his footsteps for a means of distraction. George's words about numbers giving Words protection helped her fend off the lightning bolts of despair and thunderous rumbles of sorrow until she passed through the worst of the storm.

Emerging from the gloom of the shelving, Hannah shielded her eyes from the dazzling sun, the distant outer walls visible through a shimmering haze. Passing between mace-wielding sentries, they entered a huge grassy field strewn with tents and guards practising armed combat drills with swords and morning stars. They marched away from the camp, up a long, gentle incline, the neat lawns changing to scrubland, the dusty road growing rougher and rutted. As it levelled, they entered a stunted wood choked with nettles and thickets of brambles. The dark trees on either side remained eerie and still; no birdsong or rustle of leaves intruding on the silence. As she scoured the creepy shadows and sensed eyes lurking behind every gnarled trunk, she was almost thankful to have the burly Guards surrounding her.

After an hour of monotonous trudging, they emerged onto a grassy plain dominated by something more of her world than anything she'd yet seen. Although frequently obscured by the foliage of trees and hedgerows lining their sunken dusty track, infrequent glimpses of it in the distance distracted her from their plight. Emerging from an avenue of lime trees, she drank in her first unsighted view of the majestic lichen-covered steeple reaching for the heavens. With a slatted belfry, black and gold clock faces and weatherworn limestone walls, the parish church was

136

a thing of architectural beauty. Lifting herself onto her toes, she found it wasn't alone.

CC Order marched them around a gentle curve into a quintessentially English village oozing with nostalgia. Peering between the guards, she spied thatched-roof cottages, a village shop, a watermill, a Red Lion Pub and a church hall with bunting in the windows. She heard the babbling trickle of a nearby stream and the calls of the mallards on the duck-pond, the heady perfume of roses from the cottage gardens filling the air.

Despite all that'd happened, these pleasures and the warm kiss of late afternoon sunshine on her skin melted away some of her anxiety.

Past the vicarage, they veered right over a small humpback bridge and marched alongside a thick, prickly hedgerow laden with berries. Rounding a large oak, Order turned left and raised his hand to halt the Guards. He sneered at Hannah and Alex before opening a white five-bar gate and heading for another small guard hut.

Hannah stared beyond the emerging Prepositioner and felt an icy, tingling sensation creep across her scalp.

CHAPTER TEN

Beyond a tall wire fence lay the village cricket pitch, or rather what used to be the cricket pitch. On either side of the gate, armed guards peered down inquisitively from two makeshift wooden towers. More guards sat behind sandbags on the balcony of a pavilion and on the roof of a scorer's shed. Their machineguns pointed threateningly at the four wooden huts positioned around the roped-off wicket.

A face appeared in one of the windows of the nearest hut. A second and third swiftly followed until within a handful of seconds a crowd of faces pressed their noses to the glass. The Prepositioner beside C.C Order also looked back at Hannah, leering as he licked the tip of his pencil and eagerly scribbled on his clipboard. Task complete, he stepped back inside his guard-hut leaving Order to turn his anger on the sentries behind the gates.

'Why are these not open yet? Do you know who I am?'

The sentries duly swung the gates open, one rushing so much he dropped his rifle onto the soft muddy ground much to Order's disdain.

The Author-tarian Guards prodded Hannah and Alex forwards through the gates, her focus on the nearest hut as the first of the faces emerged through the door. Words in a mishmash of discoloured green, blue and khaki uniforms tumbled out after him.

CC Order crossed the lush grass, sidestepping cautiously over the white hemp rope marking the pitch's boundary line, as if it buzzed with a million volts. The

Author-tarian Guards copied him and although it looked harmless, Hannah and Alex did the same. Ten paces inside the line, Order stopped and smiled grimly at them.

'This is Undesirables One - Word Internment Camp. As you're not on the Official Court listings, I'll hold you here until I find out what I'm to do with you.'

'We've not done anything wrong!' Alex spat through gritted teeth.

'I'll be the judge of that.' He snarled before mocking in an Old Etonian voice. 'I'm sorry, it's just not cricket, is it old chap?'

He diverted his gaze to Hannah who crossed her arms, less in defiance and more to hide her nerves.

'Now, what to do about you?' He grinned unnervingly.

'You touch her and I'll find you and…' Alex leapt forward, getting within inches of an unflinching Order before two guards lifted him effortlessly off the ground.

Hannah gawped, body quivering.

'And you'll what exactly?' Order sighed and shook his head, rapidly becoming bored with the pair of them.

'Press him in the book for a few hours, that'll take the edge off his courage. As for the girl…' He sniffed and nonchalantly flicked his head to the huts.

Two arms grabbed her by the elbows, marched her forward twenty paces and threw her down to her knees. She whipped around as the guards retreated, CC Order menacingly sucking another pipe into life.

139

Alex futilely resisted Killer and Malevolence as they dragged him towards the Scorers shed. She knew he'd instinctively tried to show them he was the dangerous one, not her. Despite what they'd endured, beneath all the levels of angst and fear, blame and irritation, Alex had still tried to protect her.

She swallowed hard and tried to get up.

'Don't. He'll be back, that's when he'll need you most.' A soft voice warned her.

A wiry man with round glasses and persuasive eyes had crossed from the huts to crouch five metres away from her. Back by the huts, a staring crowd stood warily with hands in pockets. Camp guards rushed nervously from the pavilion towards them, machine-guns clutched tightly in their hands.

A fat man bulging out of his authoritative grey uniform came wobbling out after them, flanked by two youths fumbling with their carbines. He tugged at the stained napkin tucked into his collar, wiped his mouth and brushed self-consciously at the epaulettes on his shoulders as he waddled across the grass towards CC Order.

Hannah got to her feet, wiping grass from the knees of her trousers, her eyes flicking across to Alex as they dragged him into the windowless shed.

'This way. Your friend will be fine, many of us have had time in the Book but we all come back. Maybe with less fire in our bellies, but we come back, you'll see. Sorry where are my manners, I'm Vincent Convince, but my friends just call me Vince. It's easier, you'll see.'

Hannah silently fell in beside him, her attention on Killer and Malevolence as they locked up the Scorer's shed and trudged back towards the camp gates. CC

Order stood there prodding the fat Officer's chest with his pipe, chastising him over some misdemeanour or other.

Ahead of her, the wide-eyed men outside the huts alternated between whispering amongst themselves and shrugging. As several camp guards rushed behind Hannah and formed a semi-circle bristling with rifles, the whispering stopped.

'…middle of my afternoon nap man!'

'Sorry Major.'

'I've said it 'til even I'm bored of hearing it…'

'Sor-'

'…I'm not to be disturbed in the middle of my afternoon nap.' A booming malt whisky voice approached from behind the back of the hut, a soft effeminate voice accompanying him like a splash of apologetic soda. The crowd noticeably stiffened as the pair pushed through to the front.

'What's all this nonsense? Let me through. What's going….oh!' His face froze in exclamation.

He was a jowly man with intensive brown eyes and a large hooked nose; a feature he was obviously proud of, as he'd underlined it with a bristly dark moustache. He wore a peaked blue cap with black trim and four yellow exclamation marks across its front. Four more were on the shoulders of a dark blue uniform, buttoned up incorrectly in his haste to get dressed.

'But…but you're a girl!'

Everyone looked at Hannah and back at the Major as if to see if they'd missed some vital detail. An unshaven man wearing his jacket inside out and his hat back to front spoke up.

'A girl in the camp. Whatever next? A rhino? We must put a stop to this right now!'

Another man with a steely stare and chiselled chin stepped forward, 'If she's here, she must be an enemy of *them.*' He spat the word as if it was sour. 'And any enemy of *them* is a friend of ours I say.'

'I'm with Radders here.' Vince piped up at her side. 'I think every one of us can agree what he's said there makes the most sense.'

There were more than a few nods and murmured agreement.

'But she's a girl! We can't have a girl here in the camp! It's just another indication of the wanton oppression we're all suffering as…' The unshaven man bleated until without looking, the Major raised a hand.

'That's enough for now Private Rebel.' The Major stared at Hannah, his demeanour becoming softer and less ruffled by the second. Everyone stood silently awaiting his verdict.

'It's most irregular and we'll have to make changes around here but as Corporal Radical and Sergeant Convince said, any enemy of theirs is a friend of ours.' He nodded towards the Scorers shed. 'Same goes for your companion too.'

His moustache twitched as he smiled and his face changed instantaneously from stern leader to friendly uncle. He glanced at the palm of his hand, rubbing it on his trousers as he stepped forward. 'Now Miss…'

'Hannah. Hannah Curious.'

'Curious eh? Right, welcome to Undesirables One - Word Internment Camp or Worditz as some of the wags in here have called it.' He shook her hand vigorously. 'I'm Major Form-Class, in charge of these misfits. If you need anything, anything at all, you come see me or Lieutenant Apologist here.'

'Nice to meet you. Sorry.' The sensitive man whispered, shaking her hand almost guiltily.

The Major looked disenchanted with Apologist's manner before his eyes shifted to over her shoulder. 'Ah! Now if you'll excuse me, I must have a few words with the Camp Commandant. Come along Lieutenant.'

He swept past her towards the fat guard who was returning from his dressing down at the gates, the Major's sidekick scurrying along in his wake.

The guards with the machineguns dispersed and the crowd dissolved into small chattering groups, until a brown, leather football appeared and became the new centre of attention.

Hannah stood alone, numb, home a distant intangible idea.

You can't do this...

The voice in her head was cold. Mocking. She'd so often been *that* girl, the subject of surreptitious stares and hands covering shared whispers. *That* girl, with the missing mother and broken home. *That* girl, who wore a thousand rumours.

Yet here, *that* girl was drowning in open water. Sinking into the surreal abyss alongside the calm, logical introvert that *that* girl had become.

She let her chest rise and fall, staring at the dry grass beneath her feet, staying in the now lest she entirely lose her grip on what was real or not.

'Hungry? Of course you are, after your long journey. Come on, this way.' Vince questioned, answered and guided her forward before Hannah could even answer.

As the cries and boisterous shouts continued behind her, Vince led her around the first hut, its door bearing a crudely painted number one.

'Hut One and Hut Three are where we sleep. Hut Two is for the Major and the officers.' He pointed to the left and on to the one furthest from the gates. 'That's the canteen and games room if it's raining. The latrines and wash hut are on the other side.'

They skirted the roped-off wicket, climbed three steps and stepped into the stark canteen in Hut Four. A portly black-haired man in an ill-fitting apron was collecting plates from two rows of tables and benches.

'Partisan, got a hungry late-comer. Anything left?'

'Don't be stoopid.' He said in a heavy accent; part French, part eastern European. He paused, as he turned round to see Hannah, his face breaking into a forced toothy smile. 'Of cours I've somethings leaft.'

He weaved past them with a tower of swaying plates and sidestepped around a serving counter into the kitchen beyond.

'Private Partisan is the camp cook,' Vince told her. 'He's good too, always telling us a tall tale the P in his name had been an administrative mistake. And don't be put off by the accent, Arty is an immigrant Nouner. He came to us from the Academie Francaise via the wars in the Balkan Languages some time ago.'

Arty returned impossibly quickly carrying a laden tray. He wafted past with a breeze of tempting aromas and placed it carefully onto a clean part of the table. She needed no second invitation. The sight of the bubbling cheese-topped crouton floating in a sea of steaming French Onion soup cramped her stomach with suppressed hunger. Her eyes widened greedily at the warm rustic sourdough bread, her mouth salivating even before she sipped the swirling mug of milky tea or nibbled at the crystallised sugar carrot atop the frosted slice of cake.

'Thank you.' She managed through dry lips.

'Itsa ok.' Arty shrugged nonchalantly.

After devouring one of the tastiest meals of her life, she stuck close to Vince, wary of the crowd of strangers trailing her around camp. They followed her from the volleyball net to the card school, from the vaulting gymnasts to the theatre group rehearsing in homemade costumes and wigs. She thought of asking Vince to stop them but she didn't want anyone to think it bothered her. As the sun sank behind the tree line on her left, Vince guided her inside Hut Three.

At the far end, a washing line and several blankets formed an improvised screen. Vince held it open and she stepped through to see a rickety wooden chair next to a bunk bed, the bottom made up with two pillows, the top with none. She looked at his bashful smile questioningly and with a crashing wave of understanding realised this was her bed for the night.

She looked out at the reddening sky and realised she'd lost all track of time.

145

'What time is it?'

He ducked his head to peer out at the sunset. 'About eight o'clock, I reckon.'

She thought of her Grandmother sneering at her headmaster and Police officers, a spike of panic subsiding into resignation. She deserved any fury coming her way, but it was so distant as to be on another planet.

She sat on the bed and examined her humble surroundings; wooden floors, wooden furniture and coarse woollen blankets on a lumpy bed. It wasn't exactly homely but she appreciated their effort, especially after being chased, prodded, shoved and shouted at for most of the day.

You can't do this...

She answered with a yawn. She was tired enough to rough it for one night. Staring at the rustic floorboards beneath her feet, the words echoed in her head, mutating from a statement of fact through indecision to an alarmed question.

It was only for one night, wasn't it?

She shuddered. She couldn't open that door, couldn't walk down that path. She thought about Alex, a calming thought hijacked by guilt. However bad she felt, she knew he had it much, much worse. At dinner, Convince had explained about Alex's punishment within the Scorer's Hut.

'He's in a Book Press. It's an ancient Lexican method of punishment. They use one of the obsolete Darkhive book of records and slip you between the pages like a flower.'

She'd frowned.

'I know what you're thinking, but some of the old books are ten foot high with slate covers and contain tens of thousands of vellum pages. How deep and how long you go in the book depends on the crime. They say at two thousand pages it's like breathing inside a wardrobe, four thousand is like breathing inside a desk drawer and anywhere below six thousand....' An unpleasant memory played out across his face until he noticed her scrutiny and a fixed smile returned in its place.

After a quiet hour, feeling sorrowful as the sun went down, a sharp, tuneless bugle blasted out across the camp. Vince ushered her outside to the roped-off wickets, where the prisoners assembled for a roll call in the glare of several floodlights. The cruel-eyed Hauptmann Rottweiler – the head guard Vince had warned her about - stood spitting out their names in a thick German-accent. Even after accounting for all inmates, he left them stood to attention in the cold night air seemingly for no reason as he chatted to his guards.

Lights out came ten minutes later as she clambered into bed, the shivers continuing to rock her shoulders long after she pulled the thin blanket tightly around her. Sleep was elusive, the snores and murmurs from the rest of the hut keeping her awake for minutes or hours.

Fearful images taunted and teased her dozing mind as she sank deeper.

Clambering out of the social worker's car, she pulled the hair from her twelve-year-old eyes and stared at Bluebell House, feeling like she'd wandered into a Jane Austen novel. With peeling paint and crumbling mortar, the house's Georgian splendour had faded but it still held a brooding presence beneath the overcast skies. It belonged to a grandmother she'd never met or even known exist. The wind

147

gusted, whipping the dry leaves across the gravel and onto the parched lawn. This time there were no welcome banners or balloons, no over-excited dog charging out to lick her hand or loving family huddled on the doorstep like all the other foster homes. The large door remained shut, the windows dark.

'Another day, another front door.' She thought, not realising she was dragging her battered suitcase of books up a driveway for the last time.

She twitched awake, her grandmother's icy stare remaining after everything else faded. She blinked her away and brought the few slats of the bed above into focus, sunshine blazing through the window. Placing her bare feet into an oblong of sunlight on the warm wooden floor at her bedside, she heard a blackbird singing its favourite song.

She rubbed hard at her eyes and noticed a stacked tray had appeared under the blanket screen. Neatly arranged on it were several fluffy white towels, a bell, a toothbrush and paste, soap and a fresh set of clothes. She picked up the green army style uniform and noticed the shirt already had Curious embroidered onto the chest pocket and a single exclamation mark on each shoulder. A note from Vince sat under the bell:

Good Morning

Ring if you need anything.

See you in the canteen for breakfast.

The Major wants to see you afterwards.

Don't worry you'll be fine.

Sgt. Convince.

After her croissants and fresh roast coffee, she crossed the camp to see Major Word-Forms in Hut Two. Unlike the other open huts, the officers got their own small rooms on either side of a corridor, whilst the Major had a large room across one end. She crept apprehensively along the empty corridor. Emerging into an open area beside the Major's door, Lieutenant Apologist stood behind his desk.

'Hello there, sorry, I forgot your name, sorry.'

Hannah glanced down at her chest.

'Oh sorry, of course. Silly me!'

Hannah forced a smile.

'Miss Curious, please accept my humblest-'

'Just show her in man!' Boomed the Major from somewhere behind his door.

'Sorry, so sorry...'

Hannah swallowed hard, turned the handle and stepped inside. The Major stood behind his empty desk, a bed and wardrobe in the corner to her right, a filing cabinet and boxes of forms on her left.

'Ah Curious! Glad you could make it.' He said politely as if Hannah had any choice in the matter.

He gestured to a green canvas chair and Hannah sat down, imagining her headmaster about to quiz her about why she'd brought shame on the school. The Major retook his seat and leaned back, hands bridged together on his chest.

'How is life in the camp? Are we making you comfortable?'

Hannah nodded and found her voice. 'Very much, thank you.'

149

'Excellent. The prisoners in here are good Words at heart, unruly at times, but I like to think I keep them in line. Now, firstly here are some forms for you to fill in for my files.'

She took the pile of forms from him with a hidden sigh.

'Don't worry about them now, do them in your own time.'

'Homework,' Hannah thought, 'there's always homework.'

'Now, Hannah, why don't you tell me what's brought you to Worditz?'

Hannah spoke before she'd fully decided how much she should share. Yet the more she talked of their capture outside the Glossary, the more she sank back into her chair. He listened intently to her story, amazed and excited by their encounters with CC Law and CC Order and the hint at news from above Checkpoint Charles. As she finished with Order leading them into the camp, he nodded sagely before narrowing his eyes.

'How exactly did you meet this, Alex fellow?'

She hesitated, Alex's words of secrecy ringing in her ears.

'He's a Nouner; his real name is Alex….Guide.' She scratched her cheek and curled her hair behind her ears. 'He was just showing me around.'

The Major stared at her and grunted. Hauling himself to his feet, he crossed to the window, arms behind his back. He looked out in the general direction of Hut three, the Scorer's shed beyond just visible through its windows. He rocked on his heels, occasionally sniffing as he seemingly weighed a matter up in his mind. She wanted to speak, wanted to ease the tension solidifying in the room but couldn't think how. The Major spoke without turning round.

'You obviously have your reasons for not telling me.'

Hannah heard her brain add "the truth" into the silence at the end of his sentence.

'And whilst I find your loyalty to your friend commendable, I cannot help but feel a tad disappointed after all we've done for you.'

The shame of his words pulled her head down, her cheeks burning. They'd gone out of their way to accommodate her in difficult circumstances. Two other Words slept on the floor so she could have a bed, Partisan treated her like family and Vince did his best to keep the others at bay.

She was torn, her loyalties divided between Alex - who deep down she still hadn't forgiven for leading her down here - and a group of strangers who'd fussed over her more in a day than anyone had in a year. The temptation to run and hide – however childish – was almost unbearably tempting.

She closed her eyes and sighed. 'He's not Alex Guide and I'm not a Grade One Adjectivore from Floor 121.'

Major Word-Forms returned to his seat. 'I can assure you whatever you tell me will stay in this room. These are turbulent times, I appreciate trust is at a minimum, but I ask you to put your trust in me and I'll do all I can in return.'

Hannah hesitated before her shoulders sank. The whole story of the return of her imaginary friend, the Buzzwords, the Feds and Author-tarian Guards tumbled out, leaving the Major somewhat shell-shocked.

151

'You're a Heartisan?!' He said several times, both incredulous and alarmed. His eyes flickering over the table each time she nodded, silently ordering his troubled thoughts.

'You can't be here!' His moustache twitched.

Hannah shrugged.

'No, you misunderstand.' He shook his head. 'There's a long history of Heartisans straying accidentally through defective Number Wells, even some being lured inside by unscrupulous Words. Yet they only ever reach the top floors and are always returned to their beds before they're missed. A Heartisan, not just this deep inside Lexica but this deep in the Darkhive? That's...' He blew out his cheeks searching for the words. 'Impossible!'

'Yet,' Hannah pulled a face, 'here I am.'

'Yes, yes, here you are.' He rubbed his hands nervously. 'And despite all the stories and myths, I can see now our kind and yours aren't so far apart. Nonetheless, don't say a word to a Word in here!'

'Can't you just explain to someone there's been a big mistake? I wouldn't tell anyone about Lexica.'

He gave her a long sardonic look.

'But I shouldn't be here!'

The Major twiddled his moustache and frowned.

'Hmmmm.' He tapped a finger on his lips and sat on the corner of his desk. 'You shouldn't be here, unless of course, someone wanted you to be.'

Hannah stared.

'Don't you see? The Feds chased you and the Author-tarian Guards manoeuvred you into their trap, yet we've had no other inmates arrive in the last two days. Any other rebels tricked by them have gone...' He drummed his fingers grimly. '...elsewhere. Meanwhile you were only charged with breaking and entering and put in here with us at Worditz.'

Hannah bit her tongue at the *only*.

'On whose orders? And why did Alex think you were in great danger in Pandemonia.'

'I don't know! Alex hasn't told me anything!'

'Hmmmm. Well, perhaps you're a danger to them, perhaps you have something they want. Perhaps they just find you...Curious.'

Hannah's eyes widened.

'Hmmmm, perhaps you should go now Curious. Forget those forms and get some rest.'

She got up and opened the door.

'Thank you Major.' She mumbled without reply.

As she crossed the soft turf outside, Hannah sensed the Major's eyes boring into her back every step of the way.

CHAPTER ELEVEN

Hannah lay staring up at the bed-boards on the underside of the bunk above, a speck of dust buffeted by hidden draughts floated across her vision. She envied it greatly. The Major's dismissal of her situation being accidental hadn't surprised Hannah, yet laying there she realised how unconsciously she'd still clung to it, hoping common sense would prevail.

What did they want from her?

Her frustration grew at the injustice of it all.

After half an hour, Vince appeared asking if she fancied a bite to eat. More from concern about her, she sensed, than her hunger.

In the half-filled canteen, she nibbled at a chicken Caesar salad, Vince beside her, telling her she'd be alright in a soft voice. Tipping back her mug of cocoa, she spied Defy through the window, helping Alex across the outfield.

The mug thudded back onto the tabletop, but as she rose to her feet, a familiar face blocked her path.

'You'll see him soon enough.' Radical said, clutching his laden tray.

'Radders is right, plenty of time for that.' Vince smiled, hand on her arm.

Alex stumbled up the steps of Hut Two and disappeared inside, Hannah reluctantly settling back in her seat.

'Is he ok? I want to see him. Need to….'

'You will, but he must see the Major first. It's important, you see?'

154

Hannah poked indifferently at the salad with her fork.

'He's out the press, that's what matters.'

She gazed idly outside at Hut Two and blankly on to the rooftops of the village beyond.

'What did the Major say to you?' Vince asked.

Hannah's stomach lurched but she tried not to let it show on her face.

'Oh you know; house rules and the like.' She saw his intrigue awakening.

'Did he not ask you about news from above Checkpoint Charles?'

'In a way.' She reached for the cocoa.

'If only we knew what was truly going on upstairs in the corridors of Wordminster.'

'Why, what have you heard?' Hannah asked, seizing the chance to shift the conversation away from her.

'I keep forgetting you're only a Grade One Adjectivore, you seem much brighter than that.'

Hannah smiled dimly.

'Well, according to a friend of Propaganda's in the Insight office, there's talk of a powerful group that has secretly seized control of the Authortarian Guards and Feds, leaving Prim, Proper and the rest of the Cupboard Ministers as a puppet government with no authority or power.'

'What?'

'Yes, it's rumoured the Language is being deliberately tipped into chaos, while the Blondeshirts of the NGP wait in the wings.'

155

Hannah frowned.

'The Nationalist Grammar Party, they're a minority protest party, a horrible group of small-minded Words, who despise anyone who disagrees with them. They wear blonde shirts and are just as cowardly as their uniform.' He sighed wearily.

'They've been around for a long long time, but were practically extinct until the Heartisans got use of the internet. Their leaders have never convinced the masses about their grudge-fuelled policies. Only now there's rumours of the return of him; Millard Bellwether.'

Her frown unmoved, he continued without judging her ignorance.

'He's a dangerous Word. He has the power to gauge the mood of a group or even a Language and influence them with a warped reflection of their own thoughts.'

'He sounds like a politician. And a liar.'

Vince's half smiled cynically.

'Throughout the 1830s and 1840s Bellwether notoriously led the Anti-Reform League up in Pandemonia; a dissident group campaigning against Loanwords coming into the Language from the Heartisan's growing empire.'

Hannah groaned.

'They say he was masterful at tapping into the fears of Heartisans, especially as the industrial revolution turned their world upside down and inside out. My friend was part of the campaign against these dissidents and he said there were lots of these groups of ragtag idealists around but Bellwether was the toughest to counter. He led the League out of the back rooms of taverns to vast open air meetings all

156

around the land preaching to thousands at a time. Large enough to continually trouble those in power.' He shook his head and smirked. 'Leading or convincing others can be a dangerous business.'

She didn't doubt it. 'What happened?'

He lifted his eyebrows. 'His luck ran out. There was yet another assassination attempt on the Heartisan Queen.'

'Queen Victoria?!'

Vince nodded and pulled a face. 'No-one really knows for certain if it was Bellwether – he always denied it – but he'd become such a nuisance up in Pandemonia and an embarrassment down here in Lexica, not many were going to fight his corner. Prim and Proper linked him to one of several dastardly plots and had Bellwether and several of his treasonous contacts arrested and swiftly led away for trial. In many ways, he was a victim of his definition.'

'But weren't his followers outraged, the ordinary pe...Heartisans-'

Convince's eyes sparkled mischievously. 'Anyone can be persuaded of anything given the right words and enough conviction.'

Hannah didn't doubt it for a second.

'What happened to him?'

'They fanned the furore and rode the tidal wave of outrage to make an example of him,' Vince sighed, 'sentencing him to a thousand years in the Darkhive.'

She gasped.

'He appealed it at the U.R.L Court of Word Rights, claiming temporary insanity. If I remember rightly, the court overruled the first decision and he was

157

transferred to a secure place well out of sight called Bethlem Hospital in Pandemonia. You might know it better as Bedlam.'

Hannah swallowed, trying not to think of the images that word conjured.

'So what's he got to do with these Blondeshirts?'

Vince pulled a face.

'Maybe nothing, maybe everything. They've certainly become more focused and organised these last few years. Now, some even go so far as to say Bellwether himself is back in Lexica as the Blondeshirts leader.'

'What?!'

'No-one seems to know where he is or what happened to him, so they make things up, the more outlandish the better. He's the bogeyman of our times. But, without a doubt the Blondeshirts have more confidence than before, more open in their hatred; inciting the populous to rise up against Wordminster corruption and overthrow those in power. They're even openly targeting Heartisans.'

Hannah's breath caught in her throat.

'I know!' Vince empathised. 'The thought of all those Blondeshirts gleefully correcting Heartisan's grammar mistakes on the internet turns my stomach. Such pedantic and condescending behaviour to Heartisans is alien to us English Words. We're renowned for our patience and civility, I hope the NGP aren't going to ruin that too.'

'I'm confused,' Hannah hesitated, choosing her words carefully, 'I know tyranny is wrong but, shouldn't Heartisans try to spell correctly and use the correct grammar?'

158

Vince pulled a face. 'Well, yes and no, without blinding you with thousands of years of Lexican politics there are two main trains of thought. People on the left think the English Language is alive and should evolve and change with the needs of the Heartisans. People on the right think the English Language is sacred and requires correct grammatical use at all times, changes only coming through committee and legislation.'

'Where do you stand?'

'Like most Words, I'm somewhere in the middle, seeing good in both sides. The NGP though are on the far right, not only do they patrol online forums and message-boards they're also prepared to take direct action in their pursuit of a purer Language.'

It took a few seconds for Hannah to take in what he meant. She looked around at the others eating humbly.

Vince nodded. 'Yes, only - believe it or not - we're the lucky ones; we've only been down here three months. According to one of the guards we've befriended, they abandoned this place when they completed building Undesirables Camp Two, but now the slave labour are building an even larger third camp as it too is overcrowded.' His voice slipped before he regained his composure.

'Sorry. We've not heard from our offices since we were rounded up, the grim rumour is they lay empty.'

She searched his face for meaning and gasped. 'You mean...?'

He nodded furiously, lips tight. 'Erased without trial.'

'But why?'

'Because of whom we are. The Major believes the Blondeshirts are targeting the unhappiest Words of society, those without regular use or popularity. He's chipping away at the foundations of the Language, hoping to generate an angry majority that turns against Wordminster.'

'Like a...revolution?'

'Exactly. Only Bellwether's clever, making sure to seize all the Words like us who could challenge his views or organise resistance to his plans before he goes public.'

She looked blank.

'I'm Convince, what I don't know about manipulating opinion isn't worth knowing, I can assure you about that.'

Hannah believed him.

'Only Propaganda knows more about changing people's minds, he's over there sat next to Defy.'

A man with slick black hair heard his name, leaned forward and gave a wave.

Hannah copied him and waved back.

'Mislead and Deceive can make anyone think twice.' Vince nodded to two Words down the table.

'You've just missed them.' The nearest said without turning his head.

Hannah instinctively looked out the window before confusedly turning back to Vince.

'-Radical, Resist, Flout, Disobey, Contravene, all of us are the ones most likely to form a resistance if - or more likely when – Bellwether or whoever makes a deadly move for power and implements their sickening plans.'

'What plans?'

Vince looked at her uncomfortably. 'Nobody knows for sure, there's talk of stockpiles of weapons and erasure bullets hidden in the Appendix warehouses-'

'Law said something about the lower floors being out of bounds!'

'Really? Interesting. And very suspicious.' Convince pouted. 'I wouldn't have connected it with the GNP, but if they have Bellwether and the Author-tarian Guards turning a blind eye, who's to stop them cleansing the Language by force, erasing any Words deemed not of English origin.'

'They'd do that?'

'They're not shy in their hatred of Loanwords brought in from other Languages. One Bellwether with the right words...'

'...and enough conviction...' She shook her head incredulously. 'Even with you all in here, surely others will step forward to stop them. Everybody knows the difference between right and wrong, don't they?'

Vince tried to smile but his eyes betrayed him. 'Heartisan history tells us differently. We Words aren't naturally brave or defiant, we just do our best for the Language. So when Words who speak out start disappearing, Words learn not to speak out. Despite the disappearances and broken glass underfoot, the majority will turn a blind-eye, keep their heads down and hope it all blows over.'

Hannah made to speak but stopped.

161

'Go on.' Vince said.

'I'm sorry if this sounds insensitive, but why has Bellwether kept you all alive. I mean why hasn't he simply erased you all if you're so dangerous?'

Vince smiled coolly. 'It's a good question. We believe we're his insurance policy, his get out of jail free card.'

She frowned.

'Look around you Hannah; Resist, Disobey, Rebel, Defy, Insurgent, Confront, Radical, me. Now put yourself in the shoes of the Lexican Council looking in from the outside. Who else would be at the centre of a dangerous revolution against the authorities of the English Language?'

Her eyes flared. 'He'd set you all up to take the blame! But…but…'

'No Ifs, no Buts in here, just us troublemakers. Besides we'd probably do most of the work for him.' He half-smiled. 'The Words in here aren't exactly known for their patience and self-control. Only the Major's discipline stops them all rushing the nearest Guards in a valiant but pointless show of defiance. Without him and with the minimum of mistreatment from the Blondeshirts, they'd become a riotous mob within days, leaving Bellwether to call for action from the Author-tarian Guards and walk away the saviour.'

Despite the blazing sun outside, a shiver shook her shoulders.

'I'm sure it'll all work out for the best in the end, you'll see.' Vince tried but she could see his heart wasn't in it. His eyes had a faraway look and his voice none of its usual vitality.

The prisoners drifted away in ones and twos towards a game of volleyball. They'd all lost colleagues, but they buried their hurt deep. It reminded her of the care homes she'd washed up in; stories untold, pain unshared.

'I bet you're wondering about the village over there.' Vince appeared calm once more, as if she'd imagined the previous conversation. 'Did anyone tell you where you are?'

'The Darkhive?'

'No, here in the village of Lighthope.'

'Lighthope?'

He nodded out the window. 'It's the village where the archaic Words take their recreation time. Every Word stored on the shelves here gets a week in the village, once a decade.'

'Once a *decade*!' Hannah blurted.

Vince nodded. 'It used to be double that before they built more inns and repaired the football pitch. Once a decade may seem a long time but if you're in here forever, it'd be regular enough believe me.'

'It still seems a long time.'

Vince looked at her sympathetically as if explaining to someone much too young to understand.

'Perhaps, but it's still better than being erased from existence.'

Hannah swirled the dregs of her cocoa sheepishly. As conversation stoppers went, it was up there with the best of them.

'Oh no!' Rebel groaned, rising off the bench.

163

Vince and Mutineer also got to their feet, all peering out the windows towards the main gate.

Outside the barbed wire, a group of machinegun-wielding Words had surrounded the officious Prepositioner. Pushing him and trying to prise the clipboard from his hands were about ten or twelve fair-haired Words wearing pale yellow shirts. Several camp guards rushed out from the Pavilion to join the nervous sentries on the gates, the rotund officer in his grey uniform waddling out last, pulling on his jacket.

'What's going on?' Hannah asked.

'Blondeshirts!' Vince spat beside her. 'What are they doing in here?'

'They're not allowed in the Darkhive, are they? It's neutral territory!' Rebel cried.

'Maybe they've brought more new arrivals?' Vince said, to many nods.

'I doubt it.' Defy snapped.

'What can they possibly want in here?' Rebel said.

Nobody answered.

Dissenter, Deceive, Propaganda and some of the others stepped outside to get a better view, other prisoners spilling out of the other Huts.

A Blondeshirt in a peaked cap laughed over the cowering Prepositioner before turning to threaten the Camp Commandant through the wire gates.

'Whatta all the fuss?' Partisan joined them from the kitchen, wiping his hands on the chequered tea-towel hanging from his belt.

164

'Blondeshirts at the gates, but the Commandant won't let them inside.' Radical said.

'Quite right!' Rebel said. 'They've no authority here.'

'They're not here for a coffee and a chat, that's for sure.' Mutineer said.

'They get no coffee outa me!' Partisan spat disgustedly.

'But what can they be after?' Rebel said.

They nervously searched one another's faces before collectively turning her way.

'What? Me?' Hannah spluttered.

'You or your friend.' Mutineer said. 'You're the only change to the camp, it must be you two.'

'Non! They coulda be here for any of us.'

'Exactly! Don't pick on her, she's one of us now, don't you see?' Convince said.

They eyed her suspiciously. The Blondeshirts couldn't be after her, could they?

'Well, I say we hand them over! Give them what they want.' Mutineer said boldly.

'Noooo!' Vince and Rebel both protested.

'Get outta my canteen! Go, go now! How dare's you...' Arty whipped Mutineer out of the canteen with his tea-towel.

A gunshot rang out across the cricket pitch and they all fell silent.

Beyond the gates, the Blondeshirt in the peaked cap lowered the revolver from over his head, a pall of white smoke drifting away behind him.

165

'They're coming in.' Rebel muttered. 'We need to ambush them.'

'No, we need to hide Hannah and her friend.' Vince countered.

Hannah gawped numbly out the window as the fearful Commandant allowed the gates to swing open.

'Alex!' Hannah pushed forward but Vince held her back.

'The Major will hide him, don't worry.'

'They're in. We need to do something.'

'Why doesn't the Commandant stand up to him?'

'This isa bad!'

'Alright, everyone stay calm and keep your discipline. Remember what the Major said; don't attack unless he says so!' Vince said to a few mumbled groans.

Hannah tried to block them out, the blood throbbing in her ears.

'Now, we must hide Hannah!' Vince cried.

'But, where?' Rebel said.

'Somewhere they cannota find her.' Partisan gestured with his hands.

'Well obviously!'

'How about down the-' Radical began.

Vince cut in. 'And risk everything?! No, we-'

An out-of-tune blast of a bugle stopped them all dead.

'A rolla call, oh me, oh my!' Partisan exclaimed.

'Let's not go!'

'Rebel, we have to go, it's for the best.' Vince said without vigour as he led them towards the door.

'I justa putta the muffins in too!' Partisan moaned as he and Rebel stepped outside.

As the rest of them walked away, Vince paused, one hand on the door.

'Hannah, hide somewhere, somewhere real good, we'll do what we can.'

The familiar crushing feeling of abandonment returned, leaving her soul brittle and empty.

'It might not be alright this time.' He said with empty eyes.

Hannah simply stared, her brain whirring with ridiculous ideas.

With a formal nod and a forced smile, Vince stepped outside.

As the door thudded shut, the maelstrom of thoughts parted in her mind.

'Vince!'

The bugle sounded again outside.

'Vince!' She moved to the door. 'Vince!'

He reappeared, eyes wide.

'Vince! I have an idea.'

He listened as the words tumbled from her mouth, his eyes narrowing as he looked her up and down.

'How did...?' He shook his head. 'Never mind, I'll tell the Major right away!'

The door slammed and he'd gone.

The room was quiet and empty, the benches and long tables still covered in plates and bowls from lunch, only the muffled cries of Hauptman Rottweiler drifting in through the walls. She peeked out the corner of a window as Vince rushed across the grass to whisper in the Major's ear. He glanced from Vince up to the canteen before beckoning Deceive and Mislead to his side. Within seconds, they'd scattered to play a rowdy game of tag.

The Blondeshirts angrily waited for the Camp Commandant to return order as prisoners boisterously weaved in and out of the huts. Amidst the chaos, Hannah noticed the peaked cap gripping one of his Blondeshirts by his collar and flicking a finger up to the canteen.

'Oh no, no, no.' She groaned, realising none of the prisoners had headed her way.

By trying not to draw attention to the canteen, they'd drawn attention to the canteen. She sagged as two of the Blondeshirts rounded the cricket-wicket in her direction. She jerked her head back from the window, her pulse beating a twenty-one gun salute in her ears.

She scanned the dining tables, cast-iron stove and serving table with its dented tea-urn and stack of mugs. Wincing at the lack of hiding spots, she rushed on hands and knees to the swing door and entered Partisan's realm.

Narrow and small, it more resembled a ship's galley than a restaurant kitchen. Two sinks half-filled with plates and foamy suds stood beneath a window on her left, two ovens and a hotplate beneath an extractor hood on her right. Cupboards, fridges and wooden work surfaces sat along the longer walls. Breathing in a heady Mediterranean scent, she glanced up at the copper pans, dried herbs and cured sausages hanging from the ceiling marvelling at how Partisan could feed them all from such a small kitchen.

A noise spooked her back from wonder, eyes jolted from awe back to panic. With a sense of dread, she picked her spot and concentrated on lowering her rate of breathing.

'Come out, come out wherever you are!' A muted voice said eerily.

A dread-filled silence followed.

'You do out here Actual, I'll search in there!'

'Alright Grievous.' A grizzlier voice murmured in return.

Hannah heard the kitchen door swing open and someone step inside, the crash of overturned benches thundering through from the dining room. Her foot twitched and she tensed up.

'Look at all this nonsense!' A voice grunted.

She flinched as a huge metallic crash went up and her body revved its engine. She breathed deeply through her nose and tried to lower her surging pulse with calm thoughts.

'It's only the pans...'

Another shattering explosion of noise made her jump again, the sound crackling in her ears long after the sound subsided.

'...and the stack of plates.'

She heard a grunted chuckle, more footsteps crunching the broken plates and a boot sending a pan skidding across the debris. Her body trembled, her cramped legs and shoulders juddering uncontrollably. Straining with her ears, she heard the hum of the oven grow louder.

'Hmmm.' The Blondeshirt murmured before a yelp of pain pre-empted another crash on the hard floor.

Hannah pictured him trying to pick up the hot tray of muffins with his bare hands and almost smiled.

'Urggghhhh!' The Blondeshirt groaned throatily before slamming the oven door violently shut.

A few seconds of silence passed, only punctuated by dull thuds coming from next door. She wondered if her Blondeshirt had given up, sulking because his fingers hurt. She tilted her head, holding her breath to catch every sound as she counted to ten in her head.

All remained silent. Maybe he'd gone?

She sagged inside, stretching her shoulders as relief flooded through her veins.

A boot moved on the broken crockery.

She froze as if plunged into liquid nitrogen.

'I know you're in here.' The Blondeshirt's calm menacing whisper cut through her like an icy wind, sucking the air from her lungs.

The Blondeshirt emitted a low, angry growl each time he threw open a cupboard door with his sore fingers. Flinching with every slammed door, Hannah closed her eyes and thought only of one person.

The noises inched nearer, her muscles numbed and mind drowning in a dread-filled bog.

170

'Any second now.' She screwed her eyes up even tighter.

The slamming of the last cupboard door vibrated through her numb feet.

Her miserable breaths came out in short jagged gasps, the feet crunching around on the floor right beside her head.

The door of the cupboard under the sink opened.

The light shone through her eyelids, filling her mind with red-tinted hell. She steeled herself for a fist to haul her out by her hair, a silent scream echoing around her head like a steam-whistle.

CHAPTER TWELVE

'Grievous!' A voice shouted through the doorway.

'What?' He grunted above her.

Hannah's eyes snapped open. Black scuffed boots stood inches away on the messy floor, two trouser legs rising upwards, twisted at the knee.

She stopped breathing, even stopped blinking.

'They've found them!' Actual boomed.

'Yeah?'

'Yeah!'

The cupboard door slammed shut; jolting her body and crackling her hearing. The retreating footsteps crunched their way out of the kitchen and shoved the swing door. Footsteps retreating, the smothering silence returning.

She sagged awkwardly against a cardboard box full of cleaning chemicals and let out a couple of sobs. Her torso shook, scrunched ribs squeezing her like an accordion, the rim of a washing-up bowl cutting into one side, a stalactite of pipe-work digging into her hips on the other.

The silence stretched out into minutes, but she resisted the orchestra of dread playing throughout her body, too scared to move her limbs or unfurl her twisted spine.

Footsteps.

The screaming knots down the back of her cramped legs battled with her fear of seeing those boots again, her body a warzone of pain and panic.

'Hannah?' The footsteps echoed across the canteen floorboards.

They'd come back!

'Hannah?'

They knew her name, knew she was there.

'Han!'

She turned her neck, a sharp pain jolting her shoulder.

'Aaargh.' She moaned, eyes watering.

'Ssssh, what was that?'

'In there I think.'

Hannah closed an eye and bit hard on her lip as the kitchen door creaked open.

'Sacre Bleu! The Kitchen, it isa ruined!'

She sucked in a breath, coughed and gurgled a faint yelp, 'Arty!'

'Hannah?' Vince yelled.

'Han, where are you?'

'Alex!' Hannah croaked pathetically and prodded at the cupboard door.

Three crunching footsteps and the cupboard doors swung open, Alex looked in at her with a mixture of concern and stunned relief.

'Hannah!'

She rolled over awkwardly, sending two tins of oven cleaner tumbling onto the floor and spilling half a box of soap flakes with her shin. Her heavy foot thumped

173

onto the broken plates, followed by a twisted knee and unfeeling fingers; emerging from her hiding place with all the grace of an inebriated swan. Wincing and groaning, Alex helped her wriggle round to sit on the floor, twitching legs in front of her.

Alex squatted and held her gently by the shoulders.

'You alright?'

Hannah pictured the guard's legs outside the cupboard – so close she could count the eyelets on his boots. She imagined him leaning in and yanking her out by her hair; the pain, terror and humiliation...

She drank in the concern in Alex's blue eyes and nodded weakly.

With Vince's help, Alex lifted her up unsteadily onto her tingling feet, her cramping legs refusing to straighten. She leaned back against the sinks and waited for the room to stop spinning. Alex held her upright until her cheeks gained a little colour.

'It's good to see you, Alex!' She opened her heavy arms and gave him an almighty hug.

'Ow, oooh, ouch, ow, ow!' Alex mumbled, tapping her shoulder like a defeated wrestler.

'Sorry, I forgot.' Hannah sank back against the sinks.

'Good to see you too.' He blushed, holding his ribs and wincing as a cough rattled his chest.

'It worked Hannah, your plan worked!' Vince looked at her inquisitively. 'Did the Guards come close to finding you?'

174

She met his eyes and shook her head. 'I hardly knew they were here.'

Vince nodded with some relief before noting the kitchen's destruction, the certainty draining from his face.

'Oh no, they even getta my muffins!' Partisan tutted picking up the tray and turning off the oven.

'Anything we can do?' Hannah said as he picked up a pan and ran a finger over its dented rim.

'Non, non, I fix, no problems.'

Hannah got the distinct feeling he wanted to be on his own.

Alex led her and Vince gingerly out across the debris-strewn floor. The canteen looked little better, with tables, benches and smashed crockery scattered haphazardly across the room. The Blondeshirts had smashed every piece of crockery into tiny pieces and even cracked the glass in the door of the cast-iron stove.

Vince helped Rebel to right some of the upturned furniture.

Alex picked up the battered tea urn and placed it back on the counter.

'Are you alright Alex? How was the Book Press?'

He wiped his hands on a tea towel. 'Great, I always wanted a flat stomach.'

His mock laughter morphed into a heaving, coughing fit leaving him red-faced and short of breath. He waved away her murmured concern. 'Alright, truthfully? It hurt, a lot, but I've had worse.'

'Oh Alex.' She murmured, remembering why he'd gone in their in the first place.

175

'Your plan worked like a charm Hannah!' Vince said excitedly from across the room. 'The Major told us to ignore the Commandant's roll-call and act up. The leader of the Blondeshirts-'

'Grammar Sergeant Malice.' Rebel stated.

'Was that his name?' Vince frowned. 'Anyway, we wound him up something rotten, he barked at his officers to search the huts, threatening all within earshot. Nasty piece of work, that one.'

'Have they gone now?' Hannah leaned against the counter and tried to shake off her dizziness, the sight of those boots dominating her thoughts.

'Yes, they found "Hannah and Alex" in Hut three.' Vince grinned.

Alex shook his head wryly. 'I'd love to see Millard Bellwether's face when the Blondeshirts arrive with Eamonn Mislead in an old shirt and Robyn Deceive wearing a black wig, polka-dot dress and a pink and yellow scarf.'

Hannah's eyes flared with annoyance before sighing regretfully. 'I loved that scarf.'

The door opened and the Major appeared beaming so widely it looked like his moustache was readying for take-off.

'Here she is!'

The Lieutenant popped his head around the door behind the Major, stepping inside with a mouthed apology.

'Bravo Curious! Bravo!'

176

Hannah raised her heavy head and straightened her aching shoulders. He stretched out his hand for her to shake and Hannah didn't know which of the three to shake.

'I think I need to sit down.' She mumbled, wobbling slightly.

'Han?' Alex said, his voice full of concern.

'This way.' Vince helped him guide her to the nearest bench.

Hannah sat, a glass of water and some biscuits appearing from nowhere.

'Sorry, I'll be alright in a minute.' She said, feeling silly.

'No apology necessary, after such a genius plan!' The Major boomed, rocking on his heels.

Alex rolled his eyes at *genius*.

Hannah sipped from her glass. 'I hope I haven't been too selfish.'

'Selfish? Nonsense! You couldn't go, could you? Give the rotters what they want? Never! No, no, absolutely out of the question.'

'Will they be alright, Mislead and Deceive?'

'Pah! Those two have been itching to raise hell for weeks on end. As I told Alex, I've been desperate to get a couple of Words over the boundary to boost morale. Two sixes in a single over is just marvellous.' His joy faded. 'We do have one stone amongst the strawberries though.'

Hannah's smile dissipated.

'I'm afraid when Bellwether finds out he's been misled and deceived, we'll reap what we've sown.'

He took off his hat and handed it to Lieutenant Apologist.

177

'What do you mean?' Alex asked.

'All in good time,' the Major unbuttoned his jacket, 'first I'd like to get Curious here somewhere more secure.'

Five minutes later, Hannah hung up the Major's jacket and cap on a hat stand in his office.

As the Lieutenant apologetically locked the office door behind her, Hannah heeded the Major's warning about keeping out of sight of the Guards and sat on the bed well away from the windows. She screwed up her face, her dizziness dissipating into a tension headache.

She kicked off her shoes and groaned at her empty wrist. As the light faded outside, she realised it was Saturday evening and she'd been missing for well over twenty-four hours. She imagined her bed back at Bluebell House and pulled the blanket over her legs, an intense sense of loneliness and self-pity enveloping her in a cold embrace.

She didn't feel tired, more drained, her body aching and stiff. She closed her eyes and tried not to think, tried not to care.

She imagined herself breaking out and rushing across the grass to the canteen. Only the door looked different, odd, the wood drier and older. The daylight changed, becoming darker and taking on more of a yellow hue. She frowned and took a step backwards, her foot stepping from soft turf to a parquet floor.

She lifted her gaze and the hut was gone.

Books.

Thousands of leather-bound stories filled the shelves of the tall, mahogany bookshelves. The muted browns, warm burgundies, formal blues and threadbare greens stood in dignified lines, slumbering books waiting to impart their wisdom to a fresh pair of eyes. Their colours shone in the warm flickering gaslight from simple crystal chandeliers and lamps on the walls. She listened to their whispering sigh, the library inviting her inside, telling her she was safe. Telling her, she belonged.

The room curved away to her left and right as if she stood at the hub of a great wheel, the two-storey high bookshelves radiating outwards like spokes. She shuffled across the highly polished floor to the nearest aisle, stretching her arm out for the books beside her. She drew in the dusty smell of old paper, savoured it, her fingertips connecting with the warm leather and bumping along several bulging spines.

A sound fogged the scene, her ears surfacing while her imagination tried to keep her under. She tilted her head to read the faded gold lettering on the spines, taking in the names of voices from the past...

A floorboard creaked.

Several parts of her brain powered back up from standby in an instant. Her eyes irritatingly snapped open and found the Major's office filled with thick, eerie shadows. Her annoyed sigh only half escaped her lips as metal connected haphazardly with metal. She kept absolutely still, eyes widening as with a loud click and a rattle of the handle, the door swung open.

Her stomach cramped as if she was back in that cupboard. Had the Blondeshirts returned to seize her?

She swallowed and shrank further under the blanket, pressing her head low into the pillows. A light grey figure drifted across the floor towards the bed, arms blindly groping in front of them, feet shuffling like Frankenstein's monster.

Hannah gripped tightly on the blanket and sucked in a deep breath, ready to release the scream bubbling in her throat.

'Hannah, you awake?'

Her tight chest subsided. 'Alex?'

'Yes, who else!' The shadow snapped, squatting beside her bed.

'Stop doing that!' Hannah hissed, swinging a well aimed pillow at his head. 'You nearly gave me a heart attack.'

Alex picked himself up off the floor. 'Feeling better are we?'

'Yes, thanks.' She stifled a yawn.

'It's time to go.'

'Go? Where?'

'No time for questions, we've wasted enough of the night already.'

Alex crept over to the window and peeked around the undrawn curtains. Hannah swung her legs out of bed, pulled on her shoes and stretched her back. The reflected light from a meandering searchlight fell on Alex revealing a silvery sheen to his hair and clothes.

'Alex? You've gone grey.'

'It wouldn't surprise me.' He said drolly before vigorously rubbing his head and shoulders. 'Ugh! That dust gets everywhere.'

She followed his dust cloud out of the office, creaking down the corridor to the hut door. She yawned at his shoulder, rubbing her bleary eyes.

'Gaaaare whe goynnn anieewhehh?'

'Huh?' Alex turned from the crack in the door.

'Aaaahhh,' she sighed, belatedly covering her mouth with her hand. 'Sorry I said, "Where are we going anyway?" It's...what time is it?'

'Ssshhhh!' He whispered. 'Just stay close to me, only move when I move and whatever you do don't make a noise.'

Reacting to the seriousness in Alex's voice, Hannah yawned silently.

'Right let's go.' Alex gently swung the door inwards, athletically placed a hand on the floor and dropped silently into the shadows beside the wooden steps.

Hannah banged her shoulder on the closing door as she exited, bounded heavily down the steps and circled round to crouch next to him.

'Sorry. Ohh!' She brought her hand to her mouth and whispered. 'Sorry, Shhh!'

Alex cradled his head in his hand.

'I have only just woken up, you know?' Hannah yawned.

The camp looked much larger to her in the twilight, the moon shining through the clouds like a motorbike headlight through fog. The huts looked dirty and menacing, the dewy grass stretching out in front of them like a carpet of black velvet.

181

Hannah squinted at the vague shadows on the Pavilion and Scorer's shed as they wielded the bright circle of their searchlights serenely over the camp. Hundreds of excited moths and insects flitted in the light, bats swooping hungrily across the beam.

Alex shifted his weight next to her and was gone. She followed blindly into the darkness, more by the noise of his feet and rubbing clothes than by vision. Rushing across the dark camp was exhilarating; knowing one misplaced foot, noise or shadow could alert the guards and wake the whole camp.

They stopped and started.

Dropped and darted.

Flopped and far from silently fell in a heap by the Canteen door.

Alex put an arm across Hannah and pushed her back into the shadows between the steps and wall as a searchlight scythed across the front of the Canteen hut. She screwed her eyes shut, but still the light blinded as it drifted silently past. When she prised them open, the circle of light was sliding serenely along Hut One. Alex twitched again and she followed him into the pitch black Canteen.

'Hannah, crawl down there and say goodbye to Vince. I need to speak to the Major.' Alex whispered before disappearing into the enveloping gloom on his hands and knees.

Goodbye? Why, was Vince…? Hope shone inside her like a spotlight.

Had Alex and the Major worked out a way to get them out of there?

Her optimism strengthened and she realised how deeply she'd suppressed her feelings whilst trapped in the camp. Maybe, just maybe she was about to take her

182

first steps out of this nightmare and back up to Pandemonia - she hesitated before correcting herself - back up to London.

She peered along the wall, eyes adjusting to the murk, splashes of opaque moonlight hinting at the rows of empty tables and benches back in their rightful place. With green and red dots from the spotlight still dancing across her vision, Hannah's hearing filled in the gaps; a shoe rasping across the floorboards behind her and tentative whispering over to her right.

What was going on?

She crawled between the bench and windows, wrinkling her nose at the feeling of the greasy dust on her hands. As she reached the far corner, a pair of fingers clicked over by the stove and she heard someone else shuffling across the floor.

Turning ninety degrees to the right along the end wall, she'd just crawled past the first table when the door dramatically flew open the door and the lights flared blindingly into life.

CHAPTER THIRTEEN

Hannah winced as the glare of eight electric lamps bleached her world with light. She squinted over the edge of the table, grubby hands shielding her stinging eyes. Along the wall opposite the door, a dozen prisoners - including Radical and Vince - rose to peer at the three figures in the doorway.

Gawping back at them, the Camp's Security Officer - Hauptmann Ernst Rottweiler and his two accompanying goons wore a similar look of surprise. Dark skinned, with a protruding broad nose, large nostrils and jowls hanging over his bottom jaw, Rottweiler bore many similarities to the dog breed of the same name. Yet stood in his Officer's uniform and peaked cap he was unmistakably a fearless and self-assured Nouner.

No one spoke, everyone frozen in the excruciating moment of red-handed capture. Rottweiler's brown, almond-shape eyes shifted and his suspicious gaze fell down onto the two men by the stove. Alex and Major Word-Forms knelt by a dark square hole in the floorboards. The cast-iron stove stood to one side, the rough-hewn wooden handles still wedged underneath the hot metal.

As the Major used the back of a chair to haul himself up onto his stiff legs, understanding dawned on Hannah. She imagined a crude tunnel dug beneath the hut and heading out to the boundary, the last scurrying prisoner clambering out into the fresh night air beyond the perimeter fence.

184

'Vot iz ziss May-jor?' Rottweiler barked, his Rhineland accent thick and full of phlegm.

The major sighed, languidly looking around at his men, at the hole in the floor and up at Rottweiler's raised chin.

'We're escaping Hauptmann.' He said.

Rottweiler furiously unclipped the revolver from the leather holster on his belt, his teeth bared. He raised the gun to the Major's chest.

'Bullets won't stop us dog-breath!' Rebel jeered.

Rottweiler turned sharply, his finger curling on the trigger. His aim wavered between three prisoners as if he was unsure who'd spoken.

'Enough.' The Major said quietly but sternly.

'Ze May-jor, yo shold lizten to. All of yo, hands on yor heds!'

He smirked as they all leisurely raised their arms and interlinked their fingers on their heads. He waved over one of his guards, conspiratorially whispering in his ear and grinning at the major as the guard scampered out of the door. Hannah glimpsed him out the window heading towards the Pavilion, a blur of movement behind the reflected faces of the prisoners.

'Ze vall! All agenst ze vall!' He flicked his gun in the general direction of the rest of the prisoners. 'Yo vill not be so insolent ven ze Kommandant arrives!'

As Alex and the Major walked around the edge of the tables, Hannah surreptitiously scurried over to hide next to Vince at the end of the line.

Despite the situation, he managed a vaguely reassuring smile.

185

Hauptmann Rottweiler nodded at his guard to cover all of them before shuffling to the hole, his gun by his side. Stood at its edge, he glanced down into the black square and sneered at the prisoners, lip curled. He sat back on the bench behind him, his revolver nonchalantly flicked at the hole.

'How meny May-jor?'

The Major shrugged, 'We're all that's left.'

The Hauptmann's eyes flared with anger. Hannah stifled a nervous yawn, averting her eyes behind Vince's elbow whenever Rottweiler looked her way. After five tense minutes, the door opened and the rotund Commandant stepped inside, accompanied by the returning guard and four more with rifles.

'Ah Kommandant!' The Hauptmann leapt to his feet, looking smug as he saluted stiffly. 'I hev kort dem escaping!'

'Iz this true Major?' The Commandant's German accent was a lot subtler, his words more rounded than the jagged shards spat from the Hauptmann's lips.

The Major removed his hands from his head and nodded without remorse.

'I see. Of course I voz fully avare of de tunnel. For some time I've been avare.' He edged towards the hole but paused to look at the Major for a reaction that never came. He frowned into the dark hole. 'I didn't kno it voz finished.'

He looked judicially at the Major, his eyes travelling along the line of prisoners, Hannah pushing her head back out of sight. She peeked again in time to see the Commandant's gaze fall back on the Major. His hand reached for his belt, fumbling for a gun holster, which was patently not there. He patted his side, seemingly frustrated at having hurriedly dressed without it.

186

'Yor gun if yo please Hauptmann.' He held his hand out behind him without averting his gaze from the Major.

The shock sucked the breath from Hannah's lungs. Someone had to stop him!

She eyed Vince, Radders, and the others, they couldn't just let him shoot the Major. This was wrong, so terribly wrong. The Hauptmann stared at his gun as if he didn't want to let it go.

'Please Hauptmann!' The Commandant flicked his hand impatiently.

Why was no one stopping him?

Icy dread seeped down through her as if she'd swallowed too much ice cream.

She wanted to jump up, wanted to stop all this, wanted to fight guns with her fists, yet she stared with all the rest. Without the courage to break the silence, she projected her fury on to the others.

How could they all sit there while the Major was about to be executed in front of their eyes?

Who'd be next?!

Why wasn't anybody doing anything?!

The Hauptmann reluctantly placed it in the Commandant's hand, an expectant look on his face as he leaned round his commanding officer to watch the Major get shot. The Commandant grinned broadly, as he gripped the revolver and pointed it at the Major.

'I've looked forward to this.'

'No! You can't!' Hannah finally shrieked, the Hauptmann's amusement mixed with confusion as he saw who'd cried out.

He was so busy glaring at Hannah he didn't see the Commandant turn around. Looking back at the Major, the Hauptmann's eyes dropped to the barrel of his own gun pointed at his chest. He frowned at it before lifting his gaze to the Commandant's face.

'Komm-an-dant?' He stuttered, all bravado gone.

'Tie him up.' The Commandant said, two of his guards stepping forward from the doorway, one pulling a coil of rope from his shoulder.

'Kommandant?' The Hauptmann cried again with a baffled expression.

'You're the only one stupit enough to vant to stay Hauptmann! So yo vill stay here with the Prepositioner.'

'Speaking of which, Commandant, may I suggest we get the lights out again. The Prepositioner has probably already noticed and recorded the incident, but nonetheless.'

The Commandant stared out toward the hut by the gate.

'Yo kan't do zis!' The Hauptmann struggled below three burly guards as they pinned him to the table. He kicked and thrashed as they looped the rope around him in a tangle of fiendish knots.

'Help! Hel-'

One of the guards pinched his nose and stuffed a handkerchief into the Hauptmann's open mouth, muffling his cries with another tied round the back of his head.

'Hmmpft, Mmmmfth!' He murmured, his face turning an incensed shade of purple as he strained against the ropes, head and the heels thudding into the wooden tabletop.   Satisfied he was secure, the Commandant flicked a finger towards the door and one of the guards turned off the lights. The darkness blanketed them all back into secrecy, everyone lowering their hands and breaking into relieved chatter.

'You alright Hannah? That was somewhat hairy wasn't it?' Vince sighed.

'Just a bit.' She understated.

As her eyes readjusted to the moonlight, she saw the silhouettes of the Major and the Commandant whispering by the window.

'Hannah?'

'Alex?' I'm here!'

The dark shape reached her down the line.

'You alright?'

'Yeah, what's going on? Are the guards on our side now?'

'Looks like it, the Major told me he's been trying to show the Commandant for weeks, not one of us is safe if the Nationalist Grammar Party take over. If anything, these guards are likely to be one of the first on Bellwether's list of undesirables.'

Hannah frowned. 'What? Why?'

'It's true Hannah.' Vince nodded. 'Commandant Wanderlust, Hauptmann Rottweiler and the guards Hamburger, Kindergarten, Kitsch, Abseil, Poltergeist and the Doppelganger twins, they're all originally Loanwords from the German

189

Language. They're all as much a part of the English Language as you and me, but the GNP see them as impostors stealing our definitions.'

Hannah watched Radders and one of the others, possibly Contravene tentatively shaking hands with the guards by the door, the moonlight illuminating their cautious faces as they lowered their rifles and exchanged chocolates and cigarettes. Perhaps not everyone down here was completely self-centred after all.

'Right, everyone sit down and listen up.' The Major stood in a patch of moonlight out of sight of the main gate.

'Mmmmpft Hmmght!'

'Yo too Hauptmann or I vill make yor zilence permanend!' The Commandant hissed, cocking the revolver for the desired effect near the German's ear.

'Good. Now the Commandant has agreed to let us complete our escape as long as we allow him and his guards to use the same tunnel.'

There were murmurings of agreement around the room.

'I'm glad you feel the same way as me. Of course as I've told you all along, our chances of getting out of the Darkhive are slim. No-one has ever escaped here before but we must try, if only to show that while every Word fears the death of the sentence, not every Word fears a sentence of death.'

He gained a few fearless nods around the room.

'Now, we've wasted enough of the precious darkness, I suggest we get on and send our newest guests through next. My Words will follow and I'll squeeze through last. After that, it's all yours Commandant. I suggest you gradually move your guards over here when the spotlights dazzle the Prepositioner's hut.'

190

'I vil. Danke Major.'

The Major nodded to the Commandant and returned to the hole in the ground, sighing as he crouched.

'Hannah, Alex?'

'Come on,' Alex grabbed her arm, 'it's our turn.'

'One second.' She said letting him scurry away towards the Major. She turned to Vince, his teeth visible in a broad grin.

'I can't thank you enough for looking after me while I've been here.'

'It's been a pleasure, a ripping yarn to tell my office about when I get back.'

She reached out and gave him a hug, his arms patting hers as she gave him a squeeze.

'You'll do great. Alex is tough, he'll get you out of here you'll see.' He said with affection in his voice.

Hannah wanted to say she hoped to see him again but couldn't bring herself to voice what seemed quite impossible.

'Take care Vince.' She pulled away. 'And good luck.'

'Good luck Hannah.' 'Good luck.' 'Safe Journey.' 'Be careful Hannah.' 'Bon Voyage!'

The prisoners echoed as she moved down the line shaking hands and smiling, the last coming with two kisses on her cheeks from Partisan.

With a mixture of happiness, dread and sorrow, she reached Alex's side on the floor.

191

'You've made a few friends here Curious!' The Major said with genuine surprise.

She blushed but didn't know what to say in response.

'Alex here will lead the way.'

'Right.' Hannah said, unsure if that was good or bad.

Alex nodded, inched his legs into the hole and without hesitation disappeared into the blackness. A few second later, she heard a soft thud.

'Clear.' He shouted up from deep below.

'Dangle your legs over and drop with your knees bent. It's not far.' The Major said as she swung her legs into the hole. 'That's it. Now, once you're in the tunnel, don't touch the sides or roof, we've not had chance to shore them up properly. After the Blondeshirts came this afternoon, we've had a rush on to finish it you see.'

Hannah liked this less and less, but nonetheless inched herself forwards over the edge.

'Good luck Curious.'

She nodded, took a breath, twitched, took another breath and jumped.

The dark swallowed her vision, her stomach lurching as the air rushed past her cheeks and tugged at her hair. She landed unexpectedly with a soft thud, tumbling forwards onto her knees and forearms before she'd chance to prepare herself. Disorientated and slightly winded, she shuffled awkwardly off the stack of mattresses towards a chink of dim light.

'Clear.' She called up softly before groping blindly forward through a thick blackout curtain.

Her eyes widened at the makeshift undulating tunnel, the walls not the thick brown clay and rock she'd been expecting but a bristly, fibrous material the dulled white colour of wet sheets. Shuffling knees and hands had smoothed a path along the soft tunnel floor like skis through grey snow, a frayed forest of stalactites hanging from the ceiling and walls. Electric bulbs on the right-hand wall stretched out ahead of her like miniature streetlights, twinkling dust swirling in the disturbed air. Between the lights, wooden boards braced the ceiling and walls from collapse. Alex's wiggling bottom blocked any view of the tunnel's end. Glaring at the rough walls and the trickle of dust falling from the precarious ceiling, her panicking claustrophobia obstinately crossed its arms and vehemently shook its head.

'I'm not sure I can do this.' She shuddered, opening her mouth to shout to Alex.

Her head sagged, but when she lifted it again, the tunnel stubbornly remained. She swallowed and with the thought of the Major clicking his fingers back up in the canteen, commenced a reluctant shuffle on numb hands and knees.

The dry, stuffy air soon left her breathless, her head pounding and chest tight. She tried to be grateful they'd dug the tunnel for bulky Words rather than her slender frame, but she still flinched and cringed every time a stray fibre tickled her arm or face.

Up ahead, Alex kept peeking under his arm and vocalising encouragement but Hannah didn't reply, couldn't. It was all she could do not to think of the tonnes of

193

ground pressing down on her, the Major's chilling words of warning ringing in her ears. She'd expected more wooden props to hold up the ceiling, the gaps between them too far apart for her nerves. A feeling not helped when she realised the props were simply boards stolen from the camp's bunk beds.

'What am I doing down here?' She mumbled, stifling a cough as the dust tickled her nose. She imagined other girls in her school slumped in front of the television, reading in their beds or secretly scribbling about their latest crush in a diary. How could life carry on whilst she risked hers tunnelling out of a prison camp?

She hadn't lost her mind.

She looked under her arm but no-one was following, no-one coming to help her. She closed her eyes and banished the thought. Others couldn't crawl for her, she had to do it herself.

Shuffling on, the tunnel floor went from smooth and flat to rough and bumpy as if part of the ceiling had recently come down, the walls narrowing around her shoulders. She tore her anxious eyes from the numerous cracks in the walls, lips pressed hard together, body tensed. Concentrating hard on matching the rhythm of her shuffling hands to her breathing, she pushed past the pinch point, glancing back to an empty tunnel. With a deep breath, she headed down a slope and around a compacted grey boulder. The sight of it amidst the fibrous walls halted her beneath one of the bulbs.

'Laura Johnson's notepad!' She murmured, recalling a bohemian school-friend's eco-friendly workbook. It had the same speckled grey, coarse texture of

194

recycled paper on its thick hard cover. She tentatively brushed the fibres with her hand, a fine dust glinting in the light.

'I'm tunnelling through compacted paper...'

The dust irritated her nose and she sneezed four times, much to Alex's amusement up ahead.

'Yeah, laugh it up.' She muttered under her breath, rubbing her sore eyes on her sleeve.

'Whad ya say?' Came a muffled query.

'Doesn't matter!' She clenched her teeth.

He peered forwards and back. 'Just six lights ahead of me, try to keep up.'

Hannah emitted a low growl, counted eight lights back from his scraping feet.

'Just six lights ahead of me, try to keep up.' She pulled a face and mimicked his voice as she put her head down and surged onwards up a gradual slope.

As it levelled, she found the next square of wood had partially collapsed, the wall bulging and prop leaning inwards. Gritting her teeth, she gingerly contorted herself through the narrow triangular gap, as conscious of all her limbs as when accidentally wandering into the fine china section of a department store.

On the other side, a calming breath broke down into several shallow coughs. Blinking away her watering eyes, something bumped her hand. She picked up a pebble the size of her thumb, the fibres whiter on one side than the other as if the air affected the hue. She was still staring at it when a faint thud came behind her, the vibrations shaking the floor and knocking dust from the walls.

She tensed, her mind full of sliding noises and pictures of tumbling rocks. She pictured the walls cascading inwards, trapping anyone nearby. Claustrophobia returned with a paralysing grip on her clenched muscles, her pulse pounding like a jackhammer. The silent scream in her head was more deafening than a steam whistle.

You're going to die here. The tunnel's collapsing into a grave, your grave.

Annoyance at the voice fired a starter's pistol in her head. Her limbs unglued themselves, fingers and toes clawing at the ground as she surged forwards. Rage propelled her over fallen blocks of paper and squeezed her between broken boards even as reason smothered her panic. Looking under her arm, she saw no blockages or clouds of dust, just an empty tunnel and lights gleaming. She stared, confused. It hadn't collapsed, her frightened mind had tricked her, conjured a calamitous tunnel collapse from the fall of a few small rocks.

She shook her head, wishing she was anywhere else in the world. A cocktail of embarrassment, fear and anger wrung the last dregs of energy from her weary, wheezing body and she sped on, head down and teeth clenched.

Chest aching and muscles protesting wildly, she didn't know she'd reached the heavy curtain until she barged right through it into Alex's legs, using her head as a battering ram.

'You took your time.' He said, stood beside a rough ladder in a narrow vertical shaft.

She panted heavily, collapsing onto her elbows and arching her back like a cat. As her head stopped swimming, she gingerly got to her feet, her back and legs

196

deeply reluctant to straighten. With his hand under her arm, she managed to stand on wobbly legs. Breathing deep in the thin, stuffy air, she wiped away the sweat dribbling from her hairline, feeling wretched.

'I'll go up and check it's all clear. When it's safe, I'll signal for you to follow.' Alex said without emotion, his face little more than a pale shape in the dim light.

'I'm fine, Alex, thanks for asking.' She said testily.

'Eh?' She made to tell him about the rock-fall but worried he might delay their escape to go see if he could help clear the tunnel. She gritted her teeth. 'Nothing.'

Alex turned back to the ladder.

'Are you going to tell me what the signal is or do I have to guess?' She said, fear morphing into anger.

'Oh. I don't know...I'll throw a stone into the hole. Alright?' He said, raising his foot onto the first rung.

'Wait...What?' Hannah scowled.

He sighed.

'Did you say you'll throw a stone?'

'Yes when it's safe, I'll throw a stone into the hole. Alright?'

'Erm...' Hannah frowned harder, 'No!'

Alex reached up the ladder again but stopped. 'Huh?'

'I said "No" it's not alright.'

Alex kept quiet, Hannah knowing he was glaring at her in the darkness.

'I mean...throwing a stone into the hole no doubt seems perfectly reasonable...but you're not in the hole, are you?' She blew upwards toward her glistening brow. 'You're not the one being pelted by stones-'

'Pelted? I…'

'You're not the one showered in gravel.'

'…' Alex tried.

'I mean what is this? Some kind of vertical coconut shy?' She vigorously rubbed the back of her clammy neck.

Alex paused before muttering indignantly. 'It's what they do in the movies…'

She shook her head stiffly. 'I'd just prefer it if you didn't throw a rock down a hole while I'm stood at the bottom.'

'I think I said a stone, not a rock-' Alex sounded increasingly confused.

'And what if you can't find a rock? If you throw a stick or a surprised small animal, am I to think it isn't clear? Is it one snail for no, two hedgehogs for wait a minute?'

'Hedgehogs?'

'I'm just saying Alex, that after leading me through a tunnel built by the world's most incompetent mole, you haven't fully thought through this pebble messaging idea of yours.' She glared at him as her Grandma would serve as an aperitif to an argument.

He paused as if she'd just quoted Shakespeare in Swahili.

'Will you stay quiet if I go away?'

'Will you go away if I stay quiet?' She snapped.

198

'Heartisans.' He growled emptily, stomping noisily up the creaking ladder, all thoughts of stealth forgotten until he lifted the turf trapdoor at the top.

The cool night air cascaded soothingly down onto her from above, and she gasped, sucking it in as if it was nectar. He scrambled through the gap, leaving it slightly ajar, a thin line of moonlight throwing shapes and shadows onto the shaft wall. It tempted Hannah up the wonky chair-leg ladder. She peeked out at a carpet of dew-laden grass, Alex silently thumbing over his shoulder to the dark bushes.

The scent of freedom brought her wriggling out of the hole and into the cover of the undergrowth, the fresh, damp air as refreshing as opening the fridge on a hot day. He scampered after her into the bushes. Rubbing the pale dust from their clothes and hair, they looked back over the prison camp. Through the barbed wire fence, the spotlight carried on the pretence of patrolling around the four dark huts. Her anxieties and fears faded, replaced by excitement, satisfaction and accomplishment. Only the light in the Prepostioner's seemingly empty hut marred her elation.

'Maybe he's just stretching his legs?' Alex said unconvincingly as she pointed it out.

'Oh sure, he's probably just popped to the pub for last orders.'

Alex didn't even bother arguing. She glanced guiltily at him and back at the hole.

'Look Alex,' she let out a heartfelt sigh, 'sorry about just now, I've never been one for confined spaces.'

'It doesn't matter.'

'It does to me. You're doing your best, you don't need me being annoying. I should bite my tongue.'

'You'd have to catch it first.' He said sardonically.

Hannah pulled a face. 'I have only just woken up you know!'

'Oh, I know!' He smiled, unnecessary apology accepted. 'Come on.'

He darted away through the bushes.

Hannah stole one last glance at the dark Canteen hut and scurried after him.

CHAPTER FOURTEEN

They scampered low to the ground for the best part of an hour; skulking along hedgerows and edging along boggy ditches. With every step away from the shrinking silhouette of Lighthope's church steeple, Hannah had expected to hear a wailing siren or barking dogs, but the cool night air remained tranquil and starry. About two miles out, they nearly bumped into a patrolling guard, but thankfully Alex pushed her back down into the grass until he'd passed on the other side of a dry stone wall. Rounding a ploughed field to rest in a small copse, much of the earlier tension eased from her tight stomach, although what lay ahead dampened any euphoria.

Whilst out of the P.O.W. camp, they remained in the inescapable Darkhive in the middle of the Emergen Sea, five hundred floors below safety. It was enough to overwhelm her with futility. Slumped within a thick bush she wished Vince could be there for encouragement. Instead, she sought solace in the stealthy meerkat stood on tiptoes beside her.

'So…what now Einstein?'

He didn't answer, so she tugged on his trouser leg.

'Hey!'

He resisted, but a second tug brought him down to a crouch opposite her.

'Still no sign we're being followed and...'

'Alex.' The tone of her voice stopped him. 'What's the plan from here?'

'Well...'

'Don't *Well* me Alex. I don't like being *Welled*. I want the truth, however ugly.'

He winced. 'Ugly is such a *strong* word...'

'Alex!'

'Alright.' He sighed. 'The Major's been planning this for weeks, but with so many Guards around, he still thinks we'll all need a bit of luck. The main way out is the way we came in...'

'Across the causeway!' Hannah gasped, absent-mindedly pulling her ankles closer to her.

'Yes, but we're not going that way. Some of the prisoners are chancing a night crossing of the causeway if they can get over the walls. A few are going to check out a rumour of some caves across the other side of the Emergen Sea. That's if the maintenance barge they're hoping to steal is still moored at a jetty on the east side of the island-'

'A barge?'

'Yes, but we're not going that way. The hardest plan involves some of the prisoners stealing Author-tarian Guard uniforms and simply walking out at dawn,-'

Hannah tried to cut in but Alex rushed on.

'-but we're definitely not going that way. The Major and a few others are hiding in a secret passage under the Rectory in Lighthope and waiting until the fuss dies down. If all goes badly, we'll fall back there. I've no idea what the Commandant and his guards will do.'

Hannah thought of all the friendly faces she'd seen around the camp also tramping through the night and the armies of coloured helmets who'd soon be turning the Darkhive inside out for any trace of them. She shuddered and licked her dry lips.

'And us Alex? What's going to happen to us?'

'We're heading for the North West corner.'

'Why, what's there?'

'There's-'

Lights came on behind them.

Alex cautiously stood up through the foliage. 'What the hell...?'

Hannah heard Edward Lost's chastising voice in her head as she squinted at the strengthening light shining through the green leaves. Carefully bending the supple branches above her, she raised herself to Alex's shoulder and seconded his astonishment.

In the distance, a patch of the dusty wasteland between them and the rows of Darkhive shelving now shone like a football pitch ready for a night match. The temporary floodlights, three on each side of a large square warmed to their task and glowed ever brighter, a faint hum reaching them from the generators.

From the surrounding darkness, hundreds of Law's Author-tarian Guards appeared, like militant moths attracted to the light. Interspersed amongst them were Order's own Guards, the glare from their silver helmets contrasting with the blue ones like a sequinned wave washing up a beach. Row upon row followed until there were hundreds of them pounding forwards, their feet kicking up wispy clouds of brown dust. They spread out to guard the perimeter, the last falling short of a podium constructed from scaffolding and black sheeting at the far right. A tight line of Words in dark trousers, yellow shirts and peaked caps marched across the gap in front of the stage, each brandishing a machine gun.

'Blondeshirts!' She murmured.

At the other end, figures came out of the dark and Hannah's eyes widened.

Many remained cautiously in the shadows, but a few strode boldly into the brightness. Some wore their finest Sunday best whilst others slunk forward in little more than rags. A man in a mustard-coloured tunic nervously followed into the light, a cloak fastened at his shoulder with a brooch. Another came forward in a fur-trimmed dark velvet gown, his fingers drumming together as he furtively looked around him. More came from the edges; a group in identical brown cowls with their faces obscured, women in long mud-splattered dresses clutching shawls around their shoulders, men in belted tunics carrying wooden weapons like extras from a Robin Hood film. Peasants came forward in dirty brown leather doublets and jerkins, rubbing shoulders with Merchants in tri-corn hats and long heavy black coats, their hands dripping in gold. Chain-mailed soldiers strode in, their bright tabards adorned with an assortment of lions, unicorns and bears. Within seconds,

204

they were pouring in, pushing and shoving like a crowd surging for the best view at a pop concert.

Alex answered before she could ask. 'Darkhivians, the inmates in all their archaic-Word glory. Although what so many are doing out at once….' He trailed off.

Hannah's lips moved but for once, the words evaded her.

These were the Words locked away awaiting their week's holiday once a decade. Words invented for a specific reason or purpose, but since deemed irrelevant or unnecessary. Words abandoned by the English Language on the whims of progress or fashion.

'There's…..there's so many.' She managed as they continued to stream forwards filling the open ground with a mass of jostling shoulders and heads.

Alex muttered under her breath, Hannah didn't hear.

'Alex, what's going on? Shouldn't all these Darkhive inmates be in their cells or whatever they're kept in?'

Rubbing his cheek, he didn't answer but shot her a sheepish glance.

'Oh no! No you don't!'

'It wouldn't take long, we could just see what was going on and…'

'Alex! Unless you hadn't noticed we're trying to escape the Darkhive not wander along to a free concert or whatever it is!'

'Hannah.'

'Don't *Hannah* me!' She snapped. 'I'm pretty sure the basic rules of escape are dark and empty good, bright and filled with guards bad. And I know I'm no expert, but that guard-filled bright area down there, surely falls distinctly in the latter category.'

'Hannah.'

'Fine, no, don't speak to me because if you think for one second I'm following you down there-'

'Hannah.'

'What?'

'Why don't you stay here?'

She stared at him lips pursed, annoyed he'd outthought her. She hated to admit it but the sight of the Darkhivians terrified her, aggravating a fear she'd become one herself if she stayed here too long. Yet she hardly wanted to sit alone in a dark bush either.

'So now you want to abandon me to…to…hang on!'

Alex broke through the branches and stomped away across the uneven ground. Hannah scampered after him, a mixture of hot angst and cool curiosity in her scurrying steps.

'I wish you'd stop doing that! Alright, but if we're caught, imprisoned and tortured to death, I get to die with a smug face.'

Alex led them along a gully through the long grass, moving to a rotting tree stump at the top of a slight slope, only thirty metres from the backs of the Guards at the edge of the crowd.   'This is too near!' She whispered.

He signalled her to keep quiet and still.

All eyes were on the podium as the stocky figure of Chief Constable Law stepped forward, leaned over the lectern and tapped the microphone with his hand. His copper coloured helmet gleamed as triumphant phrases rippled from his lips, his welcome to the Darkhivians echoing from speakers hanging on the floodlights.

'Important historic meeting…Significant time of change…Momentous occasion…' Yet despite his obvious conviction, his speech left Hannah none the wiser.

Behind him, a woman and three men sat on a row of seats between two enormous guards. Hannah recognised the nearest as the Blondeshirt Grammar Sergeant Malice. CC Order sat alongside him, smouldering pipe clenched ceremonially between his teeth. The middle-aged woman next to him sat in a long, voluminous green dress with a simple white shawl over her shoulders and white bonnet, reminding Hannah of a period drama. She clutched a small bag tightly on her lap, nervously tidying the strap, her bespectacled eyes focused on the back of CC Law's legs rather than the intimidating crowd.

Next to her sat a man who'd no such apprehension. Sat bolt upright, his chin raised and nostrils flaring like an arrogant bull, the greying man engaged all before him. Even Hannah found it hard to draw her gaze away. He appeared awkwardly tall, his dark blue woollen coat wrapped tightly over stretched limbs, hands the size of tennis racquets protruding from his sleeves.

Behind him, two Blondeshirt soldiers at either end of the stage lifted heavy looking flags from the floor, snapping the ends of the wooden poles into holsters at their waist. She squinted at the dark magenta flags as they swayed gently from side

207

to side, the unfamiliar coat of arms at the centre resplendent with two rams on their hind legs flanking a jumble of armour, swords and other Lexican symbols. Yet at its centre was the unmistakeable image of a large golden bell.

Law raised his arms as if asking the silent crowd to settle down. Glancing over his shoulder, he met the eyes of the awkward man as he got to his feet, buttoning his blue woollen coat. 'Darkhivians! I give to you the new Leader of the Grammar Nationalist Party and the saviour of the English Language: Millard Bellwether!'

Hannah curled her lip, the anger coursing round her bloodstream tinged with a desire to get as far away from there as possible. Here stood the Lexican who – if Vince was right – had already disappeared thousands of Words; their futures gone, definitions erased. The Lexican who'd sent Convince, Radders, Rebel and all the other camp prisoners to the Darkhive and sent his ruthless Blondeshirts to seize her from within their midst.

Having an idea, Hannah reached inside her top and surreptitiously brought out her mobile phone from its hiding place.

Alex did a double take as he saw her turn it on and lift its camera in front of her to record.

'You said to me you'd left your phone in the lift!'

Hannah didn't dare look at him, the heat rising in her cheeks.

Back on the podium, Law grinned and clapped excitedly to the crowd but only a handful put their hands together in return.

Bellwether stepped forward, his hands gripping the sides of the lectern as his piercing eyes glided silently over tens of thousands of upturned faces. A thin smear of fear and disgust hurried across his lips.

'They said to me I wouldn't come here.' He paused between sentences, giving his words greater emphasis and power.

'They said to me I shouldn't come here, I *couldn't* come here. They said to me, the Darkhive is a lawless island, a refuge of the abandoned and insane. They said to me a prison for Words consigned to the pages of history should be beneath my attention, if not my *contempt*!'

He paused before emphasising each quoted word with a jabbed finger.

'They said to me the Darkhive is "a waste of your time." Yet...'

He peered at the faces in the crowd, making sure he held every Word's attention.

'I *am* here. I have returned from exile in Pandemonia precisely because of the Darkhive, because of its great walls and great inhabitants. This place is a testament to how the politicians have run our Language for centuries; hiding the old, retiring the unwanted and burying the past. Discarding Words to these peculiar penal pastures where they can no longer be an embarrassment to the rich, bloated vermin in Wordminster. All the while patting themselves on the back for not erasing unneeded words like other Languages.'

'I say enough!' He thumped his fist into his other hand and again with each *enough*. 'Enough to hiding our forefathers, enough to turning a blind eye and enough to the Darkhive!'

209

Bellwether paused, his nostrils flaring to accept a ripple of cautious applause.

'A Heartisan once said, "A week is a long time in politics!" *I* say to all of you, politics has been a long time weak. The English Language has been weak on meddling interference from the URL council. Weak on those who allow foreign Words to come in and take our English definitions! And weak on the Heartisans corrupting our fine Language with text speak and the inherent use of *slang*.'

He spat the last word from his lips as if tasting something unpleasant.

'The English Language has spread across Pandemonia to become the most widely spoken second language, but we cannot live off past glories, not while the Mandarin and Spanish Languages plot against us. The English Language has become weak, but I am not.'

Bellwether became more animated, thumping his fists on the lectern much to the delight of the crowd as the eager applause generated some whistles.

'I'm strong and pure and I am here to make the English Language strong and pure again!'

The crowd clapped continually and Bellwether had to raise his voice further above the frenzy.

'My plans are coming to fruition; my schemes are preparing the ground for change. When the time comes, I will step out of the shadows and move swiftly and decisively to rescue this fine Language from itself. Operation overrun will be unleashed on the complacent upper cases of high society. Out will go the foreign words! Out will go the URL ambassadors! Out will go all those who stand in the way of progress! And out...' He paused for effect, pointing at the crowd and

210

drinking in the almost hysterical adulation of the leaping, hollering converts jostling against the Guards below him.

'Out of this Darkhive, you will *all* march!'

The field exploded with a roar as if Bellwether had scored a winning cup-final goal. The ground trembled beneath their feet, the screen shaking in her hand. The deafening noise surged through them, filling Hannah's head with a painful crackle. She glimpsed Alex pulling the same contorted face and at a suggestive flick of his head they scampered back the way they'd come.

As they disappeared into the darkness, the thunderous roar changed into the excited chanting of Bellwether's name. Glancing over her shoulder, she saw Bellwether at the front of the stage, arms aloft, his hands in tight, triumphant fists. The crowd below him were going wild, reaching for him, clamouring for his touch.

It made her feel sick.

CHAPTER FIFTEEN

The early morning hung over the red Darkhive walls like a heavy sheet of hammered metal. Hannah dropped her eyes past the burning braziers on the empty ramparts to the small building huddled at the base of the wall.

'You're sure this time?'

'Yes, I'm sure.' Alex said testily.

'It's just this blue door looks much the same as the last one.'

'We got away didn't we!' He snapped.

Hannah harrumphed. 'Only because the Guard tripped over his trousers and knocked himself out on the toilet door.'

Alex pulled a face and glared at the small building, if only to avoid her eyes. 'All the doors look the same!'

Hannah raised her eyebrows. 'I was just saying.'

'You're always "just saying."' He curled his lip and sighed. 'And I still haven't forgiven you for lying to me about your phone.'

Hannah winced. 'I'm sorry Alex, but you don't understand, it's my phone!'

'But Hannah I needed you to hide it! This isn't a game you-'

'I did hide it!' Hannah lowered her voice, 'just, not where you asked.'

'Do you realise what would have happened if CC Law had found it when you were searched by those-'

'Guards.'

'Yes,' Alex hissed, annoyed at her pedantic interruptions, 'when you were frisked by Law's- '

'Guards.' Hannah whispered distractedly.

Alex's anger flared but his venom dramatically seeped away as he followed her gaze back along the dingy and dust-filled aisle of locked chests, wooden boxes, and brass-handled drawers.

About a hundred yards away at the end of their eerie row of slumbering Darkhivians, five silver-helmeted guards had peeled off from a passing army and headed cautiously into the gloom. She figured five more were marching down the next row and each row beyond that, all systematically flushing their quarry out into the open.

She abruptly had a deep empathy for pheasants.

'Panic on the count of three?' She said calmly, defying the dread surging through her veins.

'Three?' Alex frowned.

Hannah grabbed his arm and dragged him in the opposite direction as if he'd trapped his sleeve in a car door.

Breaking from the shadows, they charged across the open ground towards the squat building opposite, whistles blown near and far. Skidding into the blue door on the dusty ground, Hannah fumbled at the loose black doorknob, leaned into it with her shoulder and they gratefully tumbled inside. Alex slammed the voices out, turned the key in the back of the lock and leaned into the wood.

'Get something for the door!'

She turned frantically from him to the warm refuge of some kind of workshop. Opposite the door, cluttered shelves of tools, clamps and oilcans covered the long red wall, three leather aprons hanging limply on hooks beside a calendar showing exotic Words.

On her left, a dirty steam engine ticked and clicked idly, a lick of flames visible through its metal door, its lime green livery unloved and peeling. A table strewn with paperwork, a wooden wheelbarrow and several hessian sacks of coal sat next to it on the floor.

On her right, a large black cast-iron tubular chamber covered with rivets protruded from the wall at waist height. With a brass wheel on the front and heavy-duty hinges, its door looked like an airtight hatch from a Victorian spaceship.

A hammering on the door and a groan brought her back to her senses. She scoured the room more objectively, eyeing the bags of coal jealously. The door thudded again, shaking Alex as he strained to keep it from breaking out of its frame. Using strength she didn't know she had, she hauled a half-empty sack of coal across the floor and shoved it behind Alex at the foot of the door.

'Now get the table!'

She dragged it over, leaving a trail of paperwork and an upturned chair behind her. Ignoring the heavier pounding on the door, Alex flipped it onto its side and rammed it beneath the door handle before resuming his position.

214

'Get me some nails and a hammer.' His voice vibrated with the pounding wood at his back.

Hannah searched the shelves, her nostrils full of grease and coal fumes. She pulled out pliers, tongs, and implements she didn't recognise, each falling to the floor with a satisfying crash. At one end, she found a pot of rough-hewn nails and a heavy hammer with a smooth wooden handle.

Returning to the door, she followed his instructions and bashed the square legs off the table. She fumbled the nails and they spilled across the floor. Muttering a mixture of curses and apologies, she scooped up a few and braced the table legs across the top corners of the door and frame. Alex took the hammer from her, picked up a couple more nails and pulling the table aside, secured the bottom corners.

The door stopped rattling so heavily in its frame and Hannah cautiously stepped closer to put her ear to the murmurings coming through the wood. Alex dragged over another of the bags of coal and waved her out of the way. She righted the chair and sat down, watching Alex stack the bags of coal one after another until they covered three quarters of the door.

With sweat glistening on his forehead, he blew out his cheeks and leaned on his knees. 'Should slow them down a bit!'

Hannah smiled proudly, but glancing around at the cell-like walls, she couldn't help see the flaw in his work.

'Yes well done Alex, but now what?'

He wiped the sweat from his eyes. 'Now Hannah, we get out of here.'

He crossed to the huge tubular chamber, turned the stiff wheel and swung open the heavy door to reveal a dirty chamber heading back into the wall.

'What the he…?' She managed before the stench hit her. Turning her head and coughing hard, she took a couple of paces backwards.

'It's our route out of here Hannah, the Refuse Disposal Duct system. Magnificent isn't it?'

'Magnificent? You are joking.' She muttered through her hand, her eyes watering.

'No?'

'Alex, the musical genius of Wolfgang Amadeus Mozart can justly be described as magnificent. The famous scribblings of William Shakespeare deserve such acclaim. Michelangelo's painting and decorating in the Sistine Chapel is undeniably worthy of all manner of superlatives, but this? This is...'

She gestured incredulously at the rusting hulk.

He frowned, only partly chastened. 'It's a fine example of robust, Victorian over-engineering….'

'Alex, it's a stinky rubbish pipe.'

He rubbed the rough metal as if she'd somehow hurt its feelings. 'How can you say that, just look at the workmanship in these joins?'

'Riveting.' Hannah scowled.

'Exactly.' Alex nodded proudly before looking unsure of himself.

A heavy thud overtook their discussion, their barricade quivering as the door shuddered violently in the frame, a faint splintering noise making them both frown.

216

The blade of a shiny axe head cracked through the wood.

'Right let's go!' Hannah said.

Alex gestured with his arm. 'Ladies first.'

With a boost from his interlinked hands, she clambered into the dark chamber. She could just stand with her head bowed, her shoes squelching in the accumulated soft sludge in the bottom. A single glance downwards turned her stomach over and she gagged as she headed to the back of the chamber. After a dozen tentative steps with a hand over her mouth, the tube narrowed and curved upwards from horizontal to vertical. A series of grimy steps rose out of the sludge, changing into rungs as they continued up the curve and onto the wall. The grease-stained electric lights opposite the ladder soared up the inside of the tube like a string of fairy lights dangling down from the edge of space.

'Grab the ladder and start climbing.'

Staring at the unidentifiable filth hanging from the rungs, her throat tightened and shoulders heaved. She steadied herself and hurled some unladylike words over her shoulder, fortunately drowned out by the echoing clang of the heavy iron door. The deafening noise sent her upwards like a startled squirrel, making it up thirty rungs before thinking about the grime squishing between her fingers.

'How far up is it?'

'Just keep going and fast!'

Hannah heaved herself upwards, feet tapping on the rungs.

'Go!' Alex bellowed up at her, the panic obvious in his voice.

217

Taking two rungs at a time, Alex's contagious fear pushed her on. She ignored the filth on her hands and tried not to think about the growing long drop below her. Five minutes of heart-thumping, finger squelching misery and she was struggling for breath, her arms stiff and legs burning with cramp. She slowed, her willpower willing but her adrenaline ebbing away.

'We need to…. keep going…Hannah.' Alex panted just below her.

'Can't…need…..rest.' Hannah hooked her unfeeling elbow around the ladder to take her weight.

'We can't…rest.'

'Why?'

His sweaty face peered up at her, dirty finger marks drawn lopsidedly across his forehead. Beyond him, the line of lights on the opposite wall drew her eyes down to the swirling lights in the dark depths of oblivion. If she hadn't climbed from the base, she'd believe it bottomless.

She tightened her grip on the rungs and sucked in great lungfuls of putrid air until calm enough again to be simply disgusted.

'Don't look down...Hannah.' Alex said helpfully. 'Just keep climbing.'

Swirling lights.

Looking down past Alex, two swirling pinpricks of yellow light flickered far below them.

'What're those?'

Alex followed her gaze and gasped. 'Torches! Must be guards...on the rungs.'

Hannah roused herself and reached for the next rung.

218

'As quick as you can Hannah.'

'Are they catching us?'

'It's not them I'm worried about. Listen.'

She strained her ears to a distant hissing thunder.

'They're stoking up...the boiler.'

'So?'

'It powers a compressor.'

'And?' Hannah gasped impatiently as she plodded upwards.

'The compressor makes...high-pressure air...released into the base chamber... blows rubbish from the tube...genius system...beautifully simple.'

Hannah took a second to comprehend. '...you mean?

'We're rubbish.'

'Speak for yourself.' Hannah murmured, more a reflex than with any jollity.

She climbed in the same manner, without enthusiasm or fear, just a sense of going through the motions. She tried to rouse herself, to shake herself into urgency but she ached too much, muscles weary and brain tired. Every brief spurt receded back into the same monotonous swaying of her hips.

The rumbling grew louder, the walls ringing with noise. The lights vibrated and flickered, the rungs humming under her fingers. She chanced a glance downwards, but the swirling lights had stopped.

How much further?

Just what was it with tunnels, pipes and the threat of impending death today?

She heard the matter-of-fact voice mumble the questions in her head and shook her head at the ridiculousness of the situation.

'I haven't lost my mind.' She muttered. 'I haven't.'

'There!' Alex yelled craning his neck up at a large circular hatch recessed into the wall opposite the ladder, complete with a grimy brass wheel and narrow ledge.

A deafening siren sounded, filling the tube with disorientating flashing amber lights.

She flinched and tensed up, white knuckles clinging to the rung beneath her chin. She heard Alex shouting over the top of the alarm as she clutched the greasy, stinky metal, felt him climbing over the back of her, his hands shoving, jostling and pulling at her arms.

'Climb Hannah! Climb!' He yelled in her ear. 'Stay here and we're dead!'

The alarms still whirred.

Reluctantly unclamping her hands, she forced her stiffening legs to push her upwards, if only to get away from Alex's pinching fingers. Her thighs screamed with cramp, her arms were leaden and reluctant to take her weight, but she gritted her teeth and pushed onwards. Fifteen tortuous rungs higher and with barely a thought of the empty abyss below, she turned her swimming head and propelled herself from the ladder with all her remaining strength.

She landed heavily on the narrow ledge opposite, skidding into a crouch amidst another thick layer of sludge. Steadying herself, she looked dizzily back at Alex's wide-eyed dopey expression. She imagined he'd been steeling himself for a "Convince style" pep talk to get her to jump. Desperate to get away from the

220

painful noise and the blinding light, she covered her hands with her sleeves, yanked the greasy wheel handle loose and shoved the heavy service hatch open.

Alex skipped up a couple more rungs and jumped effortlessly across behind her.

On the other side, they heaved it shut and tried to rotate the wheel handle but it was much stiffer than the other side and their greasy hands and sleeves couldn't get it to lock shut.

The wailing alarms died away with a pained whine.

'Leave it!' Alex urged, the panic audible in his voice.

They slipped and slid around a bend, pushing themselves off the rusting walls until they emerged at the top of a cast iron staircase spiralling around the outside of the pipe. They'd barely skipped down a couple of steps when the thick metal pipe trembled and shook, flakes of rust tumbling from the blistered tube as the vibrations grew more violent.

'Cover your ears!' Alex bellowed, dragging her down onto the vibrating metal stairs and sitting on the step behind her.

'Head down!' He said shoving her head forwards until she clamped it between her juddering knees, her elbows squeezing her thighs. Alex leaned onto her back, head between her shoulders. Gritting her teeth, she screwed up her eyes and waited with an intense feeling of foreboding as the trembling tube grew in noise and violence. The rumbling approached within the pipe like a charging freight train, growing louder and louder until almost unbearable. She heard the service hatch smash open behind them with a thunderous crash, a pained howl released from within.

Even with Alex behind her, the fetid air hit like an angry hurricane, pressing Hannah's face hard into her legs, her feet skidding against the lower step. The sound consumed her entire being, like the deep whistling roar of a grumpy lion, just inches from the back of her head. Almost too loud for her to register as noise, it filled her with a numb, disorientating feeling like an electric shock she couldn't escape. She clamped her unfeeling hands harder against her head, her fingernails digging through her hair and into her scalp as she waited for the end.

CHAPTER SIXTEEN

The crushing air relented, slowing from a tornado to the laboured bad breath of a
wheezing asthmatic. Hannah's eyes flickered open blurrily to the grubby green
cotton covering her knees. Her whole body was in open revolt. From her arched
spine to her crumpled neck, from her crunched hips to her scrunched organs, she
was as fragile and vulnerable as a snail hiding in its shell. Uncurling herself
gingerly, she drew her nails from her scalp, straightened her back and tentatively
stretched her legs.

Alex got to his feet, whooping and punching the air as he bounded down the
steps, around the corner and back. His tinny voice came to her distantly, heard
through a muffled hum. She cautiously loosened the tension in her jaw and
swallowed hard, the click gratifying. Screwing up her eyes and doing it again, her
left ear popped.

'-made it!' Alex yelled, pointed downwards excitedly.

She sighed passively as he scampered away, her own will to move, let alone
celebrate a long way off returning. They'd survived only by a tick of the second
hand. She imagined CC Order hundreds of metres below contently puffing on his
pipe at the thought of their demise. An intense heat still radiated from the corroded

iron tube beside her, warming her face and filling the air with the earthy tang of hot metal. She tried not to dwell on what'd happened to their pursuers.

Forcing herself unsteadily to her feet, she wearily trudged down maybe twenty steps, finding a beaming Alex stood on a brightly-lit flagged floor.

'We showed them didn't we? We made it!'

Hannah paused, before joining him on a dusty stone floor about ten paces across, the thick pipe and steps at her rear. She squinted upwards at the source of the light, unable to decide if the pinprick was a bright star in the sky or a tiny spotlight just out of reach. She blinked away the purple and yellow splodges in her eyes, her gaze falling on the faded white line around them.

Outside the ill-maintained, chalk circle, the darkness seemingly hung like a thick viscous curtain, absorbing all the light and sound thrown at it. It was like an empty stage, the burning spotlight giving every action more meaning, the anticipation of impending drama palpable in the air.

'Made it *where* Alex?' She said irritably.

Alex's eyes flickered from beyond her, his joy subsiding. She turned, equal parts fascinated as disturbed as the inky darkness crept across the surface of the corroded pipe like a matt black tar. It creepily devoured the lot, slithering down the cast-iron steps to the edge of the encompassing circle.

She glared at Alex, lips poised and her finger pointing disbelievingly.

'Right.' His Adam's apple jerked upwards as he swallowed, his elation gone. 'These are the Marginlands.'

224

'The where?' Hannah said distractedly, still swallowing hard to clear her blocked ear.

'The Marginlands, never been here before, but I remember reading about them a long time ago-'

She winced inwardly.

'I read the autobiography of explorer Sir Writer Raleigh, who travelled through here once. He said it's an empty no-man's land, a blank sheet of paper between the English Language and the Darkhive.'

'Empty?'

'Well…nearly empty. The only Fiends to survive in this kind of wasteland are the Figments.'

'Sounds like a rubbish boy band.'

'Not quite,' Alex said with a tone of poorly concealed ignorance, 'these Figments patrol the border attacking unsuspecting victims and scavenging their dead bodies.'

Her other ear popped.

'What?!'

Alex flinched in the full beam of her attention.

'What?' He stared until understanding dawned. 'Oh, no don't worry. I'm here, I'm sure we'll be fine.'

Hannah didn't get chance to even form a sarcastic reply as a streak of colour fell from above and banged into the stone floor. She shrieked as it bounced twice and crashed back to the ground. The spinning blur resolving itself into a battered silver helmet rocking on its side. As she trembled and twitched, the smouldering remains of a boot fell from the skies and landed beside it with a disturbing noise somewhere between a wet squelch and the crack of a whip.

She shuffled backwards, her eyes never leaving the smouldering helmet as fine wisps of grey smoke escaped its interior.

'Han.'

She flinched as he reached for her.

'Hannah, it's alright, I'm here, we'll be fine.'

Her wide eyes darted from the silver helmet to his face like a laser.

'Stop telling me we'll be fine! I'm up to here with we'll be fine!' She pulled free and stomped away around the circle, her search for an exit as futile as looking for a corner.

'Two days ago….' She paused as she realised it'd been less than forty-eight hours since her world had disappeared atop the Monument. 'Sunday, it's Sunday! Oh no, it's already Sunday!'

She raised fists to the heavens but her fury was only for herself.

'And to think, not so long ago, I actually wished you...'

She walked on, eyes searing Alex's dumbstruck expression as she turned and counted on her fingers.

'Since meeting you two days ago, I've; been attacked by a giant wasp, walked down an imaginary staircase, had tanks point their guns at me...and nearly been pulled into a green sea by some kind of evil watery, water-hands!'

'...' Alex paused as he realised she wasn't finished.

226

'I've been threatened with torture. I've been locked up in prison, chased by fascist Neanderthals in coloured helmets, nearly buried alive in a crumbly tunnel and...and almost fired out of a garbage super-gun. Now to top it all, as if that wasn't enough, you tell me I could be attacked, killed and end up a scavenged body!'

Alex's eyes narrowed. 'You make it all sound so...'

'What Alex? What do I make it sound like?'

He shrugged indifferently. 'Soooo...negative.'

As she sucked in a breath ready to explode, he realised his mistake, verbally fumbling to get the pin back in the grenade.

'Besides, anyway, listen, come on...you did say...you wanted me to keep you informed?' He spluttered.

'Yes Alex I did.' She said in a chillingly calm voice. 'Although I was hoping it wouldn't just be news updates on how I was going to die...'

He mistakenly grinned at her sarcasm.

'Why the heck are you grinning?'

'You always were funny when ...' He stopped.

'Funny when...?' Hannah's eyes burned mischievously, stepping towards him and shoving him in the chest.

'Hannah?' Alex stepped back, raised his hands and smiled nervously.

'Don't "Hannah" me!' She shoved him again.

227

Alex staggered back a pace, his right foot skidding beneath him. Glancing downwards, he noted most of the circle lay in front of him and shuffled his heel from the faded white line.

'No Hannah, wait, hang on…'

'No Alex, you hang on!' She knocked his pleading hands aside, too annoyed to care if she made much sense.

'Han…' Alex attempted before she shoved him in the chest again, knocking the breath from his lungs.

She grinned as Alex tumbled backwards over the line, flailing for his balance, the darkness illuminating behind him in an instant. He managed one lopsided step before gravity pulled him down onto a brick floor covered in old dry straw. Red and cream movement wiped away Hannah's smile. A huge fat animal waddled forward out of the darkness, its scaly tail thudding on the ground. She gawped at the winged beast, unable to move a muscle.

Alex scrambled to his feet as the dragon sucked in a deep breath through its flaring nostrils. Alex pushed himself up, a garbled yell escaping his lips as his foot slipped on the straw.

A bubble of fire erupted from the dragon's mouth in a fiery jet, chasing Alex as he rushed forward and dived for the white line. The roar of the tumbling, dancing flames approached like the exhaust of a rocket. Alex landed on his forearms at Hannah's feet as the wall of fire rushed towards them. She closed her eyes and turned her head, awaiting the wave of burning pain to hit.

Nothing.

She opened one eye and dared to peek back at him. Alex sat on his heels rubbing his arms, smouldering stalks of straw scattered around them. Beyond him, a dim glow and encroaching blackness replaced the huge dragon, leaving behind only a whiff of sulphurous smoke. Her legs gave up their rigidity and without finesse collapsed cross-legged opposite him.

Eyes wild, she tried to speak but her lips only twitched. Alex rolled up his sleeve and examined the white and red graze on his elbow. He rubbed it with a wince before rising sharply to a kneeling position and rubbing his toasted buttocks, the trousers steaming as if freshly ironed. He changed position so his soles and bottom sat on the cool flagged floor, careful not to lean back over the white line.

'I'm, I'm so sorry, I…I…' Hannah stuttered.

Alex looked furious but after a sigh managed a rueful grin, eyes sparkling playfully. 'Don't do that again, will you?'

'That was a flamin' dragon!' She glared at Alex and shook her head, not least at sounding like a simpleton. 'I'm not sure about this Alex.'

'Right first thing, the dragon doesn't exist.'

She pouted incredulously.

'I know, I know, but as I was trying to tell you the Marginlands are empty, it's just a blank canvas filled by us and the Figments. Sir Writer Raleigh described them as a "collaborative consciousness." It'll be our imagination pitted against theirs, an imagined game of mind-chess.'

She gawped at the smoking straw and shook her head. 'And this is definitely the only way out?'

He nodded. 'We have to get to the next Punch-hole along. Unless you want to wait here for someone else to pass by, you'll be perfectly safe within the circle. Someone could be here in a few minutes.'

She looked at him, a bubble of hope growing in her mind.

'Or it could be a thousand years.'

Pop!

Her shoulders sagged. 'Alright, so what do I need to do?'

Alex half-smiled and got to his feet. 'Okay, well, the key in the Marginlands has always been imagining the opposite of what you face.'

'So for the fire-breathing dragon you think water?'

'Exactly!' Alex nodded.

'A bucket, no wait a fire hose?'

'Yes, but bigger. The Major said the Marginlands were abandoned so long ago, we should expect much worse than Raleigh's expedition.'

She shook her head. 'One of those forest-fire planes?'

'Bigger.' He said patiently. 'The other-'

'Erm…a waterfall, a wave, no wait…a tsunami!' She said bewilderingly.

'That's the idea. The other rule to remember is Figments can hurt you but they can't actually kill you, they can only convince you you're about to die.'

Hannah's eyes narrowed. 'They can't kill you?'

'No just persuade you you're doomed.'

'You mean….they scare you to death.'

230

'Kind of….for instance if I'd curled up in a ball in front of the dragon I wouldn't be here now.'

She took a moment to think. 'What happens...?'

He hesitated. 'I'm not sure, I think they just...absorb you into their consciousness.'

She frowned and looked at the emptiness beyond the circle.

'You mean to tell me, their consciousness is formed from all those people who haven't journeyed safely through the Marginlands?'

Alex winced and looked as if he tried not to think about it.

'This, this is the Major's great escape plan?' She mocked, lip curled.

He wisely said nothing.

She blinked hard, making to wipe her eye before scowling at the smell and wiping them once more on her grubby, green trousers.

'There must be another way? The pipe, the darkhive, the...why are you shaking your head?'

'Even if we could find the pipe again, it'd just dump us back in the Darkhive. Besides, they probably think we're already dead like the Guards, that gives us a chance, if we get through...'

She glanced and turned away away from the debris on the other side of the circle.

'This is...this is all...so messed up.' She murmured.

Alex softened. 'I know this isn't easy for you. None of this was supposed to happen.'

231

She folded her arms, shoulders hunched.

He gently shook his head. 'That George has a lot to answer for.'

Hannah had no energy for arguing, little enthusiasm for finger pointing.

'I'm sorry Han, but we should get moving before the Figments get plotting.'

She sagged, drew in a long breath and shuffled after him to the edge of the circle.

'Stay close. Keep focused.'

They stepped across together into the midst of long grass and flowers. The sloping English meadow undulated away from them for about two hundred metres before a bank of dark mist prevented them seeing any further. All around them, the dry grass thronged with swaying yellow buttercups, red poppies and the vivid blues of cornflowers, the sweet scent filling her nostrils. Butterflies fluttered, bumblebees flitted and bluebirds twittered in the warming lemon sunshine.

'Don't get complacent.' Alex said, noting awe replacing her frown. He nodded to her side.

She stared at a toilet, bath and washbasin, the shiny white porcelain stark against the surrounding flowers, the bathroom suite amidst the flowers as fantastical as a television advert. She glanced at the grim stinky ooze drying between her fingers and gratefully stepped forwards to wash her hands and face in the hot water.

'What about these?' She said pulling at her grimy, stinky military shirt.

'What would you prefer to wear?' He asked.

She frowned.

232

He sighed. 'What did you wear to church last weekend?'

She closed her eyes as she tried to recall, it seemed such a long time ago already.

'Jeans, white t-shirt, grey jacket and funny-looking scarf?' Alex said.

Hannah's eyes snapped open. 'Yes, how did you...?!'

Alex smirked and nodded at her body.

She looked down at the clean jeans, t-shirt and jacket she now wore, pulling at her pink and lemon scarf.

'But that's...' She stopped herself, much to Alex's amusement.

Ignoring him, she picked up a clean glass from the sink, held it under the cold tap and drank heartily. As Alex washed his hands, she stared at the floor, her head shaking with concentration as a red tube materialised at her feet. The shape darkened, solidified and gained detailing on its label, pin and hose until it became real. She tapped Alex on the shoulder and proudly pointed the fire extinguisher out to him. He looked at her sympathetically, forcing an encouraging expression.

'Well done, but we won't be seeing another dragon.'

She raised an eyebrow in enquiry.

'Raleigh said the Figments get bored easily and tend to avoid repetition, did I not mention that?'

'Er no!'

'Oh sorry.' He answered non-committally, his eyes already scouring their surroundings.

'Alex, I don't know if I can do this...'

'Yes, you can. I know you can. Simply imagine you can and you're halfway there.'

She shook her head, 'I'm too tired and-'

'This is the Marginlands. Imagine you're not.'

She stared at him, the words fizzing in her brain like popping candy on her tongue.

'Come on, we shouldn't hang around.'

She followed him through the long grass, straightening her back and stubbornly willing her aching muscles away.

She realised she was still holding the glass.

'One second.' She uttered and swirled round to find all trace of the bathroom completely gone, even traces of their footsteps missing from the pristine meadow.

'But where should I put....?' She stared at her empty hand.

'Hannah! Stop dallying!'

She shook her head and stumbled onwards, barely taking three dazed footsteps before a long-eared puppy bounded through the knee-high grass and leapt up into her arms.

'Aw! Look!' She cradled the animal as it licked her face with its soft tongue.

'Put it down and keep your wits about you.' Alex said, stepping deliberately on a smouldering, discarded cigarette in the dry grass.

Hannah mimicked him behind his back and put the panting puppy down.

'Run along little chap.' She encouraged, the puppy turning and tilting its head at her, tail wagging excitedly.

'Sssssssh!' Alex hissed sharply.

She stopped and listened at Alex's shoulder, unable to hear past the chattering of skylarks and the chirp of crickets. She opened her mouth to tell him to stop being so sensitive when a breath of wind brought a chorus of yelps and wailing cries to her ears. Alex grabbed her hand and pulled away up the gentle slope. A fuzzy bee bounced off her forehead as they broke into a run, the swish of her legs through the grass drowning out much of the barking and yelping behind.

'Jump!'

Alex pulled sharply up on her hand. She leapt high and heard a loud snap like from the jaws of a metallic crocodile, glimpsing the frightening rusty teeth of a large mantrap behind her as they sped onwards.

'Wait!'

The man of few words now seemed to be down to one at a time. She stopped at his shoulder, panting hard.

'There's a sign.'

A stout oak had appeared at the junction of two dusty tracks. Alex rushed to a white signpost by the tree, the two arms pointing left and right partially obscured by the dangling foliage. At the haunting cry of a bugle, Hannah spotted the puppy lolloping after them through the tall grass, tongue lolling out and ears flapping. In the distance, a pack of ravenous beasts bounded through the grass, three brown horses and a grey cantering at their heels. Faceless men in white jodhpurs and red coats bobbed gently in their saddles.

'Alex!'

'Wait, a second...' He pushed the leaves aside on the right-hand sign.

Certain Death – This Way

'Hmmm.' Hannah murmured.

Alex brushed the foliage from the left with a sweep of his arm.

Certain Death – That Way (Scenic Route)

Hannah puffed out her cheeks. 'Choices, choices.'

The horses' pounding hooves shook the ground and filled the air with a growing rumble. Flashes of dusty red fur coats and cream chests weaved up the sloping meadow, egged on by the huntsmen on their horses. Only as one stopped and peered deviously at her did she realise they – and the puppy – were being hunted by a skulk of ravenous foxes.

'Alex?' She moved closer to him.

'Think you can outrun a horse?' He said fearfully.

She looked up the trunk of the oak and back at him.

'Alright! Go!'

She could barely hear him now above the bugle calls and barking foxes, but she didn't need to. With a boost from his hands, she scrambled up the knobbly trunk, hauling herself upwards with the thicker branches when they came within reach.

'Keep going!' Alex bellowed when she dared to look down.

She climbed higher and higher, the trunk dividing into three. Straddling the thickest, she tried to catch her breath whilst a growing wind tugged at the leaves around her.

At the base of the tree the foxes, puppy and four horses despondently milled around sniffing and snorting.

'They're all Figments aren't they?' She said humbly as Alex sat opposite her on a separate branch.

'Yes.' He sagged against the branch, his hair sticking to his glistening brow. 'Maybe we shouldn't have come this way after all. They're much quicker than I imagined.'

Hannah smirked, but his pun wasn't intended. She cursed the part of her brain busy musing at her imaginary friend not imagining their imaginary enemy could out-imagine them in a deadly imagination competition.

She hadn't lost her mind.

'We should have imagined a motorbike.'

Hannah blew out her cheeks at the thought of riding an imaginary vehicle at high speed.

'No use to us up here.' Hannah said urgently over a gust of wind, the branches swaying and creaking, leaves hissing.

He looked around and grimaced. 'Hang-glider?'

Hannah's eyes widened. 'No Alex.'

He shrugged. 'Hot air balloon.'

Hannah continued staring.

'Well I don't hear you coming up with any ideas?!'

A mechanical roar from the ground below interrupted him. Three faceless men in checked shirts glanced up mischievously as they fired up three throbbing chainsaws.

'Ugh.' She groaned, closing her eyes and concentrating hard.

'Hannah?'

She opened her eyes, Alex holding open the brown leather straps of a pulley hanging from a stainless steel zip-wire. She looked at the fading rope-ladder she'd imagined and felt embarrassed. 'A zip wire? I don't think-'

The tree shuddered with a loud crack and she scrambled across to feed her hands through the straps and grip the grooved handles. Below them, wood chips and shavings spewed from the whirring metallic teeth as they bit into the bark and gorged themselves on the tree's trunk. She pouted, sad for the tree, even though she knew it wasn't real.

A glance down through the swaying green leaves and she froze, her senses overloaded with the roaring noise, cool breeze and smell of freshly carved heartwood. High above the ground in a make-believe tree wasn't the place to imagine her first dizzying spell of vertigo.

'Go!' Alex shouted as she stared blankly out at wire stretching out between the quivering, rippling leaves.

As she stalled by rechecking her grip, Alex encouraged her with a gentle shove in the back. She half-stumbled, half fell off the branch with a small squeal, her stomach lurching upwards as she dipped a couple of metres on the sagging wire. Hiding her face behind her arms, she crashed through the thin outer branches and

238

leaves and burst into the light, the air on her face like the clasp of cold hands. Alex's weight dropped onto the line behind her and within seconds, they were tearing over the treetops and a glittering stream some terrifying distance below.

The ground fell away further as they crested a ridge and flew over the edge of a steep wooded hillside. The rush of air rapidly numbed her cheeks and hands, tugging her hair back over her shoulders and making her eyes water.

'They're deliberately lengthening the cable!' Alex boomed behind her. 'Think of somewhere soft to land.'

'Somewhere soft to land?' The thought took a second for Hannah to compute.

Above her the wheels whirred in the pulley with a terrible whine, giving off heat as she sped ever faster. Staring at the blurred ground far below, her hands dampened with perspiration. Squinting up at her wrists securely in the straps, she tried to lift herself up with one arm to free her other wrist, but she didn't have the muscles or the courage to hang on one-handed.

'Imagine away the straps.' Alex bellowed over the whistling wind and growling pulleys.

She stopped her contorted wriggling and imagined the straps were gone.

'This is stupid,' she thought, 'there's no way…'

She stopped as the straps flickered and disappeared, panic tightening her grip around the now clammy handles.

'Well done, now think of a soft landing.' The unwavering voice shouted from behind her. 'Drop on three, alright.'

She glanced at her dangling feet and regretted it, the dark green and red whir of prickly holly bushes below making her feel nauseous.

'One.' Alex shouted.

She closed her eyes, but the queasiness remained.

'Two.'

'Two already?' She sucked in a deep breath and tried to focus.

'Tim-' A bellowing voice echoed through the air.

The line twitched and slackened. Some way behind her, she heard the sharp cracking and splintering of wood.

'-berrrrrr!' The lumberjack voice finished gleefully.

'Three!' Alex screamed.

She let go, her fingers slipping off the handles as the cable bucked and twisted like a piece of snapped elastic.

'Soft...things!' She yelled as she tumbled, her body rigid with fear.

She was falling.

She plummeted on her back, her breath caught in her throat. She imagined the hard ground and bed of prickly holly leaves rushing up to meet her. Her arms flailed as she shook her head, screeching air pushing her hair up over her eyes.

She was falling.

'Soft things!' She screamed helplessly through gritted teeth.

Falling to her imaginary death.

CHAPTER SEVENTEEN

Alex crashed into a mound of soft hay, sending a plume of dust and straw up into the air. Coming to a halt in the near darkness, he sucked in a deep breath of tickly dust and coughed into his fist. Pawing at his stinging eyes, he tentatively wrestled himself upright, a sharp pain bringing his hand down to a shiny needle in his rear.

He grimaced sardonically and pulled it free. 'Not funny.'

His raised eyebrow focused his mind.

'Hannah!'

He frantically clambered up towards a slither of blue sky, the hay constantly shifting beneath his hands and feet. Breaching the top into weak sunshine, he stopped and stared like a slack-jawed yokel. Opposite his modest haystack was the largest four-poster bed he'd ever seen, possibly anyone had ever seen. The patchwork quilt covered a mattress the size of a tennis court, the headboard bigger than a cinema screen and the posts as tall and thick as carved totem poles. Displaced feathers gently wafted down like snow over a mound of fluffy pillows.

Alex slid down the haystack to a wooden floor split by dark crevasses. Brushing the itchy straw from his shirt and hair, he shuffled his foot to the edge of a wooden board and peered over the edge into the impenetrable void. After a moment of concentration, he brought a scuffed red cricket ball from his pocket and dropped it into the darkness, cocking his ear but never hearing it hit the bottom.

He leapt over several gaps and clambered up the corner of the four-poster bed. As his eyes rose over the mattress, Hannah's mischievous grin filled his vision. Sat crossed-legged on the patchwork quilt, her tongue licked a cone laden with several scoops of chocolate ice cream.

Alex pulled a face. 'Well, there's no need to show off.'

She stuck out her chocolate-coated tongue.

'You know, this isn't a game Hannah.'

'If I'm going to die horribly, I'm doing it with an ice cream in my hand.'

'I'll remember that for your gravestone.' He shook his head and shimmied back down to the wooden floorboards.

Hannah crunched on her ice cream cone and followed, looking wistfully around at the pillows one last time as she went. Back on the ground, Alex was gazing skywards, his eyes flicking between two bright stars in the dark sky.

'What're you doing?' She asked, licking the last of the ice cream from her sticky fingers.

'The stars are the lights over the punch-holes. That's where we started, that's where we're headed. I'd say we're nearly three-quarters of the way there.'

Hannah mumbled affirmatively, a blur of movement to one side turning her head.

Before she could focus on any Figments, the floor leapt up towards her and the world went black.

Hannah groaned and opened her groggy eyes, trying to focus on the blurred grain of wood under her nose.

Where...?

Had she blacked out? Had the Figments got her?

With a grimaced effort, she tried to lift herself up, but pressure in her back pushed her straight back down, her knees under her chest. Winded and bruised, she struggled to move, each breath an ordeal.

Her neck was impossibly heavy, but with some effort she placed an arm across her chest and levered herself up enough to look around. Her dream bed had gone, Alex's haystack too.

'Alex?'

She rose to her hands and knees but the weight returned, pinning her back to the floor. She kicked and screamed at her hidden foe but the pressure remained until she stopped struggling.

'...anna...'

Alex!

Hannah twitched and twisted her head, but she couldn't find him. A scuffed cricket ball pitched up out of a gap in the floor, landing with a dull thump on the wood and rolling to a stop within reach.

'Alex?'

'...ang on!' His garbled voice came up from the void between the wooden boards.

Hannah's heart sank.

She kept still and the weight in her back receded once more. Tensing her muscles, she abruptly flipped over and despite herself almost laughed.

Towering over her, an enormous black and white kitten sat on its hind legs with a look of wide-eyed curiosity on its face. Its front paw jerked forward to Hannah's stomach and pinned her to the ground, its young face rotating sideways inquisitively. She kept still and the paw returned to hovering above her, twitching whenever she shifted her weight. A wry smile formed on Hannah's lips as the kitten's ears flicked backwards at the imagined sound of a barking dog.

Hannah used the distracted moment wisely, the leather ball splitting in her hands, off-white fur bursting through the red shell. She let the catnip toy grow whiskers and a long string tail and hurled it over the kitten's head. With claws scrabbling on the slippery wood floor, the kitten bolted after it and pounced, tumbling head over tail with the mouse in its tearing claws.

Hannah turned back to the edge of the floorboard.

'Alex?'

'...on't panic...all under control!' She heard faintly, his voice distorted, almost metallic.

The black abyss had a glossy surface like a lake on a moonless night. Her tired reflection peered up at her, uncertainty in her eyes. A white cork ring bearing the name *Lusitania* appeared up from under the surface, ripples distorting her face.

'...rab ne nin.' Alex said indistinctly.

'What?'

'Grab. The. Ring.'

244

She frowned at the lifebuoy, crouching and pulling it towards her by its snaking rope, gasping as her fingers broke the unbearably cold surface. Dumping it on the wooden floor by her feet, she blew hard onto her throbbing digits, cautiously turning in case the kitten had returned. It'd gone, replaced by an impenetrable ebony curtain creeping eerily across the floorboards towards her. Her eyes widened as she realised the horizon was closing in on her from all sides, the black silky curtain creeping nearer inch by inch.

'...ut it on...there's not...time.'

It was a strain to pick out Alex's words.

She glanced down at the discoloured white and red lifebuoy and back at the oppressive wall, her whole world condensing into an ever-decreasing circle of light.

There was no way out.

She spun around, panicking as her world shrank to twenty metres across and kept shrinking.

She was losing.

'They only want me to think I'm losing!' She tried to remind herself.

Her fear shouted louder than whispered reason.

What if Alex was wrong?

What if the Figments could kill her without her consent?

She looked up to the light shining above her, feeling wretched and confused. As the dark walls crept in on her, she wanted to believe it was a trick, wanted to resist the Figments. She tried to force them back with her mind but they crept ever inwards. Sucking in a breath, she clenched her teeth, wracked with indecision.

She put the lifebuoy over her head and raised an arm through it before pausing, a ray of sanity shining through her clouded paranoia.

Alex was the one who'd fallen in when the kitten pounced! Wasn't he?

She wasn't the one needing rescuing, was she?

Was she?

The coldness closed around her, sucking away her powers of reason as well as her body heat.

You have thirty seconds to live.

She shook her whirling head. Tendrils of sooty vapour tumbled from the walls to her feet like a cascading fog of dry ice. She took a tiny step back from the edge of the abyss, desperately wanting to force the walls back but not knowing how.

'Alex?'

'...uickly...I've got you!'

The rope tautened and pulled at her, sawing the wooden edge with a deep, jagged rasp. She held onto it at arm's length, shoes sliding on the floor inches from the bleak pool.

'Stop! Alex stop!'

The rope stopped pulling but remained taut.

She stood upright, the jet-black wall of destruction less than a car length away in every direction.

A thought burned in her mind, a thought needing time and space for examination. A thought denied both.

As the Figments pushed inwards, they drew heat from her until her clothes stiffened with frost.

Her eyes widened, lips parting.

The circle.

She scrunched her eyes tight, head trembling before she dropped to her knees and untidily drew a semicircular line on the floor with the freshly imagined stick of chalk in her hand. The darkness slowed at the line, but didn't stop, eating into the chalk like acid.

Hannah sagged, shivers shaking her shoulders, muscles tightening, body numb. She struggled to think straight, falling back onto instincts, a few weak threads of deliberation ignoring the anarchic panic whirling around her brain.

'Alex, wh-wh-where...are you?'

'...hat? Hannah...Come up now!'

She envisioned a mooring bollard at her feet and with unfeeling hands placed the lifebuoy over it, just as the rope snapped tight once more.

'Al-ex, wh-what do...you see?' She shook, teeth clenched.

The rope jerked violently, loosened and snapped taut, flicking blackness off the hemp line like runny treacle.

'...oosen the rope, it's snagged!'

The black wall touched her left shoulder and she gasped sharply, muscles tightening as she shuffled nearer the centre, feet together, her elbows stuck to her ribs and fists under her chin. She stood and grappled with doubt, staring into the darkness, looking at her feet to be sure she hadn't yet closed her eyes.

'No!' She dug in, shaking her head more than her growing shivers.

She shook her head, the cold clawing at her flesh and freezing the marrow in her bones. The blackness embracing her like a cannon around a cannonball.

'Al-Alex.' She shouted through clenched teeth. 'L-Listen to me!'

The Figments reached for her with icy fingers, picking at her clothes and pinching her skin.

Sucking in a deep lungful, she screamed. 'Al-Alex! You're on...the wr-wrong side! Dive in-to the d-dark-ness.'

The rope tugged twice before going quiet and limp.

She did the same, the time for action and noise passed. The black soup eagerly devoured the last of the rope and the bollard at her feet, leaving her alone.

Defeated and alone.

'Step into the light.' Her brain hiccupped the cliché of near-death experience survivors. 'Step into the light and feel the kindness of a supreme power.'

She raised her vision to the dimming light above, her last act to be a step into the dark.   Disappointment and fear overwhelmed her, freezing her to a slow vibration, a fading spark trapped in ice. She could've been crying but she wasn't sure she still had the energy. The black world enveloped most of her stiff body, her senses too overloaded to keep track. She screwed up her eyes, trying to stop the Figments from getting inside her head. She shook uncontrollably, hoping she'd stop feeling soon before it hurt too much.

248

As the petrifying, darkness absorbed her entire body, she stopped feeling anything at all.

CHAPTER EIGHTEEN

'Han…nah!'

She couldn't move, didn't want to. Felt sick even at the thought of it.

She wasn't cold; Cold was a sapping wind on a drizzly cross-country run. Cold was waiting for a bus on a frosty December evening with throbbing fingers and a rosy nose. She was beyond cold, beyond even the idea of cold. She was at absolute zero; minus two hundred and seventy three degrees Celsius. Every molecule within her body ceasing to vibrate, ceasing to work, ceasing to be.

'Han…na-nah!' The chattering voice swirled distantly.

Maybe this was it. Maybe she'd reached her last chapter and turned the last page of her story.

'Han..nah!'

They were calling her name, guiding her home.

'Han-nah, o-pen y-y-your eyes...'

She twitched, eye straining against encrusted frost to prise itself half-open. A blurred spot of orange and yellow light seeped in, sharpening into a mesmerising flame. Behind it, two tiny reflections flickered in unison, her brain deciphering the faint outline of a cheek and nose into a face; a familiar face.

'You're a-live!' Alex trembled on a bed of black snow, his eyebrows and hair frosted with crystals of dark ice. As he spoke, the clouds of his breath instantly froze, falling sideways to the ground like a sprinkling of icing sugar.

250

'W-w-we're in t-t-trouble.' He gasped irregularly.

The flame flickered as it reached his fingertips.

'The fi-fig-ments. Han-nah-'

Energy spent, the flame performed a shrinking last dance, until even the faint red glow faded away.

'-t-think or we-we're...d-d-dead.' The desperation in his voice chilled her further.

She closed her eyes and groaned at the throbbing effort of thinking. She tired of the fight, the struggle to go on. They'd lost! It was much easier to wait for death and the loving embrace she missed so dearly. There she'd know love once more, there she'd know...

The darkness lifted in her mind like the clouds parting on a moonlit night. An obscured crowd of leering faces broke into her imagination and dispelled the picture of love she so craved. The toothless wretches closed on her like prisoners sizing up a new inmate. She got an electric shock as they pawed at her hair and tugged at her sleeves. She reared from the horrifying vision, anxious to escape, desperate for warmth.

Sand, hot sand.

She imagined something yellow but the Figments brushed it aside dismissively.

A dribble of ice-cold moisture ran down her neck like the trace of a stiff dead fingernail. Gritting her teeth, she resisted, her shoulders shaking uncontrollably as she willed her imagination to break free.

'No!' She screamed, panic riding a wall of death around the inside of her skull.

251

She chastised herself, renewing her concentration on hot sand between her toes, picturing the beach and sea from her holidays to Scarborough, holding it in place and forcing it wider until she could step into it.

Two frozen hands firmly clasped her cheeks, causing her to gasp and struggle for breath. Yet, after the initial shock, she felt a bead of water trickle over her cheek.

The Figments were growing desperate!

She tore her tongue free from her frozen teeth and peeled apart her lips.

'No!' She gasped.

Her resolve brightened and she imagined herself somewhere hotter than the English seaside.

Her feet remained in the sand, the hot sun continued to shine, but the Grand Hotel and promenade faded away, taking with them the deckchairs, windbreaks and consistently tepid North Sea. Towering dunes grew around her, airborne sand whipped up by scorching winds. The dazzling sun grew ferociously hot, beating down from a cloudless topaz sky, a sky too blue to be real. The clawing hands and leering faces retreated, her shivering slowing until she sank into a slump of deep misery. The blood rushed into her extremities; her legs burning with pins and needles, her arms readying to explode.

Her temples throbbed as she fought hard to keep those dunes in her brain, her shoulder sinking a few centimetres into the sand. When she could bare it no longer, she opened her eyes wide and gasped in the searing air. The heat on her skin never felt so good, like a roaring fire after a prolonged walk in the snow. She rolled over

252

to bathe in its rays like a basking lizard, her eyes falling onto the unmoving body sprawled next to her.

'Alex.' She croaked.

She lay drained, her mind still muddled as if she'd been woken from a deep sleep.

'Alex!' She tried again a little louder.

With some effort, she reached a hand out and clawed herself stiffly towards his still body. Slithering and groaning at uncooperative muscles, she crawled across to his back and stopped. She wanted to touch him, to shake him and rouse him from his slumber, but a large part of her preferred not knowing. With a cold feeling no sun could dispel, she tentatively gave his back a nudge.

'Alex.' He didn't respond.

She pulled at his freezing cold shoulder and he flopped limply onto his back. He lay motionless, his pale face looking at peace; lips a blue-purple colour, eyes closed and brows frosted. She prodded him but he only rocked passively.

'Alex! Alex!'

She nudged him again, his body swaying loosely as she jolted his arm with ever more urgent pushes and prods.

He'd gone, she'd lost him.

She kept shouting his name as the tears blurred her vision. She shoved him with both hands and screamed at him, punching him on the arm until she'd no more energy and collapsed sobbing on his chest.

They always leave you.

253

She'd only just found him again and now he'd gone forever. She cried for Alex but mostly she cried for herself. Whenever she cared about someone, she lost them, whenever she believed in someone they disappeared.

She wasn't a curse, she wasn't!

A noise lifted her gaze.

'Alex?'

He sniffed, his nostrils flaring.

'Alex?' She wiped her nose with a finger and blinked away her blurry eyes.

He murmured, twitched and looked up at her groggily, a grimace on his face.

'Alex, you're alive! I thought... Oh Alex!' She hugged him tightly, his moans of resistance temporarily ignored.

He coughed and grimaced again as she laid him back down.

'Feel...tingly.'

'I had that, pins and needles? Oh Alex I was so worried. Are you sure you're alright?'

'Yes...I'm fine.' He rolled away from her, leaned on his elbow and vomited all over the sand.

Hannah wrinkled her nose at the noise and smell, rubbing his back at arm's length. Alex rolled back around, wiping his mouth on his sleeve as the colour returned to his cheeks.

'Better?'

'A little, thanks.'

'Tingling gone?'

He nodded, but winced, rubbing his bicep. 'Arm still hurts somewhat.'

Hannah licked her dry lips and swallowed. 'Parting present from the Figments, I'd imagine.'

'Yes, I guess.' He grimaced as he flexed it.

Hannah sheepishly got to her feet.

'Don't worry about the details, you're alright that's all that matters.'

'Hmmm.'

She offered him a hand and hauled him up, dusting the sand from her jacket and jeans.

He copied her, wincing whenever he bent his elbow. When he stopped abruptly, Hannah wished he'd gone on grumbling.

'They're back, aren't they?' She groaned without turning around.

He nodded and her shoulders sagged.

'Don't they ever take time off for bad behaviour?'

An army of black scorpions, snakes and scarab beetles came over the next dune and scurried down into the gulley.

'Run?' She asked wearily.

'Not sure I can. See if you can see the punch-hole light from the top?' Alex nodded upwards.

Hannah lurched into an awkward stagger up the clogging sands of the desert, sinking in with every step, the heat toasting her feet. Two high dunes rose on either side as she trudged up the sloping gully between them. With each step forward, the dune gave way beneath her feet. Over her shoulder, Alex swatted

255

unenthusiastically with a cricket bat, leaning jadedly on the handle between great swipes at the encroaching mob.

The dry air seared her lungs, the sweat trickling over her ribs and dribbling down the back of her calves. Her feet slipped and sank, every step pushing more sand down than lifting her up. She ploughed on, pumping her arms hard but after two painful minutes she dropped to her knees exhausted and slid back to Alex's side.

He winced at her lack of progress.

'Alex, it's too hot.' She panted, her brow glistening. 'I can't do it.'

He bashed away a pair of scarab beetles the size of Hannah's head and after a strained moment handed her a pale blue ice bag and a khaki flask.

'You're only hot because you expect to be.'

She let those words sink in for a moment and realised she still had a lot to learn. This stray thought startled her more. She didn't want to learn, she wanted to get out and go home.

Didn't she?

Quick to want a distraction, she stared at the open rim of the flask and peered into its depths, Alex jabbing at scurrying scorpions, their stings quivering.

'What's in the flask?' She asked after a reflective moment.

'What do you want it to be?' Alex volleyed the question back at her.

She blinked hard and tilted her head back, an endless ice-cold stream of cloudy lemonade flowing into her mouth. She glugged back great mouthfuls, feeling it soothe down through her like nectar. She wiped her lips with the back of her hand

and soothed her flushed face and clammy neck with the ice-bag. Screwing the cap back on the cloth-covered flask, warm sand pushed on her shins and she realised she'd sank slightly into the dune.

Alex noted she stood a little shorter, his eyes narrowing as a thought morphed into a rueful decision.

'Alex?'

'Do you trust me, Hannah?'

She stopped tugging at her legs and didn't know how to answer.

'Snake.' She muttered with a gentle nod of her head.

'Huh?' He frowned.

'Snake!' She pointed.

Alex swatted a hooded viper as it reared up ready to strike, knocking it over the top of the nearest dune. He looked back at her as she tried to lift her foot out of the sand. 'Just stand perfectly still.'

She stopped and swallowed, the sand soon devouring her knees. Alex sighed and returned to his innings. She looked from him to the sand trickling serenely up her trapped legs.

'This was quicksand!' The thought came like an unexpected camera flash.

'I trust him. Do I trust him?' She murmured to herself but nonetheless she kept still.

Part fascinated, part horrified, she passively watched the grains of sand cover her stomach. Only when it reached her ribs and she realised she was being buried alive did panic edge out her trust.

257

'Alex?' She tried, chest tight, the warm sand trapping her elbows.

'Alex!' She croaked but he kept on swatting away tarantulas and scorpions without a care.

If it was Alex?

The terrifying notion came at her out of nowhere, paranoid questions exploding in her mind like fireworks.

What if they weren't Alex's eyes behind the glowing match?

She kicked her trapped legs and thrashed her arms but only succeeded in speeding her descent into the dune.

What if Alex had already joined the Figments?

What if the Word in front of her was an impostor, a figment of *her* imagination?

The questions swarmed around her like angry bees.

She tried to shout to Alex for help but the searing pressure on her chest and throat became too much for her to yell. Her chin touched the sand and she strained desperately to lift it higher. As if hearing the anguished cry from her soul, he looked down at her.

'Take one last breath Hannah! I'll be right behind-'

She missed the last of the sentence as she leaned her head back, sucked as great a lungful of air as she could, scrunched her eyes tight shut and sank beneath the ground.

Once more, darkness enveloped her.

Holding her breath and a silent prayer, she endured the rough sand scouring her face and seeping into her ears, filling her head with a sharp rumbling hum.

'I'm drowning,' she thought, 'drowning *in* dry land.'

She sank helplessly into the dune, unable to move. The back of her throat burned, her head shaking as she burrowed deeper, now more plunging than sinking. Her lungs moved from suggesting to urging and on to desperate pleading for oxygen. Her temples pulsed, her throat tightened, her jaw aching with the strain of keeping her mouth shut.

As her desperation grew to a muted scream, the pressure reduced on her arms and legs, the column of sand pushing her down, falling like a barrel swept over Niagara Falls.

She hit the ground, hard.

Sky, sand, sky, sand, sky, sand, sky sand.

The world became two blurred colours as she tumbled down a steep slope. Soft impacts came on every side of her body until a clawed hand caught in the soft dune. Twisting and flipping one last time, she slid over a couple of small bumpy ridges and slowed to a stop, her feet half-buried and her clothes full of sand. She hacked and spluttered, retched and spat, coughing up half a desert from her parched throat.

Blindly stretching out her heavy right hand, she imagined the strap of Alex's flask. Hauling it towards her and unscrewing the cap, she poured the cool mountain spring water over her head and dusty face, the whistling in her ears changing to a dull crackle. She washed her bloodshot eyes in the inexhaustible stream until she could tease them open and look fuzzily at the world around her.

The fragile bumps of sand shifted beneath her feet and she leaned back nervously. The steep dune stretched alarmingly out into nothingness on three sides, tiny grains still bumping and slithering down the slope. It was as if she sat on a gigantic piece of sandpaper stretched about twenty degrees from vertical.

'Aaaaaaarrrrrgggghhh!'

She cautiously plunged her hand deep into the sand and swivelled around to see Alex re-enact the same dizzying descent she'd just endured. He tumbled and slithered down the slope, cautiously crabbing and rolling his way across to her as he gained control. Coughing once, he lifted the ski mask from his grimacing face.

'Why didn't you tell me I needed one of them?' She said, still dabbing at her stinging eyes.

'I only thought of it when you'd gone.' He sneezed and managed a weak smile. 'How are you doing?'

'I'm alive, or thereabouts.' She coughed into a pained smirk.

Alex vigorously rubbed the sand from his hair, thick wooden runners and a blue rope materialising at his feet.

'Any chance this'll work?'

'Probably not.' He straddled the wooden sledge. 'Coming anyway?'

A roar turned her head, the tumbling column of sand morphing into a swirling whirlwind snaking its way down the dune towards them.

'You know, I'm beginning to think we're not welcome.' She sighed as she sat behind Alex.

He chuckled and pointed the sledge diagonally across the slope. She leaned into his back and wrapped her arms around his waist, his stomach muscles tensing beneath her arms.

'Don't be getting any funny ideas either!' She yelled.

The sledge rapidly picked up speed, more so as Alex dug a heel in the soft sand and they turned directly down the slope. Pressed into his back, Hannah rested her head and watched with one eye, as the slow twister shot back up the mighty dune.

She closed her eyes and clung on, strangely wishing her life were more like the Marginlands. The Figments were rather trying, not to mention life threatening, but they did simplify things. They forced her to live in the present, the past erased behind them, the future a blank canvas. Here, in the Marginlands she was more alive than ever before.

Subtly the slope evened out from mountain to hill and from hillock to gentle slope, but their speed remained frighteningly high.

'Hang on!' Alex shouted redundantly.

Hannah raised a squinting eye over Alex's shoulder to see the front becoming more cockpit-like with every second. Bodywork enveloped them on either side, a plastic bubble sweeping over their heads to become more like a jet fighter bobsled than a child's toy. Ahead of them, a thick wall of glass reaching to the heavens sped towards them, reflecting the vision of their swift approach.

'Brace yourself.' Alex shouted.

'You're not...' She said before burying herself in his back and tightening her grip.

The sled jolted as the metal nose cone punched its way through the thick glass, her head jarring against his back. Skidding on into the darkness, Hannah dizzily looked back through the plastic canopy, the cracks shooting up the glass wall like frozen lightning bolts.

They skidded away over a shiny black surface, the restrictive darkness of the Marginlands disappearing for the first time.

Looking through the glass and up the slope to the streaming cascade of sand, she saw another inverted dune hovering above and her mouth fell open. Even as they sped away, it didn't get any smaller.

Pale shapes appeared sat on the ridges of sand. Nearer still, ghostly figures stood pressed against the glass. All watching them leave. They'd tried to convince her she was better off giving up, that freedom was a gift she didn't deserve. Yet she'd seen through their facade to the desperate, loneliness the Figments suffered here in a prison of imagination. No doubt they rarely saw visitors, let alone those who could challenge them. With no outlet for their collective creativity, it was little wonder they were all so angry.

Beneath her, the soft hush of the runners changed to a hard grating noise as they sparked across stone flagstones. They slowed, but she didn't avert her eyes, somehow knowing the gathered Figments were honouring her and Alex's bravery.

She didn't know why, but she was compelled to raise her hand to gently lift an imaginary hat and give the Figments in their colossal hourglass acknowledgement

262

of their efforts. Some strange kinship in their dignified respect between friend and foe touched her deeply and she didn't know why. Yet, she knew instantly she'd never share the moment with anyone else, not even Alex.

They crackled over the stone floor to a dusty-flagged circle, trickling over a faded chalk line towards a pair of oak doors in a granite archway. With a soft thud, they bumped into the two sparkling granite steps at its base.

As the sledge dematerialised around them, Alex did an impromptu victory lap around the circle as if he'd just won a title fight. Hannah chose to sit on the stone floor and remove her shoes and socks, forming a small pile of sand as she tipped them out and brushed between her toes.

'I told you we'd be fine, I told you, you didn't need to worry. I did it; I got us through the Marginlands safe and sound!' Alex smugly circled around her.

'*You*?!' Hannah snorted. 'You'd have been filling out Figment Induction forms and getting shown where the Marginlands lockers are right now if I hadn't seen through the lifebelt illusion.'

'Yes well, but my training as a Knight Watchman would have…..' Alex lowered his hands.

'Not to mention, my warming desert when we were about to get hypothermia!' She pulled her socks and shoes back on.

'Yes, of course but…'

'Or the four-poster bed I produced to land on. Or the toy I produced to distract the kitten.'

'Kitten?' Alex frowned.

263

She got back to her feet and gave her jacket and jeans a shake.

'Oh sorry yes, that was when you'd stumbled into that inky soup of yours.'

'Soup?'

'Yeah, that thick black broth that a somewhat depressed chef might label, Cream of Oblivion.'

Alex pulled a face and scratched at the floor with his shoes for a second or two, searching for a reply that wouldn't cause Hannah to snort derisorily or laugh wildly. After several seconds, he raised his chin and met her eyes.

'Ah yes, but who trained you?'

Hannah paused, stifling an ironic smile at Alex's riposte. Revelling in her unusual silence, she allowed him the swagger in his walk as he leapt up the steps. He was right; they'd reached the Punch Hole together, a team triumphant.

Hannah followed him, a shimmering wall of the thick syrupy blackness now sliding up to the perimeter of the circle. Alex turned the brass-ringed handle, opened the creaking door and disappeared inside. Hannah paused on the steps, an impish smile dancing across her lips.

She sidestepped to the white line surrounding the circle and cautiously shuffled a foot over it. A hand grenade skidded over the flagged floor towards her foot, followed by a second and third. She gritted her teeth and briefly closed her eyes before rushing back up the granite steps and closing the heavy door behind her.

CHAPTER NINETEEN

They emerged into an eerie hallway. Withered candles on two wagon-wheel chandeliers painted a weak glow onto the floating spider webs and dark wood-panelled walls. She followed Alex's footprints over the dusty floorboards into a spectacular hall festooned with displays of old weaponry. Sweeping fans of broadswords, pikes and axe-like halberds glinted on the right-hand wall. Circles of duelling pistols, muskets and blunderbusses gleamed on the panelling opposite.

Alex crossed her eye-line and decisively jabbed a button between two sets of doors. He was dragging an upholstered armchair from one of the walls when he lifted his gaze and stopped.

'What?' Hannah licked the chocolate ice cream cone in her fist.

He made to speak but simply shook his head and shoved the chair in front of the lift. After an indicative nod of the head, he returned for a second armchair. She sat as he dragged it across on noisy brass castors and slumped down next to her.

Alex leaned back, Hannah fidgeted, her eyes everywhere, silence temporary.

'What's that?' She pointed up at a tiny red pinprick of light.

'Looks like a lift.' Alex said without moving a muscle.

'You didn't even look!' Hannah said, realising belatedly she wasn't below a matt-black ceiling but staring up into a cavernous lift shaft.

'No need, we're out of the Marginlands now, I can give my imagination a well-earned rest.'

Hannah's curiosity had no such plans.

'Where are we exactly?'

'We're in the old Hunting Lodge.'

She glanced at the weapons.

'Hunting? In the Marginlands?' She licked a stray dribble of chocolate making a bid for freedom over her knuckles.

Alex nodded. 'Yes, after Raleigh's adventures, the Royals and English dignitaries used to come down here for their sport.'

Hannah stared blankly at the lift doors. It was no surprise the Figments attacked everyone within their midst when they'd been so mistreated. She wondered if they were hunted because they were dangerous or dangerous simply because they were hunted.

'They don't come down here any more though,' Alex continued, 'not since the Marginlands became part of the demilitarised zone.'

'The...what?'

'It acts as a no-man's land between Words like us...me...on the Definition floors and the archaic Words below in the Darkhive. I can't believe I've escaped from the Darkhive. Imagine George's face when he hears about this!'

Hannah crunched the last of her ice cream cone and wiped her fingers with a tissue.

'Escaped? I'd hardly say we're...Wait! The Royals came here? Does that mean we're near that Palace George mentioned?'

'Well...'

Hannah wasn't listening, her smile broadening.

'So, we get up to Bookingham Palace, find the Number Well and I get to go home?'

He nodded. 'That's...the general idea.'

She beamed, drawing her feet up beneath her and sinking deeper into the armchair. Her eye strayed up to the twinkling red light. 'What will you do after we get out Alex?'

'Don't worry about me, I'll just be happy to get you safely back up to Bramley-upon-Thames.'

Hannah's mind snagged on the harsh punishment her Grandmother would dream up after the police and her headmaster had been ushered out of Bluebell House.

Her brain whirred further. 'Will I be safe back in Bramley-upon-Thames?'

'I hope so.'

It wasn't exactly the answer she'd wanted.

'Am I in more danger now than I was before?'

He raised a hand to his brow and peered up at the red dot.

'Alex?'

Alex's tongue poked out between his lips. 'I wish the lift would hurry up and get here.'

Hannah narrowed her eyes. 'Alex?'

'You know, that's the trouble with lifts-'

'Alex, don't make me hug you again.'

He flinched, much to her amusement.

He sighed. 'Sometimes you ask questions, I can't answer, no matter how much I want to.'

Hannah narrowed her eyes. 'Secrets?'

He nodded reluctantly and drew a cross over his heart with his finger. 'Super-Secrets.'

The memory of their childish games almost a decade ago softened the feeling of mistrust. She knew he'd tell her if he could. 'What *can* you tell me?'

'I didn't know exactly why the Guardian wanted to meet with you, but I knew it must be important or I wouldn't have been asked.' He half-smiled. 'I didn't mind of course, although I was somewhat apprehensive.'

'You?'

'I haven't seen you in so many years,' he said coyly, 'Heartisans change more than Words.'

'Have I changed, Alex?'

'In some ways, less than I imagined, in other ways more than you'll ever know.'

Hannah narrowed her eyes but he avoided her gaze and patted his pockets.

'I just remembered, Major Word-Forms gave me a card... '

He pulled out paper fibres and pieces of hay.

'...told me he couldn't help much beyond getting us out of the Darkhive...'

He drew a handful of sand and a scrunched up muffin case from his back pocket.

'...He agreed getting you back to Pandemonia was the priority, but any return to Lexica for me afterwards may be impossible.'

'You mean with all those Author-tarian Guards and Feds?'

Alex nodded. 'All the Number-Wells will remain locked down, so I might find myself trapped up in Pandemonia. The Major gave me the card of someone who might be able to help me, name of Captain Of.'

'Sounds Russian.' Hannah mocked.

'No,' He sighed. 'Captain *Of.*'

'Captain of what?'

Alex paused. 'No, not Captain of what. That's his name, Captain Of. His name is Of and he's a Captain.' He had a second thought. 'Of what Captain Of is a Captain of or rather what Captain Of was a Captain of…I don't know.'

'I see.' Hannah lied.

'The Major hasn't heard from him since he retired to Pandemonia-'

'Wait, since when do Words retire?'

Alex dipped his fingers in his shirt pockets.

'Those at the top do. Important, frequently used Words like *The, And, Of, To* and *A* are huge departmental operations akin to big businesses in your world. These Captains of industry retire with gold-plated pensions to Pandemonia to enjoy the rest of their days in peace and quiet.'

He triumphantly drew a crumpled business card from his pocket, half-heartedly flattened it and handed it to Hannah.

Captain Of (Retired)

The last light in England.

Down BUT not out.

Telephone Number: Ex-Directory

Unexpected Guests unwelcome.

'Well he certainly sounds a friendly sort doesn't he?'

She flipped it over but the other side was as empty as Alex's expression.

Her lip curled. 'That's it?'

Alex winced but ignored her disdain. 'What do you make of it?'

Hannah read it again, eyes narrowing. The card just seemed illogical. Why'd someone so obviously frosty to visitors design a business card with no contact details on it? Let alone hand it out to people. If someone wanted to retire and hide away, they just did it, telling others about it somewhat defeated the object.

Unless.

Her thinking became audible.

'Unless it's a double bluff, in case the card falls into the wrong hands? Maybe it's all there if you only know how to read it.'

'Like a code?'

'Maybe. Maybe not.' She tapped the card on her chin and looked it over again.

'*Down BUT not out?* A bit full of himself too this Captain, isn't he?'

Alex plucked it back from her grasp with a withering look.

Hannah stifled a hearty yawn with an upturned fist and glimpsed the red light arriving at speed. The dark cube slowed and descended serenely behind the ornate doors in front of them. Alex got up as they opened, Hannah following him inside.

Numbered lights covered the walls of the lift from floor to ceiling, but seemingly in no apparent order; Number four sat next to eighty-six, number fifteen next to two-hundred-and-twelve. Alex brushed his hand over the wall, a sweep of numbers lighting up.

'Go on.' He said, catching her enquiring look.

She hesitantly jabbed a few numbers before sweeping her hand over the wall in a great streak. Mischievously pressing herself against the wall, she stepped back and admired the Hannah shape.

'That'll be enough.'

The doors closed and others opened behind her, Alex stepping out into a similar hall filled with antique weaponry.

'What the…?'

He beckoned her to follow.

She frowned and stepped out, the doors closing behind her.

'What's wrong with the lift?'

'It's not a lift, it's a Number Lock; it stops the Figments escaping into the rest of the English Language.'

'But you said it was a lift.'

'I said it *looked* like a lift.' Alex grinned, eyebrow raised.

Hannah narrowed her eyes, unamused.

271

With a whirring noise, the non-lift shot upwards at great speed, once again becoming a red dot in the blackness.

As she took in more wood panelling and fanned displays of arrows and leather shields, Alex touched her arm and pointed downwards.

Two sets of footprints in the grey dust lead across their path from the left.

'What-'

'Ssssh!' Alex brought his finger tight to his lips and pointed to the right.

He led her along a hallway into another dimly-lit room, the candle chandeliers casting shadows onto the eerie landscape of white dust sheets below.

'Alex,' she whispered in his ear, 'what are we doing?'

'Just listen.' He mouthed.

Her eyes grew more accustomed to the weak light, making out the shape of a grandfather clock against one wall and a tall cabinet against another. Card tables, chairs and wing-backed armchairs sat dotted around the room, a snooker table with green oil lamps in the far corner all cloaked but barely disguised. An enormous fireplace - taking up half of one wall - escaped hibernation, its mantelpiece ornately carved with stags, wild boar and rabbits.

'What?' Alex whispered.

'Huh?' Hannah turned to his enquiring expression.

'I thought you said something.'

Hannah shook her head, 'I thought it was you muttering?'

They exchanged a back-and-forth rally of restrained alarm.

As Alex pushed on towards the next doorway, Hannah gathered herself and tugged on his sleeve.

'Alex, why are we following the footprints?'

'That's what you do with footprints.'

Hannah sighed, too tired to fight such insightful Holmesian logic.

In the next room along, they found a large dining table with twenty chairs individually covered in dust sheets Protected paintings hung on the walls over draped cabinets and side tables. The whole place gave Hannah the creeps.

She crept another five steps along the hallway towards the next room before yanking on Alex's cuff again.

'What happens if we find the person making the footprints, still in their own footprints?'

He straightened and examined his surroundings, 'Hannah, you're right of course...'

She wished she could've recorded him saying that, but noted he hadn't stopped whispering.

'But the chances of them being here at the same time as us are so slim-'

'Aitchoo!'

'Bless you.' Alex followed the footprints around the covered dining table. 'so slim in fact, it's not worth worrying about.'

Hannah stood stock-still. 'Erm...Alex.'

'Yes...?'

'...that wasn't me that sneezed.'

Alex took four more paces around the table before dramatically sweeping round to her, the candle flames flickering in his wild eyes.

CHAPTER TWENTY

Scuttling back to her side, Alex guided her silently against the wall as if late for a firing squad.

'Are you sure you didn't sneeze?'

'Am I sure I didn't sneeze?' Hannah muttered incredulously. 'Are you sure your brain's safe in there on its own?'

Alex pulled a face and scanned the room.

Hannah's eyes darted from every shape and shadow, apprehensively sensing faces and subtle movement everywhere she wasn't looking.

'I think it came from back there.' She pointed down the hallway.

Alex eyed the room one last time before creeping back over their own footprints. Hannah followed, constantly peering over her shoulder, scalp tingling from unseen eyes. Her imagination - saviour in the Marginlands – now turned on her.

Re-emerging into the room full of armchairs, something stirred almost inaudibly. Hannah ducked behind Alex, not wanting to see who'd found them.

'Can't you keep still for a second?' A voice hissed.

'Itchy nose.' Another whispered.

'You're as stealthy as a cat in tap shoes! Keep quiet.'

'Sorry George.' The murmured name drawn out.

Hannah's shoulders fell, amusement wiping away all fear. She shrugged off Alex's cautious paranoia and strode over the squeaking boards towards the snooker table. Spying a door in the corner and a trail of footsteps, she turned to a pair of high-backed, winged armchairs facing each other over a small chess table, the ebony and ivory pieces thick with dust. She stifled a giggle and beckoned Alex across, pointing to the two pinstriped legs and a cane poking out from beneath one of the dust sheets

Alex shared her grin. 'If you two were any louder, the ghosts in here would go on strike!'

The armchair sprang to life, a beaming George Found living up to his name.

'Great Scott, they're here!' He jumped up, throwing the dust sheet over his head.

'Aldwyn my dear fellow!' He smoothed his hair before heartily pumping Alex's outstretched hand and patting him on the shoulder.

'Miss Lady Hannah!' He turned and shook her hand more daintily, still beaming excitedly. 'One is so glad to see young Aldwyn has kept you safe from harm all this time. Everyone was most worried.'

Alex at least had the dignity to look sheepish.

'Aitchoo!'

All three turned to Edward Lost battling his dust sheet like a street-fighting ghost. Hannah stifled another giggle as George lifted the sheet off the armchair with a heavy sigh. Edward Lost stood up abruptly, trying to regain his composure, even though his bowler hat sat at a jaunty angle.

276

'Yours I believe young lady…' George regained her attention.

Her mouth fell open as he held out her bag, watch and keys.

'…and these I believe Aldwyn, are yours.' He continued, jangling a larger bunch of keys in front of Alex.

'Thank you…but…?' Hannah murmured.

'I find things. It is what one does.' He smiled coyly as he smoothed his moustache.

'What are you doing here George?' Alex cut in, irritation barely masked.

'We are here to steal-' Edward began.

George laughed hysterically. 'We're...we're here to steal...here to *steel* ourselves for a long wait.' He gave himself a self-satisfied nod. 'A long wait now thankfully at a satisfactory conclusion.'

'But George, I thought you said-'

'Now now Edward, you remember what we agreed about you and thoughts.'

Edward paused, peering up into his furrowed brow as if a pondering how to get a kite out of a tree.

'You only get in each other's way?' George said.

'...get in each other's way.' Edward repeated.

'Precisely, besides look, you've dropped your hat again.' George plucked the bowler from Edward's head and threw it blindly across the room into a dark corner.

'Oh dear.' Edward mumbled, patting his head and moving off in the wrong direction.

'You are mean to him George.' Hannah chided.

277

George pretended he hadn't heard her.

Alex furrowed his brow. 'How could you know we'd be here?'

Hannah made to help Edward but her curiosity kept her in the conversation.

'The Guardian met with Major Word-Forms and-' George began.

'The Major escaped?' Alex clenched a triumphant fist.

'What about Convince and the rest?' Hannah asked.

George looked from one to the other, beaming at his importance. 'I believe the Major got out over the Causeway at night with three others, making contact with the Shrouded Guild once clear of the patrolling Author-tarian Guards. He got word to the Guardian of your proposed escape route and well, here we are.'

'What about Vince, Radders, Arty and the others?' Hannah asked more firmly, stepping into George's eye line.

'Who?' George frowned.

'The other prisoners from the Darkhive P.O.W camp.' Alex explained.

'I'm not sure.' He shook his head before catching Hannah's expression. '…but I'm certain they all got out just fine.'

'Yeah, of course.' Hannah lied, stepping aside.

She slumped down onto the arm of one of the armchairs, feeling the all too familiar ache. She'd only known Vince and the others so briefly, yet the thought of any of them being caught or worse was crushing. They'd selflessly helped her and protected her when she'd been at her most vulnerable, imagining Law and Order gleefully sending them for erasure was too much for her to contemplate.

George's voice filtered back into her thoughts.

'..feels terrible about what happened. The Guardian wanted to meet the pair of you and arrange the resumption of Hannah's personal protection, this time at Bluebell House...'

Alex looked at Hannah and they exchanged a slight grin.

'...distraught that the Guild's Intelligence only highlighted the dangers on the upper floors from the Author-tarian Guards, not from the Feds up in London. Had they known, the whole meeting would have been cancelled.'

Hannah shook her head, torn between knowing some strangers were trying to protect her and the thought of what they were trying to protect her from. She absentmindedly picked up a pawn from the chess set and blew the dust from its bulbous top.

'Hannah?'

She lifted her eyes to find George and Alex looking down at her.

'Can you show George the film you took?'

Hannah fumbled in her pocket and clicking on the right buttons handed her phone to Alex, the film illuminating George's face.

'*...They said to me, the Darkhive is a lawless island, a refuge of the abandoned and the insane.*'

'Bellwether!' George leaned forward on his cane, marvelling at the moving images of Bellwether on the podium, the GNP leader's voice slightly metallic and high-pitched from the tiny speakers.

She watched Alex's cheeks colour until he had to look away.

'The English Language has become weak in my absence, but I am not. I'm strong and pure and I'll make the English Language strong and pure again!'

George's eyes became mesmerised as he drank in Bellwether's words. Hannah dropped hers to the floor, wishing she could as easily ignore the bitter sound of his voice. The crackling sound of the Darkhivian's cheers returned the uneasy shudder she'd experienced in the glare of those floodlights.

'Out will go all those who stand in the way of progress! And out…of this Darkhive, you will all march!'

The film ended, releasing George's gaze from the screen as if a hypnotist had clicked their fingers. He blankly lifted his eyes.

'Bellwether's behind the colossal Darkhive breach? Blooming heck!'

'Ladies present!' A muted voice shouted from under a dust cover somewhere across the room.

'Quite, Edward, I do apologise Miss Lady Hannah.' George bowed humbly before blowing out his cheeks and giving his moustache a thorough grooming. 'It's just…Bellwether, in person, doing what we all feared he was doing…only worse.'

They stared, his expression changed, his voice lowered. 'Of course. You know even less than me. Some Words said he'd been seen in and around Wordminster, the Guild asked me to find any evidence, but no-one's talking and those witnesses were…nowhere to be found. There are also lots of strange Words hanging around in the lobbies and corridors, the Author-tarian Guards ignoring or dismissing any queries of their origin. I'd thought they were simply new Words or evacuees from one of our Annexes, but now…'

280

'Releasing all those Words is illegal isn't it?' Hannah said.

'By jove, it is utterly illegal! United Repositories of Lexica Law states Words must be released from Lingual Darkhives on an individual case-by-case basis. What he's doing while Prim and Proper sit in Wordminster is preposterous. If the L6 learnt of this, they'd have to take action against us!'

'I can't believe he thinks he can get himself elected by releasing illegals from prison, they can't even vote?!' Alex shook his head.

George's eyes slid onto Alex, his bemused scorn only partially hidden.

'No Aldwyn, my naive fellow, I think you misconstrue his intentions. Bellwether isn't calling for an election, he's not seeking votes or blackmailing favours, he's building a loyal army. He's not organising a repatriation of Darkhivians to the Definition floors, he's planning a violent and undoubtedly inky revolution.'

Alex twitched as George pushed the point home.

'Do you think this new underclass of Archaic Words will get a shake of the hand and a new office from the leaders? Or will they confront more modern Words and try to take their positions by force? All while the Author-tarian Guards abruptly decide they only need patrol around their staff canteen.'

Alex lifted his chin; lips tight, pride dented.

'We coped before with the breakout at the Slang Quarantine.'

'Yes Aldwyn,' George countered, almost sympathetically, 'but when all those abbreviations and mutants got loose, Wordminster managed to cover it up by inventing Text-speak. The Darkhive is thousands of times larger though and none of the Words are in common usage with the Heartisans.'

The mention of Heartisans wiped the glower from Hannah's face. She guiltily bit back the self-centred question on her tongue but George caught the look on her face.

'How'd you think Heartisans like Miss Lady Hannah here are going to cope with unreadable books, obsolete dictionaries and an internet corrupted by sentences not spoken for several hundred years?'

'We don't know that will happen!'

'Heck Aldwyn, it might have already happened! I've not been topside or back on the definition floors for some time...'

He paused only for a second, but his eyes betrayed him. Hannah realising he wasn't entirely down here just for them. Whatever George had found out had come at considerable cost and worse still, now he'd found them, he had no excuse to remain down here in hiding.

'We shouldn't jump to conclusions.' Alex said.

'No you are correct Aldwyn, but if the release of the Darkhivians starts a civil war within the English Language, the Heartisans will sure know about it!'

Hannah froze as the last loop of the blindfold slipped from her mind's eye.

All the Words in their Lexica wonderland weren't isolated at all. The Words down here weren't just representative of the English Language, they *were* the English Language. If Lexica tumbled into chaos, her world would inevitably

282

follow. She tried to grasp the result of all the Archaic Words flooding the English Language and replacing those she used every day.

'What would happen in my…in Pandemonia?'

'Words in Pandemonia are all linked back to their office here in Lexica. So if Words change here or the office is hijacked, the same words in emails, books and letters in Pandemonia are instantly updated or corrupted.'

Hannah's lip curled.

'I know it is hard for you Heartisans to get your head around Quantum Grammar: Participle physics, Parallel Wordy-verses and the like.' George said testily. 'Heartisans are always so sure they're in full control, but this is how Language has evolved in harmony with the Heartisans for hundreds of years. If we left it to *your* lot and the decades you spend *revising* dictionaries, well the Language would never get anywhere.'

'Manners George!' A muffled shout came from inside a cupboard across the room.

'Yes, don't take it out on Hannah.' Alex agreed sternly with Edward.

George sensed he'd overstepped the mark and backed down. 'I am sorry, that was uncalled for.'

'Hannah is not your everyday Heartisan.'

'No Aldwyn, quite right. I apologise profusely Miss Lady Hannah.' He bowed, a hand on his chest. 'I guess I'm still a little shaken at Bellwether in your moving picture box. I was only pointing out Heartisans are ill-prepared for such great changes. Forget a few humbugs bemoaning slipping standards of grammar, this'll

283

be a descent into an anarchic dark age, a time when no-one can communicate except in oral slang.'

Hannah's mouth went dry. 'So when I get back home I won't be able to read?'

'It won't be quite that quick, but you'll find yourself looking up more and more words in a dictionary. The internet will become corrupted and your favourite shows will sound more Dickensian and Shakespearian as Victorian and Medieval Words replace modern equivalents.'

Hannah was numb, not processing the chaos unleashed by such a wave of illiteracy. Even the news reporting it would be in a language no-one understood. Confusion and frustration would become the norm, everyone finding themselves in a foreign country. Education would become worthless, books unreadable. She shuddered at the vision of millions of 'corrupted' books piled-up and burned. Language dumbing down to street slang, pictograms and emojis.

Yet worse was to come.

'I am afraid there is a more alarming implication.' George said gravely.

Hannah wasn't sure she wanted to hear it.

'The French?'

George frowned across at Alex. 'The French?'

'Well, not just the French, equally the Spanish, Russians or Mandarins. With the English foundering, another Language could seize the opportunity to become the international Language of business and commerce. The French Language has hankered to put the English Language back in its place for over a thousand years.'

George looked at Alex as if a footballer had quoted Einstein's theory of relativity.

'Quite, yes,' he tried to recover his composure, 'I was...yes...well, I thought that went without saying.'

Hannah smirked at his discomfort before the thought of the western world solely speaking French or Mandarin crushed any amusement.

George twisted the knife further.

'No, I refer to a different Pandemonia problem. The Elders believe the recorded past of the Heartisans could become so distorted, it'd be all but lost. Using unscrupulous decipherers and translators, the most powerful in Pandemonian society could rewrite history for their own gains, the illiterate masses having to accept the words of the elite or suffer the consequences.'

Hannah frowned.

'Imagine if all the Laws had to be redrafted from scratch, what changes would creep in for someone's personal gain? Imagine all the subtle amendments made to records and deeds of who owns what? Tough to argue with paperwork stating someone else now owns your castle, horseless carriage, prize sow or wife. Chaos and anarchy would surely follow with a nervous government desperate to regain control, by any means.'

Hannah's thoughts tripped and stumbled. George wasn't talking of an outbreak of illiteracy he was talking of a bloody uprising in her world too. Hannah envisaged angry illiterates taking to the streets; making incomprehensible demands on indecipherable placards. She saw the descent into frustrated violence, burning barricades and petrol bombs; a pandemic of rioting and looting breaking out across every city as direct action spoke louder than garbled words.

She numbly went to help Edward, her emotions close to overflowing. Crossing to the snooker table without feeling the floorboards underfoot, she lifted its dust sheet and found Edward peering dimly across the green baize from the other end.

'Hello Miss Hannah.' He beamed.

'Have you found your hat Edward?'

Edward patted his balding pate and shook his head.

'Come on, I'll help you.' Hannah guided him into the corner where George had thrown it, finding the hat under the third chair she checked.

'Ah! Thank you Miss Hannah!' Edward grinned, brushing the crown of the bowler with his sleeve and placing it firmly back on his head.

'Very smart.' Hannah managed to smile back, picking a hair from the brim and wishing she had an equally simple view of life.

They returned to George and Alex deep in conversation.

'.. the private Royal lift through in the weapons room. It connects directly up to the Glossary, Wordminster and the Contents terminal, but more importantly it stops at Bookingham Palace.' George said.

'Are you not coming with us George?' Hannah asked.

Guilt flared across his face. 'Ah well, of course we'd love to, but we have to...erm... finish off down here and you know...'

'Oh yes?' Alex smirked.

George smiled uneasily. 'Well, yes...you know me Aldwyn.'

Hannah looked towards Edward, awkward at George's facade and Alex's obliviousness.

He straightened. 'I mean as long as you don't meet any more Guards, Aldwyn-'

'Author-tarian Guards, P.O.W Camp Guards, Blondeshirts, Figments; I've seen them all off George!'

'He's extremely brave you know.' She said.

George's eyes flicked to hers, widening as she tried to say all she could without uttering a word. His expression narrowed and for the briefest of seconds he looked bullied.

'Oh yes, that's right.' Edward nodded eagerly.

George twitched, eyes unmoving.

'You said as much the other day to the Guardian, did you not George?'

He turned an inch and seemed to power back up.

'Yes, thank you Edward.' George forced a beaming smile, cheeks colouring.

'"Don't worry," he says, "Aldwyn's the bravest Nouner I know."'

'Yes I did, thank you Edward.' George said through clenched teeth.

'And you said-'

'Yes, *thank you* Edward.' George reached for Edward's hat but catching Hannah's glare, stopped himself and gripped his cane tightly instead, tapping it stiffly on the floor.

Hannah ached, wishing so much was different.

'Where do we go in the Palace?' Alex asked, his grin out of place.

'Well,' George rocked awkwardly on his heels, unable to meet Alex's eyes, 'the entrance to the Number-Well is supposed to be in the Narcissus Temple in the disused west wing.'

'*Supposed* to be?' Hannah leapt on his words. 'You mean you don't know?'

George almost looked offended. 'Me, trespass on Royal property?'

Hannah glanced around at the mothballed Hunting Lodge and back at George.

'Oh no, we wouldn't do that.' He said obliviously. 'Do you know what the Author-tarian Guards do with trespassers?'

Hannah bit back her reaction, her empathy and sympathy slipping as the real George shone through this tired and broken shell.

'No, we've never been in the Palace.' Edward said stiffly.

'See.' George smiled nervously.

'We wouldn't go in the unused rooms.'

'Agreed, but that's enough now, Edward.'

'No, we've never been there at night looking through the pretty things.'

'Ha ha ha, quiet now Edward,' George grinned forcedly, 'before Mr Cane has an emergency meeting with Mr Bonce.'

Edward's eyes widened and he ducked his head into his shoulders, cautiously gripping the brim of his bowler hat with both hands.

George looked at Alex's questioning face and decided denial would be fooling nobody.

'Alright, we did go in once, but it was only through intrigue at the old Narcissus legend. It is quite an interesting story actually, about Princess Eve.'

He smiled at Hannah as if he knew all little girls liked Princesses. Hannah glared, fighting the desire to kick this version of George in the shins.

'Oh I like this one.' Edward grinned.

Alex cut in. 'I think I've heard of her, didn't she disappear without a trace?'

George glared at him as if he'd just given away the punch-line to his best joke.

'Yes, back in the late 18th century there was a young inquisitive Princess called Eve who spent much of her spare time reading in the Great Library, walking in the grounds and exploring the hundreds of unused rooms around the Palace. Escaping the formal protocols of the Royal court and the overbearing strictness of her Governess, she hid herself away from the world in the west wing.'

Hannah's curiosity stirred.

'One morning, two days after her sixteenth birthday, her Lady-in-Writing found Princess Eve's bedroom empty, her bed unused. Alarm raised, Queen Literate organised all the court officials into an extensive search for her. Soon the servants and Palace Guards were looking too, all over the Palace and its luxurious gardens. Three days passed, but they found no trace of her anywhere across the English Language. There was no evidence she'd run away from home, no evidence of kidnap. She'd just disappeared.'

'What happened?' Hannah asked.

George tweaked his moustache.

'Nobody truly knows. The only clue they found at the time was in her diary from the night before she disappeared: *Curse of Narcissus: 8*'

Alex looked blank. 'Narcissus Temple? Curse of Narcissus?'

289

Hannah turned to him. 'Narcissus was a hunter in Greek mythology who fell in love with his reflection and died because he couldn't bear to leave it. I don't know what the *8* means though.'

'Ah.' Alex nodded.

'Queen Literate mourned the loss of her daughter by wearing black for the rest of her life, always waiting for her daughter to return.'

'Did she?' Hannah asked eagerly.

'No.' George half-smiled enjoying her captivation. 'She was never seen again. However, there is a footnote to the story. When they renovated the west wing at the beginning of the nineteenth century, workers discovered a secret entrance to a Mirrored Words room in the Narcissus Temple.'

'What was inside?' Hannah said.

'Inside they found a set of strange mirrors and a bizarre puzzle no-one could understand.' He reached inside his coat. 'Yet, amidst the thick dust on the floor they found this green enamel fountain pen, inscribed with Eve's name.'

Hannah gasped at the beautifully slender pen; an ornate lattice of silver gleaming over a glimmering green body. Her curiosity whirred. 'She was there!'

'How come you've got...?'

'Yes Miss Lady Hannah.' George ignored Alex's awkward question, the pen disappearing as quick as it appeared. 'She was there.'

Alex sighed heavily. 'So, this Mirrored Words room is where you think the Number Well is hidden?'

George shrugged, a knowing smile on his face.

Hannah's shoulders sank, her simple escape becoming more complicated by the second.

'Did the Workmen search for an exit?'

George thought for a second and held her gaze. 'Unfortunately, Queen Literate – perhaps reflecting on the tragedy - chose to hide all poisonous reminders of that day. All details of any secret entrance are maddeningly buried along with Eve's name.'

'A secret Number Well from a fanciful legend?! George, have you any idea what we've been through?' Alex fumed.

George feigned mock surprise.

Hannah touched Alex on the arm and shook her head. Cheeks colouring, he kept his lips tight.

'Where do we find this Narcissus Temple?' Hannah asked.

'I don't know exactly, somewhere at the far end of the west wing I'm told. Probably on the second floor, beyond the Gemstone rooms at the far end of the Long Gallery.' He paused, realising he'd been more specific than he'd intended. 'I imagine, so I've heard.'

'Right.' Hannah said. 'We'll find it.'

Alex stared blankly at the floor and ground his teeth.

George placed his hat firmly onto his head and tapped his cane twice. 'Yes well, you'll want to get going. Come along Edward!'

Back in the Weaponry room, George tapped his foot as he waited for the hidden lift doors to slide open.

'This is an express lift, it will take you up to the Palace in next to no time.'

'Right.' Alex muttered.

George shook his hand. 'Take care Aldwyn, keep up the good work.'

Alex nodded stiffly and as the doors opened, stepped into the brightly-lit lift.

'Goodbye Aldwyn, goodbye Miss Hannah. Thanks for finding my hat, I'm always losing it.' Edward bowed and gently shook her hand, his hat falling to the floor by his feet.

'Goodbye Edward, you're welcome.' Hannah returned it to him before turning to George.

'Farewell Miss Lady Hannah.' George bowed.

'Goodbye George. Take care of Edward. And yourself.'

'Of course. You too.'

Hannah half-turned in the lift doorway. She moved her hand to her thigh and turned back to George. Without a word, she held out her upturned hand.

George tried a puzzled frown, but Hannah batted it away with a raised eyebrow. He tentatively licked his lips before sheepishly lifting his hat.

He reached inside and placed Hannah's phone back into her hand. She gave him a withering look of disappointment her Grandmother would have approved with a sniff and stepped inside the lift.

CHAPTER TWENTY-ONE

Draped comfortably across a plush burgundy chaise longue, Hannah spent a long time clutching her phone, George's words circling around her head. Alex sat solemnly close by in one of twenty brown-leather Club chairs. With Persian rugs, oil paintings of old racehorses and a cocktail bar in the corner, their surroundings more resembled a small Gentleman's club than a lift.

She glanced above the lift doors, still disappointed to find it wouldn't speak to her. The golden needle sedately revolved from *Hunting Lodge* on the right to *Palace* on the left, itself one notch up from *Contents*. Hannah drummed her fingers and invaded the silence.

'I'm not sure we should've told George about the Bellwether film.'

'Mmmm.' Alex murmured.

Hannah thought about telling him more but knew it'd only add fuel to his dark mood. She could now see how George worked, his charm and wit an engaging front for his sticky fingers and manipulative nature.

'Do you believe what George said down there?'

'George?' Alex sagged. 'He's annoying and arrogant, but he's not a liar. If he thinks there's going to be a revolution, we should prepare for the worse.'

Hannah gritted her teeth and eyed the golden needle, its movements as surreptitious as the minute hand on a classroom clock.

She blew out her cheeks and fanned her flushed face with her hand. Unwinding the pink and lemon gypsy scarf from around her neck, her restless eyes settled back on her phone.

'What are we going to do with this?'

Alex leaned forwards. 'The film? I'll have to get it to the Shrouded Guild, somehow. The Elders will know what to do with it, maybe a hacked broadcast to every office over the Imperial network, maybe copies sent to the leaders of the U.R.L council. What good it'll do, I don't know.'

He looked tired, worn down by the enormity of the last few days and the responsibility the pair of them bore on naive shoulders.

'Lets' just hope I can get it to them in time.'

They shared a moment of grief for their own worlds, their own thoughts both at once mutual and selfish.

Hannah saw the darkness in his face and tilted her head reassuringly. 'If you can put up with me through the Darkhive and Marginlands Alex, you can do anything, right?'

Alex half-smiled at her and Hannah beamed back, he was an idiot sometimes, but he was her idiot.

Forty restful minutes passed until the lift slowed and she moved expectantly with Alex to the doors. It stopped with a judder and the muffled chime of a bell as the doors opened. They stepped cautiously out onto a lush red carpet, their long shadows thrown onto the portraits lining an olive green wall opposite. The bell chimed again and the lift doors slid shut, erasing their silhouettes and leaving them in the gloom.

Hannah waited for her eyes to adjust, the darkness receding to grey shapes and blurred outlines. On her right, tall doors and two sets of round windows looked out onto a gravel driveway; silvered lawns on either side punctuated by white marble statues and manicured hedges. A landing and four tall Georgian windows bridged the front door, muted moonlight keeping it all deep in shadows. On her left, two sweeping staircases curved elegantly up to a mezzanine lined with busts, more paintings and several tall, imposing doorways.

Over their heads, four crystal chandeliers hung like sparkling champagne held in invisible glasses. Even in the faint silvery light straying in through the windows, they sparkled and gleamed, their giant size making Hannah too nervous to stand beneath them. As her eyes adjusted to more form and detail, she speculated this was perhaps the grandest and most opulent room she'd ever seen, making Bluebell House look like a budget doll's house in comparison.

'Wow.' Alex understated.

Hannah shuffled after him, her raised eyes making out figures in the frescoes and golden cherubs amidst the plasterwork. Every part of her soul wanted to turn on the lights and drink in its full glory, almost as if the room realised it had visitors and wanted to show itself off.

The brightening moonlight bounced off the chandeliers and glittered across the ceiling, the pair of them spellbound as if fairies swirled amongst one another.

'What are those?'

Alex didn't answer.

The lights grew in strength, shining bright like dappled lunar light twinkling through swaying trees. A more familiar crunching noise pulled her gaze back to earth.

Shining lights came over the lawn and up the driveway, swinging in the hands of shadowy figures.

'Alex!'

She backed away a couple of strides and bolted for the stairs, leaping up the shallow treads three at a time.

'Go left.' Alex said breathily, catching up with her as the steps split and curved away onto the landing.

The lights outside grew stronger, joined by the clatter of boots on stone steps and the metallic smash and curse of dropped keys. The faltering moonlight cleared the clouds and streamed starkly through the windows above the front entrance, casting slanting rectangles of light onto the red carpet below.

'Keys!' Hannah hissed to Alex, nodding to one of the closed doors.

He shook his head and sped away in a crouch, keeping close to the cabinets and chairs by the walls. Glimpsing between the balusters of the wooden balustrade, Hannah saw the windows downstairs go dark as shadows pressed against the glass, their hands clamped around their eyes.

A key rattled and jarred in the lock, until reluctantly withdrawn.

Hannah scampered after Alex, joining him around the corner at the end of the landing.

More muffled curses and a further rattling of keys preceded the lock turning, letting all the noise inside.

'...inside five minutes ago! Get your act together Prepositioner or you'll be replaced!' A familiar voice chastised, his disdain tangible.

The room filled with light, the chandeliers sparkling brilliantly and making Hannah squint.

'I say, steady on. Alan is doing his best, what?'

'Colonel Etiquette, for the last time this is not an armed jamboree. Security isn't about doing one's best!'

'I say, that's rather strong.' The Colonel muttered.

'There, there's the lift. It set off my alarm.'

'Yes, I know what a lift looks like Prepositioner. Brute, Hooligan, go check it out.'

'I must have the names of its occupants, I simply must, Rule 14.8 clearly-'

There was a whacking noise, a brief yelp and a calamitous smash filled the cavernous room.

An angry silence followed, only punctuated by a whimper, porcelain broken underfoot and scurried footsteps running down the steps outside.

'I say, I'm not sure that was called for-'

Hannah caught her first whiff of smouldering tobacco, the aroma triggering a dark memory, her stomach tightening like a wrung out mop.

'Listen to me Colonel, let me make this absolutely clear. You're not in charge any more You and your Palace Guards come under the command of *my* Words. I'm the Law round here now!'

'I say...' The Colonel exclaimed before meekly adding. 'That seems quite reasonable.'

'Boss!'

'What do you have there Hooligan?'

'A scarf boss, found it in the lift boss.'

Hannah brought a hand sharply to her bare neck, a jolt of panic shooting through her body.

'I've seen this...somewhere, where have I seen this before?'

Alex's eyes bored into her cheek.

Doors clicked open and several scurrying footsteps rushed onto the landing, followed by the sharp creak of a door thrown wide open.

'Cyril, what in all of Lexica is this hullaballoo about?' The voice shouted from off to their left, on the other side of the first floor landing.

Hannah's muscles turned to lead.

'Bellwether.' Alex winced, peeking one eye around the corner. 'And several Blondeshirts.'

'Sorry to disturb you my leader. The Prepositioner clumsily knocked over one of the vases.'

'For crying out loud! After all I've done for the English Language in the last few months; bureaucracy smashed, economy emboldened, rivals fearful...you'd think I could get some peace and quiet!'

'Humbly sorry my leader!' The Colonel chimed.

Bellwether simmered, shaking his head as he glared about him.

'I...It was-' The Colonel blustered.

Bellwether gripped the dark balustrade before flinging a silencing arm aloft. A single finger pointed to a large garish painting behind him on the wall. 'Does this mean nothing to you? The power of Words, the power of control, the power of change.'

Hannah ducked and shifted her weight, leaning out to take in the masterly painting of a scholar at his desk, studying a book, hand resting on two more. It looked vaguely like Bellwether, but the paint on the face was fresher and lighter than the rest as if overpainted by another artist.

'Han!' Alex hissed drawing Hannah back to cover.

'May I remind all of you, our enemies are everywhere. It's not just the Latin and English assassins you need to expect.'

'I am sorry my leader.'

'Well! Why are you all here, sneaking around in the middle of the night?!'

'I say, there was a faulty lift alarm.'

Alex clicked his finger and motioned for Hannah to get up and get moving.

'One second.' She mouthed as he nodded behind him down the dark corridor.

'Be quiet Colonel!' CC Law's voice echoed noisily around the hall, reverberating in the crystal chandeliers. 'My Leader, there are smugglers in the Palace.'

'More smugglers...Or more assassins?! I brought you and your Guards here to stop this kind of nonsense!'

'Sorry, my leader.'

'Cyril, what are you hiding behind your back?'

'Oh nothing...just some lost property left in the lift-'

Alex pinched her arm but Hannah pulled away, closer to the corner, swallowing hard at the sight of the Blondeshirts' rifles pointing down into the hallway. Bellwether clicked his fingers, an Author-tarian Guard scrambling up the steps towards him with her scarf. He snatched it from him, rubbing it between his fingers and holding it up to the light.

'This is the work of Figments. A crude imagining of a Pandemonian weave...' Bellwether stared fiercely down to the floor below.

'I...It...couldn't-' Law blurted desperately.

'How can Figment-made...?'

'I don't know... My Leader.'

'Wait...that bothersome pair from the Darkhive, what were their names...the trespassing girl and her guide!' Bellwether fumed.

'It couldn't...I executed them personally.'

'Personally? You did, did you?' Bellwether growled.

Law's voice crumbled, his bluster a high-pitched croak. 'As good as! I chased them into the Marginlands, nobody could survive that!'

'And yet, the girl's Figment-made scarf turns up within metres of my bedroom?'

'My Leader, if Reginald Order had done his job-'

Bellwether snatched up a marble bust in his huge hands and hurled it angrily off the landing. The thudding down the steps and crumpled smash at the bottom turned Hannah's fear up several notches.

'She may look like a weak and feeble Heartisan but she's a dangerous rebel and she's here, in my home. Bring her to me immediately Cyril, or bring me your resignation!'

'Sorry...my...Leader.'

With unfeeling limbs, Hannah turned away from the corner, the zips on her bag scraping against the wall.

'Who's there!' Bellwether rasped.

Hannah winced.

Alex snarled and dragged her away as hurried footsteps thudded across the entrance hall below.

'Immediately Cyril, and don't spare their ink!'

'Yes my leader.' Law said respectfully before screeching. 'Don't just stand there Colonel! Empty the barracks. My Guards, the Blondeshirts, even your pathetic sentries; get them all in here now!'

The voices disappeared when Alex led her into a dark reception room and quietly pulled the door shut behind them. He ran straight for the grey doorway on the far side, Hannah following, her mind racing with guilt.

Through the doorway they bumbled, eyes adjusting enough to make out heavily laden bookshelves and the dark rectangular shape of a desk, everything a shade of grey. On they went through two more studies and a lavish sitting room, never pausing longer than locating the next exit. Passing through a set of gilded double doors, Alex closed and locked them before his head slumped on his arm.

'The scarf...the bag...I'm so sorry Alex.'

Alex didn't move.

'It was an accident. I'm sorry. Alex?'

He wearily pushed himself off the door and grabbed an ornate wooden chair, wedging it under the doorknobs.

'We should keep moving. These doors are thick and sturdy but they'll only slow the Guards by a few minutes.'

'How did CC Law get here so soon? And what's Bellwether doing here?'

'I don't know. Getting you to that Number Well, that's all that matters now.'

Hannah wanted to argue, but Alex stomped away without looking back.

'I loved that scarf too.' Hannah muttered, hand absent-mindedly rubbing her bare neck.

Ten minutes of stately hallways, grand staircases, painted ceilings and several more locked and barricaded doors later, Hannah broke the silence, if not the tension.

'Is this the Long Gallery George mentioned?' She asked Alex.

'I guess.'

Hannah followed him along the creaking floor, lines of moonlight spilling from the shuttered windows and illuminating the lines from Shakespeare hand-painted along the edges of the floorboards. Curves of fine porcelain caught the light, painted faces looking disapprovingly down on them from golden frames.

'Stop dallying. We'll...' Alex stopped.

He dallied, transfixed by a glint of green through a doorway. Gleaming in the weak light from her phone, the pair of them headed for it like moths to a lamp. Prodding the door open, they stared in on a bewitching sight. A dark green crystal-like stone carved into the shapes of animals and plants covered the walls of the small room. The different shades and textures glinted wondrously, rendering both of them speechless.

Alex stepped closer to the wall, running his hand over the fine details of a soaring eagle.

'It's Jade, I think.'

Hannah slumped down on a circular, green velvet seat in the centre of the room. She'd never seen anything so beautiful, so perfect and so impossible. The Jade was flawless, almost translucent, every inch of the room full of mesmerising detail from the bark of an oak to the curled fronds of a fern, from the wing-feathers of an owl to the whiskers of a mouse. She sat spellbound, the wonder of it lifting her spirits.

A bright flash and shutter noise from her phone broke the spell for Alex.

'No, no, we can't stop here. We have to keep moving, have to find that Number Well before the Guards catch us up.'

He averted his eyes from the walls and frogmarched her out the room, gripping hold of her arm so tightly he pinched at her skin.

'Ow, Alex you're hurting me!'

He let go back out in the Long Gallery. 'We can't stop here.'

'Alright, I get it.' She said rubbing her arm.

'No Hannah I don't think you do!' He snapped and stomped away.

Hannah fumed, ambling down the gallery after him, rebelliously shining her phone into the adjacent rooms.

Next to the Jade room was a Ruby room with a red phoenix emblem on the door, followed by a Sapphire room, diamond stars and constellations glimpsed in the dark blue interior.

As her phone shone in on the lemon walls of a Citrine room, Hannah stopped. 'Alex.'

He tramped onwards, shoulders hunched.

'Alex, I've had an idea.' She spoke softly.

'Hannah!' Alex wheeled around.

Hannah held up her hands. 'No, listen, I know these rooms have delayed us, I just thought they might delay the Blondeshirts and Guards too.'

Alex stared at her and sighed. 'Sometimes, you're too clever for your own good.'

Shielding his eyes with his hand, he threw each of the doors open wide, leaving Hannah in the doorway of the last of the gemstone rooms. Multicoloured sea creatures swam amidst the soft blue glow of the Aquamarine walls. Tropical fish shimmered amidst the coral, rays and sharks soaring overhead, silhouetted against a shimmering light. With difficulty, she kept her feet glued to the floorboards until Alex returned.

He stood at her shoulder.

'We should go.' She muttered.

'Mmmm.' Alex murmured before tensing and pulling her away from the door.

Rushing on towards the dark-panelled double doors at the end of the Long Gallery, Hannah looked enviously back at the soft rainbow glow spilling across the floorboards. It was crushing knowing she'd never see their beauty again.

As Alex pulled out his keys and busied himself with a dusty padlock and chain wrapped around the brass handles, a painting caught Hannah's eye. A princess in a flowing blue dress stood defiantly staring out at her, at once humble but knowing. She stepped closer, drinking in the fall of her ringlets, the string of pearls round her neck and the slumbering dog at her feet. An intensity in her expression enthralled Hannah; a lost, distant look captured in the oil paint, trapped potential glinting in her familiar eyes. She wondered if it could be the mysterious Princess Eve.

The padlock clicked, the chain unwound.

They entered a much less-loved part of the Palace. The floorboards lay unpolished and bare, the plaster walls cracked and in places crumbling. He chained and padlocked the handles on this side of the door, propping several loose floorboards under them for good measure. She wandered along the hallway, turning right onto a wider gallery, a warren of small rooms and hallways on either side, the devastation of neglect widespread.

'Nasty.' Alex murmured as he returned to her side.

'Gemstone Rooms.' Hannah said. 'Nobody gets further than the Gemstone Rooms.'

'Let's hope so.' Alex replied.

They rounded a patch of swollen, rickety floorboards, reluctantly using the mouldy, crumbling walls for support. Brown water stains bulged in the ceiling, light fittings dangling precariously from their wiring. What little furniture remained in the surrounding rooms was unloved; dust sheets cast aside, drawers and cupboards left open. Hannah stepped closer to Alex, the air of the Palace changing from one empty of life to one empty of soul.

A door creaked.

They pressed themselves against the wall at the corner of a side passage. Hannah strained her ears to pick up every sound. Surely Law's Guards hadn't got ahead of them?

'Yes Hannah,' a voice mocked in her head, 'because a big Palace like this would only have one big entrance, wouldn't it?'

As the silence stretched out, Hannah's imagination filled the void with Yellow-helmeted Author-tarian Guards waiting impassively behind every door in every room around them. She blinked the unhelpful thought away.

A floorboard squeaked, someone sniffing before a dragging noise drowned out everything else. She moved to peek around the corner, fighting off Alex's cautious hands with a mild curse.

The noise stopped and Hannah froze, a vein throbbing in her temple. Twenty agony-filled seconds passed before there was another sniff and the noise of scuffed friction returned.

Ever so cautiously, Hannah pressed her nose to the corner of the wall and peeked down the hallway, eye widening at the ambling figure walking away, hauling a bulging hessian sack along the floorboards.

Twisted awkwardly from the great weight hauled behind him, the man wore a scruffy brown leather trenchcoat that dangled down to his knees, long lank hair hanging limply from beneath his black tricorn hat. He stopped and stretched, his hands rubbing his aching back. As he sniffed and turned around to grab the sack once more, Hannah drew back out of sight.

She waited until the dragging noise was in full flow before signalling Alex to follow her across the end of hallway. Tiptoeing away, they progressed whilst the stranger moved and paused when he stopped as if playing a deadly game of musical statues.

As the noise became fainter, they clambered over the debris of a fallen ceiling and tugged open a stiff oak door peppered with woodworm, the wood squeaking across the floor. As Alex shoved the door closed behind them, Hannah picked up a small black plastic square from the floor, finding a white printed Z on the other side.

'What's a *Z* from a computer keyboard doing here?'

'A letter smuggler probably dropped it, maybe even the one we just passed back there.'

'A letter smuggler?'

Alex locked the rotten doors. 'The taxation on letters makes smuggling lucrative for those prepared to take the risk.' He prised a crooked skirting board from the wall and shoved it under the handles. 'Underground alchemists buy letters on the black market and change them into all kinds of prohibited items with Imagination powder. '

A muffled thud from upstairs caused them to pause, staring down the deserted hallway and up at the dilapidated ceiling. After a minute with no more noise, they relaxed a little, Hannah wrinkling her nose at the peeling and mildewed blue wallpaper, the air tainted with mould. She pulled a piece from the wall and dropped it to the floor with disgust, her curiosity as to what was through the many doorways on either side of the hallway exhausted.

'Right,' He whispered, 'let's find this Number Well before the smuggler or Law's Guards painfully erase us out of existence.'

Hannah grimaced. 'It's a mystery how you remain so positive Alex.'

His lip curled. 'I'm just telling you the truth.'

'Yes Alex, but sometimes a tiny little white lie helps the medicine go down.'

Alex glared at her and although he didn't say a word, Hannah clearly heard him exclaim 'Heartisans!' in his head.

CHAPTER TWENTY-TWO

Moving carefully and methodically, they looked in dozens of dilapidated rooms and made several wrong turns before Hannah found herself at the end of a shadowy hallway. As she made to retreat, two identical curved marks on the wall caught her eye. Moving nearer and illuminating the grubby paintwork with her phone, she allowed herself a faint smile. Despite several coats of paint, the carved laurel wreaths couldn't be so easily disguised. Between them was a paper-thin crack in the paint, the faintest of draughts seeping through.

'Alex!' She hissed.

His head appeared from a room further up, a wave of her hand bringing him to her side.

'What?'

She smirked and nodded to the wall, enjoying his confusion.

His eyes narrowed and twitched. 'What?'

With a devious smile she pushed at the wall. The secret door moved an inch inwards, before closing.

Alex gawped at them and her, head shaking. 'How did...?'

He prodded it but after an inch it stuck fast on the floor. The wall beside it trembled and he tentatively shoved that too.

'Double doors!' Hannah exclaimed before lowering her voice. 'Sorry.'

He made a face and leaned against the other door, although it took several shoves of his shoulder before he'd made a big enough gap to slip inside.

She stared, pursuers forgotten.

After so many warped floorboards and decaying ceilings, the pink and white marble colonnades, sculpted plasterwork and frescoes overwhelmed their senses. Moonbeams slanted through two lines of broad skylights leaving bluish pools of light on the mosaic floor and reflecting off a rectangular mirror pool at the centre of the room.

They exchanged amazed glances, Hannah ambling forwards in the cool half-light as Alex eased the doors closed behind her. She marvelled at the walls behind the colonnades, glimpsing painted figures forming papyrus from strips of reeds, carving pens from bone and scribing on wax-coated tablets. Higher up the walls, letters of the Greek alphabet punctuated a carved frieze of fruit and animals like an A-Z border in a nursery.

Alex moved ahead to the mirror pool, leaning forward and blowing at a plaque on the top step, wiping away the last of the dust with his sleeve. She skipped across and read over his shoulder:

These temple rooms are a gift from the Ancient Greek Language
to the English Royal Family for their unswerving support and friendship
throughout many turbulent centuries. The Words of the Greek Language
will forever be in debt for the salvation of so many Loanword refugees
during the Constantinople Crisis of 1453.

Hannah looked wide-eyed at Alex.

'About five percent of English Words are derived from the Ancient Greek Language. Together with the Latin and Germanic Languages they form the bedrock of English.'

Hannah nodded and looked back at the plaque. 'What was the Constantinople crisis?'

'I think it was when they were invaded by the Ottoman Turkish, thousands of Greek Words sought refuge here, many of them allowed to stay.'

On either side of the plaque, she noted smaller brass notices attached to the marble. She wiped away the dust with her sleeve to find the warning:

Quicksilver – Do Not Touch

Hannah frowned and looked at the shimmering liquid in the pool more closely.

'A pool of liquid mercury?'

A faint crackle of gunfire made them both flinch, eyes like owls.

'It's alright, that's still some way off.' Alex lied.

'If I can hear it, it's not far enough.'

He winced slightly, saw the intention in her face and nodded. 'You search that side and I'll look on this.'

Alex darted off behind the columns and down a side passage, eyes all over the walls but plainly not seeing. She eyed the closed doors as she crossed to the colonnades, gazing up at the Alpha, Beta and Epsilon letters she recognised and the oddly shaped ones she didn't. She dragged her fingertips across the smooth marble pillars, reading the Words picked out in exquisite mosaics underfoot: *Antiqua – Old, Biblos – Book, Cyclos – Circle.*

'Narcissus, Narcissus.' She muttered as she examined each of the rich frescoes, a particular bright green reed reminding her of Princess Eve's pen.

She absentmindedly tapped a finger on her lips, George's words returning to her from the Hunting Lodge.

'...Queen Literate – perhaps reflecting on the tragedy - chose to hide all poisonous reminders of that day...any secret entrance maddeningly buried along with Eve's name.'

She narrowed her eyes and crossed back to the Mirror Pool. Kneeling on the marble step, she glanced around her before cautiously leaning over the edge of the pool.

She stared at her reflection in the silvery liquid and smiled.

It smiled back at her.

Despite all they'd been through, she looked good; her hair shone, her skin looked soft and supple, cheeks coloured. Her eyes looked bigger, her cheekbones higher and lips fuller. Even the shape of her nose no longer bothered her. She lifted a finger to a beauty spot on her top lip she'd forgotten all about. Her glistening smile grew wider even as her scepticism coughed in its fist and gingerly raised its hand.

'Hannah?!'

She turned her head to find Alex frowning, hand on her shoulder.

'I called you several times.'

'Sorry.'

'This is ridiculous, we don't even know what we're looking for!' Alex bristled.

'Maybe we're going about this wrong.' Hannah said.

Alex placed his hands on his hips with a heavy sigh.

'What if George needs us to help him?'

Alex frowned, lips still severe.

'What if he's using our skills to his advantage?'

'That sounds like George.'

'Seriously though, you're a Claviger, who better to ask if he found an entrance or chest he couldn't open?'

Alex's eyes twitched.

'And I'm Curious, who better to find a hidden entrance and solve a mysterious riddle?'

Alex's eyes narrowed. 'He's arranged for us to be here, all along.'

Hannah tumbled back through all they'd been through, imagining George's hand in manipulating Alex and her to come specifically to this Number Well. Was that the real reason he'd gone to the Monument to meet them? To trick them into Lexica and divert them away from all other exits for his own means?

'That can't be true, can it?' She sighed, too tired to evaluate such dreadful thoughts.

Alex paused before shaking his head. 'He'd risk my life in a heartbeat but not you Hannah. The Guardian wouldn't look too kindly on that. No he's just a lucky opportunist.'

'So why's he want to find this Narcissus Number Well so badly? Letter smuggling?'

313

Alex shook his head. 'Not his style to get his hands dirty. More like sell the secret to a gang of smugglers or set up a toll. Who knows with George, but fair to say he'll make Lexican Credits from it one way or another.'

Hannah curled a lip.

He shrugged. 'But it's irrelevant when we can't find it.'

Hannah gave him a look.

'What?' He shrank. 'Go on.'

She glanced at the pool and back at him.

Alex stared. 'Under there?'

Hannah twitched a cheek and nodded.

'You think the Mirrored Words room is under a pool of poisonous quicksilver?'

'Yes, only I don't think it's a pool of quicksilver, I think it's just Queen Literate's way of keeping people away from the secret entrance, like the coats of paint over the doors back there.' She glanced at the pool apprehensively. 'At least I think it is.'

'You *think* it is?'

She nodded.

'You realise what'll happen if you're wrong?' He said gravely.

A distant crash punctuated the silence making Hannah stiffen.

'Do you have any better suggestions?'

He pulled a face.

Hannah stood up on the marble and licked her dry lips apprehensively.

314

'Wait!'

She looked at him as he leapt up onto the step opposite, forced a smile at her and stepped forward into the deadly pool before she could argue.

He sank into the heavy liquid without a sound, no ripples radiating out from his splash even after the mercury moved across to fill the void over his head.

She brought a hand to her mouth and stared at the still surface.

What had she done?

Her veins thundered, head pulsing.

'Alex?'

The moon and stars through the skylight shone perfectly in the mirrored surface.

She clenched her fists as panic screamed in her head. Had she just killed her friend?

Looking blankly around her at the marble columns and friezes, her eyes settled back on the mirror pool at her feet.

Her frightened face smiled back up at her, although she was sure she'd not moved her lips. She marvelled at the shine in her soft hair until the sound of more gunfire made her flinch. With a heavy sigh, she screwed up her eyes, held her nose and stepped off the marble.

The surface gave beneath her like viscous metallic custard. It pressed on her more than the weight of water, but not the crushing pain she'd feared. She sank slowly before dropping out the bottom onto a tiled floor. Had she been thinking properly, she'd have reasoned a human jumping into a dense pool of mercury would probably have floated, not to mention broken their ankles.

'Alex?' She opened her eyes, but it was still pitch black.

'Hannah! Are we dead?'

'I don't think so.'

'Oh good.'

'One second.'

She dug out her phone and turned it on, the screen illuminating Alex's face. He winced and held up a hand.

'Sorry.'

She shone it around the vault under the pool. About a metre overhead, the silver surface reflected their tired, drawn faces. Hannah winced and pulled her gaze away. Behind them, a narrow set of steps headed back to the surface, while in the far wall a stout oak door stood secured with two bulky cast iron padlocks.

Alex dug out his keys.

Hannah imagined George and Edward arguing exactly where they now stood; Edward losing his footing and tumbling into the pool, George following with a duty-bound sigh and a curse for the locked door. She wondered how they avoided the patrolling guards and letter smugglers.

'Hold the light steady!'

'Sorry.'

She chewed on her tongue, thoughts meandering.

'Alex, you know the letter smuggler we saw back there?'

316

'Hmmm.' He blew the loose rust from the top lock and struggled to turn it with a platinum key.

'Do you think we should've warned him about the Guards?'

The lock clicked and Alex lifted his eyes bemusedly to hers. 'Of all the Words to worry about?!'

'Just saying.'

He shook his head derisorily. 'Yes Hannah and afterwards we could have sat down with the letter smuggler for a nice chat over afternoon tea.'

He rolled his eyes and held three near identical keys up to the light, sliding the middle one into the second lock.

'Hannah, letter smugglers are amongst the most ruthless and dangerous Words in all of Lexica. The punishment for smuggling is erasure without trial, so they don't tend to think twice about disposing of those who get in their way.'

The key ground around inside the mechanism, metal scraping against metal until the padlock clicked half-open.

Hannah didn't say a word, her tongue snagged on the daydream of afternoon tea.

Putting his keys away, Alex lifted the lock clear and tugged jerkily at the bolts across the door, dragging them out of the stonework. The door opened an inch, a pale blue glow streaming in through the crack. Alex pushed it wider and they stepped onto a circular stone floor, fine sparkling crystals in the granite emitting the blue luminescent light.

Hannah murmured a noise somewhere between wonder and a sigh.

Twelve huge mirrors stood around the outside of the room, each taller and wider than a person. She caught sight of her blue-tinged reflection, the angles of the mirrors making her feel a little odd as if she found herself in an otherworldly kaleidoscope. All the frames pointed to the centre where a silver disc lay on the floor.

'Mirrored Words.' Alex murmured distractedly at his reflection.

She was a little on edge, the room overwhelming her senses with a presence beyond sight, sound or smell, more a feeling of anticipation trapped within the walls, neither wicked nor benevolent, just there.

'Han?'

Hannah started at the sound of her name. She looked down at her foot hovering over the silver disc and looked around guiltily.

'What are you doing?'

'Nothing.' She lowered her foot back to the granite.

'You were going to step on that silver disc.'

'I wasn't!'

'Yes you were.'

'I was just...curious.'

'Hannah, have you not learnt by now you can't-'

There was a whooshing sound and hundreds of twinkling stars lit up the domed ceiling, bringing the room to life.

Alex lowered his dumbfounded gaze to Hannah stood on the silver disc.

'Sorry.' She mouthed with a shrug of her shoulders when she met his glowering expression.

'It's like trying to teach an Alphabet farmer to spell!' He said wearily.

'You love me really.'

Alex puffed out his cheeks as if to say, 'don't bet on it.'

Hannah's reflection stared back from every mirror and repeated back into the darkness, seemingly forever. The optical illusion caused by mirrors facing one another made the room look cavernous, like a Hall of Mirrors at an egotist's funfair.

Each of the twelve mirrors bore a number picked out in iridescent mother-of-pearl and shimmering in the light like oil in a puddle. A black circular panel stood opposite the entrance, splitting the mirrors into two halves. The coating of thick black paint had dried and peeled in places, hinting at a shiny orange surface underneath. The stars faded as she moved from the disc and pulled at a curl of black paint.

Alex joined her, both scratching bits loose with their fingernails and scraping them from the wall. As the polished panel gave up its secrets, Hannah sent Alex back to the silver disc. The lights revealed a legend etched into the deep mesmerising swirls of the amber:

The Mirrored Words Gallery

Hides a secret not all can see

Round and round is the key

To find the Symbol of _____

319

Despite her curiosity, part of Hannah sagged. 'Here we go again.'

She shook her head ruefully and tried to think of symbols within the English Language. Reading the legend through twice more, Hannah surveyed the room and recalled Princess Eve's last diary entry:

Curse of Narcissus: 8

With a heavy frown, she crossed over to the number eight mirror, glancing at her reflection and Alex grinning over her shoulder from the centre of the room. She stopped by the mother-of-pearl number.

'What's it with you Words and your riddles?' She glared at Alex's reflection in the mirror. 'Why can't you just have a *No Entry* sign and a locked door?'

'You mean like the *Quicksilver – Do Not Touch* signs and the three padlocks?'

'Yes, just like that.' Hannah's lip curled and she looked over to the Legend again.

Round and round is the key

To find the symbol of _____

'Come on Hannah.' She chastised herself, eyes narrowing at the number eight. 'What had Princess Eve seen that she couldn't?'

She absent-mindedly traced her finger around the shimmering white shape, marvelling at the warm pink, green and blues subtly radiating from the surface. Her eyes sparkled as her digit returned to where she'd begun. She did it again, her finger going *Round and round.* She froze and stared at it wild-eyed.

Mirrors numbered one to twelve.

Numbers.

She narrowed her eyes and heard George again in her head. 'In Lexica, Text and Numbers mix about as well as oil and water.'

Numbers.

Numeracy.

Mathematics.

She saw Mr Harvey shuffle into her Monday morning Maths class with all the enthusiasm of a condemned man.

'Morning class, today we're going to look at Infinitesimal Calculus until I spontaneously combust and leap dramatically aflame through the window, or I run out of coffee, whichever comes soonest...'

Hannah paused.

'Infinitesimal Calculus! She murmured.

'Huh?'

'Infinity!'

Alex gave a bewildered frown.

Hannah drew in a sharp breath.

'What?' Alex bit.

She pointed back at the amber legend.

Round and round is the key. To find the symbol of infinity!'

'Right.' Alex said without conviction.

'Do you know what a Mobius strip is, Alex?

Alex floundered further. 'A kind of dance?'

'No it's...' She frowned at Alex before continuing. 'No we did it at school. A Mobius strip is a three dimensional shape with only one side. It goes round and round infinitely because its shaped like two circles side by side.'

She drew it with her finger in the air, but still he looked blank.

Hannah pointed to the number eight on the wall and traced her finger over the mother-of-pearl.

'It looks just like a number eight on its side...' She stopped.

She tried to grip it and forcibly rotate it from vertical to horizontal but it wouldn't budge. She tilted her head over to one side to confirm to herself she was on the right track, before prodding at the number with her fingers, at first tentatively but rougher as annoyance took hold. With pursed lips, she shoved at the number, pulled at it, gripped it and twisted it without effect.

'Stupid number!'

'Alright Hannah, don't-'

Attention distracted, her thumb slipped from the shiny surface into the top hole of the number eight, pushing the granite in a few centimetres. Hannah gasped as it gave against a rigid spring. She spread her fingers and pushed the bottom loop in at the same time.

'Try giving it a twist.' Alex said redundantly.

It turned stiffly, the number eight grinding coarsely against the granite wall until horizontal. A dull thud sounded as Hannah removed her fingers, a heavy grating noise of stone on stone filling the air. As it ceased, ratchets whirred and cogs ticked mechanically behind the wall.

322

After an ominous pause, the mirror serenely slid upwards, spilling a dull grey light in around their ankles. The rising glass revealed an opaque liquid wall similar to the one she'd experienced in the Marginlands, only this shimmered like a pearl-coloured sheet of satin. The cloudiness cleared, faint lines at the centre resolving themselves into the horizontal edges of six steps.

'Is that...?'

Alex nodded. 'You've done it Hannah! You've found it!'

She squinted at the jumble of shapes and blurred patches of light until the image sharpened into a shaded alleyway leading out to a hazy road.

'Is that...?'

'Time to go home Hannah Curious.'

As a red blur with two lines of windows pulled up on the opposite side of the road, her stomach lurched.

Pandemonia.

London.

Home.

The sound of heavy footsteps overhead stuck them to the spot, both listening intently, eyes wide.

'What was that?' Hannah mouthed like a paranoid mouse.

Alex shrugged and they both sneaked back to the doorway.

'...around here somewhere.'

'Dunno. Prob'ly just heatin' comin' on?'

'Maybe. But why is it still so cold?'

'Plumbin' then. I dunno. Whatever it wer' it stopped nar, annit?'

'I suppose...'

They listened to the footsteps recede, waiting beneath the shimmering ceiling for a couple of minutes, but whoever it was didn't return. A grinding noise drew them shuffling back into the mirror room, the dulled sound of ratchets and cogs signalling the descent of the glass back over the Narcissus Number Well.

'It must be on a timer.' Alex murmured.

A surge of panic flooded her chest. She returned to the mother-of-pearl digit and turned it, only relaxing when mirror eight rose once more.

'Can we go now, before it closes again?' She said, trying to sound calmer than she felt.

He nodded and forced a smile. 'Yes I guess we can't wait around here forever.'

She narrowed her eyes. 'Are you alright Alex?'

'Yes, of course!' He beamed brightly. 'You're so clever. Even George Found couldn't find this Number Well.'

'Thanks Alex.'

'So this is it...' He faltered. 'I mean...your first step back outside of Lexica. Think you're ready?'

She nodded sceptically.

'Big moment. I mean, we're pretty safe in here now, but who knows what lies on the other side? Feds, Blondeshirts, Fiends?'

She frowned again. 'What is it Alex? Would you rather go first?'

'Oh no, no, that's...no.' He rubbed the back of his neck uneasily. 'No, I just wanted to thank you for all your help down here and if there are Feds on the other side I might not get chance.'

Hannah relaxed a little.

'Never mind the Feds, I've got to face my Grandmother yet, not sure I'll be able to get through her punishments without my friend there beside me.'

Alex looked back towards the door.

Hannah's smile faded, thinking maybe he'd heard footsteps again. 'Alex?'

He sniffed and turned back, his smile not as convincing as Vince's.

'I should secure the room again. If you do see any Feds and we become separated for any reason, I'll meet you back at Bluebell House.'

'Separated?' Hannah frowned. 'Wait, you are coming with me, aren't you?'

Alex's cheeks twitched. 'Of course! I'm just saying...I best go lock the padlocks on the door. Can I borrow your phone so I can see what I'm doing?'

Hannah stared at him for a few seconds before handing it over, her eyes drawn back to the frosted glass vision of Pandemonia.

'Right.' She licked her lips unenthusiastically. 'I'll see you on the other side. Don't be long.'

'See you soon Hannah Curious.'

She glanced back at his serious face, nodded and with a deep breath stepped forward through the cool surface.

With a shake of her shoulders, she emerged on the other side with teeth clenched and body tensed.

'Ugh!'

She rubbed her arms and stomped her feet amidst the crisp wrappers, leaves and empty cans of pop blown down the concrete steps. She turned to find the silky portal sat in the middle of two blue doors, each bearing a green fire exit sign. Dragging her finger through the icy surface, she puffed out her cheeks, whirled on her heel and climbed the six steps into a brick canyon.

No Feds stepped out to apprehend her.

An electronic beeping noise pulled her onwards, softening fear with images of frustrated drivers, little green men and idling pedestrians. She shuffled wide-eyed down the gentle slope like a time-traveller returning from the past, her nose wrinkling at her first whiff of food rotting in the large bins on either side of her. At the end of the alleyway she hesitated, a loose manhole cover rattling rhythmically underfoot as the pedestrians passed oblivious to her presence. Beyond them, flashes of colour and glass rushed by to the soundtrack of impatient traffic, the vibrating burr of a taxicab and the warble of a distant siren.

She drew in a deep breath of exhaust fumes, warm tarmac, discarded cigarettes, earthy grime and the faintest hint of fresh coffee. After the dangers of Lexica, the intense noise and fug of everyday street life was as inviting as an oasis to a thirsty Bedouin. She took three more steps down the slope and looked back, the top few centimetres of the Narcissus Number Well just visible.

'See you soon Hannah Curious.' Alex echoed in her head.

What had he meant by that?

Why didn't he just say he'd see her in a moment or a few minutes?

Now she thought about it, she realised Alex had been funny with her ever since they'd first stepped in the Mirrored Words room, a little like he'd been on the causeway over the Emergen Sea.

A road-sweeper swished past, its flashing orange lights dancing blindingly onto her retinas.

Hannah Curious.

Could she still be Hannah Curious out here?

The thought paralysed her with fear.

Even with Alex by her side, could she simply go back to the drudgery of Bluebell House?   Could she return to a life of servitude and blind obedience to her Grandmother?

She glanced back at the blue fire exit, standing on tiptoes to keep a slither of the Number Well in sight.

'Come on Alex!' She hissed, guilt stopping her venturing further.

Despite a considerable detour and questionable motives, he had guided her safely back to Pandemonia, against great odds. It seemed wrong not to wait for him.

Another double-decker bus rushed past and parked up just out of sight on the other side of the street. Her feet shuffled her nearer to the pavement, her curiosity urging her to find out where this secret Number-Well had emerged and to scan the area for Feds.

'Come on Alex, how long does it take to lock a couple of...'

Her stomach turned over.

She peered back up the alleyway to the fire doors, the Number Well out of sight.

Padlocks!

The thought upset dozens of niggling concerns she'd suppressed, spilling them chaotically in her mind like an upturned basketful of apples.

Alex had been saying goodbye in his own way ever since he'd seen the Mirrored Words legend. Maybe ever since George told them about it and Princess Eve.

Eve.

Eve and Hannah.

Mirrored Words.

'Oh Alex! You knew, all along and kept it to yourself!'

Hannah whirled around as the grinding noise returned.

She was already too late.

CHAPTER TWENTY-THREE

Lurching into a panicky run, her foot slipped on the dusty concrete sending her world whirling and jarring her ankle. She stumbled downwards, knee banging the ground, palms scraping over the floor as they broke her fall. Fighting gravity, she pushed herself back upright, ignoring the flashes of pain and looking unseeingly at the throbbing silver and red grazes streaked across her dusty hands.

The grinding noise behind the distant fire doors changed to the sound of ratchets clicking and cogs whirring, renewing her urgency. She clumsily pushed forwards, shoulder bouncing into the brick wall beside her as she shuffled into a laboured uphill run. Pushing herself past a dented metal bin, she gained momentum through air as thick as molasses, time dawdling tortuously as the Number Well inched closed with every pace. She fought the pain from her trophies of misadventure, eyes unblinking amid the maelstrom of anxiety. As the slight slope levelled out and the steps sped towards her, self preservation kicked in. She tensed and skidded towards a halt on the top step. The shimmering Number Well was already two-thirds closed...

She couldn't make it.

The thought struck with a flash of immediacy. The slow rumbling torture of evidence and argument followed, her brain plainly summarising all the evidential visual cues and mental calculations with the cruel sneer of an indifferent lawyer. She was simply too late.

Hannah left the dithering courtroom of her brain at the top of the steps. With clenched teeth, she pulled with her toes and leapt down the rubbish-strewn steps without choosing where she would land. Arms flailing widely for balance, she plummeted from the sky, eyes only on the shrinking Number Well. Her left heel caught an edge, stubbing her toe into the step below and propelling her forward past her centre of balance. Her right foot rushed through beneath her and smacked into the floor, the shuddering impact jarring her hip and pitching her forward towards the knee-high portal in the fire doors. Blanking out the consequences and the alarm of her brain still at the top of the steps, she threw herself toward the closing Number Well. As her outstretched fingers touched the silky liquid portal, she abandoned herself to fate, luck and anyone else in the universe with a passing omnipotent interest.

She hit the ground with a crunch and skidded, the silky portal sucking all the heat from her body and all thoughts from her mind.

A dark numbness pervaded her thoughts leaving her adrift in a void between action and consequences, trapped between her past and her future in a present she couldn't control.

She waited, time indifferent to her impatience.

Unceremoniously, she slid out onto the hard granite floor, gasping like a fish beached on a sandbank. Lying winded in the gloom, she dragged her feet clear of the mirror as it closed with a delicate thump.

'Ugh!' She croaked, her ribs hurting, body fizzing with pain and spent adrenaline.

She rolled onto her side and struggled to entice oxygen into her lungs.

'Alex!' She strained agonisingly up onto an elbow, scouring the empty room.

He'd gone.

'They always leave you.'

The voice of abandonment hit like a punch to the stomach and she dropped onto her shoulder, head on the cold floor, eyes closing. The familiar plummet into emptiness returned. The sour ache of existence in a world of muted indifference. Love and hate, fame and notoriety were all at least proof of existence, far worse was the invisibility of the ignored, the weightless forever of the forgotten. She'd dragged herself out of that hole in recent months, putting the years of being the new girl, the angry misunderstood stranger behind her. Despite her home life with Grandma Johnson, she had friends at school, even if she sometimes doubted they said the same about her. She had Magda who always saw the good in her and spoilt her with sweets, treats and perpetual kindness. She had Alex...

The thought jarred, the tremor of reality shaking the idea her imaginary friend had ever returned to her life for more than a cruel nanosecond.

'They always leave you.'

'No!' She spat, forcing herself awkwardly up onto her hands and knees, before rising atop unsteady feet. 'Not...today.'

Her head swam, a fuzzy grey fog swamping her vision. Staggering towards the entrance, the dizziness lingered as she leaned on the door, pounding with a fist.

'Alex! Alex!'

She screamed his name several times before dropping back to her knees and sagging against the wall, the tears no longer restrained. The deception too hard to maintain.

'Alex!' She mumbled, her hand barely rapping on the door beside her. 'Oh Alex.'

She shrank further, mood plunging like a stone dropped in a lake; light fading as it sank deeper into the murky darkness of despair.

The pain of her sobs echoed through her hollow soul, jolting her body like a defibrillator on a broken heart.

'He's gone.' The mocking voice swirled through her head.

'Shut up.' She murmured.

'They always leave you in the end.'

She scowled and shook her head angrily.

'Shut up! Shut up! Shut up!'

A noise came from the other side of the door, scything through her self-pity.

She froze, listening hard before sniffing and wiping her stinging eyes roughly on her sleeves.

'Alex?' She croaked.

She tilted her head, waiting to hear Alex's voice, for him to tell her he was there and she'd be fine.

Metallic noises.

She stiffened, stomach lurching, stray thoughts attacking her curiosity. Maybe it wasn't Alex. She'd been shouting in a Palace full of Guards and Blondeshirts, all of them searching for her.

'Hannah, what have you done?' She muttered, clawing herself silently back to her feet. 'You've...led them right to you.'

She heard a scraping noise in one of the padlocks and backed away, blinking away her blurry eyes.

A click came through the door.

She rushed back to the glass mirror and twisted the number eight beside it.

Another metallic noise came from outside, followed by a second click.

Hannah listened to the gears grinding behind the wall, pulse and breathing racing one another.

'Come on! Come on!' She muttered dropping to her hands and knees.

After a silent pause, the top bolt rasped out of the stone frame behind her.

Hannah clawed at the base of the mirrored glass as the clacking ratchets continued their sedate mechanical sonata.

The bottom bolt scraped out of the stonework behind her.

'Oh no. No, no, no!' She pushed desperately up against the glass.

The door creaked ajar as a final click heralded the glass of the mirror rising from the ground.

Hannah crouched lower on quivering hands and knees, side on to the growing slither of blackness beneath her reflection.

'Just three or four more seconds.'

333

'Stop!'

Hannah grimaced, frantically pushing and heaving, desperate to wriggle through the gap.

'Hey! Han?'

She twitched forward, stopped and peered round her arm. Alex frowned heavily in the doorway, a padlock still clutched in his hand.

'Hannah, what are you doing?'

Her name. His voice. Her eyes widened as belief cut through her fear. 'Alex!'

She bounced up and charged across to him, hugging him so tightly, he staggered back against the door.

'Hannah?'

'Oh...Alex.'

He tried several times before prising her head from his chest. 'Hannah! What are you still doing here?!'

She struggled to find the words. 'I couldn't...go. Oh Alex I'm so glad you're here.'

'Couldn't go, why? Is it blocked?'

She shook her head.

'Feds?'

'No.'

He stared incredulously. 'Hannah! You have to get out of here!'

She shook her head, but the words wouldn't come. His face was ablaze with frustration.

'I can't believe this, I got you out...Why would you...?'

'Sorry.'

'I got you out! You were home...sort of. You were safe. Out and safe...ish.'

'I'm so sorry Alex, I just...I couldn't.'

He shook his head and paced the floor, he turned and made to speak before walking away once more. After several pained sighs, he jabbed a finger towards the door. 'I heard you all the way from out beyond the Temple doors!'

Hannah's eyes widened. He'd left the Temple and still come back for her. He could've left her, but he hadn't.

His voice dropped with his hand. 'I can't have been the only one. You have to go, now.'

Hannah shook her head. 'I don't want to escape without you.'

His eyes narrowed slightly and Hannah nodded.

'But...'

She reached down and took the padlock from his hand. 'The padlocks are on the outside of the door Alex. You never intended to follow me, because you knew you couldn't. You knew all along, didn't you?'

He lowered his eyes to the floor.

'Would you've stepped through if I'd told you?'

Hannah thought for a second and sagged.

'Exactly.' He sighed. 'Look Hannah, it's my fault you're here, my fault we got caught and locked up in the Darkhive. You've seen how dangerous it is down here.

That's why if I'm going to risk getting the news to the Guardian , I need to do it knowing you're safe.'

'You don't understand Alex, I need you.' Hannah's shoulders slumped. 'I'd rather help you and risk going back to the Darkhive than escape on my own and return to my old life.'

Alex's eyes snapped up to hers, making her hear her words anew. Even as she saw the impact of them on his face, she realised the truth within them and nodded.

'How can you say such a thing after all that's happened?!'

Hannah glanced at the mirror and back at Alex stubbornly.

'I heard what Bellwether wants to do to the English Language and I...I can't let that happen. I love books, they've always been there for me when reality gets too...real. The thought of Bellwether taking that away - not just from me, but from everyone else in the world. It-' She snatched at a breath and shook her head. 'It's all too much.'

'It's not your fight Hannah! You don't have to-'

She shook her head. 'I don't know why all this is happening to me. I wish I had the cool oblivion of not knowing about Bellwether and all this,' she noted his grimace, 'not that anyone's to blame, but I do know.'

Alex's mouth twitched as his eyes beamed, the sound of grinding gears and ratchets jolting the pride from his face.

'Hannah! You have to go, it's not safe-'

'No, Alex you don't understand, if I do it's all been for nothing.'

He looked exasperated. 'Hannah, you *have* to go. If you *stay* it's all been for nothing!'

She shook her head, obstinately folding her arms.

Alex sighed heavily and glared at her. 'Hannah, it's safer we split up. We can meet up later, form a proper plan. Look, it's not you...it's me. It's for the best, you'll see.'

Guilt gnawed at her stubbornness and she had to look away. Eyeing the descending mirror, her whirling mind cleared. Beneath the untidy hair and behind the tired, dark eyes she saw a familiar stranger. Unlike the beautiful illusion she'd witnessed in the quicksilver pool, she looked upon a vision of the past she'd almost forgotten.

As the mirror thudded back in place, the padlock weighed heavily in her hand, a faint mischievous smile curling the lips of her reflection.

'Well?' Alex asked, misinterpreting her stance.

Hannah turned her head. 'I'm sorry Alex.'

A frown furrowed his brow.

She smiled at him guiltily, gripped the cold metal tightly and in one fluid motion pitched the padlock hard across the room.

'Hann-'

A great crashing noise drowned him out.

The surface of mirror eight shattered into a spider's web of splinters, the fractures trembling in the frame before smashing to the floor. Hannah turned her head and shielded herself with her arm as hundreds of jagged shards tumbled from the Number Well and skidded across the hard granite.

As the noise of tinkling glass died away, Alex rubbed a hand through his hair and met her shocked eyes. 'Brilliant!'

The opaque liquid bubbled and fizzed, the image of London evaporating from the wall in a silvery gas. The surface boiled away, leaving behind only stationary cogs, gears and coarse granite blocks.

She swallowed, self-doubt nibbling at her resolve.

'Alex.'

He paced, hands on his head, refusing to look her way.

'Alex, I'm sorry.'

He crouched and carefully picked up a long shard of glass.

'Please don't be mad at me.'

He shook his head.

'Have you forgotten the Causeway and the Darkhive already?'

'No Alex and I realise now I don't want to forget.'

He glared at her.

'I'm not making any sense am I?' She tried to order her thoughts.

'Han, I-'

'No, Alex listen, see it's not just Bellwether. All these years since...' Her eyes glazed for a moment. 'Well, since that time, I've tried to forget it all. Buried all the waiting, all the empty days and the angry tears-'

His fury fizzled and faded as she lost herself in a memory.

She stroked her ear absentmindedly and returned. 'It's only now, I guess, I forgot the happy times too. I blocked out everything, buried the good with the bad.'

His eyes narrowed as she poured it all out.

'I've been trying to get by, to get my head down and *not* be that girl again. Yet, somehow I let Bluebell House become my own kind of prison camp and Grandmother Johnson my guard. I don't have barred windows in my bedroom...well, because they...they were all in my mind.'

He still looked blank.

'Don't you see Alex, I've lived more in the last three days than I have in the last three years. I've been more alive, more like myself. To you I was never Hannah Darnell; studious inoffensive mouse.' She grinned, eyes sparkling. 'I've always been Hannah Curious; sarcastic genius with a hint of mischief.'

Alex tossed the piece of glass noisily to the floor. 'Genius? Right.'

She pulled a face cheekily. 'Hannah Curious has already escaped. And she's not the kind of person to leave her friends behind when they need her help.'

He stared at her anew for several seconds.

'Is Hannah Curious the kind of person who always talks in the third person?'

Hannah smiled back. 'She most definitely is not.'

He kicked several more shards of glass across the floor and released a heavy sigh. 'So I have to babysit you a little while longer?'

Her reddened eyes flared.

He smiled ruefully and she returned it with interest.

'Now,' Alex rubbed his chin, 'as certain exits appear to be somewhat out of order. Does Miss Sarcastic genius with a hint of mischief have any ideas of how we're going to get out of here?'

'I do, but first I'll need my phone back.' She held out her hand.

'Why?' He stiffened.

She beckoned with her fingers.

He reluctantly pulled it out of his pocket and placed it in her hand.

'Because Alex, it's my phone.'

Hannah self-consciously led him out the Narcissus Temple and back the way they came. He fumed, but remained stoically quiet. By now the Palace's West Wing was alive with noise; every creak underfoot, shout and thud rapidly eroding Hannah's newfound positivity. Reaching the woodworm-riddled oak doors Alex crouched in the darkness to peer through the keyhole, before loosening the floorboard and pulling out his keys. As the lock turned with a loud click, they heard approaching footsteps in a side corridor somewhere behind them. Alex drew Hannah deeper into the shadows beside a stack of leaning floorboards, hand raised, eyes wide. She heard a murmured exchange of words, silence and quiet footsteps before two silhouettes stepped out into the hallway by the Temple.

'Why Sebastian, I don't recognise any of this at all...' A voice whispered idly through a yawn.

'You obviously never got put on dustcover punishment by the Lieutenant?' The other whispered tentatively. 'He'd march us in here or the abandoned North

Wing behind the stables, throw down two dozen books in the dirt and then make us clean them meticulously with a tiny toothbrush.'

'Sounds grim.'

'Grimy more like. Sometimes, the Lieutenant would find a single mote of dust between the pages and we'd be back to do it all again...and again...'

Silence lingered before a thud came from somewhere on the floor above.

'What-' The first voice croaked.

'Ah, don't fret. It was...probably nothing.'

'Well, *nothing* sure sounds heavy.'

'It'll be a Blondeshirt dropping his ego.'

The first guard snorted quietly. 'Don't let any of those champagne fascists hear you say that!'

The second giggled nervously.

Hannah might have smiled, but for the sniffle in her nose growing into a lingering tickle.

'I despair sometimes Sebastian.'

'I know. Seems only weeks since we were patrolling the palace orchards for hungry crows or taste-testing the feasts for fear of poisonous seasonings.'

'Quite. I mean, I know the Royals were sometimes abrasive and snooty but at least their rudeness had a poise and dignity.'

'Agreed! When Queenie glared or curled her lip at you, at least you were only psychologically scarred. That Bedwetter meanwhile, well he'd more likely smash you in the face with a silver platter.'

341

'Or set fire to your boots and push you off the roof.'

Hannah quietly stretched her face and wrinkled her nose. The growing itch in her nose making her eyes water.

The guards murmured respectfully in the silence. 'Poor Tristan. He never could control that runaway mouth of his. No dustcover punishment for him.'

'No. Nor Grayson. He always respectfully spoke the truth, even to those who disagreed.' He sighed. 'Terrible way to go.'

'The creative cruelty of the Blondeshirt officers is sickening. Mind you, I don't blame the Hy-phenas in the Royal Zoo, they were already half starved...'

'Or Wilby. Rather unfortunate how he left us, he was always a good egg.'

'Wilby? Oh yes, that was quite sudden. You know, I really didn't think he'd clear the outer moat, that trebuchet was an antique!'

'Bedwetter. He's got it coming to him, you know! One day, you'll see.'

'Quite. He doesn't scare me.'

Hannah's stifled sneeze erupted deep into her shoulder; a smothered squeak echoing back down the dusty corridor.

A forbidding silence hung in the air for the best part of a minute.

'Shall we go search the letter garden?' The first guard croaked.

'Someone should.' The other murmured.

Their quiet footsteps grew noisier as they accelerated down the corridor and barged through some doors.

Alex said nothing, yanking open the stiff, squeaky doors and locking it noisily behind them with a wince.

'Right now what, Miss genius?'

Hannah rubbed the end of her nose with the palm of her hand, blinking away the lingering soreness in her eyes.

'Well?'

She ignored him.

'Han?'

'Alright, just give me a second!' She snapped.

His silence was weighted with anxiety.

'I think...' She checked her words. 'I know...at least I'm pretty sure, there's another way out.'

'How can you possibly know that?' He frowned, anger restrained.

She bit her lip and scrunched up her left eye. 'You won't like it...'

He let out a groan and shook his head, tiring of her. 'Well, before you screamed the Palace down, I was planning on exiting through the grounds and moving from cupboard to cupboard back up to the Definition levels. I have some friends in the B offices that can hide me until the heat dies down.'

Hannah narrowed her eyes. 'O...Kay. But even imagining we could evade the hundreds of Guards – of varying competence - in the grounds, how do you propose we even get outside?'

'We climb out of a window.'

'The windows? Alex, we're on the second floor!'

He pulled a face and shrugged. 'You'll probably only break an ankle or two.'

'An ankle or two is all I've got Alex! And I've become somewhat attached to both of them over the years.'

'Han-'

A great booming rattle along the hallway killed the argument.

The crashing din thudded for a second time, the violence making Hannah flinch. This wasn't the tiptoeing caution of the Palace Guards, this was the violence of confidence and obedient anger.

Silence returned.

'What was that?' She gulped, a tremor in her voice.

'Law's Guards must have reached the doors at the end of the Long Gallery.' He whispered.

'They've stopped.' She murmured.

'They'll return, they're probably looking for something heavy to break it down.'

The oak doors rattled in the frame behind them making Hannah jump and emit a little shriek. The handles twisted redundantly in the locked doors, muted voices coming from the other side as fists and boots pounded the wood.

Alex swallowed hard as they backed away. 'Trapped.'

CHAPTER TWENTY-FOUR

'We've had it.' Alex muttered despondently.

Hannah tore her eyes from the mesmerising doors, an unseen shoulder or boot making them shudder rhythmically like a heartbeat.

'You should have gone when you had a chance.' He mumbled, head dropping.

The truth of his words stung like a whip of nettles. She'd been right there on the streets of London and she'd turned her back on it. Returning to Lexica for...for what? To recapture something already gone from her memory, something already erased by...

Bellwether appeared in her mind, leering grimly.

'No!' She snapped angrily, dispelling the image with a shake of the head. 'No! We've still time.'

He glared at her as if at a deranged stranger. 'Han, we're surrounded. Those doors won't hold, there's no other way out. We need to hide and get ready to fight.'

Hannah tilted her wrist and stared blindly at her watch. 'No! We've still time...Oh I hope we've still got time.'

Weaving in and out of the broken drawers and crumpled dust sheets on the floor, she dragged him around a corner to the left, away from both the thudding oak doors and the barricaded ones leading back to the Long Gallery.

Hannah stopped.

Alex skidded past her, bouncing agitatedly on the spot as she leaned over three bulging hessian sacks by the wall. He glared at her as she opened the nearest one and brought out a handful of multicoloured, magnetic fridge letters.

'Leave them!' Alex backed away nervously. 'We've got to hide or get out a window!'

Hannah ignored him and opened the second, finding hundreds of shiny letters prised from the backs of cars, the third overflowed with thousands of cream-coloured Scrabble tiles, each printed with a black letter and a small number.

'Hannah!' He hissed anxiously.

She swallowed hard for the forthcoming storm and sat down on the middle sack.

Alex stared at her as if she'd smeared herself in barbecue sauce and climbed into the lion enclosure at the zoo.

'What. Are. You. Doing?!' He quietly raged, looking close to a breakdown.

'Sitting down.'

'Sitting down?!'

'Yes Alex, sitting down.'

He turned from her, darted into the nearest room and scurried across to the one opposite before returning to an increasingly serene Hannah.

'Hannah!' He pulled at his hair. 'The Guards will break down those doors any minute, we need to...we need to...!'

'No Alex.' Hannah calmly shook her head and patted the hessian sacks beside her. 'This is our last chance.'

346

His eyes twitched, his mind burning off the haze of confusion before they grew wide.

'Are you out of your mind?!' Alex exploded off the walls like a punk demanding a refund.

Hannah had no answer, she was no longer sure what sanity looked like. Yet, the greater the banging on the doors, the greater his fury, the calmer she became.

'Alex, the smuggler is our only way out of here. Hiding will only delay our capture, climbing out a window only speed our demise.'

Alex spluttered angrily. 'Hannah...I...we... can't wait for a smuggler!'

Hannah nodded down the hallway. 'We won't have to.'

Alex spun around as the smuggler shuffled into view.

'Stays where you is!' A husky northern voice bellowed over the din of muffled shouts and shoulder-barged doors.

The ugly, unshaven smuggler ambled towards them in his black tri-corn hat and heavy brown leather coat, Hannah's nerves sparking at the sight of the engraved flintlock pistol in his hand. He brandished it at a retreating Alex before pointing it directly at Hannah's head. She got up unsteadily, mirroring Alex's raised hands.

'Who the 'eck are you?' He boomed, his breath stinking of stale ale and pickled eggs.

The pistol looked antiquated and beautiful, but with the smuggler's cracked, dirty finger curled over the trigger, it also looked utterly lethal. She followed the scuffed sleeve of his jacket up to his grizzled features, his grubby sneering face

347

half-hidden behind his dark, greasy hair. His empty eyes caused a flutter of panic in her chest.

He swung the gun over to Alex, his thumb resting on the hammer. 'Ah said, *who* the eck are you?'

'Err...' Alex croaked.

'And what thee doing in't Palace?'

'My name is Alex Guide.' Alex squeaked feebly. 'I...I was just showing...my friend here around the Palace.'

Hannah had a familiar sinking feeling.

'Thee's just having a look round?' He rasped, his lips parting to reveal crooked teeth and black gums.

'Yes.' Alex said.

'In't middle of night?'

'Erm, yes.'

'In't part of Palace where nefarious and ne'er-do-well rub shoulders?' He gestured with the pistol as Alex nodded.

The man bared his teeth and laughed breathily, his body juddering like a dying engine.

Alex just stared at him submissively.

'Just 'ere for a look round, eh? You're a dreadful liar.'

'Ain't that the truth!' Hannah murmured without thinking.

The stranger's arm stiffened, the flintlock back on Hannah.

'We don't want any trouble!' Alex pleaded.

348

Hannah wished he hadn't, movie actors with those lines tended not to appear in the sequel. He might as well have said...

'We're totally unarmed.'

Hannah's eyes flickered irritably across to him.

A cruel smile curled across the stranger's lips as he pulled the flint-bearing cock back with his thumb. Hannah's mouth dried, her head twitching. Unthinkingly, she raised her hand and placed her finger into the end of the barrel.

The stranger's eyes crossed to look at the fleshy cork at the end of his gun, his confusion dissolving into anger.

'Gerroff my pistol!'

Hannah stubbornly shook her head enraging the stranger further.

'I'll blow your finger off!

'No you won't.'

He dragged Hannah's finger around as he waved the pistol, desperately trying to dislodge her from the barrel.

'Nobody d'unt not tell Stan Deliver what he ain't not to do!' He snarled, stepping back and bringing Hannah with him.

Hannah's surprise swelled to smother her fear. 'Was that a *quintuple* negative? Wow!'

His lip twitched as he finally yanked the barrel back out of her reach. 'D'unt tells...'

'Hannah, don't antagonise him.'

'What's dhat mean?!' Stan Deliver waved the pistol in Alex's direction, his finger twitching on the trigger.

A heavier thud rocked the Long Gallery double doors; the chain rattling and one of Alex's bracing floorboards clattering to the floor.

They all stared down the hallway.

Alex swallowed hard 'Look mister, this is crazy! Law's Guards will be through those doors in a minute or two, finding the three of us stood here arguing!'

'Wrong,' Deliver gave a chequered smile, 'they'll find the bodies of two Words with eraser wounds to their heads.'

Hannah stared down the dark barrel, imagining what kind of bullet caused an eraser wound to the head. She cursed her curiosity and refocused on the grimacing smuggler behind the pistol, wondering if his dirty features would be the last she'd ever see.

This wasn't how she'd imagined it. After all they'd been through, all the close shaves and foes they'd faced down, this felt like a pointless way to die. Maybe she didn't know best, maybe she should've listened to Alex after all. Maybe she should have waited for the Feds climbing up the Monument steps after she'd met Edward and...

George.

Amidst her chaotic thoughts, George elbowed his way back into the maelstrom, removing his top hat and caddishly twiddling his moustache.

She raised her gaze to the smuggler's cruel features, his eyes half-closing as he braced himself to pull the trigger.

350

'George Found knows we're here!' She blurted.

Alex gave a low groan, his humiliation complete.

'George Found?' Deliver snarled.

Hannah swallowed, wishing the floor beneath her feet would follow her lead.

'George Found?! The rotten, lying, cheating, good-for-nothing, scoundrel George Found?' Deliver growled with vitriol, spitting on the floor for good measure.

Hannah winced with every hurled adjective and reluctantly gave a simple nod of the head.

Stan Deliver's dumbfounded expression broke into a crooked grin as he poked the brim of his hat upwards with his pistol.

'Why d'unts you not say so befores?! Any friend of Magpie George is all reet by me.' He made the pistol safe, tucked it into his belt and set off dragging one of the hessian sack along the hallway. 'Come on, grab sacks, should'na hang 'round 'ere all day.'

Hannah blinked hard and numbly reached for the nearest sack, the rough hessian burning the cuts on her hands as she hauled it down the hallway.

'Yay! Magpie George to the rescue.' Alex said in mock celebration heaving a sack behind her.

Hannah had no strength to argue.

Following Deliver into an empty bedroom, the banging noise on the Long Gallery doors changed in intensity, the wood splitting and splintering.

Hannah looked uneasily around the small bedchamber, a pale Alex bristling beside her. The four-poster bed had long since collapsed into a heap of broken wood. The narrow windows remained closed and shuttered, the walls bare and crumbling. More importantly, there were no other exits and nowhere to hide.

The chain rattled and a panel crashed to the floor, spilling urgent voices into the hallway, the thudding replaced with the thunder of heavy boots.

'Check every room,' Law's voice rang out down the corridor, 'every cupboard, every window, every nook and every cranny.'

Stan Deliver raised a finger to his lips and led them across the floorboards past a narrow fireplace. The sound of splintering furniture and smashed windows filled the air as Deliver casually pulled at the dado rail by the fire. A section of the wall opened inwards, a hidden servant's door revealing several hessian sacks sat untidily at the base of a tight spiral staircase.

'Check everywhere! Bring them to me nearly dead or barely alive!' Law boomed.

As the thunder of Guard's footsteps grew louder in the hallway, Hannah surged forward to get inside but Deliver blocked their path and calmly reached for their hessian bags. He unhurriedly stacked them onto the sizeable pile at the bottom of the stairs, making it obvious where she and Alex were in the pecking order.

'Deliver, we need to go! Now!' Alex hissed through clenched teeth.

Deliver rounded on him, his hand on his pistol.

'Sssssh!' A voice yelled from the hallway. 'What was that?'

Hannah glared desperately at Deliver, the frozen moment swirling with betrayal, trust and fear. The smuggler leered at them with a mixture of bemusement, disgust and a glint of insanity.

'Down there!' The voices yelled.

He was throwing them to the wolves.

The revelation crushed her hope. Magpie George or not, he was going to give them over to Law's Guards just because he could, because he held the pistol, the power and a lack of morals.

He stood with one hand on the secret door, the pistol pointing cockily at Hannah.

'It was from one of these rooms I think...' The voice boomed just metres along the hallway.

Hannah's knees weakened, sorrow sucking the spirit from her strength. She'd made the wrong choice, backed the wrong horse, picked the wrong side.

'You look in there...' The boots thundered along the hallway, floorboards creaking beyond the door to the bedroom. 'Careful, they'd be stupid not to have a gun.'

She shook her head, eyes pleading, knowing the Guards were listening and she daren't speak.

'Don't do this.' She mouthed.

Stan Deliver drank in their fear as if it were a refreshing tonic.

'Nothing? Check that one next.'

Deliver narrowed his eyes at the shadows passing the door to the hallway and signalled them inside with a flick of his head. They eagerly stepped up onto the sacks, feet crunching on the letters.

'Here, someone's in here!'

Heavy footsteps rushed into the room as Deliver softly pushed the secret door closed.

Deliver struck a match and busied himself with a candle as unseen guards kicked at the broken bed and smashed the windows. During the cacophony of destruction, the smuggler led them away up the narrow spiral staircase.

Hannah trudged upwards in his wake, feeling queasy and light-headed, untrusting but submissive. Her sore hands throbbed and legs ached as they dragged the sacks up the steep treads into the servant's quarters. Following the silhouetted glow from Deliver's candle, they heaved them through a tight doorway and along several narrow, musty landings. Dusty brass bells on the walls silently awaiting the call of their masters. They trudged onwards, more by touch than sight, squeezing through a stiff door and hauling themselves up another tight stone staircase, the rough wall and stone newel almost embracing their shoulders.

'How much...further?' Alex asked breathlessly from behind a sweaty Hannah as they clomped up the worn, shiny steps.

The smuggler didn't reply or even acknowledge anyone had spoken.

They climbed to the soundtrack of laboured breathing, plodding feet and the rub of their clothes on the wall. Hannah counted the steps in her head, if only to distract herself from her exhaustion and growing hunger.

She'd neared two hundred when they stopped.

Stan Deliver drew a key out from under his hat and stooped by a low wooden door. Hannah sank onto the steps, sagging against the cool wall; her cheeks burning, and sore hands ablaze. A red-faced Alex came to a halt on the step below her, leaning on her hessian sack as he caught his breath.

'Han?'

She met his eyes and between deep breaths gave him a reassuring nod.

'Where are we Deliver?' Alex queried.

'Way oot's through 'ere.' The smuggler leered at their condition.

'Onto the roof of the Palace?'

'Nah.' The smuggler returned the key under his hat and pushed the door open, hauling the sacks up and tossing them inside.

Alex helped Hannah to her feet.

Intrigued, more than frightened, she followed the disappearing candlelight through the door into a cramped box room. The clouds of their breath made the dim orange flame flicker, the chill of the stone floor seeping into her toes. After Alex closed the door, Deliver handed the candle to Hannah and pulled down a folded tube of piping from the low ceiling.

'What's that?' Alex queried suspiciously.

'Perry-scope. Dunt wanna appear t'audience does thee?'

Alex pursed his lips. 'Just dunt...don't try anything.'

Wiping his nose on his sleeve, Deliver pushed the tube back up and crossed to the far wall. Drawing two bolts back, a hatch in the wall popped open an inch,

355

bringing with it a cool breeze and the smell of rain. Alex stepped through first, holding it open for her to follow.

'Go on, get outta 'ere.' Deliver said, wafting a hand at her.

Hannah moved to the trapdoor but didn't like turning her back on him. 'You're not coming?'

'Nah, them noisy Guards scared orfs my contact. I'll bring up dhem other sacks and rest up in 'ere for week or two 'til fuss dies down.'

Hannah looked at the cramped floor and her eyelids grew leaden.

Two weeks of sleep, albeit in a cold stone box, almost sounded quite tempting.

'Han, come on.' Alex hissed through the gap.

Despite her feelings toward this lunatic, she couldn't just leave without saying something. 'Thank you Mister Deliver for helping us.'

He looked as surprised as if she'd slapped him.

'Fank yoo?'

'Yes.'

He thought for a few seconds, a faint smile curling his lips. 'Fank yoo. It been many a year sin' I hears anyone's say dhat to me.'

She gave him a coy nod. 'Well, thank you Stan Deliver.'

'My pleasures.' He grinned toothily. 'Been a while since I said dhat too!'

She lifted a leg through the hatch.

'Tell Magpie George ee owes me one!' Deliver said eagerly.

Hannah got the feeling now he'd rediscovered his voice, he didn't want her to go.

356

'Of course. Bye now.' She bowed her head and scrambled through the gap.

She emerged in a small square devoid of prying eyes, helmeted Guards or loitering Feds. Warming streetlights reflected in the dark windows of a sweep of office buildings, trees littering the pavements and benches with their leaves. Looking up at a tall bronze of Abraham Lincoln, Alex had briefly panicked, paranoid they'd emerged onto a floor of the American Annexe. Yet, as he frothed, a wry smile crossed her lips. Maybe it was a smell on the frigid breeze or the subtle murmur of traffic, maybe it was the fine rain tumbling out of the dusky sky, but Hannah knew this wasn't just another floor of a Lexican skyscraper.

The chimes of a large clock rang out an intro to the hour, drawing her up the pedestrianised hill like a child after an ice cream van. Hair streaming over her shoulders and aches forgotten, she gleefully rushed past closed sandwich shops and recruitment agencies, a grin broadening across her damp cheeks with every stride. The huge gothic town hall in Albert Square loomed into view as the chimes fell silent and the big bell boomed. Alex catching up as it rang for a seventh time.

'You know you shouldn't run off-'

'Alex!' She shrieked and launched herself at him, arms wrapped around him in a smothering bear hug.

'Han! What now?'

She drew back from him, eyes alive. 'We're out Alex! That's Manchester Town Hall...'

He gawped at the statues, taxis and hardy souls ignoring the drizzle.

'...I've made it home.'

CHAPTER TWENTY-FIVE

Hannah snatched at a shallow breath, a slither of brightness prising her eyes open and mocking her muddled brain. She resisted, but the morning wasn't to be ignored. She rolled away from the light, stretching her shoulders with a groan, a yawn closing her eyes as she roared like a mute lion.

'You're awake?'

Hannah flinched and rose onto her elbow, duvet clutched to her neck. A shadow stood at the window, peeking outside between the curtains.

'Alex?!' She rasped huskily.

'What?'

Hannah didn't reply, couldn't, her eyes drifting to the unloved teddy bears lined up on a half-empty bookshelf and the peeling posters of long-forgotten pop stars.

With a single blink, her chest tightened and she tumbled back six years.

The crisp leaves of a blustery autumn afternoon swirled on the pavement, the flaming foliage cascading from the trees across the road. As all the other pupils drifted away from the school gates, the impatient wind whipped her long hair across her face, hiding the tears on her chafed cheeks. After twenty-five minutes, a teacher twirling his car keys around his finger stopped mid-stride across the staff car park and headed her way, throwing his jacket around her shivering shoulders. Her dad appeared forty minutes later, bursting into the school office where Hannah

358

sat in front of an untouched plate of biscuits. He swept her up with angry arms, a worried frown and muttered thanks.

Her father said nothing all the way home, his hands wringing the leather steering wheel. Hannah knew something was going on, but not what she'd done wrong. As her father paced the kitchen floor at home, she'd buried her head in her pillow and cried until sleep came.

The following morning, she'd crept silently down the stairs and found her father still wearing his work clothes, a half-empty bottle of whisky on the floor and his wedding photos clutched to his chest. She'd made him a cup of coffee and some toast, which he devoured without thanks before staggering out the door, car keys in his fist.

It was after dark when she heard a key in the door once more.

Running from her bed and pawing at her puffy eyes, she looked down the stairs to her father's empty face. His gaze lingered on her in an intensely connected moment of extinguished hope and shared hell. Slumping on the top step, she listened to him pick up the phone and call the police.

'Hannah? Are you alright?' Alex said.

Hannah twitched, sniffed and blinked, refocusing on her bedroom window.

'Yeah, just...oh shut up.'

Alex poked his nose back between the curtains.

A whiff of sausage and bacon drifted up the stairs, her stomach gurgling like a hungry whale. Snug as she was under her pink duvet, she knew her hunger would win out in the end. 'What are you going to say to your dad?' Alex said without turning round.

Deja vu dropped her on the doormat the night before, Alex asking the same question as he used his keys on the front door.

'I have no idea.' Hannah said, still eyeing the pavement where a sympathetic line of bouquets once leaned against their low front wall.

Alex turned the lock, opened the door an inch and looked back at her expectantly. She nodded, rapped on the glass and stepped inside.

'Must be working late.' Hannah murmured, running a hand through her damp hair as she flicked on the hall light.

A flood of happier memories rushed from the walls. She saw Mr Bloggs and her other teddies sat on the stairs at one of her 'concerts'. She saw Alex leaning on the cupboard under the stairs counting to a hundred as she tiptoed carefully upstairs to hide. She saw herself running giddily into the kitchen to tell her sleepy dad Santa had visited during the night.

'Been a while.' Alex said beside her.

Hannah met his eyes and mirrored his smile. Her gaze drifted upstairs and drew in a breath.

'Dad?'

Nothing.

'He must be out.'

Heading for the kitchen, she gasped at how little had changed, dumped her bag on the floor and busied herself with the kettle. Alex sat at the kitchen table, running his hand over the smooth pine as she splashed boiling water, milk and sugar into a mug.

'Heartisan Alchemy.' He muttered nostalgically.

As she lifted it to her lips, the kitchen door burst open.

'Hannah!' The word bounced off the walls like an angry wasp in a jam jar.

She gawped at her wide-eyed dad in his pyjamas and dressing gown by the door, cricket bat clutched threateningly in his hands. Unshaven, wild-haired and dark-eyed, he looked terrible.

'You came back!' The cricket bat clattered to the floor as he reached for her, his voice cracking as the tears tumbled down his cheeks. He enveloped her in his arms, hugging her so tightly she could barely breathe.

'You came back.' His body shook with emotion as he gently rocked her from side to side.

'Dad.' Hannah gasped into his chest.

'They said I shouldn't get my hopes up, they said…'

'Dad!' Hannah wriggled and strained until she could break free from his grasp. She smelt the stale alcohol on his breath, the look of joy in his glistening eyes unnerving her.

'Where have you been? What happened? Why did...?' He sharply shook his head. 'Never mind, we'll deal with that later.' He dabbed his reddening eyes on his sleeves and forced a bewildered grin. 'Sorry, it just came as a bit of a shock.'

She grinned back guiltily. 'I'm sorry I made you worry. Did Grandma Johnson phone?'

'I'll say, accused me of hiding you she did, even got the police to come search the house.'

'Police or Feds?' Alex asked nervously.

Hannah stared at Alex, having forgotten he was there. She gulped and repeated the question. 'Were they...uniformed police or just plain clothes?'

Her dad frowned. 'Both, I think, but-'

'Did the plain clothes ones wear hats?' Alex said, Hannah echoing so her dad could hear.

Her father's unease grew as he nodded. 'Yeah, very strange. Trilby's or Fedoras I think. Must be back in fashion.'

Alex caught Hannah's gaze.

'They probably traced you from the Monument after everyone realised you were gone.'

Hannah thought of the hat-wearing Feds watching her teachers call her name and frantically search for a missing child. She meandered on through memories of CC Law, CC Order, the Author-tarian Guards and her descent into the terrifying Darkhive.

'I don't want to go back.'   She shuddered.

'Oh Hannah,' her father clutched her shoulders, 'I don't want you to go either, but Grandma Johnson is still your legal guardian, so you'll have to return to Bluebell House sooner or later. Still, beats me where've you been hiding all this time?'

'All this time? Dad I've only been gone a few days.'

Her dad's eyes widened, the air crackling with an intense silence.

'A few days? Hannah…you've been missing for six months!'

Time itself took a breath.

She was aware of her brain recording every detail; the whoosh and murmur of the boiler, the homely aroma of tea, the way her bedraggled reflection appeared in her father's staring eyes. Her mind saved the entire fragmented scene for torturous replaying and painful over-analysis over the next few days, months and even years. The wall clock ticked ever louder, a noisy invader of a still silent scene. Her dad gazed deep into her eyes but she saw no warmth or security, only panic and confusion.

She twitched her head first, murmuring denial without conviction. 'I...I can't...'

'Hannah, you disappeared back in April!' He cried as she stared blankly. 'It's now October!'

Her dad paced across the kitchen to a crowded noticeboard by the back door. He tore down a curling newspaper clipping from the Manchester Evening News and thrust it into her hand. Her photo staring back from the yellowing page.

GIRL STILL MISSING

She grew dizzy, phrases pulsing from the article:

"Hannah Darnell, Manchester girl still missing after three weeks..."

"Met Police have so far drawn a blank ..."

"Daughter of Anna Darnell, who herself went missing back in..."

"Last seen on CCTV exiting coach with other pupils..."

'Ah.' Alex said sheepishly.

363

Hannah sank back against the sink and glared at him.

'Yes, well…'

His discomfort only irked her more. She stiffly folded her arms.

'Now, don't get mad but…'

'Alex?' Teeth clenched, dawning of threat.

'Hmm?' Her dad frowned.

'Sir Writer Raleigh mentioned suffering some time dilation after passing through the Marginlands. The Figments cause you to lose track of time, like being lost in a daydream although obviously for much longer. Sorry, I forgot to mention it.'

Bruised and broken, she nonetheless managed a weary death stare towards the kitchen table.

Hannah blinked and pulled the duvet up to her shoulder, refocusing the remembered glower on the loitering curtain-twitcher at her bedroom window.

'Alex.'

'Yes.' He said absentmindedly peering up the road.

'Alex, I'm getting up now.'

'Right.' He said indifferently.

She stared at his back, eyes narrowing. 'Alex, will you get out of my room?'

'What?' He frowned.

She ground her teeth and nodded to the door.

Still he stared.

'Fine,' she continued, 'the ten main reasons why I love George Found. Number one: He always looks a very smart dapper gentleword. Number two-'

Alex pulled a face and crossed the room. 'Alright, alright. I'll...go check on your dad.'

She sighed as the bedroom door closed behind him.

After five minutes, she reluctantly slunk out from under the warm duvet.

After fifteen, she reluctantly skulked out from under the hot shower.

After thirty, she yawned her entrance back into the kitchen.

'Sleep well?' Her dad said shaking the sizzling, popping frying pan.

'You bet she did, snored like a little piggy!' Alex chirped from his seat.

Hannah held out her arms out in a sleepy stretch, clipping him on the back of the head as she crossed to kiss her dad on the cheek.

'Yes thanks, guess I needed it.'

'I checked on you last night but you were still out of it.'

'I haven't slept well for...a few days.'

'You look...different.'

'I haven't slept well for a few days.' She smiled.

He smirked. 'No, I mean...I meant...you know, you look more...grown up.'

His cheeks coloured as he turned and cracked an egg into the pan.

She saw he was different too; standing taller and he'd run a comb through his prematurely greying hair. Behind him the clock ticked round to half nine.

'Not painting and decorating today?'

Her father grimaced, 'Dave's been great, let me take a few months off work, just until...'

Hannah winced at the trouble she'd caused and looked away, her gaze falling on a flashy prospectus amidst a stack of magazines.

'Thinking of going back to college?' She asked sarcastically.

He turned and she held it up. 'Ah! Not quite, no.'

Her dad placed the mouth-watering plate of sausage, bacon, eggs, tomatoes and mushrooms in front of her.

'It'sa ok.' Hannah heard Arty's approval in her head and smiled.

'Are you not...?'

'I've had mine.' He said, hugging his mug of tea.

'Thanks. This looks amazing.'

He laughed nervously. 'You know...I did have...long before all this happened. I mean, I was getting ahead of myself. I was going to wait until you'd finished your exams and left school next year, but-'

'What?'

He nodded back towards the glossy college brochure.

'Now, you don't have to decide right away - but I wondered, I mean- it doesn't matter if you don't, of course, but maybe-'

'Dad!?'

'Sorry.' He swallowed. 'I just had an idea, that maybe you'd prefer to study at a college up here after finishing school, rather than back down...'

Hannah's eyes widened. 'But, Grandma Johnson...'

Her father smirked as she cut into a gristly piece of bacon. 'It's up to you, not anyone else. Mrs Johnson ceases to be your guardian now you're sixteen.'

Hannah thought for a second and realised if it was now October, she'd missed her birthday by a month.

'I'm sixteen!'

'Yes, but don't get any ideas; you finish your exams down there first!'

She nodded and smiled.

Her father beamed back.

'Your next escape?' Alex murmured wryly beside her.

They chatted aimlessly about the weather and nosy neighbours until he stood and cleared away her plate.

'Funny thing happened this morning,' He turned the taps on and squirted washing up liquid in the bowl. 'Milkman not only left the wrong milk, but a parcel too.'

Hannah followed his gaze to a brown padded envelope on the windowsill.

'Addressed to someone called Aldwyn...'

Hannah almost fell off her chair.

Alex twitched up to Defcon three.

She crossed to the window and tore the parcel open.

'Hannah! I don't think you should...' Her dad started.

'He's...a friend of mine.' She managed, pulling out a smooth silver box about the size of a Rubik's cube.

'What the…?' Alex gasped. 'That's a United Republics of Lexica level four Secure message-cube!'

She stared at him.

'Level four!' He exclaimed.

Hannah put it gently on the table, her dad looking over from the sink. 'What the heck is it?'

'George!' Alex exclaimed belatedly. 'George must have been the milkman. Clever. Annoyingly clever.'

Hannah was more concerned on how he knew they were here and who else knew.

Alex reached a similar conclusion. 'Bit worrying he reasoned he had to sneak it to us.'

'What is it? Who's Aldwyn?' Her father read the concern on her face.

'Put it away.' Alex hissed, eyeing her father's curiosity.

She put it back in its envelope and pushed it to one side, trying to ignore her dad's raised eyebrows.

'You can't tell him.' Alex chirped.

She squeezed her hand through the handle of her mug, cradling the tea as she drew it up to her lips. She knew she couldn't tell him the truth, he'd never believe a word.

'I don't want to lie to you dad, but if I told you everything, you'd only worry.'

He wiped his wet hands on a towel. 'Hannah, I'm your dad, worrying comes with the job.'

The weight of truth behind his words squeezed on her heart.

'I've been futilely pacing up and down ever since that balmy September night at the maternity ward...' He petered out.

Her stomach cramped. She wished she could tell him, but knew it was pointless, even if he believed a word. Bellwether and his dark intentions drifted into her thoughts, sullying her apprehension with his malevolent pollution. School, college and the future drifted away from her like the horizon in the Marginlands, Lexica's grip on her unceasing. What was the point of college if Alex and the Shrouded Guild couldn't stop the GNP? The turmoil of Bellwether's revolution would destroy everything she learnt anyway.

The sight of the suds sliding off the plates and cutlery on the draining board unsettled her, the futility of such mundane chores akin to a health and safety officer putting a wet floor sign out on the deck of the titanic.

Vince's chilling words returned. 'Despite the disappearances and broken glass underfoot, the majority will turn a blind-eye, keep their heads down and hope it all blows over.'

She tried to shake her head, tell herself Heartisans would react differently to Words, but she knew that wasn't true. By the time the English-speaking world realised what was happening, it'd already be too late.

The doorbell rang.

The three of them froze, questioning eyes going unanswered.

'Who the heck's that ringing at this time of the morning?' Her father sighed.

He headed for the door, but Hannah stood and blocked his path, raising a finger to her lips. He frowned at the young woman standing where his curious child once stood, the steel in her gaze dissuading any protest. She sensed his intrigue, the narrowing of his eyes at the melding of the old and the new, the return of her curiosity imbued with a fiery strength he'd last seen in another they'd both lost. She silenced any argument with a knowing look before crossing over to the kitchen door and peeking around the edge.

Two silhouettes stood on the other side of the front door's frosted glass. They moved and the doorbell rang again.

Alex joined her and peered through the crack between the kitchen door and the frame.

'What d'you reckon? Feds?' Hannah whispered, ignoring her dad behind her.

'No doubt.' Alex whispered back as one of the silhouettes lifted his hat and a distorted face appeared pressed to the glass.

As the other shadow squatted, Hannah whipped her head back out of sight.

The letterbox snapped open. 'Mister Darnell, it's Detectives Maverick and Hunch, we called several months ago about your daughter. Are you there Mr Darnell?'

The letterbox snapped shut. Alex glared at Hannah and her dad and she realised what he was thinking.

'The milk!' She covered her mouth with her hand.

'What? Who are you...?'

'Ssssh!' Hannah hushed him. 'Did you lock the front door?'

Her dad stared before gently shaking his head.

The bottom fell out of her stomach. Alex pinched the bridge of his nose before meeting her eyes and looking on towards the back door. She reluctantly nodded and crept from the kitchen doorway to give her bewildered dad a hug and a kiss on the cheek.

'I'll phone you dad. Don't tell them I was here, they're not on our side.'

He looked at her as if to say, 'Sides? Since when were there sides?!'

As she tried to reassure him with an uneasy smile, she heard the front door handle pushed down and the door squeak open.

'Hello? Mr Darnell?'

'Time to go.' Alex murmured.

'Love you.' She mouthed silently to her father, forcing the corners of his mouth to curl upwards nervously.

She listened and smiled as he disappeared into the hall.

'I'm sorry to keep you, something curious just happened in the kitchen...'

By the time, he returned to the kitchen, Hannah and Alex were gone.

THE END

Other books by the Author:

* Hannah Curious and the Last Knight Watchman *

372About the Author:

Growing up in a house full of books, it was almost inevitable Neil would tumble

head first into the imagined worlds between their covers, emerging only for cake,

hot chocolate or the inconvenient regularity of trips to school or an auntie who

smelled of pot pourri. A lifelong writer, creating fantastical worlds and peculiar

inhabitants since a young age, Neil is devoted to bringing curiosity, humour and

high-stakes adventure to his characters, whether they like it or not.. When not

herding letters and words onto a blank page, Neil likes to make his friends laugh,

run half marathons and explore museums and castles for inspiration.

Printed in Great Britain
by Amazon